The Undertaking of Billy Buffone

a novel

By David Giuliano

We acknowledge the support of Nathan Niigan Adler for his sensitivty read.

Library and Archives Canada Cataloguing in Publication
Title: The undertaking of Billy Buffone : a novel / David Giuliano.
Names: Giuliano, David, 1960- author.
Identifiers: Canadiana (print) 20210091630 | Canadiana (ebook) 2021009169X | ISBN 9781988989334
  (softcover) | ISBN 9781988989341 (EPUB)
Classification: LCC PS8613.I845 U53 2021 | DDC C813/.6—dc23

Printed and bound in Canada on 100% recycled paper.
Cover Design: Heather Campbell
Author photo: Jeremiah Giuliano

Published by:
Latitude 46 Publishing
Sudbury, Ontario, Canada
info@latitude46publishing.com
www.latitude46publishing.com

The production of this book was made possible through the generous assistance of the Ontario Arts Council and the support of the Government of Canada through the Canada Book Fund.

ADVANCE PRAISE

"In The Undertaking of Billy Buffone, Giuliano conjures small town Northern Ontario, the shame that allows harm to carry on well past due, the way tragedies can overlap and intersect, as can our healing trajectories, bringing folks together in a universal human experience of loss and redemption."

— Nathan Niigan Noodin Adler, author, *Wrist* and *Ghost Lake*

"In a narrative that unfolds like old time rock-n-roll Giuliano delivers a pitch-perfect, whip-smart glimpse into the lives of highly memorable characters in a small Northwestern Ontario town."

—Dayle Furlong, author, *Lake Effect & Other Stories*

"David's writing is infused with love for the landscape of Northern Ontario, and for its people. There is beauty and brutality in the narrative, which is rendered with honesty and compassion."

— Darrow Woods, finalist, 2019 Arthur Ellis Awards,

"Matthew is a practical, matter-of-fact narrator, telling us about his best friend Billy, his hometown, and oh yeah, the fact he's dead and watching Billy's life from beyond the grave. The Undertaking of Billy Buffone is alternately tragic, sensitive, and portrays the strength of friendship with great tenderness."

— Alison Manley, The Miramichi Reader

"The Undertaking of Billy Buffone is a fearless journey into the troubled souls of the citizens of a northern Ontario town. The traumas simmering within this close-knit community are real, gritty — and often spiral into greater problems. One by one, each character discovers that life's burdens cannot be carried alone forever; the cost is too great. Truths are revealed and shame loses its power. There is redemption."

— Jocelyn Bell, Editor/Publisher, Broadview Magazine

The Undertaking of Billy Buffone

a novel

By David Giuliano

Dedicated to the boys who survived, and to the boys who did not survive.

Grief is the price we pay for being close to one another.
If we want to avoid our grief, we simply avoid each other.

~

There's no easy way to do this.
So do it right:
weep, laugh, watch, pray, love,
live, give thanks and praise;
comfort, mend, honor,
and remember.

~

Thomas Lynch, *The Undertaking: Life Studies from the Dismal Trade.*

- 1 -

SCOUTER CHURLEY'S CAMP
1975

When I woke up on the floor at Scouter Rupert Churley's camp, there was a pilled blanket tangled around my ankles. I was otherwise naked. My head thrummed. My mouth tasted like a squirrel had slept—and possibly shit—in it. Eyes clamped shut, against the splintered shards of light raking my eyeballs, I rolled onto my side and buried my face in the crook of my elbow. I stank of alcohol, smoke, and adolescence. Beer and wieners curdled in my belly. I lay as thick and as still as a puddle of spent oil and repeatedly swallowed the acid seeping up my throat into my mouth. A film of perspiration coated my body. It dripped from my face, and pooled in the small of my back.

On hands and knees, I crawled across the gritty cabin floor, out the flap of torn screen hanging in the frame of the sliding door, and vomited from beneath the bottom rail of the porch. A stew of beer and pink meat spattered down onto a flat rock and the dirt around it. *Technicolour yawn.* That's what we called vomiting.

The summer of 1975, Larry and Anthony and I were doing a lot of technicolour yawning. A lot of it for Boy Scouts anyway. Officially we were Venturers, because all three of us were older than fourteen years of age. There was, however, nothing Boy Scout-like in the values espoused, or the activities engaged in at Churley's camp. We were decidedly not trustworthy, loyal, helpful, friendly, courteous, kind, obedient, cheerful, thrifty, brave, clean or reverent.

Larry was the sort of kid who jabbered in a non-stop conversation with himself, while knitting his fingers in front of his chest like a mad scientist. His eyes bulged, and he never seemed to blink. Acne bubbled on his face like a burn victim.

Anthony was a chubby, sweaty kid with hair perpetually matted to his forehead. His pathological lying, and need to be liked, were embarrassing. He lied badly, constantly, and without reason. He claimed, for example, that Bobby Sherman was his cousin. He was bullied at school and cried easily. I didn't consider either of them friends. In town we never spoke to one another. We were camp mates and accomplices in deviance.

Until that summer, Billy Buffone was my best friend. I was probably in love with him, though I would never have admitted it, especially to him because I was afraid he would reject me. But it was me who made the irreparable—and ultimately fatal—mistake of disconnecting my life from his.

Billy refused to come to Churley's camp when I extended a half-hearted invitation. Even if he had been willing his mother, Mrs. Buffone, wouldn't have stood for it. "Matthew," Billy warned to me, "I smell something up with that guy." It sounded exactly like something his mother would say. "Let's just go up to Jackrabbit Lake," he pleaded. "I got a new tent." I turned my back on his tears, and what, at the time, I considered his immaturity, and we drifted apart. It wasn't a decision, more like a snap departure. I didn't even acknowledge it had happened to myself, until everything fell apart. We were inseparable and then we weren't.

My hand slipped on the algae-covered decking boards and I fell flat on my chest. My head snapped forward and my face slammed down hard on the deck. I lay there inhaling the stink of rotting wood and nose blood. Nausea washed over me again and I puked up the remains of the previous night. Then I puked yellow bile and then dry heaved like a cat with a hairball. My abdominal muscles spasmed long after my stomach was empty. I pressed one nostril closed to nose-jet blood out the other nostril, along with snot and a piece of hotdog lodged there from vomiting. My body shivered. Were it not for the mosquitoes drilling for blood in my unprotected flesh I might have curled up and gone back to sleep on the porch.

Instead, I rose to my knees and, with the help of the railing, pulled myself to my feet. Still gripping the handrail, my bare feet slipped on the slick boards. As I stood, gravity caused my insides to drop, and I felt the bruised tenderness of my anus. I had been the "drunkest boy" again. Drunkest boy was sort of a game Scouter Churley introduced to us.

⌜

Our first trip up to Churley's camp was on the May 24th, Victoria Day Weekend. Everyone around here calls it the May two-four Weekend. We went to Churley's camp every weekend after and, when school let out, in the middle of the week, too. As a grade school teacher, Churley, like us, had his summers free. It was half-an-hour trip up Birch Lake in Churley's aluminum boat, the old Johnson belching a trail of two-stroke-engine-oil-rainbows onto the surface of the water all the way.

The bay on which Churley's camp was situated is an exceptionally isolated one, even for Birch Lake where cottagers guarded their privacy. There was only one other structure on the nameless inlet—we called it Churley's Bay. From out on the lake you could see the other camp, but on shore it was cut off from Churley's place by a spine of rock and fifty yards of dense bush.

That camp was built three generations ago by Dick Spanner's great-grandfather. Spanner continues to live a very private life in Twenty-Six Mile House, across the road from Billy's place. Spanner, as the last living heir, inherited the camp. As far as we could tell, he rarely boated up the lake to Churley's Bay. From the lake, the Spanner place appeared to be abandoned and in considerable disrepair.

Churley's camp was in use, but not much better. It was a mouse-infested, two-room cabin with shredding drapes and broken screens. There was a rusting woodstove. A framed paint-by-numbers picture of a fruit basket left by a previous owner hung on the wall. A thick layer of dust coated the black bear head mounted on the opposing wall. One of the glass eyes had fallen out of the head leaving a puckered socket in its face. Yellow Vapona Fly Paper strips, bearded with desiccated flies, hung from the open rafters above the table. The linoleum flooring was worn through to the boards in places. There was a sticky coating of grit on pretty much everything. The shitter was out back.

When Churley first invited us up to the camp he told us to bring our sleeping bags, that he would take care of the rest. I told him I didn't have a sleeping bag. "Not to worry, Matty," he said and mussed my hair. "I'll bring you something." The something he brought for me turned out to be a double sleeping bag that he and I shared on his bed. I woke in the night and felt his hardness pressing against my back. I didn't know what to do, so I didn't do anything. I told myself he was asleep, dreaming. He didn't know what he was doing. Turns out I was wrong about that and so many other things.

Churley had been taking the older Scouts out to his camp for years to roast hotdogs and marshmallows and drink beer. We glowed in his affirmation of our emerging manhood. It was a rite of passage. He nonchalantly added studying his extensive collection of porn magazines and skinny-dipping to our camp activities.

There was a coffee table fashioned from a varnished cross-section of tree, supported by three pegs. The magazines were spread out on it in plain sight, as if they were issues of *Maclean's* or *National Geographic* instead of *Playboy*, *He and She,* and *Big Boobs*. Buried further down in the pile we discovered copies of *Drag Scene* and *M.A.N.—Male Athletic Nudist*—magazines. "Enjoy, boys! It's natural to be curious," Churley giggled. "Unless you're a cat, it's not going to kill you. Nothing to be ashamed of, men."

One afternoon at the beach—apropos of nothing—he laughed so hard that his sunburned belly jumped up and down above the waistband of his bathing suit. He shouted out to us from the dock, "Don't be bashful, boys. This is a clothing-optional retreat. There's no one else around for miles!"

We treaded water, slipped our trunks over our ankles and flipped them up onto the dock at his feet. The cool water caressing our bodies in general and our genitals in particular. Felt spectacular, like in the dreams and nocturnal shame we did not talk about when we woke. At Churley's camp there was no shame.

Churley produced a Super 8 camera and began filming us from the dock, capturing images of our heads bobbing among the flashes of sunlight glinting off the surface of the water. On those early cameras there wasn't a magnetic strip on the film to record sound. So there was no documentation of what we were shouting. There were only the silent moving images of our maniacally grinning faces, captured on film deeply tinted with colour one moment and erased to white by the glare of the sun the next.

The camera became a constant presence at the camp. We mugged for it by day. At night, we squinted against the blinding light it projected while recording what we did in the dark. Kodachrome film ticking past the lens, 16 frames per second, became the sound track of our alternate lives at Churley's camp. It recorded everything.

Streaking was a worldwide phenomenon that summer. University students were dashing nude through lecture halls and across campuses. On CBC television, we saw the blurred image of a guy named Michael Angelo jumping, buck-naked, over a wicket at a Lord's Cricket Match. It was supposed to be political somehow, in ways we couldn't understand.

We were desperate to break the bonds of our parochial, isolated existence in Twenty-Six Mile House. We shed our bathing suits and, with them, the provincial inhibitions of our backwater town—a town that, by virtue of its geographical remoteness, was perpetually a decade behind the sophisticated world we saw on Channel 9, our only television channel. We felt as though, by our nakedness, we were "slipping the surly bonds of earth." Churley implied that we too were making a statement.

We floated on our backs and dreamed of flying off to Europe or California on one of the rare jets that crossed the heavens above us. Their white contrails cut across the perfect blue sky, like a scar, tugging at an ache in my chest.

It was on the third trip up to the lake that Scouter Churley introduced us to the masturbation game. We had been flipping through porn magazines, and feigning intellectual curiosity, when Anthony went outside to pee and—in all probability—to jerk off. Churley taunted him from the window that he wasn't allowed back inside until "You choke that chicken!" Larry and I—our damp swimsuits bulging—joined Churley at the window. We couldn't see Anthony in the dark shadows among the trees but cheered him on. When he returned we slapped his back like he had scored a hat trick for the Thunder Birds. His face flushed, he grinned, both grateful for, and confused by, our congratulations.

From then on, if one of us went outside while we were "partying," we were barred from the camp until we had masturbated. Churley continued to cheer from the window. After a while, we didn't bother going outside. Mosquitoes. It was pretty dark inside, too.

At the end of the night, we would take a raucous poll as to who would be knighted "drunkest boy." This was the boy who was often already passed out or close to it. Churley and the two other boys would chant "Drun-kest! Drun-kest! Drun-kest!" and carry him into the back room and drop him on the lumpy mattress to spend the night with Churley. The drunkest boy "slept" with Scouter Churley.

The less drunk boys bedded down on the two dusty couches in sleeping bags lined with flannel printed with birddog and hunter patterns. They pretended not to hear the whispering and groans on the other side of the panelled wall. As though the fraying drape pulled across the doorway to the bedroom could keep a secret.

The following morning we avoided one another's eyes. Churley was quiet in the mornings as well. We claimed we were too drunk to remember the preceding night. In my case, that was becoming frequently true. Some mornings I really couldn't remember much from the night before.

- 2 -
ONE POINT FOUR MILES AT A GO
1995

"Do you want the sander?"

"Uhm, maybe? The what?"

Billy passes a brass cylinder over to her. It's about the size of a shotgun shell. He blows cigarette smoke from the corner of his mouth toward the cracked-open, driver's side window. A pillar of tobacco ash tumbles down the front of his vest before he notices it—too late to tap it off in the ashtray. He flicks at the ashes on his vest, managing only to blend them into the dove-grey fabric. Eyes on the road, still brushing at his vest, Billy explains, "You use it to pour a cross on the casket. That little knobby doo-dad on the top? It screws off so you can tip the sand out in neat lines. Pastor Josh at the Pentecostals likes to use a handful of dirt—the town guys always leave some by the grave. Father Mike likes the sander. Makes no matter which way you do it, but people like it if you make a cross when you say the 'ashes to ashes' bit."

Ashes to Ashes by David Bowie starts up in Billy's head. He is also remembering he needs to clean out the woodstove in his living room.

✍

I can see Catherine, but she cannot see me, given that I am dead and all. Besides, she is too busy checking Billy out to notice my ethereal presence. She's guessing he's what? Maybe five years younger than her. Even in late March, after the short days and layered clothing of winter, his skin is still smooth and as brown a shelled peanut. His tangle of curling black hair could use a trim. Substantial sideburns—artifacts of the seventies, the decade when Billy's socio-cultural clock stopped ticking—frame his face. His jaw is straight and cleanly shaved, his chin dimpled. To say it is "cleft" or "chiseled" would be too manly a description. Billy is, in many respects, still a boy. His Italian heritage is as plain as the ample nose on his face. His lips are full, almost feminine. He is wearing white-framed plastic sunglasses with black lenses. From the side, Catherine can see his long eyelashes are sweeping the inside of the lenses.

Billy's morning suit is immaculate—the ashes a mere shadow on the vest now—though it appears as if it might have once belonged to a smaller man. The knees of the pin-striped trousers are carefully hitched up to preserve their crease. Dark hairs peek from the gap between the pant cuffs and his black socks. The bottom vest button is undone. He is bobbing his head rhythmically, moving his lips. He stops abruptly, returning the David Bowie vinyl record to its sleeve in his mind.

Billy flicks his eyes toward Catherine without turning his head. She busies herself with the brass sander. Billy, I assure you, has no awareness of her surreptitiously scrutinizing him. Nor does he notice the blush spreading across her neck above her clerical collar. Billy has been, as he so often is, elsewhere.

§

The hearse continues to crawl up toward the cemetery, situated half way up the hill, on the right hand side of the road. The road that links the isolated town of Twenty-Six Mile House to the east-west Trans-Canada highway, tracing the north shore of Lake Superior from Sault Ste. Marie to Thunder Bay. The Trans-Canada stretches over 7,000 kilometres across the country from the Atlantic to the Pacific. The unremarkable strip of pavement, curving up the hill to intersect with that nation-spanning ribbon, is the only way in or out of town.

Billy doesn't hurry the hearse. Propriety, and the dignity of the deceased, to Billy's mind dictate that no one should be rushed to the grave, not even no-frills, government-funded funerals such as this one. The procession of vehicles is short, counting a single rusted-out, half-ton truck and a battered Toyota Tercel, following behind Billy's polished hearse. The four functional headlights among the three vehicles are lit to alert pedestrians and passing traffic to the solemnity of the occasion. Drivers of approaching vehicles no longer feel compelled, as they once did, to pull off onto the shoulder of the road as the dead rolled past. An elderly man sitting on a bench does remove his toque. He remains seated but his hair stands on end.

⌘

The hearse was already a decade-old when Billy bought it immediately after graduating with his embalming certificate. It took another ten years for him to settle the loan with the Superior Credit Union. It's a 1972 Millar Meteor Cadillac. "Mint condition," the salesman had assured Billy. "A lot better shape than 'Mort'" he chuckled. Sensing Billy's confusion, he added "You know, the old hearse Neil Young and the Squires cruised around Port Arthur in?"

Billy rode the "The Hound" down to Detroit to pick the car up, and drove it back up the I-75 humming *Long May You Run* until he crossed Mackinaw Bridge.

The hearse is silver-grey with a black rag-top roof and white-wall tires. Clean lines flow from the front end into a hint of fin-tails at the back. It boasts a bit more chrome, and a lot more horsepower, than a funeral procession calls for. The Cadillac rep promised Billy it would do 100 miles per hour, easy. Billy has never put his claim to the test. The speedometer needle has never drifted east of sixty with Billy at the wheel.

The odometer tallies a paltry 7,932 miles. Most of those accumulated by Billy were in increments of 1.4 miles at a go. He has never calculated the distance up the hill from the funeral home to the cemetery in kilometres. The math isn't difficult for a guy like Billy. He could easily divide 1.4 by five and multiply that sum by eight. He could have easily checked the distance in kilometres while driving the '86 cargo van he uses for recoveries and transfers. It has just never occurred to him to do so. The trip between town and heaven or hell, as far as Billy is concerned, is rightly measured—like distances in blues songs—in miles. He is agnostic regarding the existence of heaven or hell, but is steadfast in his belief that the metrics of getting there are imperial.

§

Catherine is tracing the gold cross embossed on the leather cover of her Bible with fine white sand, when it dawns on her that there is nowhere to dispose of the sand she's pouring. She can't just dump it onto the spotless floor mat. Nor does it seem right to roll down the window to fling it out of the hearse. So, she balances the Bible in her lap, and wills the hearse toward the cemetery gate.

She slips her notes from between the pages of her Bible to review the words of committal and the prayer. The notes had been book-marking the scripture passage she intends to read at the gravesite—about God's compassion for falling sparrows and His or Her concern for the exact number of hairs on individual heads. Matthew 10 something. She's confident she can find the page without a bookmark.

St. Luke's United is Catherine's first congregation. She pulled into the driveway at the manse on Canada Day last year. During the eight months since, her palms have been damp more than dry. This is her second funeral. The first involved a cremation done in Thunder Bay. The cremains were shipped back to Twenty-Six Mile House on the Greyhound and the service took place at the church. So, the services of Billy Buffone's Funeral Home were not required.

"Where you from?" Billy's eyes still on the road.

"Most recently, Toronto. Originally, Tupelo, Mississippi."

"Elvis," Billy nods. *Just a hunk, a hunk of burning love* drops a dime into his mental jukebox, and Billy has left the building.

§

"Toronto. Originally, Tupelo, Mississippi," is Catherine's *Reader's Digest* reply to inquiries regarding her place of origin. Given her present condition of near pathological loneliness, the slightest priming on Billy's part would have produced a flood of autobiographical details.

To summarize: After Tupelo, on the run with her mother, from said mother's brutal boyfriend, there was a stop in Indianapolis, followed faster than the Indy 500, by two short, mean and childless common-law relationships of Catherine's own. Both of these hasty, and legally non-binding betrothals, were to autoworkers who relocated her first to Cleveland, Ohio and then Windsor, Ontario. Not long after her border crossing, she quit the second man, and her job at the Windsor Raceway— sulkies instead of Formula One cars—and moved to Toronto where she found work at Woodbine Raceway, and Jesus at Trinity Church on Bloor Street.

Five years of waiting tables at the track lounge, and parttime studies at the Toronto School of Theology, concluded with her assignment by denominational authorities to the congregation of St. Luke's United Church of Canada in Twenty-Six Mile House. She loaded a U-Haul trailer and drove the 13 hours, north and west of Hog Town, on her own.

The shy, green-eyed, trailer-park-poor girl in the Princess-Jazzy jeans and the pink tube top, is now a Birkenstocks-and-socks-wearing preacher. She no longer chews her nails to the nub and spends most days smiling like she's got a secret.

ॐ

This, slightly less abridged, chronology of Catherine's life would be entirely wasted on Billy, who is currently preoccupied with an inner dialogue along the lines of: *Tupelo? Isn't that a tree? Or is it a fish? Tupelo? No that's Tilapia. Never tasted it. They say it tastes like walleye. Who was it? Rick? Maybe. Maybe Donny. Doesn't matter. Said it was a lot like pickerel. Frozen though. Lakes are still frozen. Sure good to have winter almost over. I'll have to say that if I go into* Robin's *for coffee:* "Sure good to have winter over." *Then I'll say,* "The *robins* will be out soon."

Not that Billy ever utters a word, to anyone, on the rare occasions when he slips through the social gauntlet at Robin's to pick up a cup of coffee, or a box of donuts. Still, he smiles at his avian witticism and begins to hum in his head. *All the birds on J-Bird Street, loved to hear the Robin go tweet-tweet-tweet, rockin' Robin.*

When Billy runs out of lyrics he can recall, he turns to Catherine and asks, "Ever been to the Rock 'n' Roll Hall of Fame?"

"Actually, yes. When I lived in Cleveland," she says. "You?"

"Nope, but I plan to some day. Maybe drive this baby down there," says Billy as he strokes the top of the steering wheel like the back of a beloved cat.

- 3 -

NEW YEAR'S BABY AND THE ALIGNING OF EIGHT PLANETS THE DAY AFTER

Billy was born on February 1, 1960. Given the diminutive population of Twenty-Six Mile House—two thousand souls if everyone is in town—he was the first baby of the New Year. He was also the first child born to Mr. and Mrs. Angelo Buffone.

In the black and white photograph on the front page of our local paper—*The New North Shore News*—Billy is cradled in his mother's arms, her hospital gown sliding off one shoulder. His father, chin pushed out with pride, stares directly at the camera. In the grainy photo, it is apparent that Mr. Buffone is crying and trying not to. His smile, captured by the camera, is misshapen by his quivering chin. The doctor's head is tipped down toward a clipboard he's holding, so he is peering up from beneath his bushy grey eyebrows, giving him a somewhat sinister appearance. By all accounts, though, he was a kind physician. The laughing face of a nurse, her starched cap askew, pokes into the frame from the left. Three proprietary members of the Ladies Hospital Auxiliary of The J.T. Anderson General Hospital, jockey for position around Mrs. Buffone's metal-railed bed and the first baby of 1960.

The Auxiliary gifts to the Buffones are inventoried in the story that accompanied the photo. It was typed and submitted by the secretary of the Auxiliary to *New North Shore*: "Mrs. Angelo Buffone, mother of this year's New Year's Baby, was presented with 24 neatly folded cotton diapers; a package of six plastic pants; two sets of safety pins; a container of Johnson's Baby Powder; four flannel sleepers; six undershirts; and a blue receiving blanket by Mrs. Anders Burke, Ladies Hospital Auxiliary President. All items were neatly arranged in a sharp, new bassinette."

Billy Buffone did not spend the first months of his life like the rest of us, sleeping in a dresser drawer on the floor.

⅋

I was born inauspiciously the day after Billy. Years later, I discovered that February 2, 1960 was the day upon which, for the first time in 400 years, eight of the nine planets aligned. No notice appeared in the *New North Shore* regarding this astronomical phenomenon, or my birth. I am the fifth of what eventually became seven children in the Mad Collins family. My mother's name was Madeline. Everyone called her Mad for short. Thus, we were known as the Mad Collins. That is the kinder etymological account of our family moniker. We were also considered by our fellow citizens to be quite nuts.

While my mother convalesced in hospital, my older brothers, Roger and Mickey, were in charge of Gail and Danny at home. Roger and Mickey treated Danny like a cross between a household pet and an indentured servant. They sent him to RJ's corner store with the grocery money to buy them shoestring licorice. When Danny got back from the store, they amused themselves, while eating the licorice, by throwing an Indian rubber ball from the back stoop for him to fetch. Gail was a toddler at the time but she somehow survived our mother's absence in spite of Roger's and Mickey's almost complete disregard for her needs or whereabouts.

My father celebrated the siring of a fourth son with a week-long bender, making the week of my birth pretty much indistinguishable from all other weeks of my father's "adult" life. For my mother, the three days in hospital were like an every-other-year spa retreat, or mental hospital visit. To my knowledge, she never visited a spa. She did once sign on for a brief stretch at the Lakehead Psychiatric Hospital. Family lore has it that upon Mad's return she reported that the institution was a lot like home, but without the cooking and cleaning.

My mother checked out of the hospital after the birth of her last baby and fled Twenty-Six Mile House, dad, and five out of seven of us kids. She hitched a ride with a medical supply salesman ten years her junior. She took the two youngest children with her; my younger sister Jane and the new one. I was four years old at the time and can't recall, or wasn't told, if it—that is the new one—was a boy or girl. I've always assumed it was a girl because Mad took her along.

She stopped by the house to pack a suitcase and left a note on the kitchen counter alongside the unwashed dishes: "I need a rest." It was written with a green crayon on an envelope containing a second notice warning that our heating oil invoice was overdue. Like the invoice, her note went unnoticed for a several days. We thought she was still at the hospital.

It must have been Roger or Mickey who stuck the note to the fridge with a magnetized Black Label bottle-opener. When my father saw it there on display, he lit it on fire with a Zippo lighter; the olive-green refrigerator paint blackened and blistered. Dad burned his hand employing the opener before it had cooled. He never spoke of our mother again and stared, dead-eyed, at any of us kids who dared mention her name. We learned quickly that his silence was not golden. It was explosive and could trigger violence, necrotic to our fragile child-sized souls. Nevertheless, in our family silence persisted as the go-to pain management strategy. It was the lively conversations at the Buffones' place that healed the gaping wounds inflicted by silence in my father's house.

In my earliest memory, I am three years old and fleeing one of my father's plate-smashing-fist-through-the-dry-wall tirades. There were dandelions, so it must have been spring.

I remember the dandelions because my brothers had been plucking up fists-full of those harbingers of summer and grinding their yellow ink into my face. "Do you like butter? Huh? Huh? Look, he likes butter." It was usually Roger who held me down, while Mickey rubbed my face strawberry raw.

I didn't know the Latin word for dandelion—Taraxacum—yet, but I did by the time I was six. From the time I learned to speak, I collected words for power, for magic, as if saying the right words—*abracadabra*—could make everything better. A quiver of full words and a bow of stoicism were my primary weapons against the cruelty of my brothers. As a young child, I believed the proper incantation would transform my life, or at least shield me from it. I still do, but I have yet to hit upon the perfect string of words. Of course, *life* for me, no longer means what it used to mean.

I never cried or begged my brothers for mercy. When I was old enough, I confronted Mickey, recounting his brutality toward me. He laughed and said, "We thought you liked it. You never said anything." He claimed he thought I liked it when they stuffed me in the dryer and turned it on, or liked it when—as part of some sadistic game—he and Roger tied me to the weeping willow in the yard, and flayed me with whips cut from the tree. He was lying when he said they thought I liked it. Mickey knew it was a lie, but we were a family cobbled together by lies. This was just another one, another nail driven into the trap door leading down to the cellar, where our familial dark truths were badly potted, like rancid meat stored in Mason jars.

- 4 -

MEANWHILE BACK AT THE CEMETERY

The hearse rolls through the open wrought-iron gate into the cemetery—Catholics to the right and Protestants to the left. There is no monument marking my grave, still I visit here often to wander among the headstones and read the names etched into them. I like to imagine that Billy senses me nearby, ethereally present in the shadows of the forest that begins where the manicured lawn ends. I like to imagine he catches glimpses of me, darting in his peripheral vision, among the grave markers.

It has been an unseasonably warm March. The green knobs of daffodil and tulip heads are breaking the soil on the south side of some of the stones. They will no doubt be snuffed out by an inevitable late frost. At the back of the cemetery, a bear snuffles the ground in search of tender blades of spring grass. Startled by the sounds of tires crunching on gravel, and by the truck's deficient exhaust system, the bear gallops a short distance into the bush.

Billy leads the procession around the back of the cemetery first, to confirm that the bear has in fact been frightened off. He squints beneath the low boughs of black spruce, where shallow drifts of crusty snow persevere in the shade. Billy can't make out the dark shape of the bear, blending as it does into the shadows, but suspects it is still there, watching.

Maybe it's the same bear Billy remembers from the previous summer. After dark it will lumber down into town looking for half-full Cheezies bags and greasy pizza boxes to lick. Maybe it will knock over some trash cans. Shuffle over to the dump to forage. Visitors, and the rare tourist to Twenty-six Mile House, go to the dump to see the bears. They bring cameras. It's the closest thing we have to a zoo.

The other two vehicles pull up behind the hearse, where Billy is parked in the lane nearest the open grave. Before he gets out, Billy says to Catherine, "Hope you don't mind giving me a hand. I couldn't get any pallbearers."

"You mean help carry the casket?" Catherine laughs, assuming he is playing mess-with-the-city-slicker-preacher. It's a popular local past-time. However, given that the average age of the mourners appears to be about eighty years, she quickly concludes it's no joke. She watches a man—built like, and moving at the pace of, a heron fishing in the reeds—make his way to the back of his truck where two walkers are stored.

"Mr. Martin was a little guy, 120 tops," Billy says, "but I can't move him by myself, not without a dolly and it won't roll on this wet ground. Rev. Paul helped me out a couple of times. Sorry, I should have checked sooner." He pauses, still scanning the bush line for the bear, hand resting on the door handle. He says it again, "Sorry, really."

Catherine's clerical predecessor, the Reverend Paul Dirksen—who had apparently "helped out a couple of times"—turned thirty years old just before leaving St. Luke's. He marked this milestone birthday by competing in a triathlon in Duluth, Minnesota. Catherine is thirty-eight, and more of a contemplative swimmer than a competitive one. She has no idea whether or not she can lift a casket with a dead man in it, even a small dead man. She is praying that the casket is not made of the same dense particle-board as her IKEA furniture. *What kind of casket,* she wonders, *does one get on a veteran's pension?*

"Sure." She smiles gamely at Billy. Catherine opens her door, tipping and brushing the sand from the cover of her Bible onto the ground and rolling her eyes, "No problem-o, I'm from Tupelo."

It takes a full ten minutes for the mourners to assemble and settle themselves at the grave. A woman in an army surplus parka sits on the seat of her walker. The orange cuffs of her work socks are neatly folded over the rims of her green rubber boots. She makes several unsuccessful attempts to cross one leg over the other, and then plants her feet, side by side, on the brown grass.

The man standing next to her sports a dusty beret, soup-stained regimental tie and blazer. A bar of medals is pinned to the blazer above his heart. He has positioned his walker in front of himself, but parade-square dignity prevents him from leaning on its handles. He stands at attention, his back curved like a question mark, causing the medals to swing from his chest like rock climbers beneath a ledge. A long, fine strand of clear mucus sways from his nose in the breeze. Billy places a hand on his shoulder and squeezes gently.

Four other mourners constitute the geriatric honour guard. The youngest among them is Norma. Earlier in the week, she made the arrangements with Billy by telephone, on behalf of the Legion. "I can't think of anyone to ask," she told him when he enquired about the availability of pallbearers. "I'm still south of seventy, but a bad emphysemic. I sure as hell can't lift a God-darn casket. Jesus, Billy, I can barely lift the little kegs anymore," she wheezed. "Put your head on straight."

Billy has known Norma all his life, and was stunned to be reminded that she isn't yet seventy. She's bartended, drank and breathed the smoky air at the Legion for at least forty hard years.

Norma yelled into the phone, as if the funeral home located on the edge of town was long distance. "God's honest truth, Billy, between you and me and the gate post, no one really knows the guy. I'm as close as you get, and that's not close. He used to work up in the camps or something, after the war. When they shut 'em down, he just sort of stuck around out there in the bush, you know? Had one of them trappers' cabins at first, 'til Natural Resources knocked 'em all down. Ev'ry one says he's been living in one of them old mines since, eh? Hikes into town once or twice a month for supplies. Always stops off at the Legion for a beer. Just one. Never says a word, eh? Just nods at the tap, drinks his pint, and goes."

Fortunately, Mr. Martin had collapsed in the grocery store on his final trip into town. He would be a long time being found—if ever—had he died in the bush. He was rushed—in the small-town sense of the word—to the hospital where he died the next day, officially of pneumonia. There being no locatable next of kin, the charge nurse called Norma. Other than "In the bush, likely somewhere up past Black River Road," no one at the Legion could say where he lived, or who should be called. When things warmed up, the police would likely poke around a bit up that way to see what they could turn up.

Neither Norma nor the regular afternoon drinkers at the Legion could tell you Mr. Martin's first name. On the rare occasions when they talked about him, never *to* him, they referred to him as Jack. Shaking snow off their hats and stamping their boots on the rubber mat inside the Legion doors, they'd say, "Wonder if ol' Jack up there's froze to dead yet?" They called him Jack—like some people said "buddy" or "bub"—because no one knew his name. At the Legion, someone's name is not something you ask, because you should already know it. It's embarrassing, awkward, to have to ask.

The Legionnaires attending the funeral are doing so more out of a sense of duty to God and Queen than out of any affection for, or even familiarity with, the man they called Jack. "He put his life on the line for freedom," they reasoned over beer. "He deserves some respect in the end. Even if he was crazier'n a grouse drunk on ash berries." They toasted him, "To Jack, whoever the hell he was."

Billy found a veteran's pension stub, and the remnants of a birth certificate, tucked into a thin wallet among Mr. Edison Oscar Martin's personal effects. It would have been a bureaucratic labyrinth of forms and lawyers had Private Martin not maintained the soldierly discipline of keeping on his person the necessary documents with which to identify his corpse. Billy called the provincial registry in search of kin, but had turned up none. After the funeral, he will mail the death certificate and his invoice to Veterans' Affairs.

Billy swings the tailgate open, its freshly greased hinges sigh. "I put him in feet first, so I can grab the heavy end here. Be sure to get a hold underneath, you can't trust the handles on these cardboard models."

Catherine wants more instructions, wants to talk over the plan, wants to reconnoitre the ten yards of thawing turf they will traverse. Billy is more of a jump-in-rather-than-wade-in-to-the-lake sort of person. He takes hold of the underside of the fabric covered box and rolls it out of the hearse. Catherine doesn't have a choice: take her end, or let Mr. Martin crash down onto the gravel. Her initial grip is partial and slipping, but with a quick bump of her knee she gains a solid hold. She can see that it won't take more than a few seconds to reach the lowering device positioned over the open grave.

Shuffling backwards, Billy's face turns bright red and then ashen. His forehead beads with sweat. His sunglasses slide down his nose. He moves quickly and Catherine keeps up so the casket won't be yanked out of her hands. They squat and drop the box the last six inches onto the canvas straps. The straps sound like a soaped leather saddle as they receive the diminutive remains of Mr. Martin and the burden of his budget coffin. Billy wipes his face with a handkerchief and waves off Catherine's look of concern. She heads back to the car to collect her Bible, notes, and the sander.

ℰ

When the ceremony is finished Billy says, "I've gotta stick around until the guys from the town come out to fill in." He motions to the honour guard. "You want me to see if one of them can give you a ride down?"

Catherine watches them, slowly retreating to their vehicles, likely on their way to the Legion to raise one last pint to the Unknown Soldier. "That's okay," says Catherine. "I can wait."

Billy squats on his heels beside the grave, flips a lever on the lowering mechanism and the straps lower the remains of Mr. Edison Oscar Martin into the ground. The cross that Catherine poured with the sander, remains fixed on the fabric lid of the casket. Billy unclasps the straps on one side of the lowering device, tugs them out from under the casket and cranks them back up with the detachable handle.

"Does it go back in the hearse?" Catherine asks. Billy nods and they each pick up an end. "It's sure lighter than Mr. Martin."

"Sorry about that," says Billy.

Catherine laughs, "It'll be good story to tell my friends in Toronto. What about you? Are you okay?"

By the time they load the contraption into the back of the hearse Billy's forehead is beading with perspiration, again. "Fine, fine, just need to do some more aerobics, I guess." He secures the door, gently with his fingertips, then rests against the bumper to wipe his face.

"You're sure?"

"Oh, yah. I'm fine. No need to dig my grave yet." Billy lets out a single huff of laughter and tells her. "You do a nice funeral."

"Thanks," says Catherine. A blush rises from beneath her collar.

The sound of a backhoe, with the town logo and motto—*Superior Pulp,* even though the mill is long gone—painted on the side, draws Billy's attention away. The digger bounces into the cemetery and stops beside the open grave. The driver wears a flash-orange vest and Toronto Maple Leafs ball cap. He jumps down, hitches his jeans up, pulls the faux-turf carpet off the pile of dirt and stones, climbs back up, deploys the two stabilizer legs, and pushes the mound of earth into the hole with the side of the bucket. He finishes up, scraping the last clumps of dirt onto the grave with a hand shovel, waves to Billy and Catherine, and then bounces away. The whole job takes three minutes, four tops.

A clay-coloured rug of clouds unrolls itself across the sky from the west, smothering the sun. The temperature drops several degrees and a cold wind from the north stirs the soggy leaves on the ground. Perched on the top of a stand of raggedy spruce trees, ravens caw and then stop.

The sound of the diesel engine fades down the hill, restoring the reliable silence of cemeteries everywhere. It is the kind of silence that seeps into and settles a body. Catherine inhales it, parses it with her nose for hints of spring, leans into its peace-filled generosity. Billy stands beside her, facing the opposite direction, peering into the woods at the back of the cemetery. He can make out the bear now, a block of darkness lingering in the shadows ten feet beyond the tree line.

Bears are like memories. We mistakenly think hibernation means they are completely asleep, as if in a coma, but they aren't. Even on the longest, darkest winter nights bears, and lost memories, continue to stir in their dens. They just sleep longer in winter, opening an eye now and then, anticipating spring.

Billy and Catherine take shelter in the hearse. He slides the heat control across to maximum, turns the fan up to high and starts down the hill toward the blackening waters of Superior, down toward the boarded-up pulp mill on the shore of those wind-troubled waters. "Looks like winter's not over yet," says Billy.

- 5 -
My First Home

In that earliest of my childhood memories of Billy and I, in
the season of dandelions, I am still wearing my pyjamas, and
am walking across the front lawns on our side of Miles Street.
I'm wearing socks but not shoes. It must have been early in the
morning because I remember the grass being thick with dew.
My socks are wet. Through our neighbours' open windows,
I can smell coffee and toast, can hear the clatter of breakfast
tables being set.

Three yards down the street from ours, Billy is sitting on the
wet grass in front of his house, basking in the early sun. He is
wearing short pants and no shirt. His smooth legs are crossed in
front of him. We called it sitting Indian style, never making the
connection to Pickerel River First Nation, only twenty-minutes
from town. Billy's legs are already turning brown even though
summer is just starting. His belly is round. His eyes are closed.
The drops of moisture glittering on the grass, and the dandelions, give the appearance that he is floating on a green pond of
yellow lilies. A prayer-bell of peacefulness encircles him. I am
drawn by the soundless bell, toward him.

I stopped a few feet away, waiting for him to notice me. I
stepped closer, circled him. I got close enough to smell the baby
shampoo in his hair. If he heard me approach, felt me breathing close by, he was undisturbed by my presence. His eyelids
remained soft and closed, his eyelashes dark and full. His hand
hovered over the cap of a single dandelion, among the hundreds
dotting our yards, allowing the slender yellow petals to touch
the centre of his palm. It must have tickled because, as his hand
almost imperceptibly moved above the flower's golden crown,
his eyelashes fluttered and his lips tipped up in a smile.

I continued to watch him, waiting for his eyes to open. When they didn't open, I knelt down on the grass beside him, closed my own eyes and swept my hand around at my side. A dandelion caught between my fingers and was decapitated. I wiped its milky sap on my pyjama pants.

I winked an eye open to locate one particular flower and closed my eye again. This time I slowly lowered my hand until I felt the glowing energy of it in my palm. I was not so much touching the petals as sensing their warmth, cupping its life force in my downturned hand. It was as if light entered my hand, trickled up my arm and spilled into the empty cavity of my chest. Tears rose in my throat and moistened my eyes. Some of the light from the flower spilled out of my eyes onto my cheeks.

The sound of my father's roostering and slamming disappeared down a dark and closing hole. The cry of seagulls, the gentle morning surf down at the shore, and warmth of the sun washed over me, over us. It was as if Billy and I were safe, together in a sphere of serenity, a place defying words I didn't know then, nor have found since. Something unspeakable held us and in that moment we became best friends.

It is difficult to say how long we sat there on his lawn. An hour? A minute? The mysticism of childhood defies the violence of chronological time. I learned, later, that the Greeks called this qualitative measurement of time, *kairos time.*

By unspoken agreement, we simultaneously unshuttered our eyes. Billy smiled a sleepy smile, took my hand, led me along the warm concrete walkway to the back door of his house, and into his mother's kitchen.

Billy's baby sister, Mary, would have been about a year old then and was buckled into a high chair at the table. She and Billy had the same smooth skin, round faces, the same dark-chocolate eyes and black, lamb's wool hair. She was wearing a flannel nightshirt, and was eating pieces of cinnamon toast that Mrs. Buffone had cut into quarters. Her fingers and face were sticky with butter and sugar, and tinted by the cinnamon. She smelled of baby, and exotic scents, unfamiliar to me.

After that first day, on countless mornings, afternoons and evenings, Billy and I sat at his mother's Formica table eating fresh macaroons or biscotti and drinking sweet tea cooled with cream.

At my house, I awoke most days to the sound of the back door slamming. When my father was on dayshift, he left for the mill at 5:50AM. After night shifts, he returned at 6:10AM. It was less than a ten-minute walk down to the mill, even drunk or hungover. In my father's case, not much time elapsed between those two inseparable states of alcoholism. On the days he did not work or was on evenings—so at home during the early morning hours—I slept lightly, rose at the first hint of dawn, and crept out of the house. I pulled the door closed behind me, slowly releasing the knob so it would latch soundlessly. I dreaded the consequences of awakening the sleeping beast.

I crossed the grass to Billy's house as if travelling from the hostile planet of the Mad Collins to what, by comparison, seemed a fairy tale world within which I hoped to one day reside. If the kitchen was dark when I arrived at the Buffone's back door, I sat on the stoop to wait. I cradled their quart of milk—delivered earlier in the morning by Mr. Leveret—in my lap.

As soon as I heard Mrs. Buffone's slippers on the linoleum inside, I tapped on the aluminum door with the bottle and held it up to the screened window for her to see. "Well," she would say and put her hands on her hips, "who shrunk my milkman?" I had to avert my eyes, because there was so much kindness in her voice that it embarrassed me.

"It's me," I'd say, shuffling my feet, "Matt." Mrs. Buffone would laugh, and hold the door open so I could deliver the milk. "Oh, it's you, Matthew!" I beamed with pride carrying the heavy glass bottle, and at being fully named while doing so. She and Mr. Buffone always called me by my full name, Matthew. Mr. Buffone pronounced it, "Machew." When I think back to those bottles of milk, heavy and slippery with condensation, I realize what an immense act of trust it was on Mrs. Buffone's part to allow the four or five-year-old me to carry them into the kitchen clutched to my chest. I never dropped one. Her love, I think, provided the necessary strength. That, and the trust that, even if the bottle dropped from my arms, the glass splintered, and milk washed across the floor, it would have in no way diminished her love for me.

On mornings when Billy wasn't yet awake, I would clamber on all fours up the narrow staircase to lie beside him on his bed. Early on, he shared a room with Mary. She was often awake when I arrived and without lifting her head from her mattress would watch me through the wooden slats of her crib.

Sometimes I fell asleep next to Billy. Sometimes I grew impatient and ran the tip of my finger along the top of his velvety ear, until he yawned and opened his eyes.

Mrs. Buffone made us porridge with as much milk and brown sugar as we wanted. On Sundays, we had pancakes with corn syrup. Mr. Buffone sat on the counter smoking, drinking black coffee, and urging us to "Mànge, mànge. You be big boys!"

Billy's mother scolded his father, "It's *eat*, Angelo! This is Canada. You are going to confuse the heads of these boys! They have to go to the school soon. What will the other children think? What will the teacher say? She will ask, 'What? Are you peasants from the hills of someplace?'"

Mr. Buffone would hop from the counter to strike a dramatic pose, raising his arms and shouting, "Yes! I am a peasant from the hills someplace!" He laughed and, seated back on the counter, pulled Mrs. Buffone to him. She would make a show of struggling against his hugging arms and his legs wrapped around her. He pressed his lips to her ear and murmured, "Non mi resistere al mio amore, la mia amante!" Billy and I didn't know what Mr. Buffone was saying, but we would cover our ears and plead for him to stop.

When they were alone, or didn't want us to know what they were saying, Mr. and Mrs. Buffone spoke Italian to one another.

The tenderness in the round tones of their voices was as foreign to me as the words themselves.

"It was like my second home." People say that about the home of a childhood friend: "Theirs was like my second home." When they say it, they mean they felt as comfortable, as welcomed, and as cherished as they did in their own home. They mean, in this second home they experienced the same ease of familial patterns, safety, the same unbreakable bonds of family ties. They mean, there is no strangeness to the smell of this second home. Its inhabitants are blood. This second home is where one spends as much time as they do in their own home. If all those things are true, if that is what people mean when the say "It was like my second home," then the Buffone's house was like my *first* home.

Their home was where each year, on the first day of school, my photo was taken in front of the rose bushes that kept pace with my growth as they climbed the cedar-rail fence; where a mother licked her thumb to wipe jam from my face, or to tame my unruly hair; where a father showed us how to straighten bent nails and supplied us salvaged boards with which to build our forts in the trees at the end of our street; where teasing was rare, and what teasing there was, was kind, good-natured, and more often than not, self-deprecating; where my birthday was celebrated every year with Billy's; and where they knew me well enough to give me books as gifts, rather than a second-hand shotgun, as my biological father did the Christmas I was thirteen.

Billy and I were like brothers. The Buffones were my family. Their home was my home.

6

ERASING FOOTPRINTS

Billy is vacuuming. The forty chairs that, when set out, fill the funeral chapel to capacity are stacked against the wall. Mr. Martin's funeral didn't create much fuss or muss. A little sand was tracked in. Billy vacuums the morning after each funeral as a matter of principle. He vacuums to lift the sand and to resurrect the pile of the rose-coloured broadloom where it has been pressed flat by shoes and walker wheels.

Routine, one thing systematically following the next is, as far as Billy is concerned, the balm of Gilead. His mind is calmed by the predictability, the formulaic nature, of funerals. Their sum totals as reliable as a mathematical equation. Funerals begin with a phone call from a distraught family member, or a no-nonsense night shift nurse at the hospital. They conclude with vacuuming of the carpet and the re-setting of the chairs, readying everything for the next call.

Bigger funerals take place at one of the three churches in Twenty-Six Mile House, where the pews can accommodate a larger congregation of mourners. Less notable—not to say lesser—undertakings like Mr. Martin's, are conducted in the more intimate environs of Billy's chapel, where the posted Fire Marshal's Notification declares the maximum capacity of the room to be fifty persons. Billy doesn't always know who vacuums or sweeps up at the churches after funerals, but is consoled by a steadfast faith that somebody does.

Billy's chapel is not much bigger than the living room at what used to be the Mill manager's house. The Mill is shuttered now, the last of the managers emptied his house and slipped away under the cover of night. Of course, Billy's chapel is, technically speaking, a dying room. The dimensions of the two rooms are similar, that's all I am saying.

To the left of the draped casket-dolly, there is a blonde oak podium fitted with recessed castor wheels. The wall behind dolly and podium is draped with a burgundy velvet curtain. The wide vertical stripes of the wallpaper, affixed to the other three walls of the chapel, are the same hue as the draping but several shades lighter.

The sound system, behind the curtain, is wired to mini-speakers mounted in the four upper corners of the room. Before and after each service, and during visitations, Billy plays cassette tapes from the *Solitudes Collection,* which blend Pan flute with the sounds of birds singing, brooks burbling or gentle surf. The music mutes the sharp edge of sobs, nose blowing and, on occasion, wailing laments. It also helps to fill the awkward empty silences, when there is really nothing worth saying.

Sometimes during the service, a keyboard player accompanies hymns. Other times, Billy uses the *Abide with Me and Other Favourite Hymns* tape. Most people choose "The Old Rugged Cross" or "What a Friend We Have in Jesus" and always, unfailingly, "Amazing Grace."

"Mom loved those old hymns," her children recall. "We should include one or two." Billy dutifully types and makes photocopies of the lyrics, even though he knows only the preacher and maybe a clutch of steadfast churchgoers will sing along.

An elderly widow once requested that a disco song by the Whispers called *It's a Love Thing* be played as she recessed from the chapel behind her husband's casket. Her adult children were mortified, and tried unsuccessfully to dissuade her from playing the song. On the night before the funeral, she dropped by the chapel with the cassette for Billy. He slipped it into the player and the two of them sat in the front row to listen. Billy assumed it was the "talkin' in my sleep about the love we made" line that made her kids want to whinge. Maybe they just didn't like disco.

Billy rested his arm across the back of the woman's chair,

and she leaned into his shoulder and cried. When it ended they played it again. "It's perfect," Billy assured her.

Dick Spanner's house is across the street from Billy's home and business. Spanner's place is one of the newest and biggest houses in town. Spanner, like most men in Twenty-Six Mile House, was employed at the mill until it went down. By all appearances, however, Dick remains quite flush. There are rumours he won a lottery, or that he made millions selling the Pascal computer program he wrote to operate the gauges at the mill. Spanner has never said. In fact, he rarely says anything to anyone and, in the way of small towns, his silence spawns— among the coffee drinkers at Robin's Donuts—even more sinister speculation about the source of his unaccountable wealth.

To Billy, for reasons he could not explain if he had to do so, Spanner's house is also the most malevolent looking house in town. Creepy. Looking at the house, out the window above his kitchen sink, gives Billy an uneasy, sick feeling in his stomach. Its two-story flat face projects a blank expression, as though it is hiding something. Not a single accent or trim of any colour interrupts the facade. On foggy days, the front slope of the shingled roof looks like it is floating, as if suspended in the claws of the unkindness of ravens, that regularly occupied its crest. The windows float unmoored in the thick mist.

The sick feeling Billy gets looking at Spanner's house is the same nausea he felt awakening from a fevered dream as a teenager. He had dreamt of an infinite darkness, in the middle of which floated a tiny, yellow, raw egg yolk. In the yolk was a pulsing spot of blood. He woke from the dream, his pyjamas soaked with perspiration, and vomited in the ice cream pail next to his bed.

While he cleans, Billy is wearing a set of immense headphones. They look like the polished halves of a black coconut, connected by an adjustable bridge that flattens his hair on top of his head. The headphone jack is connected to the sound system by a long, coiled extension cable. Billy's Bob Seger and his Silver Bullet Band cassette is in the player. He cranks the volume control knob on the left coconut up to eight. He fingers imaginary frets on the vacuum cleaner wand and strums air guitar strings across the carpet-beater attachment. The Electrolux canister, jerked along by its hose, mimics Billy's strutting performance.

Eyes closed, Billy grimaces with emotion. His lips pressed tight, he hums song syllabics in the back of his throat. Old time rock and roll is the kind of music that soothes his soul.

He pictures the light show, the pyrotechnics, the deck of amplifiers and the mixing board, raining thunder from three storey high stacks of speakers. He is playing Cobo Hall, in Detroit. Motown. The Motor City. The fans roar and crowd surf. They wave Bic lighters above their heads. The smell of pot, teenage angst and hormones hang sour and heavy in the air. Billy is wearing dark glasses to shield his eyes from the blinding stage lights, but is pretty sure he just saw a kid jump over the rail from Tier A. He shakes his head and hopes the crowd down on the main floor, egging him on, broke his fall.

His security guys are wearing black leather vests and merch-T-shirts emblazoned with Billy's picture; each one of them, weighing in at 240 pounds plus, are pushing back against the surging crowd. Two crazed and tanned girls, wearing hotpants and kerchief-halter tops, clamber over the security line to dance on the stage. His bodyguards are on them like flies, but Billy waves them off between chords. It's cool.

Billy chicken struts to the front doors of the funeral home and plops the rug-whacker attachment down on the floor, ready to vacuum backwards into the chapel to erase his own foot prints from the carpet pile. There—framed in a window of the double-doors, staring, mouth agape in a perfect round O to match her wide eyes—is Catherine, the preacher.

7

CATHERINE TURNS AND BOLTS

Catherine turns and bolts. She takes two steps in the direction of her parked car and turns back, irrationally trying to make it look like she has just arrived, that she did not see what Billy clearly saw her seeing: Billy, the funeral director, wearing a massive pair of headphones on his head, rooster strutting and playing air guitar on a vacuum cleaner. Her shoulders slump. She steps up to the door, facing the fact that she can't pretend not to have seen what she saw because—as I said—Billy saw her seeing it. She raises her knuckles toward the door. Then, rather than a redundant knock, she opens her hand and gives Billy a queenly wave.

Billy opens the door and raises his dark eyebrows like questions. "Hi?"

Catherine's fair complexion mottles, again, as though she has been caught peeking between the drapes into Billy's bedroom. *Why am I the one who's embarrassed here?*

"Sander." She pulls a canvas bag off her shoulder and begins to scrabble around in it.

"Sander," Billy repeats. He pats the chest of his white V-neck T-shirt with both hands, instinctively checking the breast pockets of the morning suit he is not wearing, for the sander. He searches the front pockets of his jeans. Looking down at his feet, Billy sees that his big toe is poking out through a hole in his sock. He slides his foot forward to draw the offending hole under his foot and clenches it there with his toes.

Catherine is still mining her bag. "Yes, your sander. I forgot to give it back yesterday." Her face feels hot. "I'm sorry... I... well, I should have called before coming by." She locates the sander and hands it to Billy. He closes his fingers around it but does not lower his arm. His fist continues to float between them. *Is he waiting for a fist bump? See ya. Peace out.*

Catherine's mortification—waving a white flag—surrenders to giddiness. She looks away, ransacking her mind for epically sad, or tragic, or grotesque images with which to cork the pressurized hilarity bubbling up in her throat. She inhales through her nose, exhales from her mouth, and meets Billy's confused brown eyes.

Laughter, suppressed in socially inappropriate situations—in church or at a funeral home, for example—like gas under pressure, inevitably leads to an explosion. The more you compress it, the more unstable the gas becomes. Once the tab is flipped on a shaken soda, there is just no putting it back in the can.

Catherine sprays a mist of saliva into the woolen mittens she is mashing into her mouth. Her eyes spill over with tears. Her body heaves. She shakes her head side to side. Her cinnamon coloured hair falls across her face. She holds up her free hand—the one not stuffing her mouth with her mittens—her index finger extended. *One moment please.* Could she utter a coherent word without a howl of laughter, she would plead with Billy, "I'm sorry. Sorry. Please wait. I'm sorry. I'll be okay. Just give me a second. I don't know what's come over me. Sorry." And so on. But, given her possession by the gremlins of hilarity, and mittens-stuffed mouth, she is unable to speak.

Catherine chastises herself: *Grow up. Grow up! For God's sake, grow up! You're a grown woman, a minister, for the love of God!* Did she not herself, from time to time, dance around the living room with a hairbrush microphone? Doesn't everybody? What is the big deal? Recovering her composure, she looks up at Billy, wiping her eyes and nose with the mittens, composing an apology.

Billy taps the muted headphones, now hanging around his neck, and says, "Silver Bullet Band. Old Time Rock 'n Roll."

"What? I mean pardon?" Catherine strains to decipher his coded message. It's as if Billy is speaking a language of which she has only a rudimentary grasp. Mercifully, the words "rock 'n roll" and "Bob Seger" collide in her frantic mind. "Oh, right. RIGHT! YES! Great song!"

"Yep," Billy nods. An awkward silence expands between them. Billy nods again, "Uh huh."

Catherine notices his fist is still raised—fist bump ready— the brass cylinder cap is visible above his thumb. She touches a finger to his hand and Billy watches his arm lower itself to his side.

"OK, then. I guess I better get going," says Catherine. "Thanks for the sander. Hope I don't see you soon." Catherine grins, anticipating Billy's chuckling acknowledgement of her witticism. "For a funeral, you know. I hope I don't see you for a funeral, too soon. I guess you've heard that one a few times. Anyway." She is dying. "Not that I don't want to see you. Just not, you know, for funerals. I'd love to, you know see you, get together, you know hang out or whatever, you know, another way. Up town or whatever." Even to herself, Catherine is starting to sound like a stalker.

Billy nods, raises the sander, like a champagne flute for a toast. "Okay. Uh huh."

Catherine scurries toward her car, then looks back over her shoulder. Billy has disappeared from the door window. She returns to the door, for the third time in as many minutes, and notices the doorbell for the first time and rings it.

"Do you want to go for a coffee? I mean go for a coffee or get one and go down to the beach and look at the lake or something?" She rattles the words off before she lets herself chicken out.

Billy looks at the vacuum cleaner, at his footprints, awaiting erasure. The stacked chairs need to be reset in their orderly rows. He looks down and notices the cold air has hardened his nipples. He crosses his arms over his thin t-shirt, gripping his shoulders. "No thanks."

"Okay," says Catherine. "It's a bit nippily out and I can see you're busy right now. Maybe some other time. Me too. Busy, I mean. Easter coming up and... well, see you later... maybe after that, after Easter and Good Friday and everything." She turns to leave, drops her keys, picks them up and hurries to her car. From the driver's seat she looks back. Billy is gone, again. She says, "Sure, I'm pretty busy, too. Let's take a rain check, shall we? Did I say nippily? Nippy! NIPPY! SHIT!" She bounces her forehead off the steering wheel.

8

LONELY

Catherine reflexively rummages through the detritus covering the passenger seat—a Bible, her Week-at-Glance calendar, scraps of paper scribbled with notes and phone numbers, empty coffee cups, sermon outlines—looking for cigarettes. She quit smoking years ago. She cranks the steering wheel hard to the left, because the key won't turn in the worn ignition if she doesn't. Her twelve-year-old Impala barks to life and she drives back into town toward St. Luke's. The snow tires hum on the dry pavement. She's waiting to get paid before getting them changed over to the summer tires. God willing, they've got one more season of tread left on them.

Behind the church, the parking lot is a minefield of potholes that put the car's shock absorbers to the test. A test they predictably fail, with a bottoming out clank, but they will have to do until Catherine's student loans are repaid, sometime around the Second Coming.

St Luke's is pretty much what you would expect when picturing a post war, Protestant church building—white clapboard siding, a steeple crowned with a cross, modest bell tower, and some stained glass windows dedicated to the memory of the local boys who marched off to war and didn't come home. Due to budget shortfalls, a few of the windows remain paned with clear glass.

"The church is the community of people, not the building," Catherine regularly reminds her dwindling flock. They all nod, compliant as lambs, but she has no doubt that—if fiduciary push came to budgetary shove—the building would stand and she would walk. The building has, after all, outlasted a parade of preachers. It houses more memories—baptisms, weddings and funerals—than do any one of the twenty or so preachers who've stepped in and out of its pulpit over the years. In Twenty-Six Mile House, preachers generally come and go on a three-year cycle. The little white church has stood faithfully against the vagaries of time. It has borne all things, believed all things, hoped all things, and endured all things—including all manner of financial calamity.

Catherine unlocks and heaves one of the heavy, double doors open. The church office is located in an addition, tacked on to the sanctuary, as an afterthought. In a cathedral, this bit at the front is called the apse. St Luke's building has little in common with a cathedral, beyond their constant need for roof repairs. The addition serves mostly as Catherine's office. The recently purchased safe, a fleet of burgundy choir gowns, a set of thirty-year old Sunday School curricula books, and a fairly new photocopier are also stored there.

The green indicator light on the answering machine stares, unblinking, back at Catherine. Just to be sure there are in fact no messages, she pushes the "play" button. The machine remains mute.

While training for ministry at Emmanuel College, across from Queen's Park and the Planetarium in Toronto, Catherine and her fellow seminarians pledged themselves to ministry *with* the people, *alongside* the people, to supporting the people in *their* vision for ministry. *The people* of St. Luke's are warm, kind-hearted, and encouraging folks. They are also stalwart in their resistance to change. And they are encamped behind an impenetrable wall, beyond which she has been granted only a visitor's visa.

Catherine gets it. Most of the clergy—professing their great love for the town, winter and St. Luke's—logged their years, x-ing out the days on their calendars like prisoners, only to decamp to greener pastures, gentler climates, bigger flocks, and more sophisticated versions of civilization. They find churches with paid administrators, big choirs, praise bands, youth ministers, and compensation above the minimum pay scale. They head south to cities with art galleries, live theatre, shopping malls, restaurants, and a degree of anonymity.

"We should have a revolving door for ministers." Catherine overheard that remark during fellowship time, on the Sunday Beverly Anders, Chair of the Board, introduced her to the congregation. The person who said it, and those who chuckled thought Catherine was still upstairs.

That first summer, Catherine joined a co-ed soft-ball team, and represented herself well at bat. After the umpire called the last out, she was thanked profusely for coming out, but was never invited to join the rest of the team for a postgame beer at the Legion. One night, she imposed herself at the cramped team table. She squished in, between the Pac Man game and the wall, and talked too loudly, tried too hard. Her teammates visibly squirmed, trying to get comfortable on the familiar, wooden chairs. Eventually Catherine begged off, "Saturday night. I guess I better go finish getting ready for tomorrow morning." A hearty, and clearly relieved chorus rose among her teammates, "Thanks for coming out! See ya!" She left a half-finished Coors Light in a puddle of condensation on the table.

This emotional distancing protects congregants and ball teams alike, from predictable heartbreak, brought about by the departure of yet another preacher. They've come to know that this preacher too, will pass. Catherine gets it, and she intends to prove them wrong. She wants to stay.

For now, though, she is lonely. It was her loneliness which led to the humiliating and stuttering response to Billy's blunt rejection of her invitation to coffee. What else but desperate loneliness could have compelled her to extend the offer in the first place?

There are three or four bachelors of Catherine's generation in town. Sure. Reclusive, guarded men, unconcerned for their personal hygiene. They are men who live alone in houses where small-engine repairs are made at the kitchen table. A few of them are quietly gay. There are also men, who continue to exist, left broken by Rupert Churley. Catherine doesn't know about all that. There is something different about Billy, something to which she feels drawn.

She finds him handsome, and curiously, vulnerable. There is a sense of substance, depth to him. Catherine has always been confident of her intuition and, these days, maintains a fierce trust in her inner voice. Her two misbegotten, and unlicensed, marriages only serve to reinforce that confidence. She entered into both unions by tamping down her misgivings. There is something different about Billy Buffone and she intends to find out what it is.

She hangs her coat on a wire hook screwed into the back of the door. Catherine keeps her journal locked in a drawer of the grey metal desk. She retrieves it, along with a ball-point pen, and plugs in the electric heater to chase the chill from the office. Zipping up her thrift store cardigan, she heads down stairs while the heater's glowing coils warm the room.

She takes the steep wooden staircase down to the kitchen. Everything in the kitchen from the counter tops, to the stove and refrigerator, to the rose patterned china, are original and impeccably preserved by the United Church Women.

She pours the coffee she brought from home in a mayonnaise jar into a ceramic mug embossed with the school board logo. She puts it in the microwave to warm it. Early on, Catherine had microwaved her coffee in one of the gold-rimmed teacups. Who knew there was actual gold on teacups? The consequent electrical storm in the microwave pitted the plastic door and shattered the cup. She had secretly disposed of the cup.

The Sunday following the flaming teacup incident, carefully worded recriminations began to fly among the ladies regarding the whereabouts of a missing teacup. The cups, it turns out, are inventoried regularly, and a single lost cup, among the exactly one hundred, is investigated with all the prodigal love of Jesus seeking the lost sheep.

Catherine confessed, before things got out of hand, and offered to replace both the microwave—the damage to which had so far gone unnoticed—and the cup. "Oh no, don't be silly," replied the ladies, one and all. "That isn't necessary." "The kitchen fund is in good shape, dear." "We should probably be ordering a few extras just to have on hand."

For the United Church Women, there is no greater pleasure than the opportunity to extend dispensation to a repentant sinner. Catherine was not only genuinely forgiven, but her small culinary offence and her contrition cracked open—just a little—the emotional door between them. It also happily established Catherine's reputation as a kitchen-klutz, best suited to the pulpit when it came to teas and fowl suppers. Four new cups and saucers were ordered from a china shop in Kitchener-Waterloo. They are only available in sets. So, there is one spare saucer should one become necessary.

- 9 -
BILLY BOLTS THE LID BACK DOWN

Billy, meanwhile, is gasping air the way a drowning man gulps water. He inhales—the air laden with the smell of Lysol—but cannot breathe. His lungs have turned to splintered glass. Billy is certain that he is choking to death. Panicking is too ineffectual of a word. He has fallen through the ice and can't locate a pocket of air from which to sip. His heart hammers against his sternum, trying to break out of his chest. His face is on fire. He is drenched with perspiration, and he is shivering. He has taken refuge in the unisex bathroom outside the chapel. He has locked the door, with the blue and white and Braille restroom sign, behind him. He presses his cheek against the cool ceramic tiles on the wall beside to the sink.

He opens the cold-water tap. His hands flap spasmodically, splashing his face and combing his fingers through his hair. He lays a cool hand on the back of his neck and continues to shiver. He wets a paper towel, presses it to his forehead. Another wave of vertigo swamps him. His legs go numb. He collapses onto the toilet seat. He leans forward with his head between his knees. Maybe he should throw up and get it over with.

Instead, Billy lurches down the hallway—past the display room and the kitchenette—balancing himself against the wall. He stumbles through the office, trips up the two steps, and through the door, leading into his kitchen. He makes a circuit of his apartment, closing the kitchen and living room blinds, locks the front door and the one to the office.

Finally, he drops onto the couch in the kitchen. He turns his back on the rest of the room, draws his knees up to his chest, and pulls the throw-blanket down from the back of the couch to cover his shoulders. He presses his face into the crack between the seat and back cushions. He inhales the familiar smell of the couch through his nose.

The couch is from his mother's home. The texture of the worn green, corduroy fabric, and the smell of it, soothes him. It evokes better days in Billy, days before that last summer.

This is how Billy bolts down the lid on his panic attacks which increasingly, and without warning, jump him like a gang of muggers. It feels like the panic will kill him. When this irrational terror has him on his knees, like it does now, death would come as a relief.

Billy once made an appointment to talk to a visiting physician about these spells. She told him, "It sounds to me like an anxiety disorder, Mr. Buffone," wrote a prescription and offered a referral to a Thunder Bay therapist. Billy flicked both the prescription and the referral off like spruce-beetles landing on his shirt. Assuring the doctor that such extreme measures were unnecessary, he thanked her politely, and fled the examining room.

The doctor was left sitting on her rolling stool, open-mouthed, finger raised at the ready, to offer Billy reassurance and a contrary view, but he was gone. She telephoned his house later that evening. Billy did not pick up. She left him a message asking if he was all right and inviting him to be in touch so they could talk more. At the time of this follow-up phone call, Billy was on the couch, back turned and nose buried. He did not return the doctor's call. She left town for a stint in Sioux Lookout the following week. Billy has not sought further medical assistance for his attacks.

Billy is lying on the couch coaxing his brain like a small frightened animal into its tranquil place. This diversionary tactic is a trick he has played on himself since his teenage years. It has been his escape route from the emotional chains and cinder blocks trying to drown him below the dark waters of our shared past.

Billy fantasizes that he is a famous musician or a producer or sometimes a painter. He pictures a house built on the red cliffs of Cavendish, Prince Edward Island. He first saw the house in a photograph on the September page of the 1975 Superior Credit Union calendar—the month after I died and Billy started panicking.

The lane leading up to his imaginary house is surfaced with yam coloured gravel. The front of the house, visible from the road, is clad in traditional east coast, white-washed-wood shakes and multi-paned windows. There is a detached garage where Billy stores his Triumph 100T Bonneville motorcycle. In the driveway is parked an older model Porsche 911, its once silver paint faded to grey. The aluminum-alloy engine pings as it cools. Billy—the musician, producer, maybe artist—is wealthy but he doesn't care about money.

The other side of the house faces out toward the ocean, and is ultra-modernist because anything is possible in fantasies. Floor to ceiling, stainless-steel framed windows reflect the cerulean sky above and the sea below. There is a hot tub, hammocks, a barbeque and several tables with umbrellas and cushioned chairs on the deck where he entertains his celebrity friends. A set of switch-back steps lead from the deck down to the beach. Billy begins each day at sunrise doing yoga on the beach. Naked. It is very spiritual.

Inside, there are stairs descending from the living room to a recording studio carved directly into the cliff face. Famous studio musicians come to hang out and record the new songs Billy writes. In his mind, Billy outfits the studio with top-end sound equipment, a drum kit, and an assortment of other instruments. The polished red stone that forms three walls of the studio are fitted with acoustic tiles. The fourth wall is made of expansive sheets of glass looking out over the ocean. On summer days, the panels of glass are swung open to channel the warm ocean breeze inside. In the winter, Billy finds his inspiration gazing out on the moody sea. He steps out onto the lower deck to smoke and brood over deep philosophical thoughts.

Back inside the studio, he slides buttons up and down on the mixing board, or noodles a tune on his vintage Les Paul electric guitar. Today he's working on a project with a young protégé discovered and brought to him by Meg Ryan. Billy fell in love with Meg back when he first saw her in the Burger King commercial. She's with him in the studio, watching him work, or is upstairs making lunch. Meg trusts Billy to help the troubled girl straighten out her life by launching her career as a popstar.

Sometimes it is Jodie Foster, instead of Meg Ryan, who brings Billy a protégé and is making lunch upstairs. In line at the grocery store recently, he read that Jodie might be a lesbian. It doesn't matter to him. That's the kind of person he is.

In one of Billy's fantasies, Jodie is preparing to play Janice Joplin in a biopic about the singer's short, tragic life and career. Jodie and Billy drink a lot of Southern Comfort, work through Joplin's repertoire, and have sex. The sex is wild and fierce in the act, and tender afterwards. They both regret it, the sex. The awkwardness dissipates quickly, though, because of their mutual respect and platonic love for one another. Thereafter, they continue to sleep together, platonically.

Lately, it's been one of the Hemingway sisters with him at his September calendar page house in Prince Edward Island. He can't remember if her name is Mariel or Margaux. She's the one who was in *Manhattan*, the sister with the hurt eyes. Not the one who was a model before she was in *Lipstick*. Billy imagines helping her too, maybe with an addiction or an emotional breakdown, caused by being too beautiful and famous and misunderstood and driven by inner self-hate and by her father's suicide. These women stay with him and get strong. They want to be his lovers but he always tells them no. It would be wrong. It would be taking advantage of their vulnerability.

At night, Meg or Jodie go with him to a nearby roadhouse, where he sits in with the house band. It's a big deal for the band because he is famous. Some of his high school classmates—the cool kids, the hockey players and rink bunnies like Sonny Neilson, Deborah Doret, Mike and Grant Tiltner, their sister Brenda—are there, sitting at a table covered with pint glasses of draught beer and wet paper coasters. They are on summer holidays with their kids, and have stopped into the pub by chance. They are stunned to discover Billy performing there on the stage. They see him, with Meg or Jodie or the hurt-eyed Hemingway sister, and regret the provincial cruelty of their youth. They wish they had been more kind to Billy when they had the chance.

He welcomes them magnanimously. "Hey folks, some old friends are in the house tonight!" he shouts into the microphone. "Let's give them an East Coast welcome!" The crowd explodes with applause as he launches into one of his new songs. The song is a bit like Van Morrison's *These Are the Days of the End of Summer,* but better.

I slip into the roadhouse, take a stool at the bar at the back, and nurse a beer. Billy doesn't see me—the ghostly presence of his deceased best friend dropping into his fantasy—at first. I can see through the scrim of Billy's fantasy. I can see him, curled on the couch in his kitchen in Twenty-Six Mile House. If I still had a throat it would constrict with tenderness, it would strangle a sob and my eyes—had I eyes—would sting. Had I arms, I would wrap them around him and carry him back to his kitchen from this make-believe place. Lay my body down to spoon him on the couch. Hold him and stroke his ear like I did when we were children. I want to weep, but I have no tears to spill, no longer have eyes from which to pour out my sorrow.

Billy notices me, inhabiting the shadows of his fantasy. In spite of the cost to my dislocated soul, I smile and raise my glass to toast his success. He tries to erase me with the chalkboard brush of his imagination. In his urgency to be rid of me, he hastily sketches in my place a burly bear of a potato farmer, laughing with his friends after a tough day in the fields. A dark-bearded man wearing coveralls. A man built, and dressed entirely unlike me—wiry, barely five-foot-seven, smooth-faced, angular and, when Billy last laid eyes on me, a natty dresser.

Billy is having trouble deploying his fantasy shield today. His happy place keeps giving his brain the slip. Catherine's face keeps displacing Jodie's or Meg's. He pinches his eyelids closed but that's where she is, inside his eyes. She takes the stool next to mine at the bar. The picture of the roadhouse and the red soil of Prince Edward Island begin to shred, like a bear is raking its claw across the thin fabric of a nylon tent. Billy is losing focus. He presses his nose further down between the cushions, inhaling their musty scent. In this half-dream state, his mind vacillates between the imaginary, charmed life in Prince Edward Island, and Catherine, the ethereal me, and the harsh realities of his life in Twenty-Six Mile House.

I try teasing him the way I used to do. "She said, 'Let's get a coffee. Go down and look at the Lake.' And you said 'No?' Billy. Seriously? Tell me that did NOT just happen.

"Remember how I used to call the big Lake 'Mother Superior? Remember how I used to say, 'Let's go consult Mother Superior on this matter, my friend.' Remember how you would roll your eyes?"

Billy can hear me. He concentrates on getting back to P.E.I., but bumps into Catherine waiting for him there. Are they Catherine's eyes? Is she the one with the hurt eyes, or are they his own eyes mirrored back at him in Catherine's?

When Billy manages to block the memories of our last summer—by retreating into make believe—the shredding pain behind his eyes, the weight of wet clay in his belly, and the caving in of his chest, gentles. The exhaustion, caused by the conjuring of increasingly unreliable fantasies, carries him off to sleep, a sleep still troubled by dreams he will elect to forget when he wakes. He will sleep for an hour or two, and wake, feeling refreshed. He will don his headphones, turn the knob back up to eight or even nine, and finish the cleaning. Walking the vacuum cleaner backwards into the chapel, he will erase his own footprints from the carpet.

- 10 -
Are You There, God? It's Me, Catherine

Back upstairs in the sanctuary, Catherine settles into the front left-hand pew where she sits most mornings to write in her journal. I am seated across the aisle, on the right. She cannot see me, of course, because I'm dead. My family would be shocked and derisive to find me, of all people, here in a church of any denominational flavour. Neither I nor my kin were churchgoers, but as they say, "Once a Catholic always a Catholic." If that is true, we Mad Collins remain very distant associates of His Holiness the Pope. During my short life I attended only one service of worship. I'll come back to that.

I am not drawn to St. Luke's on Sundays. The songs and homilies seem like noisy affronts to the sacredness of the space. I prefer to come in the middle of the week, craving silence, the sunlight fractured by stained glass, the cross and the candle—which, by extreme concentration, I have twice caused to ignite. I am drawn on winter mornings by the crack of the frozen beams thawing. Early on, I came to pray for Billy. My prayers for him have been marginally efficacious, but in the sanctuary, I experienced a kind of peacefulness previously foreign to me. So, I've kept coming.

Catherine spies the offering plate left on the Communion table since Sunday. She gathers the sheaf of envelopes—each one numbered for tax purposes—along with loose bills and coins, puts them in a manila envelope, and locks it in the safe for the treasurer.

A scattering of stale bread crumbs also remain on the Communion cloth. She brushes them into her cupped hand and, from the side door, scatters them onto the frozen ground for the birds. As if it had been waiting, a raven drops from the roof and pecks up the meagre remains of the Body of Christ from the snow.

Catherine's movements are lovely to watch, a ballet of embodiment, the elegance of her reaching arm, the turning of her long, freckled neck, the shifting of her hips. There is grace, a physical kindness even, in the way she draws the door closed. Homesick for my own once vital body, I allow myself a melancholy sigh and Catherine is startled by the intuition humans sometimes have, that they are being watched. She scans the sanctuary, the air alive with motes of dust dancing in the sunshine. Having reassured herself that she is alone, she returns to her pew.

Since arriving in Twenty-Six Mile House, Catherine has, with varying degrees of success, attempted to write in her journal every morning. She's batting about five hundred. Some days she feels too busy to write—overwhelmed by sermon preparation, visits to the hospital, Bible study, preparing her column for *The News*, fundraising dinners, community organizing, and drinking tea with powdered seniors.

On those days, her inner productivity judges bang their gavels, circumventing her best intentions. The road to Hell is paved with them. Lately, those judges sound like Ernie Caird, Chairman of the Property Committee. She hears him insisting that "the church needs to be run more like a business," and how it must be "nice for Catherine to have all day to just scribble in her journal." Ernie has never expressed any such sentiments, never said anything even remotely like them. His stiff collared Calvinistic demeanour, and his self-flagellating Protestant work ethic, cause Catherine to suspect that Ernie would consider her a superfluous line in the annual budget. A cross laid on the back of St. Luke's to bear.

She knows these thoughts are manufactured by her own insecurities, but a word of reassurance from Ernie now and then would be nice. She laughs along with folks who tease her about only working one hour a week. Sometimes she beats them to the punch line. Inwardly, however, she is determined to make them appreciate the demands and value of her daily sacrifices; prove to them that what she does matters. That she matters.

Dear God, This is the salutation with which Catherine begins each journal entry.

I just asked Billy Buffone to go for a coffee and sweated and stuttered like I was thirteen! I forgot to give his sander back yesterday after the funeral—Ed Martin. The way he reacted, you'd think I'd asked him to marry me or hook up at the motel. (Not necessarily in that order ☺). Probably just embarrassed—I caught him playing air guitar with his vacuum cleaner. It was hilarious. Actually, he didn't seem embarrassed at all. I did! Crazy!
Is this how it's going to be? Are guys going to be forever freaked out because I'm a minister? I am not a nun, for crying out loud! I would like to date every now and then. I get horny. I know that's OK with you. Honestly, at this point, I'd settle for a friend, God. Help!

"You are surrounded by love."

When Catherine feels she is hearing the voice of God, rather than her own ego, she writes what she hears in quotation marks. Her tests for authenticity are: 1) She hears God responding before she has formed her own next thought, and 2) It sounds like something God would say. If she is not positive about whether it's God or her ego, she adds: *I'm not sure if that's you or me talking.*

Well, that might be true, maybe I am surrounded by love, but I am lonely; more alone than I've ever been. Everyone is "nice" to me. I trust that I am where you want me to be, but I don't have a single friend, not really. It's like I'm not human.

I think the women worry I'm out to steal their men, most of them are old enough to be my grampy. Besides, no need to worry, ladies, your men are scared to death of me. They assume

I'm sworn to celibacy or a lesbian. A couple creepy dudes like to flirt with my nun-like-ness. I get an icky feeling that one guy—Ray Graham—has a full-blown clerical fetish, fantasizes about getting a peek up the Alb at the bad girl underneath. I *definitely* miss sex, but it's not what I miss most.

Billy's a bit odd. Different. Like he might be lonely too. Maybe we've got that in common? Maybe that's just wishful thinking because, since the funeral, I've been thinking about what it would be like to kiss him. I'm not hearing you chime in on that, God.

Everyone in town knows Billy. He's lived here all his life, but he's out there on the edge of town, in more ways than one. He's an old- towner, but at the same time, an outsider. When people talk about Billy, it's like he grew up here, but left or like he used to be a real person, but isn't anymore. A real boy who turned into wood. That's not quite it, either. They respect him, I think, but unlike most old-towners, mentioning his name doesn't blow the doors off a collection of stories and memories. Tight-lipped generalities would describe what I got when I asked around about Billy, before the funeral. "Billy? Good guy. Grew up here." Smile. End of story.

Last night, I dreamt about rescuing a little girl who had fallen in the lake between the slabs of ice. There were other people there too. Everyone was running, hopping from one raft of ice to the next, like the ones the wind blew into the bay last week. I fell between two of them. A lot of other people were falling too. I found the bottom with my feet and crawled out onto the ice. I came up on the shore with a baby—a little girl—in my arms. I don't know where she came from but she was blue, so I blew in her mouth. Just once, and she started to cry and I started cry. I fell down and cut my knees on the jagged ice. People were pulling me, taking me someplace warm. Then I woke up.

Not sure what it means. Maybe it's me who needs rescuing? The dream didn't feel like that, though. It felt like it was someone else I'm supposed to rescue. When I woke up, I was thinking about Billy.

Well, I have to go by the hospital today and put together the bulletin for Sunday. Tonight is B.S. Bible Study. God give me what I need today to be your will in the world. Amen. Catherine signs off each of her journal entries with that prayer.

She bookmarks the page with a blue jay feather she brought with her from Toronto, closes the journal, sets it down on the pew, and sips her coffee. The sunlight bends through the two stained-glass windows on the south side of the sanctuary—JESUS the Good Shepherd and Suffer the Children to Come Unto ME. The other five, south facing windows are clear glass. The north wall has one stained-glass window—If I but Touch HIS Robe I Will be Healed. Mounted on the sill below each window is a brass memorial plaque engraved with the name of the benefactor family and date of their donation.

The sunlight, refracted by "Suffer the Children to Come Unto ME," paints the back of Catherine's hand. The rainbow of colour illuminates and magnifies the pores of her skin, the fine hairs there. Her fingers wrapped around the handle of the mug. It feels like a miracle to us both, the way her fingers bend and move with such ingenuity. The light. Her hand. The navy cuff of her Salvation Army Thrift Store sweater.

She moves her fingers contemplatively. They are dancing. Her chest fills with wonder, with a soft longing for something beyond naming. It is not magic so much as it is being awake. It is seeing what most of us never stop long enough to take in—the intensity of colours, the scent of coffee and waxed wood blending with the smell of a million extinguished candle wicks. Catherine absorbs it. Her lungs inflate with gratitude and joy and wonder and love. Something bigger even than love. She calls it Presence or Mystery but knows from experience the futility of trying to domesticate such moments with words. Capturing them with words is like trying to chain the wild dogs of her soul. They cannot be kept staked in the yard. Holding on only limits their wildness, the very thing by which she is so moved.

Catherine observes her fingers with childlike wonder. The whole universe is present to her—no, it is she who is present to it—in the miracle of their movement, in the instant of fingers, skin, light transformed. Flesh and bone and blood, inspired.

From across the aisle, I watch her body softening and a wave of nostalgia for my own lost corporal being washes over me. She senses me near again and shivers.

In the sky outside, clouds drift across the sun. The luminous presence fades. Catherine rolls her head from side to side, rotates her shoulders forward and back, and heads for her office, her journal under her arm and the empty cup dangling from a finger. She smiles, determined to carry the fleeting moment into her day. I will stay here in my pew a little longer.

- 11 -
FRIENDS FOR LIFE

I knew from our first encounter that Billy and I would be life-long friends. I just didn't know at the time how truncated "life-long" would be for me.

On our first day of school, Mrs. Buffone walked Billy and me up Anderson Avenue, past the post office to Twenty-Six Mile House Elementary School. The building was a utilitarian yellow brick box. It sat in a yard, mostly of packed dirt and tough weeds mowed short. There were six bucket swings suspended by chains and hanging from a steel-poled structure. A chain link fence kept us in and the bears out. The bears were drawn by the scent of our littered sandwich crusts and apple cores, and—we were warned—small children.

The more frightening predators were enclosed with us, inside the fenced school yard. Bullies, like my older brothers and their friends, stalked us in packs, sniffing the air for the weak, the pants-peeing, the nose-picking, and the easily-brought-to-tears. They chased the girls and flipped up their skirts, guffawed and chanted, "I see England, I see France, I see Martha's underpants." In the winter, they stuffed snow down the backs of our parkas. Those boys—bored and frustrated by school rules and wounded by dysfunction at home—inflicted their pent-up anger on us.

Looking back, I can see it was just a cathartic game to them. They really didn't understand how afraid we were, how defence-less we felt in their menacing presence. Two of those bullies continued to master the mathematics of power after graduation. One is in jail and the other is a Conservative Member of Parliament. The rest were just broken kids, lacking imagination and biding their time until they were old enough to work at the mill.

In our kindergarten classroom on the first day of school, our miniature desks and chairs were arranged in groups of four. The vagaries of alphabetical seating meant Billy and I were assigned to separate foursomes. This unanticipated injustice flustered he and I all year. There was an open, new box of eight thick crayons, placed squarely at the upper right-hand corner of each child's desk.

The front edge of Donna Benson's desk was aligned with the front of Billy's, so they sat facing one another. She wore a plaid jumper and sobbed to the point of hyperventilation. Mrs. Del Bello, our teacher, tried to jolly Donna out of her torment, then scolded her, and finally ignored her. Donna worked herself into such a snotty, gagging mess that she eventually threw up all over her and Billy's desks and, to his great consternation, directly into his box of pristine crayons.

Mrs. Del Bello and Mr. Gruètte, the janitor, wiped their desks and mopped the vomit up from the floor. They rinsed Billy's crayons in the sink at the back of the classroom, dried them with a paper towel, put them back in the box, and re-squared it on the corner of his desk. He leaned forward and sniffed the wax sticks, now wrapped in soggy paper tubes. He sat back and, elbows on his desk, covered his eyes with one hand and pinched his nostrils closed with the other.

The teacher gave us all a big piece of paper on which to colour, while she left the room to escort Donna to the principal's office. They must have called Donna's mother because she didn't return to kindergarten until the following week. While Mrs. Del Bello was gone, I slipped out of my chair over to Billy's desk and exchanged his box of crayons for my own.

The girls thought my action quite chivalrous and told me so at recess. "That was really nice of you to trade with Billy, Matt." Maureen Small rewarded me with a bite of her Twinkie, packed by her mother for snack.

There was a vulnerable fragility, a tenderness, about Billy, that I instinctively felt the need to protect. Not because I felt sorry for him or because he couldn't take care of himself. He was a gentle kid, but strong and tall for his age. Bigger than me. Smart, too. Throughout our elementary school years, he was an above-average athlete and earned better grades than most of us.

No, this drive to defend Billy was lodged in a need of my own, not his. My desire to be noble, to be good, spurred my protectiveness of him. I liked who I was, and how I appeared to others, when I was sticking up for him. I felt at once powerful and self-sacrificing. Defending him preserved what was good in me. Without Billy, anything good in me merely flashed, like a hummingbird, in and out of my peripheral vision; as soon as I tried to look at it directly, it was gone. Innate goodness perpetually eluded me. Protecting Billy helped me to locate it. Without him, I couldn't find it in myself. Standing up for him, I can see now, was my attempt to collect the tattered threads of grace and mercy for myself.

Needless to say, I could not have explained any of that as a six-year-old, or even at ten, by which time I was pummelling any kid reckless enough to bully Billy. I didn't need to split too many lips, or bloody many noses, before it was understood that Billy Buffone was off limits. If one of the bigger boys was giving him a hard time, the inexhaustible fury with which I retaliated frightened them so badly that, even if they triumphed over me, they didn't come back for more. They left me and Billy alone.

An unspoken understanding also emerged among our peers, that Billy and I were a single entity. In the manner of small towns, it became the accepted and invisible natural order of things.

We had other friends, naturally. We joined in the games of British Bulldog and dodgeball on the playground. That we would play on the same team, however, was never questioned or remarked upon. When captains were picking teams, we were picked together. "We got Matt and Billy." Then the captain of the opposing team selected two players. Once a new kid asked, "Hey, how come you picked two?" Everyone just shrugged, as though he had asked why there are three strikes in baseball. It's just how the game is played. Those are the rules.

After school, Billy and I did our homework and ate cookies at the Buffones' kitchen table. I slept over at their house several nights a week. When Mary moved into a bedroom of her own, Mr. Buffone bought a second-hand, twin-sized bed and set it up in Billy's room for me.

My father's shame about his failure to provide an actual home for his kids, prompted him to occasionally march me back, by my ear, from the Buffones' place. Looking over his shoulder, he would shout at me, so that Mr. and Mrs. Buffone would hear: "You've got a house and family right over here, mister."

Unlike me, Mr. and Mrs. Buffone never gave up hope that my father would one day quit the bottle. Whenever Billy's dad encountered my father on the street, Mr. Buffone insisted on shaking hands with old-country formality. He would expound on the weather, or pulp production levels at the mill. He overlooked my father's cynical distrust of, and seething anger toward, just about everyone, especially "foreigners." Mr. Buffone never remarked upon my father's halitosis, or commented on his equally foul mood, both of which reeked of alcohol.

Billy's mother, cognizant of my own motherless state, would regularly send me home with homemade soup and warm bread or a pie. Out of earshot—after those formal handshakes, or while wiping pie from his chin and licking it from his fingers—my father would demand of me, "Jesus H Christ, who the fuck do they think they are? The mayor and Betty-fucking-Crocker?" And other witticisms to that effect.

Billy and I were eleven years old when Mr. Buffone fell from the top of the scaffolding surrounding a digester at the mill. My father was working the same shift and took morbid pleasure recounting, to anyone willing to listen, that "Buffone's head sounded like a bowling ball hitting concrete." I wished it was my father who fell, whose head cracked open on the cement floor. I made sure he didn't see me cry, to avoid his ridicule. At the funeral, I sat up front in the pew reserved for family with

Billy, Mary, and Mrs. Buffone. That was my only experience of church. Back at their house, we cried easily and held one another.

There was no insurance policy to redeem or legal papers to be sorted. The Buffones had no contingency plan for tragedy. In those days, most people in Twenty-Six Mile House didn't have a plan for unforeseen injuries, illnesses, or deaths, even though they occurred often enough. After the funeral lunch, hosted in the church basement, Mr. D. Rickman, the company president at the time, came by the Buffones' house. He offered his "personal and sincere condolences on behalf of the company." He assured Billy's mother that she would continue to receive her husband's pay packet every two weeks, for the rest of her life. "We'll make sure you and your kids are looked after, Mrs. Buffone," he promised. He shook her hand and then shook Billy's. Billy was, said Mr. Rickman, "the man of the house now."

It's different now but back then, in company towns, handshakes were as binding as any contract. A mill employee dropped off those pay packets of cash every two weeks without fail until more than a decade later when Mrs. Buffone died of uterine cancer. Her frugality, and investments at the credit union, funded Mary's teacher's degree from Lakehead University, Billy's diploma, and the down payment on the funeral home, the first in Twenty-Six Mile House.

CHEMICALS IN OUR HAIR AND DRIFTING
FROM THE DOCK

By the time Billy and I were in high school, we had each mapped out our vocational trajectories. Billy would be a doctor and I would be a writer. He liked to read biology, anatomy and chemistry text books in bed at night. "They help me relax," he insisted, though I couldn't see it. Math came easily to him, too.

In grade eleven—just before everything fell apart—Billy won first prize in the Science Fair Competition for Northern Ontario. The project also won him, and by extension me, some notoriety for eccentricity among our classmates.

Billy's science fair project was an experiment he designed to measure the chemical precipitate levels raining down on us from the short-stack at the Mill. In Twenty-Six Mile House, it was a taboo topic to broach, even conversationally, let alone scientifically. If visitors or new comers to our town had the temerity or bad manners to remark upon the sulphurous stink we inhaled daily, the trope at the ready among locals was, "Smells like money to me." It was traitorous to empirically measure, as Billy proposed to do, how much of those chemicals were in fact falling on our heads, how much were we snorting up our olfactory-desensitized noses into our lungs.

The protocol Billy designed to test his hypothesis—chemicals are falling on us from the sky—was simple, and even more shocking to our provincial sensibilities than the hypothesis itself. His plan was to compare the level of chemical residue found on head hairs with levels found on pubic hairs; that is, hairs exposed to acid rain and hairs that were not exposed to anything, ever.

I had never even heard anyone say the word "pubic." In the

boys' changeroom we called those emerging or longed for genital hairs, "pubies." In tenth grade health class, Mr. Inglis (Ignite for Inglis!) our red-faced, stammering, stump of a Phys. Ed. teacher, told us that during our teen years: "Well, men, you'll start to get hair under your arms and in your, ah, public area." He couldn't make himself say the word pubic. When he asked if we had any questions, you better believe there were none. Mr. Inglis clearly did not want to talk about our public or pubic hairs and neither did we. Billy's experiment—for crying out loud—involved harvesting the stuff.

We were at our lockers when Billy explained his methodology to me. Seeing the incredulity on my face, he thought I didn't understand *how* the experiment would prove, or disprove, his hypothesis. "The pubic hair," he said pubic out loud, like a normal word, "isn't exposed to precipitates, but the head hair is. Get it?"

"Yes! Keep your voice down. Holy crap!" Then I hissed, "And how are we going to get those pubic hair, doofus? Off the urinals?"

Billy was genuinely confused by my failure to arrive at the obvious answer to my own question. "Well, ask people for it. Duh." This conundrum clarified, he turned to rummage in his locker for his algebra textbook.

And ask he did. He asked our painfully adolescent classmates for some of their pubic hair. He asked Donna Benson for some of her pubic hair first. By high school, she one was of the most popular girls in town. Maybe Billy felt they had a special bond after she puked on his crayons in kindergarten. Maybe he knew that if a popular girl, like Donna, acquiesced to his request, everyone else would clamour to follow suit.

He showed her two envelopes—one labelled "Head" and the other "Pubic"—marked with the same random four-digit number, say 4231 for example. He assured her that he wouldn't track the numbers. So, even he wouldn't know whose hair was whose, but he could compare the two hair samples from the same anonymous donor.

"If you put a few strands of hair from your head in this envelope and a few pubic hairs"—he said it just like that, "pubic hair," without lowering his voice or tripping over the words—"in this one, you can slip both envelopes through the vents on my locker when you're done. It's for my science fair project on precipitants from the mill."

Donna's cheeks blushed cherry-bomb-red, but Billy's guilelessness and, I suspect a degree of lascivious titillation on Donna's part, trumped any embarrassment she felt. I couldn't believe it. "Ohhh, kaaay." She drew out the oh and the kay, but she was in. I was totally jacked by the idea of an envelope full of Donna Benson's pubic hairs. Billy was unmoved.

With my help, we collected pairs of hairs from the head and pubis of thirty-two, Twenty-Six Mile House teenagers. In the methodology section of the report, Billy listed me as his "research assistant." Reading his final paper, I discovered that *pubes* is in fact the plural for pubis, not pubies. Who knew we were so close to being right in the locker room?

Billy proved his hypothesis: Yes, in fact, a veritable cornucopia of chemicals showered down on our heads each and every day. Locals began to take note of how quickly the paint on cars, parked exposed to the elements outdoors, faded from candy-apple red to construction paper red, or from glossy-navy to mottled baby-blue. Citizens loyal to the mill continued to deny—all of Billy's evidence to the contrary—that the fading paint jobs were connected to sulphide ion dust. Fading paint resulted from planned obsolescence in the auto manufacturing industry. Most of our neighbours insisted "acid rain" was just dreamed up by tree-hugging granola eaters. We did not eat granola in Twenty-Six Mile House, nor did we care much for people who did. We didn't talk about trees. We talked about available fibre. Nonetheless, there were quite a few garages built and car-tarps purchased the spring Billy's results were reported in the *New North Shore*.

Late May, Billy and I (as his research assistant) rode the train down to Toronto with Mr. Eid, our science teacher. Spring in Southern Ontario arrives several weeks before it does in Northern Ontario. It was hot and sticky when we disembarked from the train. We were wearing our new corduroy slacks, sweaters, and our polished shoes. Billy and I carried new, two-toned vinyl Adidas gym-bags. Billy's was navy on baby-blue. Mine was dark brown on beige. Mrs. Buffone ordered the clothes, and the bags, for the trip from the Sears catalogue by telephone. She was stressed for days, until everything arrived at the Sears outlet on time for our departure.

I had never been farther than Thunder Bay from Twenty-Six Mile House. Toronto was another country, another planet. I craned my neck until it hurt and I had to stop. I was enthralled by the tall buildings and by the panhandlers leaning against them. The bustle on Front Street. The hippies smoking pot under the trees and on verandas in Yorkville. The strip joints on Yonge Street, right there where anyone could just walk right in. My brain hurt when Billy pointed out to me there were more people inside the Royal York Hotel during the Science Fair than the entire population of Twenty-Six Mile House. Try as I might, I could not visualize *anybody* from our town chatting science beneath the chandeliers in the Royal York ballroom. Not even Billy and me, but there we were.

Billy's display board was accompanied by a pair of micro-scopes set out on his table. One microscope was loaded with a single strand of precipitate encrusted head hair, fixed between two glass slides. The other one held a pristine curl of pubic hair. One of the judges, a University of Toronto professor wearing the requisite houndstooth jacket with elbow patches, scrinched up his face and put an eye to the viewer of the microscope—displaying one of Donna Benson's or someone else's pubic hairs—and exclaimed "Brilliant."

Maybe I was disorientated by the city, or lack of sleep, but the word "brilliant," applied to someone's pubic hair, struck me as unbearably hilarious. I stifled my juvenile laughter and beat a quick retreat to the anonymity of the hotel lobby. There

I fell sideways onto a velvet sofa and snorted and giggled until my face was wet. I sat up and dragged my shirt sleeve across my eyes. A bearded guy with long hair and granny glasses and his brassiere-less Asian girlfriend were sitting on the red couch across from me. They both smiled and flashed me a peace sign.

That night, I lay awake on the wide bed next to Billy, listening to Mr. Eid snore in the bed next to ours. Three things occurred to me: 1. The couple looked a lot like John and Yoko, 2. They assumed I was stoned, and 3. Life was passing me by in Twenty-Six Mile House. I needed to get to Toronto, somehow and soon.

When I had recovered from my laughing fit and returned to the ballroom, Billy raised an eyebrow as if to ask, "What's with you?" And I fled again, possessed by the general hilarity of life. Was I the only one who could see the humour in this whole crazy situation? I imagined the *Toronto Star* headline: "Northern Pubic Hairs Under the Microscope at the Royal York." Come on! I ask you, is that not hilarious? Maybe it's just me. I was just fifteen years old at the time.

Billy's project was awarded first place in the senior provincials. As the champion, he was expected to compete at the nationals in Ottawa. Our District School Board—no doubt under pressure from Mill management—refused to cover the costs for travel to the capital. They sent Billy a letter which read in part "Irregardless of the Toronto judges' opinions, we as a Board are not convinced that the findings of your research are sufficiently reliable for further dissemination. We believe this issue requires more study, and replication by qualified scientists before we, as a Board, can endorse sharing them in a wider arena." A scientific prophet hath no honour in his home town, especially if it's a mercury dumping, sulphur oxides spewing, mill town.

ℒ

As for me, I planned to be a writer. I worshipped the Americans, like Kerouac, Vonnegut, and Steinbeck. It was like J.D. Salinger was writing for me personally. Although the specifics of Holden Caulfield's life could not have been more distant from my own, Salinger plumbed the depths of my own angst in ways that kept me awake at night, wondering if I too was making a steady decent into madness.

The Pietà of dark hopefulness with which Steinbeck concluded *Grapes of Wrath,* caused my chest to literally ache. The rain washing the Earth, Rose of Sharon—her infant dead and gone—nursing the starving man from her leaking breast, like Mary cradling her crucified son in her arms, broke me open. The first time I read the end of *Grapes of Wrath,* I sat stunned and staring at the last page in disbelief. It was the first book I ever read that did not offer anything resembling a happy ending. *Thank God,* I thought. Reading it, I dreaded that, after all the suffering, Steinbeck might pull some cheerful rabbit from his hat. I loved every sad book, every character, he wrote.

I read out those final paragraphs of *The Grapes of Wrath* to Billy. "If I could ever write something like that, I will die a happy man." As I've said, I didn't live long enough to write anything even close. Nor did I die happy or a man.

❧

How did Billy and I, bound as we were, so effortlessly slip away from one another, like two boats untethered and drifting from a single dock? No, that's not a fair description of our drifting. Billy did not slip at all. He remained steadfastly faithful, anchored in his loyalty to me, right to the end. It was me, not him, who did the drifting.

Billy reasoned with me, threatened and pleaded, about my trips up to Scouter Churley's camp that last spring and summer. He did not endure my abandonment with quiet stoicism. He badgered me, not so much desperate to save our friendship as to rescue me from myself. "Just tell me, Matt. Tell me what's so great up there," he demanded, his hands splayed out at his sides. Unashamed tears wet his cheeks. "Churley's creepy. He's not right, and you know it! You know what he wants!"

Billy didn't know that—by the time he said those words "You know what he wants"—Churley was already getting what he wanted from me. Billy dared speak the truth that everyone else, silently, pretended was not happening. By then, by that last summer, most everyone knew who Churley was, and what he wanted. People kept their own kids safe and their mouths shut.

"Let's go camping," Billy cajoled. "Let's go to Sturdy Cove, or up to Jackrabbit Lake, like we used to." In spite of my sullenness, secrecy, quick temper, and evasiveness, Billy could still see goodness in me, long after I could see it in myself.

My ears were too stuffed up with adolescent self-absorption to hear him. I couldn't feel how painful it was for Billy to helplessly witness my descent into hell. I resented him for saying what I didn't want to hear. He naively believed the damage done to me could be healed, could be undone. I lacked his faith. I did not believe. I could not hear him. I was too far gone already.

Once, I extended a half-hearted invitation to Billy to come up to Churley's camp with us. I was relieved beyond measure when he looked down at the sidewalk, shook his head, and declined my clearly phony offer. I was glad he didn't want to come. Had he come with us, my two worlds, my two spectral planes, would have collided. Had Larry and Anthony, and my experiments in hedonism, been put under Billy's microscope, they would have never withstood his rigorous examination. The flimsy pretense, that evil was good and good was evil, would have been shredded; all the foul-smelling poison of it would have run out of it like puss.

Billy's presence at Churley's camp, in and of itself, would have punctured our illusion of freedom, would have shattered the fun-house mirrors of our distorted ideas about maturity. He would have wafted the stench of our pollution to his nose, as if assessing the toxic contents of a beaker. It would have been too painful for either of us to bear. His gaze would call me back to the self I had already lost.

I did not want to see the truth, and convinced myself that Billy did not want see it either. I am ashamed to admit that I was, in a sick way, drawn to what was happening up at Birch Lake; to the seduction, the titillation, and the delusion of it. The pure light of Billy's friendship would have illuminated those dark impulses in me. There is no more painful judgement of our darkness than the judgement cast by the light of love.

- 13 -

EVERYONE KNEW

There had been gossip and coarse accusations, for more than a decade, about Churley and his boys. Kids gouged variations of "Churley's a fag" into the bathroom stall paint at both schools. Primitive depictions of oral sex and "Churley does boys" were spray-painted inside the pedestrian culvert that passes under the train tracks.

A 13-year-old, named Donald Burke, broke into the town's cable TV studio and typed "Churley Sucks Cock" into the Community Announcements broadcast. Charges against him were dropped when Churley—being such a decent guy—agreed to an undisclosed out of court settlement with Donald's father. Donald's punishment was the beating his father gave him afterwards.

Churley was a stand-up citizen: Scouter, hockey coach, teacher, businessman, active member of the Knights of Columbus and the Chamber of Commerce. It was a rare issue of the *New North Shore News* that didn't include a photo of his flabby smiling visage; his thick, rubbery-lips and heavy hooded eyelids. Like a toad. Churley cutting a ribbon on behalf of the Chamber of Commerce. Churley cannon-balling into the newly opened swimming pool, built and paid for by the mill. Churley dropping the puck at a hockey tournament.

The rumours were dismissed as mean-spirited gossip about a decent, if somewhat eccentric, bachelor. A round-shouldered, soft guy who selflessly served the community since his arrival in town, twenty-years ago. Having no children of his own, Churley reached out to kids around town. He took a special interest in boys judged to be destined for Reform School or—even more shameful in the eyes of their fathers and mothers—Hair Salon College.

To those of you who weren't there, this probably seems impossible. You are no doubt asking questions like: Why did you go along with it, Matt? Why didn't you tell someone? Where, in God's name, were your parents? Well, you know where Mad and Dad were. Why did you keep going back out there? How could it go on all those years without anyone noticing? How could the whole bloody town miss what was going on? A better question might be: How could they see it for years—long before Larry and Anthony and I were recruited to the ranks of Churley's boys—and turn a blind eye?

I've asked myself some of those same questions. They are reasonable, rational questions that, at the time, believe it or not, never popped across the synapses of my hormonally captivated brain. Probably not Anthony's or Larry's either. Our adolescent inexhaustible sexual drives, our socially isolated lives, our desperate hunger for adult affirmation, our collusion with the conspiracy of silence, and our shame, all contributed to it, I suppose. Not that we could have articulated any of that then.

We liked how Churley related to us: like adults, we thought. He was genuinely kind to us when he was not perversely violating us. I think, in a twisted way, he loved us. We were teenage boys. Churley was the only adult who didn't make us feel like criminal sex-offenders about the testosterone raging in our veins and laying siege to our minds. He made it okay. Instead of shaming us for our guilty urges and our wet-dream soiled sheets, he fanned the fire, knelt down and blew on the embers like the Scouter he was.

We first met Churley when we were round-faced and scab-by-kneed Cub Scouts. He was our Akayla. The Wolf Cub Pack obeys the Alpha Wolf. We squatted down and "dyb, dyb, dybed and dob dob dobbed." We got used to the way his hands lingered, inspecting our uniforms and fingernails, smoothing the back of our grey, canvas shorts. Personal hygiene and grooming are important for Wolf Cubs.

At Churley's camp, a new pack culture emerged. At camp, the social structure was different, less repressive, and freer than the one that had governed our lives in the basement of St. Luke's Church on Tuesday nights.

Churley's camp was liberation from the prudish taboos, forbidden questions, and conversations that ruled our lives back in town. We took pride in claiming our independence, of being unshackled from the musty conventions of our repressed elders. Our bodies responded in undeniably exciting ways, ways that would have scalded our faces with shame elsewhere. The alcohol blurred the black and white lines of morality, rendered those lines more permeable, less absolute. The porn magazines aroused our bodies and desensitized our minds.

Churley could spot boys like me a mile away—boys from chaotic families, whose parents were too drunk, or wounded, or preoccupied with their own bed-hopping, to notice the cheerful evil devouring us. Our parents lacked the capacity to see. Some of them were flattered that a man of Churley's standing had taken an interest in one of their sons.

It was a different time. Twenty-Six Mile House, everyone believed, was insulated from pedophiles and criminals of the cities. Mill security met every train and made sure no one got off without a good reason. Assistance to transients who drifted down the hill from the highway looking for help, involved putting them on the next bus out of town. Our town was a safe place where children could run free, their parents confident that they were under the watchful eye of good neighbours.

"Yeah, he's a bit odd, but he sure keeps those kids from raising hell all over town," people said about Churley. "What d'ya think would happen if he didn't take those boys under his wing? Lookit Erik Ojanen. Never would've made the AHL, not without Mr. Rupert Churley."

Last year, Eric Ojanen, fresh out of rehab and working on his 12 Step program, called *MacLean's Magazine* and told them about Mr. Rupert Churley. He described the tight-lipped conspiracy of the citizens of Twenty-Six Mile House. He told the interviewer that there were other men involved. Ojanen kept those names to himself, but allowed that they were old men now and some of them still lived in town. He blew the lid off it all, pointed out the high number of suicides among young men, and of men referred to around town as "bachelors." *Maclean's* did their research and discovered that there were in fact 30 per cent more suicides than the national average among that demographic in Twenty-Six Mile House and among those who had left town.

No one still living in Twenty-Six Mile House was willing to go on record for the story. There were a few quotes, attributed to sources who wished to remain anonymous. Most people insisted it was a long time ago. The long-time Mayor and the Chief of Police both replied to phone call inquiries by steadfastly repeating, "No comment." The President of the Historical Society spoke on behalf of the Board, and for many citizens, of our bucolic little town when she insisted, "You can't rewrite history. Why dig old gossip up now? What's the point?"

When the journalist told Ojanen about the Historical Society's President's position, he shook his head. "If they were really in the business of conserving the history of Twenty-Six Mile House, there'd be a bloody Scouter Churley pedophile display at their friggin' museum. Let me tell you, absolutely nothing, and I mean nothing, has impacted that shitty, lying town more than what that freak did to us. And what they didn't do about it."

The day after she was interviewed for the story, The Historical Society President is rumoured to have burned two cartons of old photos and files in her backyard fire pit.

- 14 -
We Weren't There

That morning in '75, the sun was already hot and high by the time I crawled through the flap in the screen door back into Churley's camp. I was looking for my underpants. Churley hadn't moved on the bed. I glanced in his direction and resumed my search. *The guy looks dead to the world.* That's what I thought. There was a motionlessness about him that was beyond sleeping. His chest wasn't moving up and down, not even a little. There was none of his usual snoring, or the laboured whistling coming from his nose. I looked again, and clearly, he was dead.

My legs turned to water and I dropped to my knees. My heart stopped. My vision blurred. A deafening moan—like an air horn carrying through the fog from a lighthouse–went off in my head. I instinctively covered my ears, but the horns were coming from inside. Then, at the moment when I was about to uncoil a scream that would have shredded my trachea, a welcome quilt of numbness wrapped itself around me. My whole body felt like my lips did after a dentist appointment. A disturbing but calming sensation infiltrated my body. I watched myself, watched the scene unfold from above, as though I was not part of what was happening, not part of Churley being dead.

Still on my knees, my eyes—even though I wanted to shut them—snapped rapid images, and burned them indelibly into my mind. Churley's head floating on a pillow. The pillow soaked with gelatinous blood. Beneath his jowly cheeks, across his blood-smeared neck, a crimson slash of meat hung slack, like the belly of a gutted sturgeon, or like its gills. A dead fish, its gills no longer making quivering gasps for air.

Inside the white fat and purple flesh of his neck I could see bone. The bone looked like a lure lodged there in his throat. I thought: *We'll need needle nosed pliers to get that out.* His eyes were open, as if in shock. His jaw was open, making a black cave of his mouth in the middle of his face. His corpulent body, the colour of day-old porridge, was naked. Blood pooled in the divot of the concave sternum of his hairless chest. The nub of his penis was retracted into a clump of steel-wool that disappeared beneath the dough of his belly.

I told myself to look away, but my eyes were morbidly spell-bound by the meaty slap of Churley's neck. The mattress and sheet must have been blood soaked, too, but I don't remember seeing it. The green blanket that he and I shared on too many nights was still on the floor where I left it. The splitter—the big maul-headed axe—was tipped over on the floor at the end of the bed, where I must have dropped it.

I was paralyzed for what felt like hours, but was likely only seconds. People say that about car wrecks: "It happened in slow motion, seemed like hours, but they tell me it was just a few seconds." The shock, with its concomitant calm, continued to buffer me, to shut my thoughts down and compartmentalize the horror, allowing me to function. What I was seeing was a grizzly puzzle to be solved, a riddle for which there might be a Scouter's challenge badge awarded for its successful resolution. Steadied, I went into the main room, woke Anthony and Larry to tell them what I had done. Given the situation, it is odd that I was scandalized to find them sleeping together on one couch.

What followed I remember in flashes. Shaking Larry and Anthony awake. With sleep still crusted in their eyes, looking to and away from the doorway, while I talked. Them, listening to what lay on the bed, trying to understand what was happening. All three of us saying, "Fuck. Fuck. Fuck." Over and over. Fuck. A word we did not normally use, even out at Churley's camp, but no other word would suffice, or come to us, given the circumstances. We were fucked.

Larry, hyperventilating. Inhaling from his puffer. Running outside. Running back inside. Anthony, eyes pinched tight, pulling the curtain, separating the back room from the front, closed. Then sweeping it open again to check again what he could not absorb. First-aid was out of the question. The sound of flies buzzing on the other side of the curtain. The metallic smell of blood wafting out of the bedroom. It was a smell we recognized from the butcher's shop at the Tomboy's grocery store. Picking up and dropping our scattered clothing. Larry puking on the linoleum floor. Falling over and hitting my head on the wood-box while pulling on my jeans. Larry looking for his shoes, which were already laced up on his feet.

Arguing about what to do. Pushing the boat off the beach into the water. Flooding the motor with too much choke. Arguing about what to do. Anthony puking in the boat. Rowing the boat back to the dock and tying it up. Our faces, drained of blood and illuminated by the harsh sun, were white as ghosts. Arguing about what to do. Kicking lifejackets around in the sand. Anthony, who was only fourteen at the time, sobbing, saliva flying from his mouth and nose, screaming, "Matt, oh fuck, Matt. Why'd you do it, Matt?"

Me saying, "Shut the fuck up, Anthony."

At first, Larry—always the voice of reason—was adamant that we take the boat and go to the police. "Look, Matt, fuck. We can't just leave him," he urged me, all the while doing the evil scientist thing with his fingers. "Just say what happened, Matt. They're gonna find him and know. Just say he was attacking you. He went crazy. It was self-defence."

"Yeah, yeah," chimed Anthony. "Just tell what happened. What he did to you. Oh man, oh fuck, we're so dead."

They were ready to hang me out to dry. They sure as hell didn't plan to hang with me, but reconsidered their options when I started yelling back at them, "And you're gonna back me up on that? You gonna tell your old man you're out here queering with Churley?" Larry's father was a coward and failure who took his shortcomings out on Larry in the form of relentless belittlement, and the occasional beating with his belt. Larry's dad was much like my own. Larry told me that, since the trips with Churley started, his father no longer called him Larry. "He calls me Farry." And Larry's dad was a sweetheart compared with Anthony's old man.

It was nearly noon when we agreed to leave the boat and hike out on the backcountry snowmobile trails to an access road, which eventually connected to Highway 17—The Trans-Canada Highway.

In the winter, a network of snowmobile trails, frozen hard as pavement, provided access up the lake to the camps by skidoo. In the summer, those trails are an impassible mess of buggy marshes and beaver ponds. No one in their right mind would consider walking them. We were not in our right minds. In some places we sunk in the mud up to our thighs. The clouds of flies and mosquitoes were thick, but we barely noticed them in our eyes, behind our ears, stuck in the sweat on the backs of our necks, or flying into our open, panting mouths.

The further away from the camp we got, the more unreal it all seemed. I wondered if we should go back to check, make sure that Churley was actually dead. Maybe it was some macabre practical joke he had pulled on us.

We walked in a trance, without speaking. It was a long way and took all afternoon, and a good slice of the evening, to get to the access road. I was surprised to find myself standing on the shoulder of highway when we finally got there.

In the north, days are long in the summer. So, it was still light, and at the sound of each approaching vehicle, we ducked down into the ditch to avoid being seen. It took almost another three hours to walk to the intersection with the road leading down into town. By then it was dark.

We stopped partway down the hill, next to the cemetery gate. A sliver of moon and a billion stars lit the sky above us. Down below, however, clinging to the shoreline, a dense fog had rolled in off Lake Superior. We could see the red light on top of the mill stack, pulsing. We smelled sulphur from the digesters drifting above the fog. We couldn't see much else through the soupy mist. The diffuse glow of a yellow porch light here and there penetrated the gloom. On the hill, above the fog, by the light of stars and the sliver of moon, I could make out the silhouette of a raven not far from the gate, sleeping on a gravestone.

"We weren't there," said Larry, staring down into the fog.

"What if the cops come and ask?" sniffed Anthony. "They're gonna find him eventually. My mom knows we were there. Lots of people probably know." His eyes were wide with terror.

Larry took a step closer to him. "Just lie. You do it all the time. We weren't there. Churley brought us back to the dock in the boat, and we hitched back into town. We've done it before. Nobody's gonna believe we walked the trails this time of year. Who'd think we made it out that way? Not possible. He was alive when we left. He took the boat back up to camp. By himself. End of story."

"Okay. Okay."

"Say it."

"I said, Okay. Okay? We weren't there. Fuck. He dropped us off." Anthony tried out the lie, his voice teetering up and down the vocal scale of adolescent boys. "He was alive when we left. Man, I'm never gonna be able to stop seeing it. Fuck." He was crying again.

"Wipe your face," said Larry, "you're covered in mud."

I swore to it, too. "We weren't there." When I said it, they both stared down at their running shoes. The mud from the bogs we'd crossed was dried on them, and caked up the legs of our jeans. You didn't have to be a mind reader to know what they were thinking, or what they were wishing—that I would turn myself in and leave them out of it. Confess. Say that I was there. Alone. But I wasn't alone.

I was apparently just the drunkest boy again. With an axe. Scouter Rupert Churley was dead. By the end of the week, so was I.

- 15 -
FOLLOWING THE TRACKS

Larry and Anthony and I walked into the impenetrable fog draping the coast of Superior, and settled in on Twenty-Six Mile House. As we made our way downhill from the cemetery, the fog swallowed us up. First our feet, then legs, then our torsos, disappeared as we descended into the thick ominous murk. It closed over our heads. The stars above us winked out.

The sound of our running shoes on the pavement was amplified in the fog. In spite of our invisibility, stealth was futile. The swishing of our pant legs drowned out the sound of the surf tumbling the round stones on the shore. We walked heel to toe, but every step reverberated like the slaps of a beaver's tail on flat water. The temperature, as we neared the lake, dropped too. My crusted pant legs became wet and muddy again. A chill penetrated my body. My teeth clattered like a woodpecker on hardwood.

I wished I could merge with the fog, dissemble and disappear. Billy once told me human babies are 78 per cent water at birth. I wanted to be water, wanted to evaporate and vanish in the mist. I spilled down the hill in a daze. Gravity pulled me toward judgement, and the inevitable gallows of my own creation.

The closer we got to town, the further apart we walked from one another. We separated. Without a word, or an exchange of nods, we parted ways at the streetlight outside the post office, disappearing ourselves into the night. Looking at one another, I suppose would have shredded the thin gauze of denial in which we had wrapped ourselves. Even a cursory glance at each other's physical presence would have confirmed our realness—confirmed the night and the fog and the body laying on a blood-soaked mattress up Birch Lake were all real. We would have seen that the lie to which we had agreed could save us was an illusion.

I wanted to lock eyes with them, wanted to gauge their resolve, take measure of their capacity for deceit, but didn't because I already knew what I would see. I chose not to observe the betrayal that the sound of their scuttling shoes muttered. I opted, instead, to deceive myself a little longer, pretending that this night could resolve itself in a way that made it possible for to me to go on living.

I knew the house would be empty when I got home. Still, out of habit, I opened the door with the quiet stealth I perfected as a boy. I don't know where my father was when I climbed the steps to my bedroom. He and I were long past concerning ourselves with one another's whereabouts.

By the time I was in my teens, my brothers had traded school for well-paying jobs at the mill. They bought their own houses. My sister, Gail, ran away with a carnival of personal hygiene challenged hippies. She headed west with them in a school bus painted with peace signs, happy faces, and marijuana leaves. I saw Gail's glowing face—framed in one of the bus windows as it rolled out of Twenty-Six Mile House—and figured she liked the odds of a raffle ticket on free love better than no love at all.

I collapsed onto my narrow bed, mud-caked sneakers still on my feet. I yawned, adrenalin ebbing from my bodily tributaries. Aching from the long hike back to town, I felt certain I would immediately drop off into a bottomless, if troubled, sleep. My closed eyelids, however, became screens upon which closeup images of dead Churley were projected. They clicked from one ghoulish snapshot to the next. Neck. Mouth. Belly. Steel wool. Toe nails, thick as hooves and the colour of nicotine. I kept my eyes open, and the bare bulb hanging from my bedroom ceiling lit, all night. Switching it off switched the images on.

I sat sideways across the bed, my back against the wall. I dipped in and out of sleep for one or two seconds at a go. During those seconds of unconsciousness Churley yelled at me, his voice shrill with rage, his words spewing, not from his mouth, but from the slash in his neck. It flapped open and closed, like an angry puppet's mouth. Blood and pink foam leaked from between his liver-coloured lips.

I bolted awake, scrubbing my face with the front of my filthy T-shirt. My clothes were saturated with perspiration and mud, and in my delirium, I mistook their viscous wetness for Churley's blood. I shivered with fever. I wanted morning to come and, at the same time, dreaded what it would illuminate.

Morning came. The dense, ground-level cloud continued to press down on Twenty-Six Mile House, intensifying the nightmare-like state in which I passed my final days. I kept to my routines. Each morning I rose, showered, and went to my summer job at the lumber yard. My body loaded board-lengths, assembled trusses, weighed bags of nails and screws. I rode inside my physical self while it carried out these tasks. Beneath my skin there was a constant, low electrical hum of panic. My brain raced in all directions, never arriving anywhere. My thinking was scrambled, chaotic. It left me dizzy and nauseated.

The jagged blade of the big circular saw wailed out in the wood yard, all day. With each board I guided across it, I considered pressing my wrist into its spinning teeth. I might have done it too, were it not for Hank who, years ago, cut his own hand off. It did not kill him, just doomed him to a one-handed life of unresolved despair.

Hank insisted that completely severing his hand from his wrist on the table saw had been an accident. The sawdust was soaked with blood, spackled with bits of bone and skin. His amputated hand—it is recounted by those first on the scene—moved spasmodically on the mitred table. I was still in short pants when Hank's "accident" occurred, but had heard the story recounted enough times to see it as vividly as if my legs had been among those sprayed by Hank's blood.

I also heard it often enough to know that amputating one's hand did not guarantee death. Whether or not Hank amputated his hand with intent, or by accident, was not my primary consideration. What mattered to me was it didn't kill him. They saved Hank's life and he still worked—single handed—in the lumber yard.

Larry and I avoided each other back in town, like always, but Anthony kept phoning our house. "I can't sleep," he told me. "My Mom keeps asking if I'm okay." I told him to quit calling and slammed the handset into its cradle on the kitchen wall. He phoned once more after that. He didn't say anything. I recognized the sound of his whimpering. He hung up after I warned him that, if he called me again, I would slit his throat, just like I slit Churley's. It was for his own good.

The next night, lying in bed not sleeping, I remembered Churley's home movies. He never showed them to us, but I knew what was burned onto those looping spools of Kodachrome.

The back door to Churley's house on Alexander Street was locked. Strange, people in Twenty-Six Mile House don't lock their doors. It is a matter of pride to live where you don't need to lock your doors. When we do lock our doors, we aren't securing possessions or keeping strangers out, we're keeping secrets in.

I splintered the door frame with a kick and left the lights off. Using a flashlight, I searched every drawer, cupboard, cardboard box in the basement, closet shelf and under Churley's king sized bed. I felt around for loose wall panels and floor boards. It took hours, and I found nothing. The grey light of morning was dawning by the time I gave up. If the movies were there, I could not find them. Hopefully, no one else could find them. Churley didn't last twenty years in town without being careful. I slipped out the back door, along the lane behind the houses, and cut through the bush out onto Main Street.

Later that morning, a customer at the wood counter asked me, "You knew Rupert Churley, right?" That's when I knew someone had found the body. I was weighing up two pounds of shingle nails for the customer, Mr. Jordan. His question unspooled six yards of barbed wire dread in me. You *knew,* not you *know,* Rupert Churley, he had asked.

Mr. Jordon was bent forward at the waist, elbows splayed, and resting on measurements scribbled on scraps of paper, littering the counter. His thick fingers were interlocked, forming a single calloused fist. One of his fingernails was blackened. "You're a Boy Scout, right?"

"Yep. Mr. Churley is my Scouter." I put too much emphasis on the present tense—is—as though I was willfully contradicting Mr. Jordan.

"They found him dead, up at his camp. You been up there, eh?" Was it a question or an accusation? Was he was testing me, scanning my face, from beneath the peak of his cap, for a tell? "Some fellahs out for walleye along shore, near Churley's place? Heard a commotion up at his camp, eh? Landed for a look-see, and found Churley dead, and for a while. The place stank, I guess. Two bears were fighting over what was left. Sounds like Churley was a mess."

"You want me to put these nails on your account, Mr. Jordan?" I tried to sound disinterested, busy. I sounded *too* unaffected. Of course, I would be interested. Did he detect the evasiveness in my voice? I doubled two brown paper bags, and poured the nails from the scale scoop into them. My hands were shaking.

"Ya, sure. Anyway, I guess they got the cops up there to shoot the bears and check things out." Mr. Jordan looked over his shoulder, then leaned over the counter and lowered his voice. "Between you and me,"—as if he had not divulged this same information to five of his buddies already—"by the smell, they figure he'd been dead a couple days at least, and it looked like it wasn't the bears that killed him first. See Donny, my eldest, boated the cops up to fetch the body. He's got that flat bottom dory, eh? Donny told me Churley looked as if his head had been hacked almost off. Axe was still lying right there on the floor. Now you don't kill yourself with an axe, do ya, Matty? Somebody else done that. Am I right?"

I tried to vocalize a sound that would convey a suitable level of shock, but only managed to clear my throat. I fished out Mr. Jordan's account card from the open drawer of the filing cabinet. Yellow bile bubbled up from my stomach, burned at the back of my throat and seeped into my mouth.

Mr. Jordan cradled the bag of nails in the crook of his arm and leaned over the counter again. His voice still lowered, said, "Between you, me and the gate post, Matty, I never trusted that son-of-bitch. Sneaky, if you ask me. Shouldn't talk ill of the dead, I guess."

His breath smelled of stale nicotine and coffee. I suppressed a gag, my lips pressed tight. He winked and whistled a few short notes of a common nursery rhyme, the name of which in my state of panic I could not recall. The bell above the door jangled and he left.

I watched him though the sawdust coated windowpane beside the counter. He tossed the bag of nails onto the bench seat in the cab of his truck and climbed in. He backed out of the parking space and drove past the window. Before I could turn my attention to some other task, before I could close my mouth or avert my eyes, Mr. Jordan looked directly at me. His lips were a tight line across his weathered face. He touched the brim of his cap, and drove away.

Relief washed over me, the kind of relief that irredeemable defeat brings, the kind that sighs, sags its shoulders, rests its chin on its chest and says, finally, "Fuck it. I'm done." Days of pent up tension flowed out of my body, down through my feet and into the floor, granting me permission to stop running, to stop fighting for survival, to lay down my sword and shield and wave a sad white hanky of surrender. Enough. Enough. I was too tired, too defeated, to keep dragging the boulder of what had happened up at Churley's camp that night.

I untied my apron and folded it into the cardboard box beneath the counter. I smoothed my work gloves flat on top of the apron. I walked out the back door, into the heavy fog, a red builder's pencil stuck behind my ear.

The railway tracks run behind the wood yard. When Sir John A.'s transcontinental railway was under construction at the end of the nineteenth century, there were 12,000 men, 5,000 horses, 1,000 dogs and an indeterminate number of prostitutes bivouacked at Twenty-Six Mile House. Those men and the ladies took a prideful bow or curtsy when in 1884, *The Sault Herald* referred to our town as "the baddest town in the north." Our current population is barely 1,200 souls and fewer than half as many dogs. There are no horses or prostitutes, to my knowledge. The rails, however, remain a permanent scar cutting through our community.

Other than the pleasurable terror induced in children by the quaking earth and thunder of a passing train, other than the soulful longing evoked in melancholic insomniacs by its distant horn, other than those benefits, the tracks are simply a daily inconvenience. For five minutes several times a day, the town is severed in two. Red lights flash, and bells clang, warning of the imminent passing of yet another freight train. The safety arms lower themselves across Main Street like elementary school crossing guards. These trains do not slow down, or in any way acknowledge, Twenty-Six Mile House. We stop for them. They do not stop for us.

During my lifetime, six young men in Twenty-Six Mile House died by locomotive. Each *accident*—that's what we called them—occurred at about the same location along the tracks, a mile east of the crossing. It was as if those boys had convened a summit in the dark woods of shame, and negotiated their terms of surrender. The tracks cut through Twenty-Six Mile House, like the truth we all pretend not to know, like the lies to which we were accustomed. We no longer noticed the truth, felt the wind of it as it roared past us. Each boy's death was a testimony to what cut our town in half. We got so used to it, we hardly noticed.

A few of the citizens of our shiny town connected the dots, of course, between the dead-by-train boys and Scouter Churley.

They elected, however, to mind their own business, attend to the welfare of their own children, and let well enough alone.

The subsequent seasons, the rain and snow, have rinsed the blood from the slag that beds the rails and ties. But faded plastic flowers, and glass from broken beer bottles, mark the location of private memorials to the dead.

Honestly, I had no plan to kill myself after putting down my apron and walking out of town between the rails. I was in a fog. I didn't have a plan, no intention of any kind. I had pushed myself though the fog in those final days, deceiving myself with misguided notions of adolescent invincibility. I understood that I could be hit by a train, but did not fully comprehend the certainty of death it would bring. I had not yet attained the maturity to acknowledge the frailty of the human body. I just walked.

The air was wet and still, and the soupy fog shrouded everything, in a dreamlike, half-darkness. I adjusted my gait, stepping from one creosote-treated railway tie to the next. Eyes down, I concentrated on landing one step at a time. In the distance, I heard the faint sound of an air horn. The iron horse was galloping across the bridge, at Pickerel River to the east. Even hearing it, I wasn't committed to killing myself. Resigned to it, I suppose, surrendered to the inevitability of it. My mind shut down. I just stepped from one tie to the next until the towering wall of iron burst from the mist, and I could go no further.

Confession: It was not guilt about killing Churley that kept me walking between the two rails. I might have been able to wear murdering him like a badge of honour, a source of nobility, of pride. It was what I allowed him to do to me that killed me. The truth about our perversions would inevitably come out. Only death could alleviate my own shame, and only death safeguard the secret with which I died. In that sense, I did it to spare Billy, too.

Above the roar of the diesel engine, the sound of my light frame bouncing off the front of the train barely registered with the crew. Looking up from their gauges, and squinting out into the fog, one asked, "Did you hear something?"

"No. You?"

"Probably nothing. Maybe a bear cub."

It was around dinnertime, when the mosquitoes were starting to hit hard, and the fog was lifting, a small boy and his mother were picking blueberries along the tracks. They found my body lying in the weeds. I am sorry it was them.

- 16 -
A Telephone Ringing, Beneath a Boat

Billy can't reach the telephone because it is ringing under the boat, upturned on the beach. The ringing is obstinate. The phone keeps ringing, over and over, beneath the rotting wooden boat. He tries to lift it, but it is too heavy. He digs, dog-like, flinging sand out behind him from beneath the gunnels, frantic to answer the phone. Grit packs up under his fingernails. The nail on his middle finger tears away from his skin and Billy gasps at the starburst of pain. He digs deeper into sand, to where it is wet. He scoops with the side of his hand, protecting the flapping fingernail from snagging. He reaches up under the boat, up to his shoulder, sweeps his arm back and forth, feeling around for the ringing telephone.

His hand touches something. It is not a telephone. It is not something made of the familiar smooth, Bakelite plastic. There is no coiling cord linking the handset to the rotary dial, nor is there is a touchtone keypad. Billy thinks—hopes—for an instant, "It must be a lifejacket." It is neither a lifejacket nor telephone. It clamps itself around his wrist, like fleshy vice. It is a hand, big and powerful, and it snaps shut, like the jaws of a leg-hold trap.

There is someone, or some thing, powerful beneath the boat. Billy frantically tries to pull his arm back and the disembodied hand slips around Billy's fingers, crushing his knuckles. It is dragging him under the boat. The side of his head slammed up against the rotting wood. The wood smells of fungus and dying toadstools. His shoulder dislocates with a pop, sending flames across his back and up his neck. The flesh between his shoulder and upper arm—between the humerus and the glenoid fossa of the scapula—stretches and narrows. His arm is torn free and dragged under the boat. Billy can hear bones crunching, like wolves gnawing on the fleshy femur of a downed moose.

Billy surfaces from this nightmare, gasping. The phone is still ringing. As with most nightmares, when they end the feeling of terror remains. Billy is electric with panic and sick with dread.

The phone keeps ringing. Billy is lying on his side, on top of the arm—the one ripped off in his lurid nightmare—which accounts for its numbness. The phone rings, again. Billy rolls over onto his back and thrashes the bedside table with his dead arm, dumb as a baseball bat. He knocks the clock radio to the floor. Rolling again, he locates the handset with his left, still sensate, hand.

It is Dr. Janzen calling. Billy sits on the edge of the bed and tips the clock up with his foot to check the time. 12:13AM. He's been asleep for an hour. Somebody is dead. That is the only reason anyone, especially Dr. Janzen, calls Billy in the middle of the night.

In addition to his regular practice as a GP, Dr. Gregor Janzen has taken on the duties of District Coroner in Twenty-Six Mile House. When Janzen calls personally—rather than directing a nurse to do it—Billy knows it is a coroner's case. The deceased require undertaking, but first, a thorough examination will have to be performed to confirm the cause of death. Somebody has died at home, or by drowning, or by car crash, or suicide, or has been murdered.

The latter is a rare event in Twenty-Six Mile House. There has been one murder in Billy's lifetime: that of Scouter Rupert Churley. And, as you know, Billy was not a funeral director, then. At the time of Scouter Churley's death, there wasn't a local coroner. The District Coroner from Port Arthur had arranged for the town police to complete the paperwork and fax it to him. It did not require that a highly skilled physician make the long drive from the Lakehead to Twenty-Six Mile House to determine the cause of Churley's death. Everyone—the Coroner,

Chief of Police and the local citizenry—was agreed that Churley's case was of the open and shut variety.

Gregor Janzen sounds, as always, tired. Like most small-town GPs, he suffers from chronic sleep deprivation. Ironically and sadly, he also suffers from insomnia. "Billy? Gregor," he commences without preamble. "There's an accident, west on the highway. One casualty. DOA. I'm finished up out there." He yawns, "It's about twenty minutes west of the turn off. I told the police I'd give you a call for a pickup. They'll watch the scene until you get there."

The ambulance can only be used to transport living persons. That's strict policy. They can't risk being caught occupied—carting a dead person around—if an actual emergency call comes in. The EMTs have likely already come and gone from the crash site. Their stretcher empty in both directions, sheets unsullied, and at the ready to serve the living. It's Billy's job to collect the bodies of those declared dead at the scene.

"Just the one then?" asks Billy. He won't need to leave his stretcher behind to make room in the van. He can transport two bodies at a time, three if he doesn't bring the stretcher. Four bodies—size depending—require some stacking.

"Just one. His I.D. says he's," Billy can hear Janzen flipping pages on a clipboard, "Gilbert Bearchild, 22 years, according to his driver's licence. Hit by a transport."

"His car was?" asks Billy.

"He wasn't in the car. Looks like he was standing on the shoulder," says the doctor. "You know him? Know who his next of kin is?"

"Uh huh." says Billy, "Well, I know his mother, I mean his grandmother, Florence Bearchild, from Pickerel River. He and his brother were raised by her, and their aunt. I think, Gilbert was away at school." Billy is accustomed to the abrupt transition of verbs, from present to past tense. Gilbert *was*, not *is* away at school.

"Let the police know about the grandmother, would you? They'll take care of the notification. Any other family?"

"Lots. Pretty much the whole community. The older brother: Clarence. He goes by Crank. Last I heard, he's in jail. Probably at The Farm."

"Okay," Janzen makes no attempt to stifle a yawn, "I guess the grandmother will have to tell the others. I'll stay at the hospital 'til you get back. I need to do a kit on him and his Grandmother—Florence right? —she might want to come in. She'll have to do the I.D. at some point. If she doesn't want to, we can find someone else in the morning." Janzen hangs up without saying goodbye.

"She'll want to," says Billy.

- 17 -
THE BAGMAN COMMETH

It had been a warm and sunny day. Waterfalls of melted snow cascaded down from the cliffs along the highway and flowed across the road. By night, however, temperatures are dropping fast, to well below freezing. The pavement is fuzzy with frost and the previously streaming water has turned to ice.

Billy taps the brake pedal to test his traction, and wonders if Gilbert slid off the road into the ditch, or was maybe pulled over to change a tire. Why else, only a few miles from home, would he stop? Why was he standing on the side of the road? Billy's van's low beams reflect back off the fog.

He rounds a curve and is at the scene of the accident. Flashing red cruiser lights pulse in the fog. Billy squints into the sudden brightness, and slows the van to a crawl. He pulls the peak of his *Canadiens* cap down to shield his eyes.

Three flares are burning along the highway, lighting a runway to a car parked on the right-hand shoulder of the road. It's facing east. Strange. Billy scratches his whiskered neck. It must have spun around and ended up pointing in the wrong direction, on the wrong side of the road.

The cruiser is parked, up tight, behind the car. Fifty yards further on, tipped up against the face of the cliff, there is a transport truck in the ditch. Beyond the transport, three more flares burn along the side of the road. Beyond the third flare, night blends with fog. Billy can see Gilbert laid out on the gravel beside the road.

The air is sharp with the acrid odours of diesel fuel, burning flares, and burnt rubber. Beneath those chemical scents, Billy detects the more subtle notes of the spring ice breaking up on inland lakes. The smell of crusting snow mingles with highway salt and soggy leaves from the previous fall. There is the odour of a fecund wetness, waking bark, soil thawing and freezing again. Nearby, water is running beneath the ice. Hints of the coming spring are faint but there—Billy can smell them, hear them, the whiff and whisper of life, in spite of death.

A police constable is leaning, arms crossed over his chest, against the passenger door of the cruiser. Shielding his eyes, against the flashing lights, with one hand, Billy offers the other, "I'm Billy Buffone, from Buffone's Funeral Home." The officer, wearing a Town Police Services issued navy parka, pulls a glove off to return Billy's handshake. His grip is firm. Billy momentarily revisits his nightmare, about a hand dragging his arm under a rotten boat.

"Okay, good to meet you, Mr. Buffone," says the officer. "Constable Ryan. Bart Ryan." Billy smiles. It still feels odd to be called mister. He recognizes Ryan. He's been around for two or three years. Rumour is that he plans to stay. Twenty-Six Mile House turns over police recruits as often as it does preachers and doctors—except for the Chief of Police who is a lifer. The story about Ryan is that he was five years on the Toronto Police Force, when his partner was killed. Ryan was wounded in the shooting. When the job opened up in Twenty-Six Mile House, Ryan and his wife, Dana, jumped at the chance of life in a quiet, small-town. They packed up their toddler and Ryan's trauma and moved north. Unfortunately, geography isn't always a cure for PTSD—wherever you go, there you are—but your odds of being re-traumatized are greatly reduced in a small town.

"There's the kid." Ryan nods toward the crumpled form lying on the side road, without actually looking. "Appears he pulled over for a leak, his fly's down, on the wrong side of the highway. Transport came around the curve, there. Probably highballing it." Ryan points a thumb over his shoulder, toward the curve Billy had just come around. "The driver says he saw the headlights coming at him on the right, and thought he must've drifted onto the wrong lane. Swerved right, and straight into the ditch, and the kid."

Billy knows Ryan's bravado is likely a fragile shield, manufactured to protect himself from the tragedy of what he is seeing. This could well be Ryan's first tough call, since relocating to Twenty-Six Mile House. Why else would he be telling the Bagman what happened? The Bagman. That's what the cops, and first responders, say when Billy arrives: *The Bagman's here.* His work starts when theirs is done. As a rule, they leave him to his business without a lot of chatter. They don't fill him in on what they think happened. They don't hang around. Billy arrives, quietly goes about his duties, alone, and departs, like a ferryman carrying the dead across the River Styx.

"It was the driver that dragged him up onto the shoulder there." Ryan needs to talk. "Tried CPR on him. Guy was out of his head, in shock. Tried to save the poor kid. Not a chance."

Billy takes in the officer's grey face and bloodshot eyes. He guesses that Ryan is only a few years older than Gilbert. "Gilbert. That's his name. Gilbert Bearchild."

"Uh, yah, right."

"Uh huh." Billy nods, "His name is Gilbert. Gilbert Bearchild. He was in university."

"Gilbert Bearchild," Ryan repeats. "Sorry. You knew him?" Billy nods.

"The other guy I'm on with tonight—new guy—caught a ride back to town with Janzen. Ambulance guys took the driver to the hospital to get checked out. He's pretty messed up. Not physically, you know, but mentally, for sure. You need a hand here?"

"Thanks," says Billy and heads around to the back of the van.

As he collects his equipment, Billy visualizes the accident unfolding. A heavy-eyed driver, head bobbing with exhaustion. Maybe he's clocking some off-the-logbook kilometres. He careens around the curve and ... holy shit. Headlights coming at him from the wrong side of the road, reflexes kick in. Flips on the engine brake. Locks up the trailer brakes. Tires burning rubber, right down through the frost to the pavement. Wrestling forty tons of truck and payload, desperately trying to avoid a head-on collision with the oncoming car. Next thing he knows, he's in the ditch, something slams off the rig's, big as a wall, grill. Sparks flying as the trailer box grinds along the cliff for another fifty yards before stopping.

Billy pulls the wheeled stretcher along the road behind him. The wheels swivel, like a shopping cart in a parking lot. A neatly folded bag rests on the thin, vinyl covered mattress. He lines the stretcher up, parallel to Gilbert's body, and releases the lever to lower it.

Billy squats down to examine Gilbert by the light cast by the cruiser's flashers: his head is flattened on one side, his arm twisted unnaturally under his back, and one of his feet is pointing the wrong way. Billy deduces that Gilbert was hit once and bounced clear of the truck. He wasn't mangled or flattened by its eighteen wheels. Billy is a professional, practiced and expert at denying his feelings. An open casket is possible.

Like a liturgist preparing a ceremony, Billy ritually unfolds the black rubberized bag. He gently lays it flat on the gravel, and unzips it—unlike a sleeping bag, the zipper runs down the top, not the side, of the bag. Ryan squats down beside Billy and together they tip Gilbert up onto his side. They tuck the open bag underneath the length of his body, allow him to tip back, pull the flaps around him, zip them closed, buckle the bag onto the stretcher and lift until the frame locks in place. Ryan does his best not to watch what his gloved hands are doing.

At the van, Billy releases the legs again as he slides the stretcher through the back doors and sets the floor locks. He gently closes the doors.

Ryan asks, "Did he, uh, feel kind of hot to you? I mean, still sorta warm? Even through my gloves. Just checking, but you know, shouldn't he be, colder by now? It's been, what," he consults his watch, "it's got to be three hours plus, since he was hit. It's crazy, I know, I know, but could he be, you know...?"

"Alive?" Billy finishes Ryan's question. "No. The heat is post-mortem caloricity. The cells keep dividing, metabolizing, keep trading CO_2 for O_2 for a while, after you're dead, but the exhaust system is shut down. So, there's no way to vent the heat and gas—no sweating, no breathing—the cells overheat for a while and quit. I wish, but he's dead."

"Huh," says Ryan, "Farts?"

"Them, too," Billy responds, absently.

Ryan clears his throat, embarrassed by his failed attempt at black humour. Unlike his fellow officers, he's never been good at laughing things off.

Billy hasn't noticed. He is preoccupied with looking down along the ditch.

"They're waiting on me at another call," Ryan says. "Those flares've got couple of minutes left on 'em. You mind sticking around 'til they're out?"

"No problem," says Billy, still contemplating the scene from the back of the van.

"Just kick them off into the ditch when they're out, if you want. We'll be back out here to finish up when it's light. I can clean them up then."

"I'll get them. It's okay."

The cruiser makes a tight U-turn and disappears around the curve. Billy savours the quiet. He stands still to silence the sound of gravel crunching beneath his winter boots. The flares cast ghostly shadows up the face of the rock cut.

Billy knows this cliff. It's The Crack. Had Janzen told him, when he called, that the crash was at The Crack, Billy would have known exactly where it was. Everybody from Twenty-Six Mile House knows The Crack; most of us have scaled this damp fracture, running vertically inside the cliff. You wedge your back against one wall, your feet and hands against the other, and shimmy to the top. Most boys, and a lot of girls, have made the thirty-foot assent up the fissure inside the cliff.

On summer nights, teenagers drive their parents' half-tons out to meet at The Crack. Boys bring girls they want to impress. Girls come with boys they love. They park the trucks in the low meadow across the highway. Sometimes they make bonfires in the meadow. Sometime they make the fire on the flat rock, at the top of The Crack. There's a path that runs up the side of the hill to the top. Those who don't want ruin their good shirts or clean jeans shimming up the inside of The Crack take the path.

If you haven't climbed it yourself, you've watched someone else do it. Debates rage around the bonfires about who holds the record for the fastest climb. Old men, over coffee at Robin's, compare their climb times. Their times get faster with every telling. There is a saying in Twenty-Six Mile House: "The older you get, the fish you caught get longer and your Crack times get shorter."

Billy and I climbed The Crack, together. Scouter Churley drove us out here the day after Billy's father's funeral. He cheered us on from the bottom, and bought us ice cream at the Shell station on the way home. Parked at the curb, in front of Billy's house, Churley told Billy, "I can't replace your dad, but I want you to know I am gonna to be here for you. Whatever you need. You too, Matt." We were all three sitting in the front seat of his car, Billy between me and Churley. He stroked Billy's knee as he spoke. I could feel Billy's body flinch.

Billy knows this: Nobody comes to The Crack by themselves. Gilbert was studying, three hours away, at Lakehead University. What was he doing here by himself—on the wrong side of the highway—taking a leak? He scratches his scalp beneath his cap.

Just then, a transport truck barrels around the curve. The driver spots the flares in the fog, and down shifts. The truck slowly rolls past the scene in the oncoming lane. The driver leans over, peering down from the passenger window. Billy gives him the thumbs up and waves him along.

The ditch is scattered with broken bottles. Billy toes the ground where it is peeled back by the locked wheels of the truck that hit Gilbert. He clambers up the far side of the ditch. At the base of the cliff, he crouches down, and pokes his head inside the entry to The Crack. Looking upward, outside the crack, the night sky is obscured by fog. Looking up, through The Crack, however, the sky is clear. The Crack functions like an asymmetrical telescope, rising above the fog. A lake of stars floats above him.

Billy stands and leans his back against the cliff. A winter's worth of cold stored up in the rock penetrates his coat. He tips his head back and looks up, but can only see the fog.

One by one, the flares yield to the darkness. The fog glows dimly, magnifying the light of the invisible stars and moon, their light refracted by a billion molecules of water.

Billy learned a prayer in college to Joseph of Arimathea, the man who placed Jesus' body in his tomb. He is the patron saint of funeral directors. A priest came in to give a lecture to Billy and classmates on stress management. The students had to memorize the prayer to Joseph for the test. The opening lines go: "Merciful God, whose servant Joseph of Arimathea, with reverence and godly fear, prepared the body of our Lord and Savior for burial and laid it in his own tomb." Billy has forgotten the rest. On nights like this, he wishes he could still recite the whole thing.

He picks his way back to the van in the dark, sits in the driver's seat for a moment before starting the engine. He whispers, "Gilbert, you weren't here alone, were you." Gilbert, however, keeps his silence, as only the dead can.

- 18 -
GILBERT WASN'T ALONE

That morning, Clarence had showed up early and unannounced at his brother, Gilbert's, townhouse where Gilbert lived with four other Lakehead University students. Clarence was relieved when he spotted Gilbert's ancient Datsun parked in one of the driveways—he couldn't remember the house number. He stamped his cold feet a few times, summoned his courage, marched up the lawn, and rang the doorbell. Clarence was wearing his only pair of shoes—prison-issued sneakers, because his boots had been "lost", as was the cash from his wallet, while he was incarcerated—so, his feet were not only cold, they were also blistered by the long walk from The Farm into the city. A second-floor window slid open, and Gilbert poked his head out. Clarence tipped his head back to shout, "Hey bro'! Surprise! Ta da!"

"Clarence? What are...? Hang on a sec. I gotta get dressed. Wait there, and keep your voice down." Gilbert ducked back inside and slid the window closed in its aluminum frame. The screen, likely blown out of the window during the winter, was trapped in a patch of hard snow against the shaded part of the house.

A moose hide medicine pouch hung from around Clarence's neck. While he waited for Gilbert, he scooped a pinch of tobacco out of it, and sprinkled it on the ground, next to the cement step.

He rocked from one cold foot to the other, and banged on the door, impatient to see his baby brother, "What the fuck, dude? Come on man. Let me in!" He laughed, "Or I'll huff and I'll puff!" It had been months since Clarence had seen his younger brother.

A couple of times, early on in Clarence's stretch, Gilbert had driven out to the prison to visit. He wanted to keep coming, too, but Clarence told him not to come back. "Focus on your school brother. I'm good. I'm clean. I'm sorting my shit out. They've got an Elder who comes in, teaches us about culture and tradition. I'll see you on the flip side."

Clarence had been making those sorts of promises to Gilbert all his life. Clarence knew he'd cried wolf too many times to deserve Gilbert's trust. He understood the doubtful smile on his brother's face, but this time it was different. He just needed some time to prove it, first to himself.

Gilbert was barefoot and shirtless, wearing a pair of fashionably tattered jeans, and scooping his long hair behind his ears, when he opened the door. Clarence noticed, for the first time, that his younger brother was actually taller than him. "Keep your voice down. Everybody's still sleeping."

Clarence flattened his cold hands on his brother's smooth chest, like they did when they were little boys—getting them cold on the picture window at Granny's, and then sneaking up on one another. Gilbert gasped and jumped back. Clarence laughed. "Bro', it must be after ten! What the fuck are you doing in bed? Remember what Granny always said..."

Gilbert cut him off, "I just finished exams. I'm beat." He stepped further back out of Clarence's reach and pulled an undershirt on over his head. Clarence stuffed his hands into his pockets, waiting on the stoop to be invited inside.

Behind Gilbert, he saw the smooth, pale legs of a girl descending the narrow staircase. She wore a plaid flannel shirt that looked like it might be Gilbert's. The middle two buttons were fastened. She wrapped her arms around Gilbert from behind, hooked a thumb into the waist-band at the front of his jeans and rested her chin on his shoulder.

"Sorry, bro," said Clarence, "didn't know you had company."

"It's cool. Good to see you. Monica, this's Crank, the brother I told you about. Crank, Monica." His voice sounded cautious, formal.

The, not *my* brother. Clarence heard it. It hurt. As if there were a whole litter of brothers and Crank was the bad one who Gilbert had warned her about. Clarence caught the carefulness in his brother's voice, and he didn't blame him for it. Gilbert spent most of their childhood and adolescence covering for him—lying to their Granny, to teachers and eventually to the cops, trying his best without success, to keep his big brother out of trouble. While Gilbert was scoring top marks at the Twenty-Six Mile House high school—and choking on a "doctrine of discovery" version of Canadian History—Crank was working the rez, selling dope and doing "B 'n' Es for Bs": Break and Enters for Booze.

As long as Clarence confined his criminal activities to Pickerel River, the cops turned a blind eye. When he started dealing and B and E-ing off the rez, their eyesight improved. By the time Clarence was caught breaking into white people's camps up on Black Otter Lake, Gilbert was already away at Lakehead University. Clarence only ever took booze. If he a broke window, gaining access to a camp, he always patched it up with cardboard, to keep the snow out. When he was picked up, he had enough grass on his person to be charged with the B and Es, and with intent to traffic. The arresting officer had asked Crank what to put down on the form under "Occupation." Clarence shrugged and laughed. "Drug dealer, I guess."

His granny—his Nokoomis—was determined to attend the trial. So, to spare her the shame of his crimes, Clarence pled guilty, without conditions. It was his first arrest, but Clarence was sentenced to a year less a day.

Had Clarence a perfect set of tissue-wringing, Caucasian parents with steady jobs and a house with a manicured lawn, no doubt he would have got off with probation, a fine and a stern talking to. A little community service at most, maybe twenty hours of painting fire hydrants or litter picking. He and his granny couldn't have scraped up the cash to pay a fine, if it had come to that.

"That's what you get for committing a crime while Indian,"

he told his fellow inmates his first night at The Farm. They laughed. "Been there, done that and didn't even get a T-shirt," as one of the others put it.

"Or, maybe for the crimes they didn't catch you doing," said a visiting Elder, when Clarence tried the line on him. "Either way, now is your time to learn to walk in a good way. Use this time to make the people who put you here see just how wrong they are about you. Don't make them right."

When Gilbert visited Clarence in jail, Clarence joked, "Nokoomis must be proud to have both her boys away at school."

Crank. "I go by Clarence now. Nice to meet you, Monica." He elongated the "o" in her name. She had the pronounced cheek bones, high forehead and the full lips of a super model. Her eyes were emerald green, and confident when they met his. Her straw-coloured hair was tangled in ways that made Clarence think he had interrupted more than their sleep. She searched his eyes, with what felt like genuine, guileless kindness.

Monica reached under Gilbert's arm to take Clarence's hand. "I was just getting ready to go." She turned and bounded back up the stairs.

Gilbert stepped back to let Clarence into the small vestibule, crowded with running shoes, flattened at the heels, and scuffed boots. Cases of empty beer bottles were stacked against a wall in the living room—Labbat's Blue, his old best friend. The house reeked of stale beer, cigarettes and hash. He examined Gilbert more closely, his eyes were bloodshot. His lips were dry and peeling and his skin was faintly off-gassing alcohol.

Clarence absorbed the room again, and turned to his brother, disappointed. "Shut yer eyes, bro', you're gonna bleed to death." He shook his head, making no effort to conceal his disgust. He raised his shoulders in a question. "What the fuck?"

"Take it easy, last day of exams yesterday. Chill. We had a party. I had a couple of beers, that's it. First time I've drank anything since New Year's Eve." Then, unable to resist a cheap shot at his brother's own habitual drinking and drugging, he added,

"Sorry. You're a day late." He saw the hurt in Clarence's eyes, and wished he could take it back.

A shadow of concern passed over Gilbert's face. "What are you doing here anyway? Please tell me you didn't make a run. You've got what? Only another three weeks to go?"

"Good behaviour!" crowed Clarence. "I knew the papers were coming down the pipe, but wanted to surprise you." He raised a hand to high-five but Gilbert—not quite able to absorb the combination of the words *Crank* and *good behaviour* in the same sentence—left him hanging. Clarence stuffed his hands back into his pockets. Gilbert looked away, the moment lost.

"Thought we could surprise Granny together," Clarence explained. "You're driving home today, eh?"

"Good behaviour?" Gilbert repeated the words, "Good behaviour?" He laughed and shook his head, "Seriously? No shit?"

"Yes, shit. Seriously." No matter how bad things got, Clarence could always make Gilbert smile, in spite of himself. "I joined up with the FNCP. That's for First Nations Cultural Program. We got a sweat lodge, and a teepee out there. Elders come in all the time to do teachings with us. I got tested, too. Turns out I'm not stupid, I'm dyslexic. Knocked off my GEDs at the *alter-native* school."

"You mean *alternative* school."

"It's a joke, bro'. We called it *alter-native*. Get it? Fuck, lighten up bro'. I'm good."

"Alter-native," laughed Gilbert. He finally delivered the hug Clarence had been waiting for. "Sorry, just getting over the shock of your turning up at the door."

In the kitchen, Gilbert boiled water and made coffee in a French press. The sink overflowed with cheese-crusted dishes and cloudy glasses. A blackened knife rested on one of the burner elements on the stove. Clarence picked it up by the handle, like it might bite him, and threw it into an overflowing garbage bag. The floor was sticky with spilt beer. He found the drain plug for the sink and started filling it with water. He rinsed the last drops of dish soap from inside a yellow bottle. "Leave it," said Gilbert. "My roommates made the mess, they can clean it up."

Finding no dishcloth, Clarence started washing the dishes with his fingers and stacking them on a tea towel, on the table. "Let's clean up a little and go bro'. You gotta live someplace else next year."

"I've already found a new place for September, with some guys from home."

"Good guys?"

"Yep. Tim and Grant and Grant's sister, Ètoile. She's Poli-Sci too. Gonna be a lawyer for the people, like me."

"Cool. Poor her, though, living with you three. Let's get going. I can't wait to see the look on Nokoomis' face. She'll scream until she pees her pants when she sees us come through her door."

"She'll probably die of a heart attack," said Gilbert. A soft smile skims his face. "She'll laugh her head off, and dance around the house like that little Chihuahua she got. Scream a little more and then die, right there beside her old stove! And it's gonna be your fault!"

"Always is bro', always my fault," Clarence hooted, then looked over his shoulder from the sink, "But she won't die before she makes us some bannock wieners, eh? Not before that. She'll come back from the dead, that one, to make you an' me bannock dogs!"

"I've got to go, babe." Monica had most of the buttons on a different shirt done up, and was wearing pants. She gave Gilbert a wet kiss and slapped the backside of his jeans. He stood at the door with her while she pulled on a pair of mukluks over her bare feet. "Gotta go mark your exams." She kissed him again, and was gone.

"She's your *teacher*, bro'?" asked Clarence? "Holy fuck! I guess you aced that class!"

"She's a T.A., for my Native Studies course."

"Seriously, bro'? No. That white lady?"

"Well, there had to be at least one." And then, "She's been teaching us Residential Schools, colonialism, treaty rights, all of it." He laughed. "She's from Germany, can you believe? Had to learn it there, 'cause they never taught it here."

"You shit me."

"I shit you not. Seriously, she's cool. She knows her stuff, and she listens way more than she talks."

"I can see she's 'cool' bro'. Is it serious, between you and her?"

"It might get that way. T.A.s aren't allowed to date students. So, we've been dancing around each other all winter. But, as of last night, the seminar is done. We'll see. I'm hoping."

"I've been in the can for a while. So right now, I'd jump a cow moose, but I swear she is the beautifulest girl I've ever seen."

Gilbert laughs. "Yep, and brilliant too and... well, kind of intense."

"Horseshoes up your ass, bro'. You always had 'em. Grades?"

"They're okay."

"Okay? Details."

"They're not out yet." Gilbert paused, and then grinned sheepishly, "Probably all in the nineties."

Clarence punched Gilbert's shoulder. A smile lit up his face and he turned his attention back to the dishes.

Up the Crack in the Dark

When Clarence and Gilbert finished cleaning up at the house, it was late afternoon. Gilbert's roommates had emerged briefly to use the bathroom, and were all back in bed when the brothers left. They tossed Gilbert's backpack, Clarence's plastic grocery bag, and eight cases of empties into the trunk to be dropped off at the beer store on their way out of the city. Gilbert needed a new battery in his car, but planned to deal with it after exams ended. So, Clarence pushed the car down the street and Gilbert popped the clutch to start it. The car lurched and the engine turned over. Clarence jumped into the passenger seat of the rolling vehicle. He was wearing a denim jacket over a grey T-shirt, his jeans, and running shoes.

"That's it? The clothes on your back and a plastic bag?" asked Gilbert. "That's all you've got?"

Clarence opened his jacket, and from the inside pocket, produced a narrow red folder. "And this," he said. He folded the flap open to reveal an eagle's feather, a tail feather from a male bald eagle. White and faintly mottled. The tip of the quill was wrapped and tied with red fabric. "An Elder gave it to me, at my travelling ceremony last night. Told me I earned it. I'm gonna make a nice carrier box for it, as soon as we get home." His voice assumed a tone of shy reverence, which Gilbert hadn't heard since they were kids. "He gave me a name, too. I can't pronounce it right yet, but he wrote it down for me. It means 'Shining Light Warrior.'" Clarence held the folder up to his nose, inhaled the scent of sage and sweet-grass clinging to the feather, and ran a finger along its vane. He closed the folder and carefully returned it to his jacket, then touched the medicine pouch hanging under his T-shirt.

They dropped off the empties and stopped on campus so

that Gilbert could submit his final essay. Clarence insisted they take the time before getting on the road for Gilbert to show him around the lecture halls, library, and food court where he had studied the past three years.

When they drove past the Terry Fox monument heading east out of the city, Gilbert said, "You look different."

"I let my hair grow long like you, bro."

"Ya that, but you're big, too. You working out?"

"Not much else to do, most days. Guys say it keeps the Posse out of your business, but the Elders say looking after our bodies, is looking after our souls, too," Clarence said. "I'm different in lots of ways. I'm not Crank anymore."

When they rolled into Nipigon, they stopped at the Husky for the meatloaf dinner special. An hour later, they were in Schreiber and it was dark. Gilbert slowed the car and asked Clarence if he needed to stop for a smoke. Clarence said he was good, but that he wanted to drive.

So, Clarence was behind the wheel when they approached the familiar rock face. "Oh man, The Crack!" he shouted. Thrilled, like he just remembered where he had buried a treasure. "I have got to climb that thing, right now! For old time's sake. I'm gonna own that sucker!" He swerved across the oncoming lane, and pulled off onto the left shoulder, still pointing east. He left the headlights on, so he could find his way to the opening in the dark and the thickening fog. He left the driver's door ajar. This climb would only take a minute, ninety seconds tops. "Time me, bro'!" Clarence leapt over the ditch and disappeared up The Crack. Gilbert shook his head and yawned, closed the passenger door, came around the car, closed the driver's side. He took a few steps down into the ditch.

Gilbert was relieving himself, and looking up for Clarence to emerge at top of the cliff, when he heard the transport truck. Clarence popped up out of The Crack, arms raised in victory and shouted "I am Fuck of the Mountain!"

Then he watched, helplessly, as the eternal instant of screeching tires and burning brake pads, unfolded. Sparks burst from the trailer as it scraped like flint against the rock cut. The bitter odour of burnt rubber and welded metal rose, like violence, to his nose. He wanted to scream. Everything in him demanded that he scream until his throat haemorrhaged and blood burst from his mouth. "Giiiilberrrrrt!" But his body was paralyzed. He could not locate his voice in time, and a second later it was too late. Gilbert was gone. Plucked up like a vole, or a mouse, in the talons of an owl, and carried off into the darkness.

Clarence turns to stone. He stands on the cement blocks that were once his feet. Only his eyes obey his brain. Through the fog, they track the man in a turban and a full black beard, the man who Clarence reasons, he will hate for the rest of his life—if he ever feels anything again. The man runs from the tractor trailer along the road. Clarence can hear his rubber sandals, slap, slap, slapping on the pavement. He looks like a ghost, running through the growing fog below. He drags Gilbert up onto the shoulder of the highway. He pounds Gilbert's chest, over and over, and blows into his mouth. The man gasps between each exhalation. He vomits. A car stops. Then another.

The truck driver is still pounding Gilbert's chest, and blowing in his mouth, when the police cruiser and the ambulance arrive. "We couldn't make him stop," someone says. The officers wrestle the man away from Gilbert's brother's body. The man is wailing, sobbing. He stops struggling and sags into the arms of the officers. They release him and the man drops to his knees, turns to the east—toward Mecca—and grinds his forehead against the pavement.

He prays, frantically, in a language that Clarence has never heard before. He guesses it is Arabic in which the man weeps. Clarence does not understand the words. He knows, though, the man is pleading for forgiveness. Clarence wishes he knew the words, so he too could pray for forgiveness, too. The man wails in a universal language.

Clarence tells his body to descend down The Crack. Commands it to go to his brother, to bring his culpability and kneel down beside the praying man. But his body defies all orders. It becomes a pile of stones—a poorly constructed trail-marker—teetering on the high cliff above his dead brother's body. He becomes the stone-marker, signifying that *this is the place*. Indicating this is the pathway of loss, grief, failure, shame, death.

Clarence floats in the sky above himself, untethered. He watches himself, standing there frozen, stunned and dumb. His arms, forgetting themselves, remain up-stretched, still declaring him "Fuck of the Mountain." He decides to push himself off the cliff, to break his body on the pavement to be with Gilbert, but his body won't budge.

Clarence can't see me there beside him, but he senses my presence. I touch his shoulder. He shivers and dissolves. I suggest, gently, that he should lie down, and he does. I lay down beside him. We lay on our backs, looking blindly upward, not comprehending the stars. Clarence weeps soundlessly, the way he cried in jail. Tears run down his cheeks into his ears. The tears baffle the sound of sirens and the voices down below. It's a small mercy. He hears instead the persistent pulse of his heart. It refuses to stop beating, in spite of his desire to die.

Had I tears, or cheeks or ears, they too would be wet. We lay there—side by side for hours, not feeling the cold stone beneath us seeping into our backs—until the red flares go black. Until the sound of Billy's van, taking Gilbert away, fades.

Clarence recovers his feet and uses them to stand up and to walk. He turns his back to the cliff and disappears into the bush heading east, heading into the night. I want to follow him, but there are places—ask me, I know—where we can only go alone.

- 20 -
FLORENCE WANTED TO BE A PRIEST

Florence Bearchild, Gilbert and Clarence's grandmother, is four
and a half feet tall. Her tear-soaked face is buried against Billy's
chest. The wetness of crying is soaking through the fabric of his
shirt, plastering his T-shirt to his skin. So many tears from such
a small person. Billy's spine, like a tuning fork, resonates with
the keening sound of her sorrow. A low rumbling fills his chest.
He becomes the boulder upon which the trilling bird can land,
drawing them into an unanticipated intimacy with one another.

Her arms are wrapped around his waist. Billy holds her. Her
brown scalp is visible in the part of her grey hair, gathered in a
braid that reaches down her back. She is wearing dream catcher
earrings, and a pink cardigan over a green turtleneck and jeans.
Balls of Kleenex bulge in both pockets of the sweater.

Billy doesn't resist the subterranean rumble building in his
chest, resonating and harmonizing with Florence's keening des-
cant. Mrs. Bearchild's shrill and unspeakable grief pushes against
the sound of the drum of Billy's chest. Together, in the hallway,
outside the funeral home office, they compose this melody of
lamentation. They harmonize a tune of the sad, soulful music, of
utter defeat.

Bernadette—Florence's older sister—grips her sister's shoulders from behind, and presses her forehead into the curve at
the back of her neck. She murmurs a prayer beneath her breath,
over and over. If she was praying out loud, neither Catherine
nor Billy would understand the words spoken. Bernadette prays
in the language of the Anishinaabeg People.

The sisters are weathered by age. Their smallness though, is
less about genetics than it is about government-sponsored, mal-
nutrition experiments inflicted on them as children taken away

to Residential Schools. Bernadette, due to the curvature of her spine, is slightly shorter than Florence. Both women, however, have expansive spirits that defy their physical stature. Their faces are deeply crevassed, soft, and weathered, like dried apple dolls. Catherine leans into the tableau, holding out a box of Kleenex to Florence.

The three women have come directly from the hospital where Florence confirmed that the misshapen body beneath the sheet had once belonged to her grandson, Gilbert. She cannot, however, connect in her mind that broken shell with her lively grandson.

The boys were raised by Florence and Bernadette, after their mother Theresa—Florence's son's girlfriend—left Pickerel River to pursue a singing career in Vancouver. The two old women have not heard from, or even of, her since. They phoned mutual friends in Vancouver and Bernadette once even flew out to search for Theresa. She reported her niece missing to the police. They listened, made a few perfunctory phone calls, and created a thin file and stored it among hundreds of other thin files of murdered and missing Indigenous women. Then, they did nothing.

Catherine had been summoned to the hospital to provide pastoral care to Gilbert's grandmother and auntie. After identifying him, Florence insisted they go directly to the funeral home. "We're here. I don't want to go home and have to come back later. I won't be able to." She took Catherine's hand and asked her to come with them. Catherine followed their big Ford LTD over in her own car. Through the rear window, the sisters' heads were obscured by the headrests. It appeared to Catherine as if the car was driving itself over to Billy's.

Billy took their parkas and hung them on the coat stand in the hallway. "I'm so sorry to hear of your loss." He said it, not with the practised professionalism of many funeral home directors, but with genuine empathy. He said it like someone well acquainted with the rending experience of loss. He had just motioned them toward the office when Florence flung herself at him.

Billy has become accustomed to this unbidden force at work through him. He accepts it now, no longer questions or doubts it. It is like the swirling of bottomless, dark waters, drawing him downward. Or like a dam, that holds mystery back from the tangible world on most days, breaking open inside him. Its floodgates unlocked by grief and the grieving. Billy becomes the still point, the funnel of air in the middle of the whirlpool of anguish. He neither resists nor conjures it. He allows it.

The first few times it happened Billy was frightened, and more than a little bit embarrassed. As the conduit, he came to see that there is great comfort for the mourner in it. If he had reason to articulate what was happening to him, he might say he feels profoundly awake, to love. He would call it love, even call it falling *into* Love, with the woundedness of all creation.

The word love, however, is bandied about with such incautious disregard for its power, so prodigally scattered, rendering it worthless as pennies scattered on the sidewalk. People love ginger molasses cookies, their cat, and their mothers—hardly the same things. The word love, to Billy's mind, is so diminished by excessive use, that it is not worth bending down to pick it up from where it has been dropped. He has thought all these things, but never talked about them.

Catherine, too, senses that she is near the epicentre of mystery, senses a door has been opened to her. It is a sensuous, soft physical attraction she is witnessing between Florence and Billy. Like their electrons are charged north and south, they snap together like magnets. She feels voyeuristic, to be imposing herself into their intimacy; until she understands that she too is part of the intimacy. The muscles of her jaw relax, her mouth falls open.

Florence's pitch is shrill, like a whistle made from the hollow wing-bone of an eagle. The sound coming from Billy is the rumbling shift of tectonic plates. Distant thunder rolls out of him. The lament echoes from the floor and the walls. The fine hairs on Catherine's arms stand at attention.

The brightness, glowing at the edge of Catherine's peripheral vision, fades. The song of lament dips to a register which maybe only wolves and dogs can hear. She reflexively looks at her watch, but can't remember what time it was when they arrived at the funeral home, or when she was called to the hospital.

Catherine clears her throat and says to Florence, "I didn't realize you already knew Billy."

Inside the office, Billy pulls one of the chairs out from the small conference table for Bernadette and then one for Florence. He falls, spent, into a seat across from them.

"I guess, in some ways, we've known one another for a long time," says Billy. "Mrs. Bearchild, I am so sorry about Gilbert," a pure, white lily in his voice. Florence takes the Kleenex box from Catherine, plucks several out, presses the box back into her hands and smiles. Catherine realizes that she too has been crying. Embarrassed, she pats her eyes and cheeks with a tissue.

Florence and Bernadette blow their noses, honking simultaneously. They wipe the tears from their faces with handfuls of tissue, then tuck them into the cuffs and the pockets of their sweaters. Seated in the padded chairs, the sisters' snowmobile boots hover above the floor.

Florence reaches across the table, rests her hand on Billy's hand, and locks eyes with him, "Can you help us, Mr. Buffone?"

"Probably not, Mrs. Bearchild," Billy sighs, "but we'll try our best. Please, call me Billy."

Probably not? thinks Catherine. *What do you mean probably not? Isn't that what you do? Help.*

"And you, call me Florence. I never was a Mrs." She smiles. Her lips quiver. Bernadette leans over and pulls Florence closer. They laugh-cry and wipe their eyes with the sleeves of their sweaters.

"You've met Rev. Catherine." Billy indicates Catherine, standing across the table, behind Florence and Bernadette, a hand on each of their shoulders.

Bernadette looks to her sister. "We want her to say the Mass for Gilbert."

Florence pats Catherine's hand. "That's right," her cheek still pressed against her sister.

Catherine crouches down beside Florence. "Uhm, Florence, you understand that I'm not Roman Catholic. I'm not a priest. It doesn't matter to me, but when you say 'Mass,'" Catherine's voice brackets the word Mass with quotation marks. "Well, I'm honoured to help in any way I can, but I thought you should know."

"We know. When we were little girls Florence wanted to be a priest," says Bernadette, "We didn't know ladies weren't allowed." She and Florence share a smile at their childhood naiveté. "She used to practise doing Mass on us, with Kool-Aid and saltines. She made us kids play church in the woods behind the house. She was kinda bossy." A flicker of remembered happiness is there and gone.

"I want a lady to say the Mass. Women know about heartache." Florence turns in her chair toward Catherine and touches her forehead to Catherine's. "I can see you know a lot more about heartache than the priest."

Bernadette turns to Billy, "Father doesn't know how to cry. That man never cries, even when he should." There is no judgement in it. She states it as a matter of fact, as if she had said, "The cold wind comes from the north."

Billy asks when the sisters would like to have the service for Gilbert, and takes their phone number down on a message pad.

Catherine asks them to tell her about Gilbert and they do, about how he was a good boy, and how he always lied to them to protect his big brother, Clarence. How he wasn't good at lying, so they always knew. How he was going to be a lawyer and fight for the treaties. How he kept up his grandfather's trap line, from the time he was eleven years old until he went away to university.

"Are there any special songs or readings you want for the service? Ones that you think would honour Gilbert, or comfort you?" Catherine asks. "You don't have to tell me now. Take some time to think about it."

Bernadette says she will offer tobacco to an Elder and arrange for a smudge and a pipe ceremony and for the community drum to be at the service. She isn't asking anyone's permission.

Florence says she wants Psalm 42 read from the Bible, and begins to recite the opening verses:

"As the deer pants for streams of water
so my soul pants for you, O God.
My soul thirsts for God,
for the living God.
When can I go and meet with God?
My tears have been my food day and night,
while men say to me all day long,
'Where is your God?'"

When Florence finishes, she presses a ball of Kleenex to each of her eyes.

Billy waits a moment, then explains, "They probably won't let me come for Gilbert for a few days. Because it was an accident, they'll have to take him to Thunder Bay for an autopsy."

Bernadette puts her arm back around her sister and says to Billy, "They already told us at the hospital. They aren't going to find no booze or dope. They think they will, just 'cause he's Indian. Gilbert wouldn't never drive drunk or high. That's how their dad died."

"I know he wouldn't," Billy nods. "I can come out to your place tomorrow to help with the details."

"Take some time for this all to sink in," Catherine advises. "There isn't any rush." But the sisters insist on taking care of what they can now. They want to sort things out, clear their minds so they can just be sad.

In the showroom next to the office, Billy says, "These are some samples of caskets and urns. There are others in the catalogue. You can talk it over a bit, about what way you want to go."

Florence glides the palm of her hand across the top of the oak casket. Her hand looks soft, like a deer hide glove and the colour of mahogany. She whispers, "Maybe something with a Raven, a Trickster like Jesus, on it." She swallows a sob, and tips her head up to say, "No, wait. What am I thinking, it has to be a bear."

"Yes," says Billy.

Florence takes Catherine's hand in hers. "That's our doodem. The bear, for protection and for good medicines."

"I'll take care of it," Billy says.

Across the hall, they stand in the open french doors, looking into the chapel. "This won't be big enough," says Billy. "Gilbert has a lot of friends. You're a big family"

"Can we have it at your church?" Bernadette asks Catherine.

"Yes, of course," says Catherine, "if you think there's enough room there."

"Maybe," says Billy, "we should hold it out at the community hall."

The sisters agree, the ceremony should be in Pickerel River.

Billy helps the Bearchild sisters into their coats. Catherine gives them a business card and says, "I'll come out later on but *please*, call me any time, day or night." She hugs Florence and then Bernadette.

Florence reaches up and takes Billy's cheeks in her hands, "Will you help me, Billy?" Catherine feels a disconcerting stab of jealousy. She is jealous of Florence's hands resting on Billy's cheeks, of the way the two of them are gazing into one another's eyes. She is jealous of the tenderness between them. Catherine feels like she is intruding on something she wants badly for herself.

"I'll see what I can do. I'll do my best," Billy promises.

"I've got to know. Help me."

"I know you do. I'll do my best. I promise."

"I know you will. I know you can do it." Then, on tiptoes, she kisses him on the tip of his nose.

Standing beneath the carport, arms wrapped around themselves against the cold, Billy and Catherine watch the women drive away, Bernadette behind the wheel and Florence in the passenger seat.

Inside, Catherine asks, "What does she need to know? What happened? She wants to know how Gilbert died?" She resists the urge to touch Billy's face the way Florence did, and berates herself for feeling jealous of a gentle old woman.

"She needs to know where Clarence is. She wants us to find him." He turns and climbs the two steps out of the office and disappears through the door leading into his kitchen.

"Clarence?" Catherine calls after Billy and waits, watching the empty door frame for him to reappear. "Clarence?" she raises her voice. "You mean Gilbert's brother, Clarence?"

Billy doesn't answer. She waits for his return from whatever pressing issue he has gone to attend to.

Billy, however, has already caught a fantasy flight to Prince Edward Island—to the recording studio, the Porsche 911, the naked yoga on the beach and Jodie or Meg or the Hemingway sister with the hurt eyes.

- 21 -
LOOKING FOR ME

By the time the police were out looking for me, I had already collided with the train. Turns out, Anthony wasn't the first to fold, as I would have predicted. He didn't get the chance. Larry presented himself at the police station shortly after hearing from his mother a version of events similar to what Mr. Jordan told me at the hardware store. Without uttering a word in response to her telling him of the recovery of Churley's body, Larry marched across town, up the wooden steps into the police station, and spilled his guts. He told them everything. Well, not everything. Obviously.

Larry's version was more along the lines of: one Boy Scout in the Apple Day bushel gone bad. One of the Mad Collins bad apples, Matt. You know how they are, officer. In his statement, Larry recounted to the constables, and to Suzie Bracken—the spellbound detachment secretary furiously taking notes—how he and Anthony had been stunned and traumatized when I woke them up and confessed to them the crime I had committed in a drunken haze. No, he didn't know how I got my hands on the alcohol. He hated to say it, not wishing to besmirch Mr. Rupert Churley's—God rest his soul—fine reputation, but the bottle might have been provided by the Scouter himself. Larry couldn't say for sure. He and Anthony were sleeping like lambs in the front room by 11:00 PM. No, they hadn't heard a thing.

Larry expressed his sincere regret for not coming forward earlier. He said he was in shock for a few days and admitted he was afraid because I threatened to kill him and Anthony if they talked. He expressed contrition, wept convincingly, and apologized for his initial cowardice, all the while twiddling his fingers like a mad scientist. The police assured Larry he was a very brave young man to come forward, even if it had taken him a few days to steel his backbone.

They interviewed Anthony next. His story was word-for-word identical to Larry's. The two statements were as consistent as a script for the school play, because that's what they were: predetermined, well-rehearsed lines. Apparently, I was not the only person Anthony had been calling on the telephone. Knowing Larry, he probably supplied Anthony with a written copy of their version of events, told him to memorize it and then eat it. And, knowing Anthony, he did exactly as he was told.

I don't blame them. Their lives were crappy enough as it was. I'm glad they made it out of Twenty-Six Mile House in one piece. Larry, single and living down east, is a rising star on the Mississauga Police Force's Crimes Against Children Unit. Anthony goes by Tony now. He runs a black-light bowling alley and bar in Thunder Bay with his wife, Elaine. They've got two great kids—a boy and a girl—who Anthony would die for. Elaine doesn't know about Churley but she's been awakened by Tony's nightmares, at least once a month since they married. Larry and Anthony don't keep in touch with each other. Since leaving town, they haven't been back. They never told anyone about what Churley did to them. I don't blame them for that either.

When the police showed up at our house looking for me, they started by asking my father if he knew where I was. Before he even acknowledged them, Dad finished a tumbler of rye—rinsed with a splash of Coke—and slammed the empty glass down on the table in front of him. Then, he replied, "How the fuck should I know? What's it to you?"

Dad proceeded to spill more rye from an almost empty forty-ounce bottle into his glass, and went to the refrigerator for more Coke and ice. By the time he sat back down at the table, he seemed to have forgotten the question during the round trip from the table to the fridge and back. So, he just stared, focusing his blood shot eyes on the wall behind the police.

"If you see Matthew, sir, please call us," said the younger of the two officers.

Eyes struggling to focus on the officer who just spoke, like it was a staring contest, Dad tipped another splash of rye directly onto the tabletop, missing his glass completely. He continued to stare, daring them to comment on the spilt liquor, daring them to remark upon his state of pre-lunch inebriation, as if he considered being a pompous and stupid drunk in the presence of the law an act of civil disobedience against The Man, an assertion of his democratic right to be an alcoholic.

"Jesus, Collins," said the older cop, shaking his head.

"Fuck you," parried my dear old dad. He was disappointed when they gave up so easily and left him to argue with himself.

The next obvious stop for the police was down the street at the Buffones' place. When Billy came in through the back door they were there, already seated at the kitchen table drinking fresh coffee from his mother's good china cups and saucers.

"Here he is!" Mrs. Buffone's voice trilled with anxiety. Never before—in Canada or in Italy—had there been police officers in her home, let alone seated at her kitchen table.

Billy said, "Hi," kicked his shoes off at the door, and padded across the kitchen toward the stairs leading up his bedroom—as if the constabulary routinely popped by for a spot of coffee and a chat with his widowed mother.

"Billy," Mrs. Buffone called him back to the kitchen, "these gentlemen wan' to talk with you." There was the hint of her long-lost Italian accent in her pronunciation. The police probably didn't hear it, but for Billy it was a telltale signal that she was nervous. She was twisting a dish towel tightly around her hand, as if to staunch blood from a cut. "They are hoping you can help them find Matthew. Something has happened."

Billy leaned against the counter, his arms hanging limp at his sides, the straps of his backpack still over his shoulders. In spite of the fine dark hairs starting to sprout above his lip, his face retained its boyishness. "What?"

Mrs. Buffone was stunned into silence by her son's impertinence.

The older officer finished stirring sugar into his coffee, gently tapped the tiny spoon three times on the rim of the cup, and rested it on the edge of the saucer. "No need for concern, Billy. No big deal," he said. "We just need to ask Matt a couple of questions."

"No," said Billy. "What. I mean *what happened*? Why are you looking for Matt?"

"Well, it's police work and confidential, at this point."

The younger officer chimed in, "Part of an ongoing investigation. We're not at liberty to..."

"It's about Scouter Churley," Billy interrupted. "Everybody in town is already talking about it."

Mrs. Buffone raised her hand, still wrapped in the tea towel, to her throat. "Is true then? He is dead, for true? Mr. Churley? Everyone is saying about it."

"Yes, ma'am. I'm afraid that Mr. Churley was found deceased up at his camp earlier today." Then to Billy, "Do you know anything about that, Billy? Or where we might find your pal, Matt?"

Mrs. Buffone interjected before Billy could answer. "What does this have to do with these boys? With Matthew?" she wanted to know.

"Like he said, we just have a couple questions for Matt, for Matthew, Mrs. Buffone. If you or Billy can help us find him..." said the younger one. He paused. A contest of who could go the longest without speaking ensued. In the silence, they could hear *Love Will Keep Us Together*, by The Captain and Tennille, playing on Mary's record player upstairs.

The older of the two officers sighed when the song ended. "Okay. Look, we know that Matt was there, at Mr. Churley's camp, on the weekend. We know what happened. I'm levelling with you here, Billy. There were two other boys there. Eye witnesses. You probably know who they are. They've already told us everything. I can't go into details, but we need to find Matt."

"Matt was with me all weekend," said Billy. "We were camping at Jackrabbit Lake."

The officers exchanged a glance with one another. Then they looked to Mrs. Buffone, anticipating her repudiation of Billy's lie. Instead she said, "That's right. They had no gone out to the lake together for a long time. I was happy, when Billy said they were go camping. They are best friends since little boys." Her words tripped over each other and over her accent. "They brought home some nice pickerel for me with them." She blushed and took hold of the refrigerator door handle, ready to produce the fish as evidence if necessary.

"Did you drive them out there, ma'am?"

"No, they ride their bicycles like always when they go. I packed up the food for them. How could Matthew have been at Mr. Churley's camp? When he is fishing with Billy?" Mrs. Buffone raised her shoulders and her eyebrows. She looked like a silent movie heroine.

"Well, there you go," said the older officer, raising his open palms, mimicking Mrs. Buffone's eyebrows, as if agreeing that it was all just one big misunderstanding. "If we could talk with Matt," he crooned, "I'm sure we can get this whole thing ironed out." Extending his stout pinkie, he drained the coffee from the porcelain cup and rose from his chair. He looked directly at Billy, foreboding in his voice, "Billy, if you know where Matt is, or where he might be, or if you see him, you *will* tell us, won't you?"

Billy stared past the officer, refusing to meet his eyes, focusing instead on the screen door leading to the garage, and answered, "I don't know where he is right now, but sure, okay." That much was true, Billy had no idea where I was then.

As soon as the screen door clapped shut behind the police officers, Billy hurried up the stairs to his bedroom and closed the door. Mrs. Buffone busied herself at the stove. She called up after him, "Supper will be ready soon. Tell Mary to turn down that music and come eat."

She bit her lip. She had not lied. It was true. She had wrapped sandwiches, processed cheese slices and cookies in waxed paper for the boys before Billy left on Friday afternoon; she put two apples, four hotdogs and buns, marshmallows and a packet of Kool-Aid in Billy's backpack. It was true: Billy brought pickerel home to her on Sunday. She opened the refrigerator, to confirm that the leftover fillet was still on a plate, covered with cellophane. Proof. She could smell the fish.

I think she was disappointed though that I didn't come inside to say hello before we left for Jackrabbit Lake on Friday afternoon. Nor had I dropped in to see her when we returned on Sunday. She must have found it strange, sad even, given that she had seen so little of me over the past few months. I didn't understand it then, didn't understand my power to hurt her, she who had adopted me as her own.

The sound of the sirens drifted over the town—carried to her ears on the dissipating fog, one wet molecule to the next, like dominos of tears. Mrs. Buffone had already prepared supper, but she chopped an onion, like she always did when she felt the need to cry.

Mrs. Buffone was scraping the onion from the cutting board into a skillet of olive oil when the sirens stopped so abruptly that it startled her. She nicked her finger with the knife. They had found me.

- 22 -

KNOCK AND THE DOOR SHALL BE OPENED

Stunned. Catherine is still pacing beside the conference table in Billy's office. She stares in disbelief at the door through which Billy has disappeared. She has been waiting for him to reappear. She checks her watch and guesstimates that he's been gone about fifteen minutes—since the Bearchild sisters left. The wall clock has ticked. Outside, the early morning sun has won a few battles, but lost the war, with a crowd of pugilistic clouds.

Catherine starts to feel like a loyal spaniel, stationed on the doormat, looking longingly at the door, waiting for her master to return. She makes a little puppy whimpering noise and then sits behind Billy's desk, in his chair. She swivels the chair. She lays her paws on the desk and pants a little.

Her fingernails need filing and trimming. She taps them on the veneer topped desk, inventing her own Morse code—she doesn't actually know Morse code—*Bi-lly wh-ere ar-e—u? STOP.* Tap. Tappity. Taaaap.

She thinks she may have heard the sound of furniture springs coming from inside Billy's apartment. She cocks her ear toward it. She squints at the open rectangle of the doorframe, attempting to manifest Billy in it. The power of positive thinking, however, fails her.

As a little girl, riding in the back seat of her mother's car—cigarette ashes being flicked from the driver's window and sucked back in the rear window—Catherine was convinced she could turn traffic lights green with her mind. She used her powers to get her mother home quickly, when her mother had one of her "like a vice on my eyeballs" headaches. Catherine believed—with pre-Eden-apple-pie innocence—that she possessed the psychic ability to turn red lights green. This childish magical thinking, and her innocence, has been severely tested, but not entirely crushed, since then.

She spins the chair around to face the wall behind the desk. *A watched pot and all that.* Billy's Funeral Director Diploma, from Humber College in Toronto, hangs on the otherwise unadorned wall. Catherine stands up, intending to straighten the brushed metal frame, but discovers it is already as level as a lake on windless day. She taps a corner and knocks it askew. She looks over her shoulder to see if touching his stuff might have summoned Billy. It has not.

The door is open. Maybe he expected me to follow him. Maybe he's in there wondering what's taking me so long? She thinks: *Maybe he wants to be followed, chased like a hurt child.* Catherine recalls her childhood tantrums, when she screamed at her mother to "Leave me alone!" ran to her room, slammed the cheap mobile home door, hurled herself onto her bed and buried her face in the pillow. A performance played out to communicate to her mother: *Don't leave me alone! Chase me! Put your hand on my back and coo that you love me.*

Maybe he's making coffee. She groans inwardly at the thought of a mug of stiff java. Catherine has been functioning without caffeine since being roused from her warm bed by the call from the hospital. Her adrenaline levels—jacked up by the call, and by seeing Gilbert's body, and by whatever was happening between Billy and Florence—have tumbled to zero. The sleepless night, and the warm office, settles on her like a fourth glass of Merlot. She yawns. *Sweet Jesus, I need a coffee. And a shower and a toothbrush.*

She scratches her head and discovers that she is still wearing her toque. She pulls it off and her hair flares in a ginger halo of static. *Maybe I should just go home, clean up, have a coffee, maybe a nap and call back later.* She flattens her hair against the sides of her head. *And use some conditioner.*

But there is the open doorway, beckoning her. Knock and the door shall be opened unto you.

The door is already open, partially. Is the door half open or half closed? Depends if you are an optimist or a pessimist. When someone leaves a door open it means one of two things: Hang-on, I'll be right back. Or—thinks Catherine—This way, follow me. An open door is either a commitment or an invitation, is it not?

Three things. It could also mean: I'm an eccentric small-town funeral director who dances the herky-jerky with my vacuum cleaner, reads minds and who grants no symbolic meaning whatsoever to doors, be they partially open or partially closed. And I'm kind of cute.

Stop it, Catherine! Sometimes a cigar is just a cigar. Sometimes an open door is just an open door.

Catherine yawns and smiles recalling her mamma's voice, loud and rattling the aluminum siding on their Tupelo trailer. "In or out! In or out! For the love of God, Katydid, you're lettin' in every fly in this high-wide-and-handsome county!"

Catherine stands on the first of the two steps and sings, "Hellooo? Anybody home?" She sets her knuckles against the doorframe. "Billy?" She knocks on the door. It is hollow veneer—so, light—and it swings open, propelled by her tentative tap. There are rustling sounds. Billy is moving about, or there's a squirrel in the attic.

She grips both sides of the door frame to lean forward, poking her head into the kitchen. "Hello?"

Billy is sitting on a green corduroy couch, five feet away. Legs crossed at his ankles, knees splayed outward, thick forearms resting on his thighs, fingers interlocked. He stares blankly at her. He looks like a child waking from his nap. His face is flushed and creased with sleep. He presses his lips into tight line to conceal a yawn.

"Are you?" Catherine stops and starts again. "Is everything okay?"

Billy grinds the heels of his hands into his eye sockets. "Uh huh. You?"

"Fine. Yes, thanks." she says. "So, we're all set? Is there anything else we need to talk about before, uhm, I go? About the funeral, I mean?"

"We've got to wait," says Billy. "Autopsy and all. There's a lot of waiting involved."

Catherine feels like she is towering over the still seated Billy. He is craning his neck to look up at her. She turns one of the kitchen chairs around from the table and sits down in front of the couch, a bit closer to Billy than she intended.

"Mrs. Bearchild, she told you she wants you to find Clarence? Or you thought that? Or felt it? Or something?"

"Us," says Billy.

"What?"

"Us. She wants us to find Clarence," says Billy.

"Us as in you and me?"

"Uh huh." Billy continues to stare unabashedly into her eyes.

Catherine leans back in the chair and resists the temptation to cross her arms. Instead, she places her hands in her lap, palms down—presenting an open body posture as per her pastoral counselling training. "Why do you say that?" Open-ended question.

"That she wants us to find Clarence?"

"Well that, and how do you know she wants *us* to find him?"

Billy tugs his lower lip and turns to look in direction of the refrigerator. Catherine follows his gaze. Unlike her fridge, there is no anarchy of photographs, no Sunday School children's drawings, no lists or reminders, suspended by insurance company and Pizza-Pizza magnets posted on Billy's fridge. Its face is as unblemished, and unreadable, as Billy's.

He meets her eyes, again. Catherine admonishes herself: *Stop thinking about his eyes.* "It's a feeling, I guess," he says. "She wants us to find Clarence, and she wants us to do it together."

Billy continues to hold her with an unblinking gaze. Her peripheral vision goes dark and there are only eyes, Billy's two chocolate eyes floating in space. Is he hypnotising her? Catherine blinks once, but doesn't look away. Her voice comes out sounding disembodied, as if it is floating out of her throat. "Well, Billy, I'll help you out if I can. I don't have a clue where to even start. I guess our first call would be the jail?"

Billy says, "First, we should have coffee."

The spell is broken. Billy goes to the counter, opens a cupboard and runs tap water into the pot. It's an old-fashioned percolator, stainless steel, with a black plastic handle, and a clear glass bulb on top. Billy says, "This was my mother's. Do you want something to eat?"

"The coffee pot was your mother's?" she asks.

"Yep. Let's eat something. How 'bout some cereal," says Billy. "I've got Cheerios." Billy sets two bowls and two spoons out on the Arborite table top. "I've eaten with these spoons and bowls at this table, in these chairs, since I was born. In a different house, though."

Catherine dutifully admires the Corningware bowls and the chrome legged table and chairs. "Nice," she says and thinks, *Am I asleep? Is this dreaming?*

Billy sets the box of cereal and a Mason jar of brown sugar on the table between them. He hums a few bars of *Brown Sugar* by the Rolling Stones, like always when he puts the sugar out. He gets a carton of milk from the fridge, opens the spout and sniffs, then puts it on the table. The coffee percolates, the brewing liquid gurgling up inside the glass bulb. "Voila," he exclaims and takes the chair across from Catherine at the far end of the table, not that one end of the table is especially far from the other.

The noisy carnality of chewing and swallowing their cereal, the clink of spoons on bowls, rather than feeling awkward to Catherine, serves to enlarge the intimacy between her and Billy. Catherine asks, "So you grew up here?"

Billy swallows. "Yep." He takes another spoon full of Cheerios, chews and cheeks the mash of crushed O's and says, "Just went away for school."

"You must really like it here." Even as she is saying it Catherine senses that Billy's lifer status isn't a question of liking or not liking; something more elemental than preference tethers him to Twenty-Six Mile House. There is an invisible gravitational pull that keeps him orbiting his hometown like a moon.

"Like it here?" Billy considers her assertion, as if for the first time. "Not really. It's okay. It's where I am. Wherever I go, there I am."

"Very Zen," Catherine smiles.

Billy pushes back from the table. The chairs have crocheted booties on their feet and whisper like children's slippers on the linoleum floor. He rinses his bowl and spoon under the tap and puts them in the dish rack. Catherine follows suit. Billy pours coffee into matching brown and green ceramic mugs. "Do you take anything in it?"

"Just black, thanks," says Catherine. She takes the cup and holds it close to her nose and inhales its promise of resuscitation.

Billy stirs milk, and several spoons of sugar, into his cup and raises it towards Catherine in a toast.

Catherine smiles and touches her mug to his. The sound of blowing across the hot surface of their mugs, and the soft swallowing seems like conversation. If later on she had cause to describe those minutes with Billy in his kitchen, she would call them "comfortable."

Billy finishes his coffee and goes through the living room into the bathroom. Catherine can hear him peeing, flushing. The tap running.

She rinses the mugs and looks out the window above the sink. There is a row of six ravens perched on the peak of the house across the road. The face of the house is unremarkable, but for some reason it unsettles her. A movement in one of the basement windows draws her attention downward. For the smallest fraction of a second, she thinks she may have seen a face peering out. The blind drops. It happens so quickly that she wonders if she imagined it. The row of small, ground-level windows grins back at her like teeth. Billy's kitchen is warm but she feels suddenly chilled. She rubs the goosebumps from her arms.

Billy returns, drying his hands on the front of his jeans. Catherine asks, "Who lives across the road?"

"Dick Spanner." There is finality in his voice, as if he has also said, "End of topic." Changing the topic, he asks, "You want to go to the bathroom before we get going?"

In his bathroom, she turns the fan on and runs the faucet so Billy won't hear her pee.

Back in the kitchen she asks, "Get going where?"

"It's up a path, I think," says Billy. "That's where Clarence is. It's a path and it's up and then down."

Catherine cannot help laughing. She touches his arm. "Well, as long as you've got the location nailed down, Billy. Do you happen to know where this up and down path is, where it starts?"

"Good point," Billy concedes and smiles sheepishly. "I'll call you later."

- 23 -
ANOTHER DOOR

They retrieved my body from the blueberry patch beside the tracks and stored it in the morgue at the old Anderson General Hospital. Not the new redbrick building with its stainless-steel morgue and automated door openers and hand sanitizer dispensers mounted on all the bathroom walls. The old morgue was rarely, and always briefly, used just to hold the deceased until Jack Garret came from the funeral home in Schreiber, an hour away, or the coroner's assistant from Port Arthur arrived to collect someone's mortal remains in need of examination.

If you want to picture the old morgue—who would want to picture it really, except that it is necessary to do so in order to picture me in it—picture the meat locker at the old Tom Boy grocery store. The morgue had space enough for two stretchers, one to each side of the heavy insulated door, with a narrow work space in between them. The chrome lever on the door was the same as the meat locker at Tom Boy's. The door at Tom Boy's, however, had a window so customers could observe the butcher at work. That's the only difference between the two doors.

The floor and halfway up the walls was finished with one-inch, grouted ceramic tiles. There was a drain in middle of the floor, like the showers at the municipal swimming pool. A large utility sink, the glaze chipped in places, was bolted to the far wall, a wooden chair beside it, and above, were shelves stocked with cleaning supplies. A string mop, metal wringer and wheeled bucket were tucked into a corner. Two pairs of fluorescent tube lights were mounted to the ceiling. The first time Billy was in the morgue, he noted that one of the four tubes was burnt out.

The day after I killed myself with a train, Billy visited the morgue twice. The first time, he presented himself at the desk of the charge nurse and announced, with poorly manufactured conviction, that he had come to identify the body of Matthew Collins. The nurse wore glasses—black, cat eye frames with rhinestones—and she looked over the top of them, at Billy. Her hair, red and curly, appeared to be more the consequence of rollers and dye than of genetics. "Sorry, Billy, no can do." Her gravelly voice testified to years of shift work and a love affair with nicotine. "Roger's been in already. The ID is done."

"Can I see him anyway?" asked Billy, the thin skin of confidence sliding off him.

"No." Her voice softened. She removed her glasses, letting them rest against her ample chest on a silver chain. "Billy, you don't want to see him."

"Yes, I do. I do want to see him," Billy's voice was as toneless as an instruction manual for a toaster oven. "If it's not too much trouble, ma'am."

"For the love of God, Billy," she lowered her voice and—checking left and right to confirm the absence of witnesses—she said, "He was hit by a train. You don't want to remember him like that."

"I know." Billy could not recall the nurse's name, but he recognized her from the bowling alley. Up close, beneath a thick application of make-up, she appeared to be older than Billy would have guessed. He detected kindness in her, perhaps kindness seeded by familiarity with loss. He heard she was divorced.

"I'd still like to see him," Billy persisted. The tremor in his voice became less restrained. "Maybe you should check with the doctor. Get his permission?" The power struggle between the nurses and the arrogant, fly-by-night doctors was a well-known phenomenon.

She pushed her chin forward and snapped, "Maybe I should check with his father, or his brothers." She reached for the phone on her desk, watching for Billy to call her bluff. Her hand hovered above the phone. It was beige and modern, with push-buttons and several unlit line indicators.

Billy's eyes stung and he blinked to dam the ocean of tears that were threatening to flood his face. A few drops slid down his cheeks. "He is my best friend."

The nurse softened. She set her pen down on the metal desk and sighed, "You're sure you wanna do this?" Billy nodded. She observed him for a beat, and then raised herself from her chair. She was marginally taller standing than she was sitting. "Follow me. And, Billy, if you have nightmares for a month, God forgive me."

"I won't," said Billy. "Have nightmares, I mean."

The charge nurse's desk was positioned to control access to the ward behind it, where on any given day, four to eight patients convalesced in their metal hospital beds. In the other direction, the desk faced a corridor leading away from the lobby. Entering the main doors of the old hospital, one could turn right to visit the ill or to the left where, at the furthest end of the corridor, the morgue was located.

The nurse led Billy past the emergency and casting rooms, her white shoes chirping on the varnished floor. They passed the kitchen, the laundry, lab, x-ray and the administrative offices before arriving at the insulated door. At the end of the hallway, just past the morgue, there was an exit door, with a wire-mesh window. Through it, Billy could see the parking lot behind the hospital.

The nurse leaned her back against the morgue door, folded her arms across her uniform and asked, "You're sure about this, Billy?"

Billy forced himself to look her in the eye. "I'm sure." She turned around and used both hands to pull the handle down. A rush of cool air escaped and Billy shivered. The nurse reached inside and flipped the light switch. They stepped into the room, leaving the door ajar behind them.

Billy looked up at the ceiling, preparing himself to see the shape of my body outlined by the sheet on the stretcher. That's when he noticed the non-fluorescing light tube. He inhaled a lungful of the disinfectant-laden air, lowered his eyes and his shoulders sagged as he exhaled. He took in the contours of the sheet, not quite able to believe it was me beneath it.

The nurse assumed a tone and volume Billy associated with libraries. "Most of the injuries were internal but there are some broken bones." She grasped the top edge of the sheet with both hands and ceremoniously folded it back. "You can tell it's him."

The face—my face—and head were raked with deep scrapes along the left side. They had been sponged off prior to Roger's visit. So, although the cuts were deep and black, they were clean looking. They weren't bleeding, of course, because my heart was stopped. A few grains of coarse sand remained lodged in my skin. My eyes and mouth had been closed, also for Roger's visit, but had slackened and parted since. Milky coloured eyes peered, sightless, between my partially open eyelids. Some of my teeth were broken. Jellied blood matted my hair and was pooled in my ears. My forehead was punched back toward my hairline. My nose was flattened; in shape and colour, it resembled the Silly Putty Billy and I used to press onto our comic books, lifting reversed images of our superheroes from the pages.

Billy reached out toward my cheek; the nurse grabbed his wrist but then let it go. She placed her hand instead, on Billy's back between his shoulder blades. To the touch, my skin was cold by then, waxy and stiff. Billy grazed his knuckles across my cheek and flattened a hand on my brow, transferring heat from his own body into mine. His lips trembled. Noiseless tears rolled down his face. They dripped from his chin, wetting the sheet that covered my body. The fan on the rooftop cooler unit hummed to life.

Billy reached for the sheet to slide it down off my shoulders. This time the nurse was firm. "That's enough."

In the corridor, the nurse pushed the heavy door closed with her backside. The latch clacked into place. "What will they do with him, now?" Billy wanted to know.

"They have to take him up to the Lakehead for an autopsy."

"Why?" asked Billy. It was pretty obvious how I died, and the books were closed on why I had died. There was no Gordian knot to be resolved.

"It's routine," she answered. "They check for drugs, alcohol, poison, that kind of thing. Just to be sure. The coroner has to rule out foul play. It's the law, Billy."

"Then what?"

"Roger says they're going to have him cremated up there. He didn't say what they had in mind as far as a funeral goes."

"He was sort of Catholic," said Billy.

The nurse nodded, "Yes, well. I'm not sure what the rules are over there with the papists when it's a. . .when the person. . ." her voice trailed off, having communicated clearly enough what she was reluctant to say. "They'll have to talk with the priest about it. If they want to. Look Billy, I need to get back to the ward. Are you okay?"

"Fine, thanks," said Billy. He stood staring at the cooler door behind her. The nurse stood guard until he had disappeared through the exit door at the end of the hall, out into the parking lot.

- 24 -
BILLY'S FIRST BODY WAS MINE

Billy went down to the basement as soon as he got home. That's where his mother kept the last of his father's clothing. He had always assumed that his mother hung onto his father's clothes because she couldn't bear to part with them, his scent, the texture of his shirts. Right after the funeral, Mrs. Buffone had boxed most of it up—a work coat, boots, heavy socks, even underwear—and donated them to St. Luke's Church to be shipped further north, to a fly-in reserve.

Over the years, Billy came to realize that she kept the navy suit, along with a white shirt and tie on a hanger, protected by a green plastic bag, hoping he might someday wear it. By the time he was fourteen, however—and with no occasion to wear a suit having yet presented itself—Billy was too tall and broad across the shoulders to fit into his father's clothes.

His mother had presented Billy with his father's watch immediately after the funeral.

In the basement, Billy retrieved the suit, took it upstairs and hung it on the rod in his bedroom closet. He stuffed a pair of his own socks and a coiled belt into the jacket pockets.

Then Billy lay on his bed, arms straight at his sides, to wait.

He got up and walked over to the drug store, where he spent half an hour in the make-up aisle, examining blushes and foundations.

At the checkout, the cashier—Shelly Timperman, one of Billy's classmates—examined the COVERGIRL foundation compact he had selected. She looked at him and at the flat plastic container in her hand. She checked the price sticker. She looked at Billy again and, making no attempt to disguise her curiosity, asked, "Is that everything, Billy?"

Having anticipated Shelly's curiosity, he replied, "Don't say anything. It's a surprise for my Mom." He added a black plastic comb from the box beside the cash register to his purchase. "Hold on," he said, "I think I'll get her some hairspray too."

"Does she like her hair stiff or soft?" Shelly followed him to the cosmetics aisle and helped him to find what he wanted.

Back at the house he lay down on his bed again, arms at his sides and stared at the ceiling, waiting. The wind-up alarm clock on his bedside table ticked. He went back out.

This time, he walked over to the hardware store. He heard someone say, "Sorry to hear about Matt, Billy," but he didn't look to see who said it. He bought a fluorescent light tube. Back home, he carefully leaned it against the wall inside his closet, next to the bag from the drugstore and the suit on its hanger.

Outside, the sun had finally burned off the three days of fog. He sat at the table for supper with his mother and sister. Mary's and Mrs. Buffone's eyes and noses were raw with grief. "I took a tuna casserole over to Mr. Collins," said his mother.

Mary's head snapped up from staring grimly at her plate. "What did he say?" she demanded.

"He wasn't home, so I just left it in the fridge."

"He was probably hiding or passed out drunk upstairs," scowled Mary.

"I'm not sure that's a fair thing to say," said Mrs. Buffone. "He has just lost his son."

Mary rolled her eyes and shook her head. Billy was accustomed to his sister's hair-trigger temper. Even as at toddler, she was given to shoe-stamping bursts of anger. As a teenager, she was tough, and didn't pull her punches. One never needed to surmise her thoughts or opinions. She dished them up hot and without sugar. She was also, Billy could see, becoming a beautiful woman, like their mother. Unlike Mrs. Buffone, Mary would never submit to stifling conventions regarding the *proper* place of women.

"Matthew's..." Mary pressed lips together. The sound of my name, spoken out loud for the first time since receiving news of my death, landed like an axe in the centre of the kitchen table. Saying my name momentarily sucked all the air out of room. Mary and Mrs. Buffone froze, anticipating an implosion or explosion on Billy's part. But he sat at the table, calm as a stone. Mary continued, "*Matthew's*—we should say his name, for crying out loud—Matthew's dad is a bad drunk and a worse father. Why do you keep pretending, Mom?"

Mrs. Buffone said, "Mary," a half-hearted scold in her voice. She reached across the table for Billy's hand.

Billy took her hand. "I'm gonna be okay, Mom."

After supper he walked down to the lake, and sat on one of the weathered boom logs marking the perimeter of the parking area. He watched the surf continue its centuries' long work of pounding stones round. It was late when first one star, and then a trillion, poked holes of light in the night sky. A fingernail of moon appeared, casting its stingy light on the rise and fall of water.

By the time Billy slipped into the hospital through the door near the morgue it was after 2:00 AM. Like I said, locked doors, even at the hospital, were an unheard-of phenomenon in Twenty-Six Mile House in those days. The hanger bearing his father's suit was draped over his shoulder. In the same hand he clutched the bag of cosmetics and the comb. In the other, Billy carried the fluorescent light tube. He wore a heavy sweater, even though it was late August and still warm. He could hear a radio playing in the nurses' lounge at the far end of the corridor—*Ol' Black Water* by The Doobie Brothers. Billy hummed along as he pulled the morgue door closed behind. In the dark, he felt for the light switch on the wall.

An hour and a half later, Billy turned out the lights and slipped out the exit door to the parking lot. By then my body had been washed, and then dressed in his father's suit and tie, and Billy's socks and belt. No need for shoes or underwear. My face and hands were powdered a not particularly natural hue. The bruises showed through the foundation, but were softened by the Band-Aid coloured cosmetic. The blood had been rinsed from my ears and hair. My hair was combed, parted neatly, and sprayed into place.

Two of the fingers, on my right hand, were broken at disturbing angles. Billy positioned it across my chest and placed my undamaged hand on top. The bone protruding from the compound fracture of my femur tented his father's wool trousers provocatively. The defective fluorescent light tube had been replaced.

- 25 -
THE LAW OF CONSERVATION OF ENERGY

Catherine leaves Billy in his kitchen—contemplating the whereabouts of the intuited upward path that would lead them to Clarence—and drives toward home. Her scalp is crawling with the ants of sleeplessness, and postponed personal hygiene. The static electricity in her hair could light a bulb. She pulls a mitten off with her teeth, rakes her scalp with her fingernails and groans with relief. Her face feels sticky, like she's walked through a spider's web. She is desperate for a shower, a thorough tooth brushing, and to fall into a coma for at least an hour.

She is addled by sleep deprivation, and by the odd comfort of breakfast with Billy. Her mind—fuelled by Billy's jitter-bug-inducing coffee—is kaleidoscoping with Dali-like images. She feels as if the car is stationary, and the world outside is rolling past it. Robin's Donuts, the arena, the Home Hardware, and the Clean Scene Laundromat all appear to be built of playdough. They scuttle past her, like cartoon images. She taps the brake pedal, but considers the possibility that the buildings have conspired to slow on cue.

The car's dash clock says it is 8:48 AM. She calculates that something like eight hours have passed, since she was roused from sleep by the call from the hospital. What transpired since has had all the qualities of dreaming. The dead boy laid out on the gurney. The tiny women crawling up onto it beside him, to lie down one last time with their grandson and nephew, pressing themselves against his cold body. Their eagle cry at the funeral home. The drone of Billy's inner thunder. The open door. Eating Cheerios. Billy peeing. The flicker of an ominous face in the window across the road from Billy's house.

It feels like something manufactured by her subconscious.

Like something in need of analysis. Maybe she imagined transcendence, weaving itself into the fabric of the mundane, in Billy's kitchen—the sacrament of chewing, of rinsing bowls with water. Did she dream his intuited conviction that they were to find an upward path leading to Clarence? She had never even seen Clarence before, who was—as far as everyone seemed to know—in a jail, so easily locatable in a telephone directory, and push-pinned onto a map of Thunder Bay. *How difficult could it be to find someone in jail?*

Catherine slams on the brakes, realising she has driven passed the manse, and almost into Lake Superior. Her car bumps up against a boom-log. Were it not for those weathered relics of logging, she might have careened off the cliff, pitching forty feet down onto Pebbles Beach. The train of logs, once corralled a winter's worth of cut timber, surfed down the Pickerel and the Black Rivers, into Lake Superior on the spring melt. These days, the timber is chipped up in the bush and transported by truck to the few remaining operational mills. The boom logs have been retired to more stationary endeavours. Instead of timber, they now corral distracted drivers, who might inadvertently swan dive their cars off the cliff onto the rocks below.

The horizon stretches out before Catherine. The long, mercury coloured undulations of the big lake mirror the slate-coloured sky. The line, where water and sky meet, is indistinguishable. In the distance they blend into one. Hybrid, rain-snow drops tap her windshield. For now, they are empty threats—easily erased with an intermittent swipe of the wiper-blades—but forecast a coming storm.

Catherine makes her way down the path from the parking lot to the beach. Along the trail, patches of snow cling to winter.

Locals call it Pebbles Beach. The brown, ochre, black, speckled, bone white and jade green "pebbles" are in fact rocks, the size of five and ten pin bowling balls. They are piled on the shore for a mile in either direction, numbering in the hundreds of thousands. These *pebbles* have been pounded smooth, and terraced five feet deep, by the force of Superior. Catherine doesn't know if calling these rocks pebbles is intentionally ironic, or accidental.

She once talked about the rocks in a sermon as a metaphor for the beauty sometimes found in suffering. "Those stones have been tumbled for centuries by the pounding of waves. If rocks could feel, I imagine it would be a painful process. Yet they have been made *more* beautiful by the tumbling of storms. And, they were tumbled together, not alone. That beauty couldn't happen without the other stones, polishing one another. They knock against each other, becoming smooth and round. When we pass through hardship together, we too become smooth and beautiful. I think, sometimes, suffering is like that."

The congregation stared in silent, and somewhat confused, ascent. Folks in Twenty-Six Mile House tend to keep their personal tumbling, and any polishing coming from it, close to their vests. Catherine wished she could have said it better, wished she could have said it in a way that evoked weeping, as it did in her.

If you ask me, I think they got it; they just don't want to talk about it.

Catherine picks her way, stepping like a fawn across the loose stones, until she reaches the narrow strip of sand dividing the terraced stones from the water's edge. The morning is still. The wind holds its breath. Wavelets tip over onto the sand, as if exhausted by the long journey across *Gichigami*. Catherine likes the sound of the Ojibwe word for the lake; *Gichi-Gami*. Big Water.

She chooses a driftwood log, its bark-less hide lightly freckled with drops of rain, and sits. She matches the rhythm of her breaths with the water lapping the sand at her feet, inhaling in through her mouth and exhaling slowly out her nose.

She worries about the pending funeral service. She wonders what she could possibly say at Gilbert's funeral, across two cultures, that might touch—let alone heal—the woundedness that comes with losing a loved one. She is relieved by the postponement, for the coroner's examination.

"God needed another little angel." That's what the priest

had said, when her friend Tammy-Lynn drowned in the Tupelo public swimming pool. "God needed another little angel." The girls were eleven years old. As far as churches went, Katydid—as Catherine was known in Tupelo—had only visited The Gospel Hall, prior to Tammy-Lyn's funeral. Never a Roman Catholic Church, and never a funeral service of any denomination. The priest's accented voice was amplified by a tinny sound system. When he began to speak, Catherine's mother leaned over in the pew and whispered none too quietly, "Sounds like a Polack."

In his sermon, the priest addressed the congregation as if they were a hostile jury, and he was the lawyer tasked with defending the wrongly accused deity. "*God* needed another little angel. So, *He* created Tammy-Lynn. But *God* is always good and always loves us, so *He* gave us Tammy-Lynn to enjoy for a little while." The priest gripped the edges of the pulpit, loomed out over it, and admonished the mourning, "Now, *God* has called her home, to be *His* angel again. We should be thankful that we had her for a while, and now, *God* wants her back. *God, The Father*, has been graceful to us, lending us Tammy-Lynn, who belongs to *Him*." The priest chided the congregation—"You should not be sad but be giving *God* thanks!"—reminding them, once again, of their failure to embrace the mysterious ways of God, of their sin-tarnished souls, in need of His long-suffering forgiveness. "You must confess your grief to *Christ*, and ask forgiveness."

In the days following the funeral, Catherine fumed over the illogic espoused by the handsome young priest. For starters, Tammy-Lyn was no angel. She was a bully. Tammy-Lynn was the alpha girl—there is one in every clique—who wielded the authority to banish other girls from the tribe. With a fickle snap of her fingers, you were gone. As it turns out, that's why Catherine wasn't at the pool the day Tammy-Lynn drowned. Tammy-Lynn had snapped her fingers in Catherine's direction. "It's nothing personal, Katydid," she told Catherine, her voice all silky and reasonable. "The three of us girls just want some alone time, without you. I'm sure you can understand, sweetie."

Tammy-Lynn was already walking away by the time she said "sweetie."

Although little Katydid's capacity for logical reasoning was still wobbly as strawberry Jell-O, she wasn't buying the priest's quarrel on behalf of an all-loving *and* all-powerful God. Had he been shilling for a capricious and malicious deity, fair enough, but an all-loving and all-powerful God doesn't lend a kid out—even an angel kid—like a library book, and then snatch her back before the due date. Besides, if God is in the business of manufacturing angel kids for His pleasure, why not just churn out a new one, and leave the not exactly angelic Tammy-Lynn be?

When Catherine asked her mother why the priest said God drowned Tammy-Lynn, her mama replied, "Because he's an asshole, and a Polack." Taking note of her daughter's cringing fear of lightning bolts, she tapped her cigarette in the ashtray and clarified, "The priest's an asshole, Baby-Doll, not God. The Pollack's a' asshole. You can't pin that on God, Katydid. Some crap just happens."

Adel died of lung cancer while Catherine was in seminary. Catherine has a photo of her mother on her refrigerator. The photo sometimes gets lost in the forest of children's crayon drawings and inspirational quotes, and Catherine forgets that her mother is dead. The photograph never fails to startle her, when it jumps out at her, from between a "Jesus Loves the Little Children" colouring page, or an Oscar Romero quote—"Peace is not the product of terror or fear. Peace is not the silence of cemeteries. Peace is not the silent result of violent repression."

In the photograph, Adel is wearing a white bikini. Catherine knows her mother has chosen a white bathing suit to accentuate her dark tan. She mailed the picture to Catherine from Florida, the year before she died. Her mother's last boyfriend, Allun, took the picture. On the back, her mother wrote, "Look at me, Katydid! Cancer keeps me thin!"

When the photo catches Catherine off guard, she finds her mother's corporeality jolting—the hair, and meat and bone of her are startling. The actuality of the absence of her mother's body from the world is difficult for Catherine to absorb. Her skeletal sternum and collarbones, the straining tendons of her neck, the loose flesh of her thighs, the knobby knees, her brittle, bleached hair, stacked on top her head, and her nicotine stained fingers, all of it preserved in the photograph, and yet gone. The stretched skin of her mother's belly is the product of yoyo dieting, but she blamed it on her pregnancy with Catherine. All of that, impossibly, gone.

Gone. A fact that does not seem possible, to Catherine.

The semester after her mother died, Catherine wrote an essay about the afterlife for her course in Systematic Theology. Rather than quoting the Germans—Bonhoeffer or Barth or Sölle—she based her paper on a theory that had jazzed her in grade eleven physics class. At fifteen, Catherine was awestruck by the Law of the Conservation of Energy: Energy can be neither created nor destroyed. It can only change in its form. She read those words scrawled across the chalkboard, wrote them in her notebook, and was excited by the idea in ways she had not previously experienced. *Nothing ends, it only changes. Holy cow!*

Therefore, she reasoned in her systematics essay—quarrelling with her own fresh despair over her mother's death—according to The Law of Conservation of Energy, the soul must continue to exist. Her mother's soul, the energy which was Adel, could change, but it— *she*—according to this immutable law of nature, could not cease to exist. Her mama's body could vanish but her energy, her *nefesh,* the thing that made Adel, Adel, must still, by law, exist in some other form. Her mother could be neither created nor destroyed, only transformed. It's the law.

And heaven, Catherine ventured further, is the continuation of this perennial, if transformed energy, the infinite congregating of souls liberated from corporeality and locationality. Heaven, the communion of saints—given the law of conservation of energy—is energy transformed.

Furthermore—Catherine was on a roll—perhaps the "being" we call "God," is Itself the sum total of all disembodied, liberated, and transformed energy. Call it love. Love can be deformed and wounded when constrained by a physical manifestation. In its unfettered state, however, it is pure. Love: The energy—"the tie that binds"—is a web of beauty, is a golden thread connecting all of creation, is the DNA of the body of "God." An orchestra swells to a crescendo in her mind; a chorus of angels declare her brilliance to heaven and earth; her professor weeps, in Italian. She typed the final words on her Selectric typewriter in a flourish: Love endures all things!

It was a consolation for Catherine, believing her mother's soul was now part of that great mysterious cloud of energy. She made no direct reference in the paper to her mother, of course, or to her own confusion and heartache, or, to the long ago, tinny amplification of a Polish priest's voice. It was strictly an academic enterprise. Her professor rewarded her with a mark of 98% and scrawled almost illegibly across the bottom of the last page: "Go further! What about the Body of the Cosmic Christ? Can energy suffer?" Receiving her highest grade ever, Catherine's first inclination was to call her mother and share the news of her academic success.

Twenty-Six Mile House and Pickerel River are a long way from the University of Toronto but—theologically speaking—they aren't that far from Tupelo, Mississippi. Would the physics of the conservation of energy preach at St. Luke's, or at the Pickerel River Community Hall? Would it speak to their sorrow the way it had hers? Would they find comfort in it? Would they rather hear about Gilbert being one of God's little angels, on loan to Florence and Bernadette, and that his due date was up? Maybe the Tupelo priest was telling, in his own simple way, the story of the conservation of energy. In the end, it is still a story of heartache.

Catherine stands up from the log, and hefts one of the polished stones into her arms. Cradling it, she sets out toward a point of whale-backed rock, jutting out into the lake at the far east end of the beach. Her boots press solitary footprints into the wet sand along the shore.

The rock grows heavy in her arms. It stretches the muscles along the back of her shoulders and the inside of her elbows. She welcomes the redemptive discomfort, like the ache that comes with probing an old wound, or memory. She invented this stone-carrying ritual soon after arriving in Twenty-Six Mile House. She walks with it, giving her prayers to the stone; whatever is weighing her down—her worry, her self-doubt, her loneliness. The stone gets heavier. She gets lighter.

She carries the stone out to the tip of the polished finger of granite to where it disappears beneath the water. It plunges down, behind the dark mirror of the lake. As it slips below the surface, it is refracted by the water. Catherine trusts its continuity, without seeing it. It is still there. Even though she can't see it, she trusts it persists, like God. It continues, like the Love, she can't always feel. Trusting it is still there, is an act of faith.

She hoists the rock above her head, widens her stance for balance, bounces a little, feeling it in her calves, and makes a prayer, "O beautiful Creator, receive my unnecessary burdens, and retain in me the ones you need me to carry." She holds the stone above her head to the sky until her arms begin to quiver with the strain.

Catherine shot-puts it, two handed, upward and outward. Her feet slip on the slick rock. She recovers her footing in time to lower herself, to sit on its damp surface at the water's edge. Her prayer breaks the surface of the lake. Unlike a curl of incense rising, it spouts a fountain and dives deep, downward.

Concentric waves flow out from where her prayer disappeared. The ripple sets off in all directions, heading for destinations unknown. The prayer, and the stone, persist below the surface.

Catherine sits cross-legged, watching the lake recover its smooth finish. A fat drop of rain explodes, like a diamond, on the black water. Then another and another, until a roaring plane of jewels stretches out as far as she can see.

She stays seated with her hands stuffed into her coat pockets. Mesmerized. The rain flattens her hair, runs down her back, soaks her jeans and parka. She thinks: *I am being cleansed. Again.*

- 26 -
Follow Me

By afternoon, the rain that soaked Catherine at Pebbles Beach is mixed with ice pellets. She decides, before the weather gets worse, to drive out to Pickerel River to see Florence and Bernadette. Sleet pelts the road, pings the hood of her car, and clatters against the windshield. The temperature is above freezing, but not nearly enough above to melt the torrent of freezing rain and sleet. Her tires slip as she makes her way up the hill out of town. A couple of times, the back end of the car fishtails. A pick-up truck is leading the way, ahead of her, carving a wake in the sleet. Catherine aims her tires into the splashed-out troughs.

Her windows fog with condensation. She turns the fan up to high and begs the heater to kick-in. "Come on, come on." She shivers, and digs a paper serviette out of the glove box to blow her nose.

After Pebbles Beach, Catherine headed home to the manse, convinced that she was suffering from hypothermia. She stood under the showerhead until the hot water tank ran cold. She cranked the thermostat up to 30 degrees Celsius, burrowed like a gopher beneath the heavy blankets on her bed, and slept until noon.

Now, in spite of the shower, heat, and sleep, a chill persists at her core. In her coat pocket, she finds a long-lost lozenge. She strips off most of the paper and pocket lint with her teeth, and pops it her mouth. The lemony softness is remarkably soothing.

Passing the cemetery, Catherine risks a glance from the road to where the bear had appeared earlier in the week and is surprised to see it is still there, or back. She is. Catherine thinks of the bear as a she, though she isn't sure how—from a distance or for that matter even from up close—one distinguishes a mama bear from a papa bear. *Sow,* she thinks. *That's what you call a girl bear. A Sow.*

The bear sits on her haunches at the back of the graveyard, a block of darkness visible through the curtains of freezing rain. *She must be caked in ice and soaked to the skin.* The bear turns her head, following Catherine's progress up the hill. The idea that the bear, this mama bear, is watching her, comforts Catherine. It warms her.

At the highway the pickup truck turns east, and continues to lead the way, down the highway toward Pickerel River. It turns south toward the reserve, weaves through the community and into Florence's yard.

Before setting out, Catherine had checked for the address in the phone book, but only a few of the houses actually display numbers. On the reserve, posted numbers on houses are considered more ornamentation than location markers. Everyone knows where everyone else lives, but newly posted numbers can bring a smile. "As if I don't know where you live, or do you get so many strangers dropping by you have to nail up a number out front, Frank?" Streets are also better known by the names of the residents living on them, than they are by their formal names.

In any case, the traffic jam of vehicles parked in the yard, and along the street, in front of the Bearchild sisters' home makes it hard for Catherine to miss it. She pulls over on the road and sets out toward the front door on foot. The lavender paint is peeling in places, revealing the house was once robin's-egg blue. There is a dog of indeterminate breed standing on the porch, wagging its whole hindquarters enthusiastically. Catherine can hear another, smaller dog inside, barking.

The driver of the truck Catherine had followed calls out to her, "They'll be out back, Rev." His window is rolled part way down. "They'll be out back," he says again, pointing toward a pathway along the side of the house. He's holding a cigarette, pressed deep in the cleft of his fingers. Catherine considers bumming one from him. "Go 'round that a'way, Rev." He is missing a thumb.

"Thanks." She flashes a half-smile, deferential to the purpose of her visit. The man reciprocates with wide grin that lights up his face. He touches the visor of his cap and rolls up the window.

The path leading around the house is hard-packed and wet. Catherine's boots slide in the thin layer of mud coating the frozen earth. A bicycle frame, its rusted chain drooping, leans against the house, beside a sofa with a hole scorched through it to the springs. The hole is likely the result of a forgotten cigarette, but given its location it may have been struck by lightning.

A teepee occupies most of the backyard. Smoke wafts out of the triangular opening between the lashed poles at the top. The ground slopes from the teepee downward to the river.

Catherine can hear a muffled voice inside the tent. It sounds far away, even though only a layer of stretched fabric separates her from the speaker. *Anishinaabe*, she thinks. She would be the first to admit that she knows nothing about the ancient traditions of the land, or the teaching, language, and stories of the Elders. *Are they secret?* She has never felt so white. *Who am I—a Christian preacher, descendent of colonizer—to be eavesdropping on such sacred words?* Inside, the speaker stops. Sleet thrums on the canvas.

Paralyzed by her whiteness, and by the settler complicity of her religious forbearers, Catherine remains outside in the rain. *What's the respectful thing to do here? Barge into the teepee or tiptoe away?* Is she an interloper, an invasive species? Barging in uninvited, unwelcome? Blundering in like the misguided missionaries of the past? *Do I knock? Call out to ask permission? Is there a password? A protocol?*

The sleet is coming down hard. *What the heck.* Catherine gulps, ducks down, and pokes her head in through the flaps. Half inside the smoky warmth of the teepee, and half outside in rain, she searches for a sign, but no one takes much notice of, or seems surprised by, her arrival.

Florence and Bernadette are holding hands, on the other side of the spindle of smoke rising from the fire. Though the smoke, they appear almost ethereal, as if carried by grief part way into the spirit world. Seated next to them, is Billy. All eyes are focused on the low dancing flames and glowing embers. Bernadette's gaze drifts up toward Catherine. She extends a nod, a sad smile, and motions with her chin toward an unoccupied lawn chair to the right of the entrance.

Catherine settles into the webbed, aluminum chair. The warmth of the fire feels good against the shins of her jeans. Steam rises from the damp denim. There are twenty or so people in the circle around the fire. Catherine has never felt quite so shamefully white as she does now. The rain continues to pour down, drumming on the shell of the tent.

Part way around the circle, there is a teenage girl folded over onto her thighs. She rests her forehead on her knees, her arms hug her shins. Across from her, a man prods wayward coals back into the fire with a stick. Next to him, a big, square of a man, in a red and black bush jacket and green rubber boots, takes a split of birch from a pile beside his chair and sets it onto the fire. Sparks spiral upward in the smoke. The man leans forward to rub his hands together above the reinvigorated flames.

An old woman, her silver hair loose and draping her shoulders, begins to hum. She is wearing a purple calico dress under her unzipped parka. She dips the thick end of a tightly bound braid of sweetgrass into the coals, then fans it with an eagle's wing. The dry blades glow orange, filling the tent with the scent of late summer. The aroma of sweetgrass mingles with the wood smoke, and drifts up through the opening at the top of the tepee.

Catherine looks across to Billy. He is motioning with his eyes toward the entryway and she is suddenly aware of a cold draft flowing past her feet into the tent. Embarrassed by her faux pas, she leans over to pull the flaps closed, and tips out of her chair. She lands on a knee, rights herself, looks around apologetically, and is greeted by several kind smiles.

The woman with the long silver hair says, "When someone—no matter how big they are—steps on a blade of green sweetgrass they cannot break it. It bends, and does not break. We will be like the grass. We will bend in our sorrow, but we will not break." She pauses to caress the wrap of sweetgrass. "We braid the sweetgrass in three—each of them with a teaching—so it becomes strong. We will be like that. We will braid ourselves together into one, and we will be strong." Heads around the circle nod at this wisdom.

She begins to make her way around the fire, starting with Florence, she offers the smudge to each person in turn. Catherine has heard about smudging with sweetgrass, or with sage, but she has never seen it happen.

She watches, trying to memorize the details. Florence takes her glasses off and sets them on the ground beside her chair. She pulls out the elastic from her ponytail and shakes the hair free. She cups her hands, and draws the sweet-scented smudge over her face, mouth, nose, eyes, and hair. She sweeps it down the front of her coat, then rests her hands on her chest. "Chi Miigwech," she sits, and continues to cup her heart in her hands.

The Elder moves to Bernadette. One by one, each person scoops the cleansing smoke over themselves. Catherine doesn't know if she should take part. Is she allowed to?

She is afraid of doing something wrong, something that might harm the spirit of deep kinship she feels flowing in the circle. She has dipped her spirit into that flow, and feels grief. She feels the paradoxical beauty in the sadness. Boundaries are somehow softened, opened, by loss. Sadness is inviting her to enter, to connect her humanity with the humanity of strangers.

When the Elder reaches Catherine, she offers the sweetgrass to her like a question. Catherine cups her hands, stiffly imitating the actions of the others. The woman fans the glowing braid with the eagle's wing. Catherine destroys the word "Miigwech." Her pronunciation of the word feels bastardized—too sharp, too angular, too loud, too white. In her mouth, it has none of the soft, round familiarity it had when the others said it.

The Elder ends up in front of Billy. He stands and places his right hand over his heart, says "Chi Miigwech"—beautifully, as if Ojibwe is his first language—then sits down and returns his gaze to the fire. The old woman nods, taps him on each shoulder with the eagle's wing, and circles the fire, back to her seat. She sets the smoldering end of the braid over the lip of an abalone shell, balancing on a stone beside the fire. *Billy didn't smudge,* thinks Catherine. *Great, was I supposed to politely pass, too?*

The man in the truck, who Catherine followed out to Pickerel River, pushes a flap aside and enters the teepee. He must have finished his cigarette, and possibly smoked another. Catherine ignores her old craving for nicotine, and pulls the flaps closed. He dips his hand into a coffee can on the ground next to the door. Catherine hadn't noticed it. It is half-filled with loose tobacco.

He squats by the fire, holding a pinch of the tobacco in his closed fist. He touches it to his lips, murmuring a prayer. When he finishes, he sprinkles the tobacco into the fire and brushes a few strands, stuck on the palm of his damp hand, into the fire as well.

He starts around the circle to the right, toward the empty chair next to Catherine. There is an audible shifting of chairs. Catherine's not sure what is up, but she is familiar with the unspoken tension in the air. Something is not right. She recognizes it, like the congregational stirring in the pews, when she is preaching something controversial, or too sensitive, or ill-advised.

The woman who shared the smudge says, "Leon, uh, uh." She circles her hand, indicating he should go the other way around the fire, to the chair. "The direction of the sun, Leon." She smiles, like a grandmother, teaching a beloved grandchild.

Leon says, "Aha, Miigwech." He makes his way, in the ceremonially correct direction, around to the empty seat next to Catherine. *Crap,* thinks Catherine, *I must have gone the wrong way.* Was her gaffe overlooked because the chair was right next to the entrance, or because she was a white lady who she wasn't expected to know any better?

The Elder motions to a teenage boy—he has Roman numerals tattooed on his neck—"Okay, Xavier." He clears his throat, takes up the frame drum and mallet resting on top of a cloth bag at his feet. He coughs, clearing his throat again, hums from the back of his throat. He grips the gut bindings on the back and taps the moose-hide skin with his knuckles, holds the drum close to his ear. He holds the drum above the fire for a moment and taps it again, listens, and warms it some more, until it is tuned by the heat of the fire.

Catherine follows the arch of the mallet with her eyes, anticipates its contact with the drum, but still she to jumps when they connect. It is like a crack of thunder, like lightening has struck close by. There are no seconds to count between flash and boom. She feels it reverberate in her chest. She is instantly awake, her soul called to attention.

The boy establishes a three-beat rhythm and then releases a tight-throated song. The high pitch of his voice raises gooseflesh on Catherine's arms, for the second time today. She doesn't understand the meaning of the Anishinaabe words he is singing, but feels their power.

Tears slide down everybody's cheeks, including Catherine's. Some of the women tip their faces upward, their tears wetting their necks. Wrenching, pent up bawls of agony fill the inside of the tepee. The men rub their eyes with their fists, and they lean forward in their chairs, low to the ground. Their lips pressed tight, their shoulders quake with silent grief.

The teenage girl, still collapsed onto her thighs, sobs. Her back spasms, as if she might retch the contents of her stomach. She bursts from her chair and scrambles outside. The man next to where she sat rights her chair, knocked over by her sudden leaving. A lanky boy, his ebony hair tied back with a piece of red cloth, scoops up a binder and algebra text book from beneath the chair, and follows the girl outside. Catherine wonders if he is her boyfriend or her brother.

The song ends. The men and some of the women respond appreciatively. "Ho." "Aho." Shuddering exhalations fill the emptiness carved out by the silent drum. The sound of rain pecking on canvas, of wind ruffling it and of the snapping fire, are amplified by the absence song.

Billy leans over and speaks quietly to Florence. She nods, pats his knee, presses her cheek to his shoulder and squeezes his arm. As he stands, her hands slide down his arm and gives his hand a squeeze. Boots are pulled back, making room for Billy to pass. The man from the half-ton pats the back of Billy's leg. Bill crouches down next to Catherine and ducks out of the teepee.

Catherine wanted to talk about the funeral service with Florence and Bernadette, but clearly, this is not the time. She decides to call later and follows Billy outside, worrying that leaving with Billy might imply that they are a thing. It's not easy to demonstrate a dignified, strictly professional relationship while duckwalking out of a teepee. She looks back over her shoulder to Florence and Bernadette and gives a little wave. Florence offers another sad smile.

Billy is waiting outside in the rain. "Follow me." He strides off—waving a hand above his head, swiping at raindrops like they're black flies—toward the front yard, where his van is parked.

Catherine starts her car and waits on the road for Billy to navigate his way out between the other vehicles. Follow me? That's it? Not even a quick, completely professional, shake of the hand? Did we not eat Cheerios together this morning? Follow me. Over and out. I heard you pee, for crying out loud, Billy. She says, "I'm fine. And you?"

The living room curtains are open. Catherine can see the girl, and the boy who followed her, sitting together in a large stuffed chair. Their bodies are entwined like the roots of a tree. He cradles her in his lap. Her hand rests on his chest. He strokes her forehead, smooths her hair back behind her ears with his finger. She closes her eyes, leans into him. His lips are moving, singing gently to her.

Catherine is startled from her voyeurism by the short bleat of a horn. She looks in the rear-view mirror. Billy is pulling away.

- 27 -
WHERE IN THE WORLD IS CLARENCE BEARCHILD?

Billy leads Catherine out to the scene of the accident, where a roadside shrine is already under construction. In the less than twenty-four hours since Gilbert has died, a white cross has been cobbled together and leans against the base of the cliff, next to the low entrance to The Crack.

Crosses are simple things to make. Not difficult at all. You don't need to be a carpenter. You just need two boards, nailed crosswise or bound together with a length of rope. That and a broken heart.

The more imperfect the cross, to Billy's way of thinking, the greater its emotional gravitas. The primitive, lopsided and wobbly crosses—the ones mashed up without skill, with only despair for a blueprint—tug at his heart the most. He pictures, a desolate soul in his garage, furiously pounding more nails than are really needed, the hammer blows pocking the surface of the wood. The builder's salty tears wetting the boards as he works. The man kneels on the cement floor, misses the nail, hitting his thumb with the hammer, and feels gratitude for the tangible, the locatable, pain bestowed by the blow.

It is almost always a man. These crosses, in Billy's experience, are constructed by men. They are cobbled together by men, unable to find adequate words to describe the vacuum that has sucked the breath from their lungs. They are crosses made by men for whom actions alone can speak loudly enough the story of their annihilation.

Women, it seems to Billy, have been granted the power of words. They use them like medicine, to draw out the poison and pain. They spread words, like a healing ointment to make the wounded whole. They use their magic to conjure tomorrow *ex nihilo* from today.

Men, lacking adequate words with which to describe the howling pain beneath their ribs, saw and hammer boards instead. They pound nails, trying to expend their inexhaustible rage, declaring the futility of love with each blow of their hammer.

The paint must be still wet on the cross across the road from where Billy is parked. Or maybe some people, so familiar with vagaries of life, keep a cross on hand in anticipation of the next soul puncturing wound. Billy has heard the inaudible hiss of hope leaking out of a grieving human, leaving the soul, soft as an empty balloon.

Across the road, two teddy bears huddle at the foot of the cross, like Mary and the disciple whom Jesus loved. One of the bears is fitted with a miniature, ceremonial headdress.

Beside the bears is the essential 8-by-10-inch framed portrait photo of Gilbert, the beloved lost. It is likely his high school graduation photo—Billy can't tell from inside the van—or a school picture day photo. There is, no doubt, an earnest, uncomplicated smile on his face, his hair neatly combed, and his self-conscious eyes not yet fully robbed of their innocence. Someone will have slipped the photograph into a plastic sleeve, or wrapped it in Saran Wrap to protect it from the weather. But Billy knows, in spite of those well-intentioned efforts, the ink will already be bleeding in the rain.

Gilbert's friends will likely come later on, to light candles around the shrine. They will put them in glass jars to guard their vulnerable flames from the wind. They might smoke a joint, or pass a bottle, in his honour and to dull the slit of pain gutting them. They will smash the empty bottle on the rocks, and weep in one another's embrace. Each of them will declare eternal fidelity to their friendship with Gilbert, and to one another.

Some couples—hidden behind the drapes of condensation coating the windows of their parents' half-tons—will resolve their virginity. They will reason with one another that life is too short to wait. "We could be dead tomorrow," a boy will say to his tearful girlfriend. And she will know, perhaps for the first time, that what he is saying is true. "If you knew you would be dead tomorrow, what would you do tonight?" she will ask. Asking and answering that question—What would you do if you knew you would die tomorrow?—was a game they played as children, while roasting marshmallows over a campfire. Tonight, it will not be a game, but a deadly serious conversation about what really matters in life.

Billy turns the key in the ignition to off and the engine goes quiet. The windshield wipers stop mid-swipe. In the rear-view mirror he watches Catherine's car pull in close behind his van. The uncoupled transport trailer remains, tilted up against the rock face. The tractor has been towed out of the ditch and into town, where the police wrapped it with yellow crime scene tape. The driver's brother and his wife are on their way from Calgary to collect him and take him home.

Catherine climbs into the passenger seat next to Billy. He smells of sweetgrass and strawberry shampoo. She says, "This is it? Where it happened?" They aren't questions, so much as expressions of her need to fill the silence.

Billy answers anyway, "Uh huh." He continues to concentrate on the cross in the ditch on the other side of the road. He holds his upper lip between his teeth, as if it is a puzzle his mind could solve. Then, by way of explanation, he says, "The Crack."

"You think Clarence will come here? That we'll find him here?"

Billy, still puzzling the cross, says, "I think he was here, already."

"Already?" A beat afterward, "You mean, are you saying, Crank was here when it happened? Isn't he supposed to be in jail?" Catherine is full of other questions, too. She is, to name just one, still wondering why Billy didn't smudge back at Pickerel River, but limiting herself to the present, asks, "Well, where could he have gone?" She motions, palms raised, toward the wilderness stretching out in three directions. As far as the eye can see, black spruce, leaf-bereft birch and poplar, needleless tamarack trees, skeletal ash trees, their blood-red berries still clinging to the branches. In the fourth direction, only the infinite dark waters of Lake Superior—the lake that never gives up her dead. Catherine is suddenly cold again.

"East or West," shrugs Billy. "Put Superior on your left or right, and stick out your thumb. East or West. Those are the only choices around here—with the sun or against it."

"Or, North I suppose," says Catherine, "into the woods. He could be hiding out in the bush up there." She leans forward in her seat and looks up to the top of the precipice. "Could he be somewhere up there?"

Billy wonders what it would be like to lean over and brush her freckled neck with his lips. "For a day. Two maybe. *Maybe*." Billy stresses the word. "It's been too cold, and wet, to survive longer. Unless you really know your business in the bush, you wouldn't last a night. Hypothermia'll kill you quick in this kind of weather—wet, it doesn't even have to be that cold—especially if you're not dressed for it. Once you're wet, there's no drying out."

A few cars have passed since they pulled over, splashing the van. This one, however, flares its brake lights. The wheels lock and it skids ten feet before coming to a stop, sideways across the highway. Its back-up lights pop white, and it reverses back along the solid yellow line. It's an older BMW.

"Jesus," says Billy. He and Catherine twist in their seats, watching back and forth, for oncoming traffic. "There's no way you could stop fast enough."

"Come on, come on, come on," Catherine pleads, and grabs onto Billy's forearm. Another vehicle wheels around the curve. The driver leans on his horn, swerving, and somehow avoiding crashing into the BMW. He wrestles his front tire out of the loose gravel and gains control. He continues to pound on his horn as he disappears below a dip in the highway to the west.

The BMW backs onto the shoulder in front of the van. A tall woman unfolds herself from the car. She is wearing an army surplus coat and boots, faded jeans, and is pulling a knitted beret down over her ears. She tucks a tangle of blonde hair up inside it. She looks like someone who used to be strong, the way she shuts the car door and strides toward the van. Her rounded shoulders, and lowered eyes however, tell a story of fatigue.

Billy rolls his window down. She steps into its frame, and he immediately recognizes a portrait he has viewed many times before. He titles it *Portrait of a Grieving Lover*. He is familiar with the sad, softened beauty of the broken-hearted. The once sharp parameters of her face are blurred; the discernible boundaries separating her physicality from eternity have been erased. Like a portrait, the edges of which blend into a dark, uncertain background. Where this woman ends, and the world begins, is no longer entirely clear. All pretence, all vanity, all concern for propriety, all certainty, have been washed out at her edges revealing the tender vulnerability that Billy spends his days wishing he could heal. It is a longed for, mystical union he sees, one that can arrive only on the broken wings of suffering.

Echoing Catherine's question, the young woman asks, without preamble or introductions, "This is the place?" Beneath the flat tone of her voice Billy hears words not spoken: *I am just barely holding it together.*

He meets her eyes and nods. They are green, swollen and rimmed red. Her nose is raw. Her lips are dry and cracked. Her breath is mixture of humbugs and coffee.

Catherine leans forward in the passenger seat, "You mean the accident?"

The woman steadies herself, holding onto the window ledge, and bends down so she can see Catherine. "I am Monica. I am Gilbert's friend. From school. Was his friend..." She swallows and, with a thumbnail, scoops tears away from beneath her eyes. There is a hint of German, or Dutch, in her accent, in the clipped formality of it. A transport truck storms by, whisking up a cloud of dampness from the road. The gust shoves Monica up against the side of the van.

Together, the three of them cross the road to the shrine. They observe a moment of silence. Two or three vehicles pass by, slowing but not stopping. A cattle truck shrouds them in a contrail of animal fear and shit. Catherine wraps her arm around Monica's waist and pulls her close to her side. Monica presses her ear down onto Catherine's shoulder, her face into the warm tangle of this kind stranger's hair. Intimacy is created quickly when personal boundaries are made permeable by grief.

"I'm Catherine, and this is Billy."

"This is The Crack," says Billy, preoccupied.

"I'm the minister at St. Luke's United, in Twenty-Six Mile House. Billy's the funeral director here," says Catherine. "If there's anything you need, Monica, anything we can do to help. Please, we're here for you."

"People climb up inside it," says Billy. He looks up toward the porridge coloured sky.

Monica takes Catherine's free hand and scans her surroundings, as if Gilbert might be nearby, as news of his death was just an unfounded rumour. "Gilbert told me about this crack. He said he would someday bring me here." She frees her hand to unnecessarily shield her eyes—as if the sun might shine at any moment—and gazes toward the top of the cliff. "There is a good view, he told me, a place for picnics on the top."

"Did you ever meet Clarence? Gilbert's brother?" asks Catherine. "We're looking for him, his grandmothers asked us to find him."

"Only one time, just yesterday morning. He got out of jail and came to surprise Gilbert. They were going home together. He is missing?"

"You were right, Billy." Catherine turns to where Billy, only seconds ago, had been standing. He is now, however, forty yards down the road, past the crumpled transport trailer. He darts down through the ditch and disappears behind the trailer. Catherine assumes that he is seeking some privacy in order to relieve himself, but his head immediately pops back out from behind the trailer and, with a wave of his arm, he beckons for them to follow.

Catherine and Monica find a trailhead leading into the trees, up the side of the hill. It doesn't take them long to catch up to Billy, who is picking his way up the wet path ahead of them. His boots slip in the loose stones and patches of snow. He grapples onto saplings and low branches to pull himself up the steep incline. He stops to catch his wind. Bracing a hand against his uphill knee, he points with the other. "Top of." He inhales. "The Crack." He circles the hand above his head. "Come down this way." Then, as if summiting Kilimanjaro, he launches himself, heroically onward and upward.

Five minutes later, they are standing on the bald pate of rock at the top of the cliff. Billy leans over, hands on knees, trying not to faint or vomit. "Are you okay?" Catherine rests a hand on his back.

"Fine," says Billy. To conserve oxygen, he is not humming *Ain't No Mountain High Enough*.... But trust me he is thinking it. And, he likes the feel of Catherine's hand on his back.

Monica crouches, balancing on her hands to peer into The Crack. Then she scans the three blending bands of topography to the south: mottled forest, gun-metal blue water, ash-coloured sky. At the very moment, when she feels overcome by the ugly greyness of it, a steeply angled shaft of sunlight spills through a momentary parting of the clouds. It's such a cliché, I wouldn't mention it, did it not actually occur. A spotlight dances on the big lake. In this circle of illumination, the water is transformed from indigo-black to mint. "*Gottes Licht*," Monica whispers. Just as suddenly as it appeared, the light hidden by the clouds, as if God had flipped a celestial light switch on and off again.

Monica sits back onto her heals, pulls an already well-used farmer's hanky from her coat pocket, and blows her nose. Catherine takes her elbow to help her to her feet. Monica says, "Gilbert loved this place." Still holding the hanky to her nose with both hands, she motions to the landscape with her elbow. "He wanted me to come to see it. I cannot believe he is gone."

"Did Gilbert tell you anything about Clarence that might help us find him?" asks Catherine. "Maybe about his friends?

"Gilbert said Clarence didn't have any friends. Not real ones, only users."

"Is there someone he might go to, if he was in trouble?"

"Is he in trouble?" Monica asks.

"No, no," Catherine assures her. "His granny is very worried though."

"Maybe he went to Martin's," says Monica.

"Martin?"

"That's not his real name, I think. When they were boys, Gilbert and Clarence found his forest house. A cave in the woods, in the side of a hill, I think. They said one could easily walk right past, and not even notice it. Gilbert said, inside he has it all fixed up. A bed with a quilt, woodstove, table, kerosene lights, everything you need. He said it was a nice place, that if people saw it, they would put it in a magazine. It has a carved door that fits into the shape of the opening to the cave."

"Edison Oscar Martin," says Billy. "He's dead."

Catherine, compensating for Billy's bluntness, adds, "We had a funeral, a celebration of life, for Mr. Martin a couple of days ago."

"Once when he was drinking quite a lot, Martin, Mr. Martin, told Gilbert and Clarence that he was an S.S. Officer. A Nazi. He was captured and shipped across the ocean to a POW camp near this place. When the war was over, he escaped before they could put him on a train and send him back to Germany with the others."

"There was a POW camp," says Billy. "Right over there." He points to a beach in the distance, bracketed by thirty acres of orderly rows of pine trees, planted over what had been the camp. "No need for a fence. Even if you escaped, there was nowhere to go. No road, only the tracks back then. A couple of guys hopped the train but were picked up in Winnipeg. You would either die lost in the bush, or the black flies made you beg to get back inside. In winter, you'd freeze to death. After the war they flattened the whole place and planted those trees over top."

"Gilbert thought it was just drunk talk," Monica says, "but Clarence told him that another time, Martin showed him a hole in the floor of the cave. There was a wooden box inside, full of Nazi things—a uniform, medals, a radio. The radio didn't work because the foreign batteries were used up."

"How did he end up with Edison Martin's papers?" asks Catherine.

"Stole them, or bought them, probably," says Billy, "from a camp guard just happy to be going home. Maybe he killed the guy. The papers cleared through Veterans Services, no problem."

"Did Gilbert say where this hidey-hole is?" asks Catherine, "Maybe Clarence went there."

"No, but in my mind, it is close to here," says Monica, "maybe just because whenever Gilbert talked about The Crack he talked also about Martin."

"Do you think he told anyone else about Martin?" asks Catherine.

"I don't think so. Not about Martin. I think he felt guilty telling even me. It was their secret, his and Clarence's."

"He's hiding." Billy joins Catherine and Monica near the edge of the cliff. "I can feel it. He's hiding." He sniffs the air like a wolf.

He begins to shuffle around in tight circles on the spot where he is standing, like a diviner taking up his sticks, getting his mojo on. Something magnetic starts to shift inside his chest. The radiuses of the circles expand, until he is making looping circuits of the cliff top.

Billy sniffs the air again. He closes his eyes, cocks his head to the side and listens, one ear toward the ground, the other pointing skyward. He can hear the brown tufts of grass, sticking up between the cracks of the rock. They are telling him something; it might be true or might be a lie. He squats to consult the rust-coloured moss clinging to the granite, runs a finger along a vein of snow, packed into one of the crevices. He continues to expand his spiralling loops.

Listening makes him dizzy. Listening, and walking in circles. Sounds come to his ears as though they are bubbling through water. He sniffs the smell of melting ice.

The loops take him to where bare rock and low leafless scrub meet—where red willow and evergreen saplings make a paltry living from the thin layer of topsoil. On the next circuit, he bulls a short distance into the scrub. The sun, low to the horizon in the west, dips beneath the clouds, washing everything in amber light. Billy and Catherine and Monica and the forest are suddenly set ablaze by the horizontal light cast by the end of the day.

Billy stands motionless, balancing his body on the soles of his boots. Through the bottoms of his feet, he can feel the earth thawing. In front of him, there are two shoeprints, stamped in a stubborn patch of granular snow. The snow is spackled with tamarack needles and snow-fleas, harbingers of spring. Everything glows, lit up by the setting sun, slicing through the opening above hills and beneath the clouds.

It took the author of the footprints only two steps to traverse the remnant smudge of snow. Then he was back onto the forest floor layered with last year's leaves, which obscure signs of his passing. The two shoeprints are enough, though, for Billy to determine that the owner of the shoes was headed east. Toward the sun.

Monica, Catherine, and Billy, their backs turned to the wash of orange light, deduce a path that disappears into the woods in the direction of morning. The trajectory of the one walking it vanishes in shadows, too thick for the feeble evening sunlight to penetrate.

Sometimes What You are Looking for Finds You

It is too late to go traipsing off into the forest looking for Clarence, footprints or no foot prints. A preacher, funeral director, and a grieving, German sociology student: they are unprepared and ill-equipped. They would be lost, without a doubt, in a matter of minutes, and when they did get lost, not one of them would have a red-hot clue about how to survive. Add to that there would be no one out looking for them. It would be days before their absence would even be registered by anyone. It is a fool's errand, dangerous and impossible, to track footprints in the dark. Nonetheless, Billy, Catherine and Monica remain rooted at the edge of the forest. They actually consider it, think it over, debating among themselves the wisdom of following what might be the footprints of the allegedly missing Clarence Bearchild.

They talk it over for so long that, by the time they come to their senses, it is so dark they can barely pick their way down the path from The Crack to the highway. Their sapling-grabbing and slipping descent confirms the wisdom of going for help, not into the bush.

Back at the funeral home, Billy parks the van in the garage and calls the police from his office. "I need to report a missing person." He explains to the dispatcher about the likelihood of Clarence being with Gilbert when Gilbert was killed, and about footprints in the snow at the top of The Crack. The dispatcher assures him that she will scramble the volunteer Search and Rescue Team. Several SRT members are at the Fire Hall already, watching hockey—Bruins verses Habs—on the big, rear-projection screen in the lounge. Billy doesn't mention the connection between the boys and the enigmatic Edison Oscar Martin. He isn't sure why he doesn't mention it, but reasons that the information is not vital to the search for Clarence.

Monica follows Catherine back into town, to stay with her at the manse. Catherine makes tea and telephones Florence to provide an update on the footprints Billy found. Looking at Monica curled up under a blanket on the couch, sipping hot tea, Catherine adds, "I have a young woman here with me. A friend of Gilbert's from Thunder Bay..."

"Monica!" Florence shouts into the phone so loudly that Catherine holds the handset away from her ear. "Tell her to come to me! Tell her how to get to my house! Tell her that she will stay here with me and Bernadette. Tell her to come soon, come now." Her voice softens, "I need her to come to me."

Catherine covers the receiver and mouths "What should I say?" No need to repeat the invitation, Monica heard Florence, as if she was there in the kitchen with Catherine.

"I didn't know Gilbert even told her about me."

"Apparently he did and she wants to meet you. It's up to you." Catherine adds, "You're welcome to stay here."

Monica says that she will go. Catherine relays this information on to Florence. Florence says, "Tell her I'll watch out the window for her," and rings off.

Catherine draws a map for Monica. "There might still be a lot of trucks out front, and there's a big teepee in the backyard."

Once she gets Monica on her way, Catherine swallows a couple of aspirin to thwart the niggling of an oncoming migraine, pecking at the backs of her eyeballs. She takes her second scalding shower of the day. She makes more tea and plows through a deck of toast with peanut butter and honey. She bumps the thermostat up and the oil furnace lumbers to life. Then she burrows into bed and a dreamless sleep.

As Catherine is closing her eyes, the Search and Rescue Team is marshalling at the Fire Hall. They huddle around a long folding-table, carpeted with maps, coffee cups, and boxes of Robin's Donuts.

Connie and the ladies of St. Luke's have arrived with the church's 90-cup coffee urn, and are scooping coffee into the filter basket and using a garden hose to fill it with water. They are ready for the long night and an early morning. The scent of coffee mingles with the smell of drying fire hoses and Turtle Wax. The search plan will be detailed overnight—maps consulted, strategic locations identified, and quadrants assigned to team leaders—and commence at first light.

At home, Billy is lying on his bed, fending off another attack of non-specific anxiety. He is distracting his mind with his new *Bodyguard* fantasy, the one in which he is Kevin Costner hired to protect a rock star played by Whitney Houston. Billy's version doesn't strictly follow the original motion picture script. He opens the back door of the limousine, shielding Whitney with his body from a crazed stalker with a gun, and pushes her inside onto the floor. He takes the bullet in the shoulder as he throws his body on top of her.

Later, Whitney comes to the hospital to thank Billy. She crawls onto the bed next to him, and murmurs that the only place she feels safe is with him.

This fantasy—like the one about the music studio in Prince Edward Island—usually pours calming oil on the stormy swells of Billy's panic. It sedates the evil, manic squirrels scampering from branch to limbic branch in his brain. Since his teens— since my death—fantasy has been Billy's dependable tool with which to tamp down his non-specific horror. They block out "the thoughts"—that's what Billy calls them—block out the memories he has dedicated his life to burying.

Eventually, the fantasies lead to sleep. Billy and Whitney— or Meg or Jodie or the Hemingway sister with the hurt eyes— drift off to dreamland in one another's arms.

But tonight? A gun shot. The force of the bullet throws Billy backward onto the limousine floor. He shouts to the chauffer, "Drive! Drive!" The car peels away from the curb, burning rubber. Another gunshot, the bulletproof rear window spider-webs, but holds. Billy looks up from the floor of the limo to discover it is Catherine, not Whitney, whom he flung into the backseat of the limousine.

Billy rolls over in his bed, bunches his pillow up under his head, scrubs Catherine from his fantasy and starts again from the beginning. It's one of his fantasy rules: No shifting gears mid-way, start at the beginning.

Whitney's manager is begging him to protect her. He reluctantly agrees to a meeting, just a meeting. Billy is disdainful of rich, prima donnas but, having recently resigned from an elite black-ops unit, he needs the work. The resignation is the result of ethical disagreement with his superiors. It is above the security clearance level of the average citizen. So, Billy cannot divulge the details, even in the fantasy. This part of his storyline is kind of murky.

Billy presses on. The shooting. Him almost dying. Whitney curled next to him on the hospital bed. He shifts his head on the pillow—the hospital pillow—and releases a heroic sigh of contentment.

Sleep is within Billy's grasp. He can feel it closing over him. In the fantasy, he lifts his head to kiss Whitney's head, resting on his chest. The hair splayed on the starched hospital sheet, however, is orange. Catherine. This does not soothe Billy. It jolts him awake. He restarts the fantasy but images of Catherine block this previously reliable escape from the haunted house that is his mind.

By the time Billy gives up on sleep, he finds himself taking a bullet for Catherine, in the sanctuary of St. Luke's Church, diving to knock her from the pulpit onto the floor behind the communion table. He shields her body with his own as a crazed parishioner sweeps the sanctuary with submachine gun fire. One of the ladies announces that, following worship, tea and sandwiches will be served downstairs in the fellowship hall. Everyone is welcome to attend.

Billy groans, throws off the blanket, pulls on socks, and pads out into the cold kitchen in his jockeys and T-shirt. He turns on a stove element under the kettle and leans back against the counter. When it has boiled, he stirs the hot water into a mug of instant hot chocolate powder.

He blows across its scalding surface. The boyhood evoking scent of chocolate helps to settle his frustrations over chronic sleeplessness. The snapping house broadcasts the plummeting temperature outside. The studs and joists crack and groan. Frost climbs up the windowpane from the sill above the sink. Peering out, above the frost, Billy sees that the clouds have been swept from the sky, accounting for the return of the cold fang of winter. The moon is nearly full. Its brilliance outshines the dimmer light of the stars, and casts a long blue shadow of his house that reaches out to the street. The shadow points to a flickering light, around the edges of the blind in Spanner's basement window. Billy draws down the blind in his kitchen.

He rinses, dries, and returns the mug to its place in the cupboard.

He decides to conduct an inventory of his embalming supplies. Inventories are calming. He knows already that there are no spaces on the shelves in need of restocking. He is well aware of this fact. Still, it will be soothing to enumerate the solutions, fixatives, cleaning products, the contents of each of the orderly sections in his tackle box of make-up supplies, bottles of hair-styling gels, and so on. He puts on a pair of jeans and pulls a sweater over his T-shirt.

Shoeless, he makes his way along the hall to the embalming room, in the dark. Billy doesn't flip on the light switches as he goes. He is remembering a winter night when he was a boy, before his father died. His father had come in through the back door, from shoveling, stomping fresh snow from his boots. Billy was at the table, in his pyjamas, drinking warm milk before bed. He could hear his mother upstairs, singing a lullaby to his sister.

His father unlaced his boots and said, "I know for sure, now I am a Canadian, Billy. I live here such a long time, I no need the light in the garage anymore, when I hang the snow shovel back on the wall, in the dark. Then I know is *my* home." He stood up straight, eyes shut, his arms dramatically outstretched like an opera singer. "Even with my eyes closed—plink—I hang up the shovel on the nail." Billy experiences a similar kind of satisfied familiarity, and pride of citizenship, in his funeral home.

He is still savouring this memory when he suddenly freezes in place, immobilized by fear. He is half in and half out of the embalming room. A thin band of moonlight, leaking in through the chapel windows, steals past him—and by that sliver of light, Billy can see that there is a body stretched out on the embalming table, where a body absolutely should not be stretched out. This does not help to settle Billy's mind.

Even in the stingy light of the moon, he can make out, undeniably, the black silhouette of a human form stretched out on its back, on the embalming table, feet pointing up, hands folded across its chest. Billy's pupils contract, vainly compensating for the darkness of the windowless embalming room.

Billy knows that he isn't dreaming but, as if in a nightmare, he is paralyzed in the doorway, his feet disobeying the commands of his brain, to run. His brain shouts orders which his body is incapable of executing. Billy wills his mouth to speak, his wooden legs to dance like a frantic puppet's. Reason defers all authority to his reptilian brain. His body is locked down, his heart, however, beats maniacally.

"Don't turn the light on," says the voice of the body "Please." Billy remains stubbornly inert.

The voice is male, a young man. It is a voice lacking the resonant timbre of age. It is also, however, a voice purified by a furnace of defeat—Billy recognizes it from years of experience with such voices. It is the voice of a beaten man, a voice seasoned early by grief and futility. Billy has heard such voices many times before.

He tries to respond by saying "okay," but his trachea remains temporarily strangled. He has been holding his breath. He clears his throat, "Okay." It comes out loud, ricocheting off the stainless-steel surfaces of the embalming room. More quietly, he asks,

"Crank? Is that you?"

"It's Clarence now, but ya, it's me. Whatever the fuck is left of me. How ya doin', Billy?"

"I'm okay. You? Sorry Cra.., Clarence. Obviously, you're not good. We've been out looking for you." Billy notices that he is still gripping the door knob with such force that his hand is cramping. He lets go and lets his arm fall to his side. He cannot, in the dark, make out the details of the mass on the table in the middle of the room. It looks like a curving geological formation, punctuated by a stand of feet, like trees, on the furthermost tip of an island. He can hear Clarence breathing. His exhalations come out shuddering, as if he is shivering. "Your grandma asked us to find you. She's worried. We're—Catherine, the preacher, and I—we're supposed to be looking for you, for her."

"Sometimes what you're looking for finds you," says Clarence. "You should write that one down and put it up on one of them inspirational posters."

Clarence unleashes a ragged bawl that stands the hairs on Billy's arms and neck on end. It is the howl of the lone wolf—the lonely wolf—not a haunting howl, echoing from some distant hill, but a chilling howl, right there in the room. It stretches out, bouncing off the walls and jangling the metal shelves and Billy's nerves. A sound that powers an electrical charge, lights up the dark. It is a kinetic green and purple sound that undulates near the ceiling, forming an aurora borealis of pain. Billy can see as clearly as if he was looking up at the night sky, dancing with sorrow.

Billy is unsure as to whether he should advance or retreat. He wonders if his socks will slip on the tiled floor, should the need for escape arise. Clarence, after all, has just been released from prison. More to the point, Billy is well-acquainted with the irrational explosions of rage sometimes elicited by grief. He is accustomed to the homicidal fury of the bereaved, knows it can sometimes vent itself upon an innocent bystander without warning. During that intensely angry, second stage of Kubler-Ross's grieving process, people sometimes need to hit something or someone. On a few occasions, Billy has been punched in the head by mourners, for no other reason than that his head was at hand. Clarence, mercifully, remains motionless.

"Can I get you something?" asks Billy. "You want a hot chocolate?"

"How 'bout a forty and a gun?"

"That won't help," says Billy.

"It's a joke, man. Fuck. You think I'd do that shit to my granny? Especially now? It would kill her more than she probably already is."

"She wants you to come home, Clarence," says Billy. "She needs you."

"I was there," says Clarence. A long silence stretches out beside Clarence on the table. Then, "I was there. *I* stopped the car. It was me. My fault." His voice trembles. "I watched the whole fucking thing from the top of The Crack. Like a fucking horror show." Clarence pinches the bridge of his nose hard. He grinds his knuckles into his eye sockets, as if putting his eyes out could erase the images. "It was my fault. I froze. Just stood there. I'm a coward."

Billy drops his chin to his chest. Mere minutes ago, in far less traumatic circumstances, he had succumbed to the same kind of paralysis. There is no point in arguing, though. A priest would have something meaningful to say after such a confession. Catherine would say something wise, or pastoral, or assign some redemptive penance. Billy's got nothing, so he asks, "Why'd you come here?"

"Looking for Gilbert. I wanted to say, wanted to tell him, I'm sorry."

Billy hears two tears fall onto the stainless-steel table beneath Clarence's head, like the sound of a dripping faucet. *Ting. Ting.* He tells Clarence, "He's not here."

"No shit, Sherlock. I figured that out all by myself. Where is he?"

"Sorry. He's up at the Lakehead. They have to do an autopsy."

Clarence laughs a jagged, bitter laugh. "The cause of death is pretty fucking obvious, don't ya think?"

"They check other stuff—blood, toxins. You know..."

"You mean booze and dope. Jesus. Gilbert was sober as the preacher's wife. I'm the addictive personality in the family."

"That still a problem?" asks Billy.

"No," Clarence sighs. "Not anymore." His voice quivers, "Right now though, it feels like it could get to be. Easy. I want to see him."

"I'm going up to get him in the morning. I'll be back later on tomorrow."

"Can I come? Go with you to bring him home?" Clarence's voice pleads.

Billy hesitates. "Okay," he says.

"Thanks."

"I'm guessing it's a long way back to Martin's cave in the dark. You can sleep on the couch until it gets light."

"You know about Martin, eh?" Clarence asks. The defeat in his voice mingles with surprise.

"Monica told us. She's come here. She's at your granny's."

"Hoooleeey shit," Clarence says. "Gilbert must have really been into that lady. Martin was like our secret. We told *no* one. Fuck it. He doesn't owe me anything. She seems like a good person. Where is Martin, anyway? Looks like he left."

"He died," says Billy. "I'll tell you about it in the morning. Come on, we better try to sleep."

"I think I'll just stay here. If it's okay. It's me who should be laid out here." Clarence taps the metal table twice with his knuckles.

"I'll get you a blanket and a pillow." Billy steps outside the door, then turns back and asks, "Can I call your granny, just to let her know you're okay? I'm sure she's awake and worried sick."

"Go ahead. But I can't talk to her," Clarence's words are choked by tears. "I can't, not yet."

"She'll understand. For now, she just needs to know you're okay."

Billy will also have to call over to the Fire Hall to let them know Clarence is no longer missing. The searchers and rescuers, Billy knows, will be relieved *and* they will be disappointed. They'll be like kids, who, having spent hours organizing an elaborate game, and just when they are about to commence playing it, are informed that it is time for bed. Not to mention all the coffee and sandwiches the St. Luke's ladies will have laid out by now. Of course, Clarence is not really found, but his kind of lost can't be resolved by Search and Rescue volunteers.

"Billy, I..." Clarence calls out, then his voice tails off. There is nothing to say. Of what use are words?

"Try to sleep," advises Billy, wishing he himself could follow it. He pulls the unmarked door partway closed, leaving a crack for the sliver of moonlight to shine into the room.

- 29 -

THE UNPARDONABLE SIN OF DESPAIR

When an ounce of, even unreasonable, doubt could be mustered, suicides like mine were ruled "accidental deaths." Drug overdoses were always determined to be accidental. Collision with rock cuts? Accidents. Over the years, a few people in Twenty-Six Mile have even died of "misfires" and "accidental" self-inflicted gunshots. If you had been happy of late, and drunk at the time, even death by trains would be ruled to be unintentional.

When a death was irrefutably suicide—hangings, or jumping in front a mid-morning train after killing your Scouter, for example—the perpetrator was denied by papal edict a place in the Roman Catholic cemetery. Indisputable agents of their own death were barred from salvation for all eternity by the wrought iron pickets separating sheep from goats. The redeemed and the damned, never the two shall meet. Attempted suicide was decriminalized in Canada a couple of years before I died. So, technically, I was not a law breaker, just damned.

Needless to say, I was judged to be the intentional perpetrator of my own demise. Father O'Mallory made a dutiful pastoral call on my father, who was handling his bereavement one bottle at a time.

The good reverend did his condescendingly best to be sympathetic. "It's a terrible, sad thing that's happened to Matthew." His voice whistled, like someone had him by the throat. "All-round no doubt, Mr. Collins, a terrible, sad thing." He rocked his head side to side, to demonstrate the genuineness of his condolences, and inhaled an asthma-like wheeze of air. "But—as I'm sure you understand—we will need to provide an alternate place of eternal rest, ah, somewhat beyond the bounds of the consecrated grounds proper per se." The priest's venous sausage of a nose, and the scotch mint clattering among his teeth, betrayed his clandestine communion with the bottle. He and Dad had that in common.

"Fuck you," my father slurred from behind a regiment of empty Black Label stubbies—dead soldiers. Dad had been conscripting and shooting them down since just after breakfast. Breakfast, in Dad's case, consisted of a coffee and a smoke.

It was my brother, Danny, who made blunt the priest's attempts to verbally stickhandle the ecclesiastical legalities of the situation. "So, you're saying we can bury Matt on the Catholic side of the cemetery, just a bit outside the fence, into the weeds?"

"Well, yes. Right up close to it. In the large scope of things, it's... I mean in the eyes of God, it's only a matter of inches. Canonical Law is quite clear on this, son. I'm not at liberty to muck... I'm afraid it is out of my hands." Again, with his peculiar tick, the side to side rocking of his regretful, bald head, he pursed his lips, in commiseration. A humble servant of Rome, he had no say in such lofty matters coming down, direct from the Vatican. No need to kill the messenger.

"So, my little brother will be just this much," Danny illustrated the distance with a thumb and forefinger, "outside the pearly gates, a matter of inches, for all eternity. Is that what you're telling us, Father?" Danny cloaked his words with earnest curiosity, but there was a knife concealed in them. "Forever, this much, beyond the redeeming love of your good Lord Jesus Christ? Maybe we should plant him over on the Protestant side." I was touched by my brother's anomalous concern for my welfare. It was, however, more his hatred for the priest, and all things Rome, than affection for me, that propelled the bolus of sarcasm dripping from Danny's questions.

"He'll rot in hell anyway," Dad roared, to no one in particular. "He'll go to hell an unrepentant faggot and murderer. Queering and killing! What does it matter whether he put himself in the grave, or whether someone else did it for him?" When it came to philosophy, Dad was a Rationalist. He dropped his forehead, with a dull thump, onto the table.

"Well," said the priest, now speaking to the top of Dad's head, "that's likely all true, Mr. Collins, but it is the sin of despair which is unforgivable in the heart of Jesus Christ our Lord and Saviour. Giving up on the *possibility* of redemption—that is, surrendering oneself to hopelessness—well that one, I'm afraid is the greatest among all sins. Technically speaking, it's blasphemy against the Holy Spirit to take one's own life, an eternal and unpardonable sin. Murder and even faggotry, being mortal sins, can, with contrition, be forgiven sins, but despair, made manifest in the taking of one's own life—playing God as it were—is beyond the reach of the salvation, even for Jesus Christ our Lord." The priest, visibly pleased with his delivery of this catechism, absent mindedly crossed himself.

"We might as well have him burned up and get 'er done with then," Dad replied, his voice baffled by his arms flung about his head which still rested on the table.

"You think we ought'a get him cremated, Dad?" asked Danny, poking the priest with another theologically sharp stick.

Father O'Mallory sputtered, "Well, I'm not sure that's such a good idea. Although it is no longer strictly forbidden by canon law, well, let's just say cremation still seems a risky option given the promise of the resurrection of the body. We could say a lovely liturgy. It's just that there would be no Mass... per se."

Dad threw himself upright against the chair back and snapped his head up, bellowing, "The boy fucked and then killed his Scouter, then he jumped in front of a God-damned train and you, you, you, pansy-papist, think cremation might be risky! You get the fuck outta my house, right the fuck now! You and the kid you rode in on!" Dad lurched to his feet.

"Now, Mr. Collins, there's no need to be like that," said the priest, scrambling out of the chair, wincing and raising his hands to ward off a blow.

Danny stepped between Dad and the priest. Dad snorted, staggered into the living room and collapsed onto the swaybacked sofa. He was snoring before his face hit the Niagara Falls cushion, its velvet cover rubbed smooth. Danny's fists were clenched at his sides. Standing too close to the retreating priest, he seethed, "We'll take care of things on our own from here, Father."

Father O'Mallory pulled his flat cap back onto his head and backed out the screen door. "If that is your preference." He was already part way down the concrete steps when he added, "If there's anything else I can do, you be sure to call me, my son."

- 30 -
SINCE MY BABY LEFT ME

Down the street, Billy was sailing the stormy and uncharted seas of adolescent grief. One minute he was cresting a wave of elation, astounded by himself and what he had done: preparing my body as he had. He felt as if a house of mysteries had been flung open within him. Riding high on the crest, Billy had the visual acuity of a superhero. He could see his true self, and everything around, him with crisp, focused clarity. Both his inner vision, and his physical eyesight, were like microscopes, remarkably magnified by loss. He could see Mary's and his mother's auras.

Billy decided he would become a funeral director, not a doctor. He would take up the sacred work of caring for the bodies of the dearly departed, and for the grieving souls of those shredded by the brutal dislocations of death. He would inhabit the world of those stripped of their emotional and spiritual armour by the virtue of loss.

Then, crashing down from the crest into the trough of grief, Billy was in the surf of a disinterested universe. He spent several days lying on his narrow bed, buried beneath a quilt in spite of the heat, weeping into his pillow. Mrs. Buffone brought him grilled cheese sandwiches and milk. She stroked his hair as she had when he was a little boy. She pleaded to God for help. In the trough, however, Billy was inconsolable.

Visions of the violent severing of our friendship haunted him until he was seized by terror—as if a spectral-being stood at the end of his bed shaking it, wailing and rattling its chains. Panic suffocated him. Had he been able to gather a breath, he might have screamed for help. His ribs crushed his heart like a clamp. A razor strop wrapped itself around his neck, strangling him.

It was during one of those wretched afternoons that Billy, for the first time, vacated reality for a budding fantasy life—a life without me, or Churley. He found himself recollecting a dream he had as a small child, at five or six years of age. A dream he found both comforting and arousing. He dreamt it on Sunday night, having attended Sunday school that morning. They had learned that King Solomon had 700 wives and 300 concubines. Mrs. Maxwell, the teacher, explained concubines were "like girlfriends" and that it was okay, in Bible times, to have lots of wives and girlfriends, but not anymore.

That night, little Billy had dreamed of Donna Benson's and Linda Pool's naked shoulders. Their whole bodies were naked, but it was the smooth skin of their shoulders that excited Billy. He was sitting on a throne like King Solomon. He too was naked. Donna and Linda were his concubines. Their naked shoulders and his naked shoulders—smooth, summer-tanned shoulders—were touching in his dream. They kissed him on his ears. It made his tummy excited, and gave him a feeling in his penis that at the time he would have described as "happy." Not that he would dare to describe the emotional state of his penis, to anyone. By the time he was five years old, he somehow understood the shame he should feel about what his penis felt.

Billy's fantasy lives were born when I died.

In those lives, the ghosts of anxiety that terrorized him faded. He was peaceful. His first visit to his imaginary place made it possible for Billy, the following morning, to descend the stairs from his bedroom and eat breakfast with his mother and sister.

"You look different," Mary said.

"Hmm," said Billy.

His mother asked, "Are you feeling better, *piccolo*?" She placed her hand on his forehead, like she did when he was sick, checking to see if his fever had broken in the night.

"I guess," said Billy.

Mary stood behind his chair and wrapped her arms around him. "I'm so sad about Matthew, too, and pissed off at him. Didn't he know how bad this would hurt us?" She laid her cheek on his head. He could feel her tears wetting his hair.

"He thought he had to do it," said Billy pushing away from the table, slipping from Mary's embrace. He went out through the back door, then said from the other side of the screen, "They would have put *him* in jail."

In the garage, Billy found some pickets, leftover from the fence that his father had built around their yard before he died. Billy wiped the dust off them with a rag. Beneath the dust the white paint was still good, only a spackling of hairline cracks marred their surface.

He took a jar of bent nails down from the shelf. As ten-year olds, Billy and I collected the nails for building forts. He chose two nails, knelt on the dirt floor, placed them on top of a concrete block, and tapped them straight with a hammer. Then, Billy nailed two of the pickets perpendicular to one other.

He carried the cross over his shoulder, past the post office to the rail crossing. He followed the tracks out of town, grasshoppers popping from the dry weeds ahead of him, to where he calculated I must have stepped into the path of the locomotive. The smell of creosote and late August filled the air. He set about erecting the cross, down below the tracks where the slag gave way to sand. He forgot to bring the hammer, so he pushed the pointed end of the vertical picket into the ground by leaning on top of it.

Billy checked its stability and found it wobbly. He found a softball sized rock and used it to pound the pointed end of the picket further into the ground. The jolt of the rock, connecting with wood, shot up his arm to his shoulder. The impact felt good. Billy hammered furiously until the flat top of the board was as splintered as a wooden tent peg and his hand burned. Spent, he dropped the rock at his feet and brushed the grit off the palms of his hands onto his pants leg.

Billy stood by the cross, thinking he should say a prayer or sing something. He couldn't think of anything appropriate to the occasion. An Elvis song came to mind: *Heartbreak Hotel.* He sang the words he could remember and hummed the ones he couldn't. He felt so lonely.

The Undertaking of Billy Buffone | 181

COLLECTING GILBERT

Billy hunches forward on the edge of his bed in the dark, the palms of his hands flattened together between his knees. He has wrestled with sleep for several hours and lost, has failed to pin his mind to the mat. His fantasies proved futile in achieving serenity, or overriding his preoccupation with Catherine. No matter where he runs—Prince Edward Island, or Cobo Hall in Detroit, or wherever the bodyguard thing is happening—Catherine keeps popping up like a Wac-A-Mole. Of course, it is the feral rodent-like memory of the summer of '75—not Catherine—he desperately wants to hammer into a hole. The two, however, are getting tangled up in Billy's mind. On the bright side: *Catherine has superseded my unwelcome cameos in Billy's fantasies. It is Catherine who increasingly interposes herself into Billy's escape plans.* "Wake up, Billy!"

It is 3:02 AM, and Billy is, indeed awake. Wide awake.

He wonders how Clarence could be sleeping on that embalming table? The sleeping bag and pillow Billy brought to him would do little to warm or cushion the cold stainless-steel table. They would be small comfort given the tragic circumstances. *He's probably wide awake, too.*

Billy dresses and goes back through the office to the funeral home to check on Clarence. An aphorism—oft-repeated by his teachers during his training—springs to Billy's mind: "We serve the living by caring for the dead." *Sometimes,* he thinks, *we also serve the living by caring for the living.*

In the embalming room, the gooseneck lamp is lit. Clarence is circling the room like a prison cell, the sleeping bag wrapped around his shoulders, and clutched at his throat. Billy taps on the half-open door. Clarence stops mid-circuit, facing the shelf of embalming supplies. "Would any of this stuff kill you if you drank it?"

"Probably," says Billy, "some of them."

Clarence faces Billy. His eyes are rimmed red and recessed in their sockets, like they are recoiling from what they've seen. Billy once saw a black and white war photograph, of a mud-caked soldier in the trenches at Passchendaele. Clarence has the same hollow look in his eyes.

"Is it time to go?"

"We might as well. Doesn't look like either of us are gonna sleep" says Billy. "I'll get my coat."

In the garage, Clarence squeezes between the van and the hearse to lift the garage door and waits outside to pull it down, after Billy drives out in the van. The headlights illuminate the disquieting facade of Spanner's house across the street. The light in the basement window has stopped flickering behind the parchment-coloured blind. Clarence climbs into the passenger seat. As he shuts the door he says, "That guy's a creepy dude. Spanner?"

Billy nods his agreement, but doesn't elaborate. He turns right, driving toward town rather than the highway. "Breakfast." The pulp mill is boarded up and abandoned, but Robin's Do-nuts remains, the last twenty-four-hour enterprise left in town. Clarence waits in the van. Billy goes inside for half a dozen donuts, and two, large double-doubles in the brown and orange paper cups.

He sets the open donut box on the engine cover between the front seats. Clarence eats three donuts before they pass the cemetery, washing them down with sips of the sweet, creamy coffee. He wipes his mouth and hands on a serviette, cracks his window an inch, and lights a cigarette. After he takes a drag, he raises the cigarette, and looks toward Billy in the dark, "Sorry, this okay?"

Billy rolls down his window. "One. I don't mind stopping if you need another." He tunes the radio dial through static, searching for WYDR, from Green Bay: "Classic rock, all day every day." At night, under the right conditions, the WYRD signal skips, like a flat stone, across the lake from Wisconsin. Tonight though, the only radio waves skipping across the lake come from an apocalyptic preacher broadcasting end-times doom from his bunker. His gleeful proclamation of the judgement of "Jeeee-*sus*"—with an eternal *e* followed by the snap of a self-righteous *us*—grates on Billy's nerves. He shuts the radio off.

As they round the curve, at The Crack, the cross flashes in Billy's high beams. Neither of them remarks on it. Neither Billy, nor Clarence, has anything to add to the testimony being made by the cross. They continue on in silence.

Clarence finishes his smoke, crushes it out in the ashtray, closes the window, and settles himself against the passenger door. A mile down the road his jaw is slack. In sleep, his face regains the possibility of lost innocence restored. He looks younger, the way he probably looked to Florence when she tiptoed in to check on her grandsons, asleep in the bed they shared. Clarence doesn't wake when Billy stops at the Husky in Nipigon, for more coffee and the bathroom.

By the time Billy is backing the van up to the Port Arthur General Hospital service doors, the parking lot lights are calling it a day. The sun glows, just below the horizon, painting the sky as red as a spawning salmon's back.

Billy coasts the collapsible gurney along the green and white tiled basement floor toward the morgue. Clarence follows close behind. A jockey-sized clerk, his grey hair cut close in a brush, greets Billy. "You're up early this morning, William." Then, taking stock of Clarence, asks, "Who's the new help?"

Observing Clarence for the first time in the light of day, beneath the unforgiving fluorescent hospital lights, Billy sees the extent of the young man's disrepair. With the scrubbed sterility of the hospital for a backdrop—even in the less polished basement of the place—Clarence is looking like tobacco spit on a wedding dress. The knees and cuffs of his jeans are caked with dried mud. His shirt front is dusted with donut powder, and his neck is smeared grey. Greasy hanks of hair flare out from beneath his Chicago Blackhawks cap. His fingernails look like he just finished digging a grave by hand. "Clarence, this is Peter. Peter, Clarence. Clarence is Gilbert Bearchild's brother."

"My apologies, sir," says the clerk, meeting Clarence's eyes with genuine sympathy. "I am truly sorry for your loss." In spite of the countless cadavers he has processed, in spite of the countless times he has spoken these words, there is authentic tenderness in his voice. He passes a clipboard to Billy for signatures, and then guides them through the swinging doors into the cold room.

On their way out of town, Billy picks up a bag of Egg McMuffins at the drive-thru on Algoma Street. "Shouldn't we have looked at him?" Clarence asks, as they pull out onto the street. "What if that," he motions with his chin toward the zippered bag strapped to the stretcher behind them in van, "What if it isn't Gilbert? Aren't you supposed to check?"

"Your granny looked already. She did the identification yesterday," says Billy. The sun is climbing low in the sky, and they are driving into it. Billy pulls down the visor and plants a pair of mirrored sunglasses on his nose. It's true, he would normally take a quick look inside the bag just to be sure, but Billy was uneasy about how Clarence might react. Besides, Billy is ninety-nine point nine percent confident of the clerk's meticulousness. "Don't worry. Peter would never let us leave with anyone but Gilbert."

"Did you call Granny last night? Tell her you found me?"

Billy nods, "I did."

"What'd she say?"

"Mostly, she was crying—happy crying, that you're okay. She wanted to come in and get you, bring you home. I told her I needed you to help me with Gilbert first."

Billy doesn't tell Clarence that she also went on at length about how she *knew* all along that Billy and Catherine would find her grandson. He told her it was Clarence who found him, but she would have none of it. "I knew it. I had the feeling, eh?

You had the feeling too, eh, Billy? Didn't you? I know you did, Billy. I'm not an old Nookomis for nothing."

Billy looks down toward the lake from the highway. There is a stand of leafless birch trees, their branches spread out against the sky. They remind him of the diagram of the circulatory system in his anatomy textbook. The tiny branches, looking like capillaries, trading carbon dioxide for oxygen with the sky. The sap in the trees—warmed by spring—will be starting to flow up the trunk, into the branches, preparing to breathe again.

Billy and Clarence make the three-hour drive back to Twenty-Six Mile House without exchanging words, each of them lost in their own labyrinths of regret.

- 32 -
First, We Take A Moment

Clarence perches on a stool, well back from the embalming tray. Billy brought the stool in from the kitchen. It is the kind with a set of metal steps that tip out from beneath it. Billy has always worked alone. He is especially uncomfortable with the idea of embalming while the brother of the deceased is there. Preparing a body is not for the faint of heart. He is even more ill at ease with Clarence's insistence that he will *assist* with the preparation of Gilbert's body for the viewing at the Pickerel River Community Hall. "That's what you told my granny, right? You needed my help. So, I'm helping. Deal with it." The bravado in Clarence's words cannot hide his misgivings.

Billy is remembering the night he crept into the hospital and into the cooler with a suit, a bag of cosmetics, and a plastic comb. "You're sure?"

"Yes." Clarence's face and neck are streaked with dirt and dried tears, smeared by the cuff of his denim jacket.

"Okay. Wash up then," Billy concedes, and points to the industrial sink bolted to the wall. "If you start to feel sick or light-headed—like it's too much—just say the word."

Clarence scrubs his face and hands with a bar of yellow soap, and dries off with paper towels. Billy hands him a rubber apron and a pair of gloves. "Flip that switch beside the sink." Clarence flips it and the exhaust fan whirs into action in the housing above the table.

Billy explains that the fan will draw any toxic fumes from the cleansers and fixers out of the room. He doesn't add that, even though Gilbert's body has been kept cool, a ripe plume of early decomposition will be released when unzipping the bag. The fan dissipates airborne toxins, and also the scent of Gilbert's departure, the beginnings of his returning to the earth.

Like his college lab instructors did, Billy positions himself facing Clarence across the closed rubberized bag. "Are you ready?"

"Let's do it," but by the end the short sentence, Clarence's voice has fallen off a cliff into trepidation.

"First, we take a moment." Billy always *takes a moment* before he starts to embalm. That's what he calls it, in his head—taking a moment—but he has never said it out loud, nor has he previously had cause to expand upon its meaning.

"I mean we take a breath. We remember this," he places a hand lightly on the mid-section of the bag between them, "is a person. We are caring for a human being, who has a name and story, and people who loved him, or her. Some people, probably most people, consider what we are about to do morbid, or frightening, or gross. We do it with dignity, and with respect for his spirit, and his mortal remains. We have to be completely here, undistracted, present to this moment." Billy is bewildered by the passion, and formality, of the words he has spoken. It leaves him a bit light-headed having, however inadequately, articulated the passion he feels every time he cares for a body. "Taking a moment is like saying a prayer, I guess."

Clarence removes one of his gloves and lays his hand on top of Billy's hand, still resting at the mid-point of the bag. The crescents of Clarence's fingernails are grey, but his hand and arm, up to his rolled shirtsleeve, is scrubbed clean. He closes his eyes and bows his head. "Gizhe-Manidoo, this is my brother who you already know. He is crossing over to you, into the spirit world. Help me and Billy get him ready. Forgive me for..." he stops, draws his free arm across his eyes and sniffs. "Just, forgive me." He stops, again. "Amen." Then he crosses himself like he was taught to do by the sisters, before First Communion at St. Ignatius School on the rez.

"Miigwech," says Billy.

Then he sets to work, a work that is both tender and brutal in its physicality. It is a work of exertion, and of ceremony, a sequential ritual at which Billy has only ever presided over alone. He unzips the bag, and Clarence swallows a sob. He helps to tip Gilbert onto one side, and then the other, to pull the bag out from under him. Billy lays a white towel across his hips to protect his modesty.

Then, he assesses the damage done to Gilbert's body by the truck. There is a flat, blackened place on the back of his head, where his skull is crushed. Billy notes the pooling blood, the irregular angularity where both radius and ulna bones of the forearm are broken, and the twisted pelvis.

The coroner had concluded that a full internal autopsy was unnecessary. Blood and urine samples had been sufficient confirmation that there were no extenuating factors causing death. So, Gilbert, and more significantly Clarence, is spared the ugly "Y" shaped incision bisecting the torso, the cracked open sternum, the thick roll of flesh—closed with quickly knotted sutures—and the jumbled organs removed and returned, to the thorax and abdomen in a plastic bag, to be mixed with formaldehyde and hardener.

Billy allows Clarence to take the lead as they wash Gilbert's body, and rinse and towel him dry. Rigor mortis has set in, making the muscles stiff and resistant to positioning. Billy shows Clarence how to massage them and manipulate the joints to restore a degree of malleability.

He passes a razor and a can of shaving foam to Clarence with which to remove the scant whiskers from his brother's face. "It helps the cosmetics look more natural, if there aren't whiskers," Billy explains.

Billy organizes a surgical tray on the stainless-steel cart beside the table—never disrespect the deceased by setting instruments on top of the body. He uses cotton balls, eye caps and stay cream, to secure the lids of Gilbert's eyes closed.

Billy's hands shake with the exertion of pushing the curved suturing needle through the right mandible, the roof of the mouth and septum, and back down to the left jaw. He tugs the suture, just enough to gently close Gilbert's mouth; tighter and it would result in a grimace. He steps aside, "You know him best. See if you can set his face to something that looks natural to you." Usually, Billy has to rely on a photograph, supplied by the family.

Clarence squeezes his arms across his chest to steady his breathing, steeling himself to remember Gilbert's face, alive. He tries a smile first, but it looks disturbingly incongruent with Gilbert's emotionless, dead face. Phoney. He tries again, but this time he perceives a look of grim judgement on his brother's face. Gilbert appears to be accusing him of his guilt in the tragedy that finds him engaged in this dark art. Eventually, Clarence molds his brother's face into a somewhat peaceful appearance by smoothing the stress lines around his eyes and jaw, shaping his mouth in a horizontal line of acceptance. Outside the world goes about its business, oblivious to the fact that everything has changed.

Billy uses a scalpel to make two small incisions in Gilbert's neck, just above the clavicle, to insert the port lines—one into the carotid arterial, the other in the jugular vein. He releases the arterial clip and the pink mixture of formaldehyde and water starts to flow into Gilbert's circulatory system. Billy waits until the fluid begins to inflate the arteries a little before releasing the second clip. The clear tube turns brownish red with Gilbert's oxygen bereft blood. The open end empties into the drain, at the head of the canted table.

Clarence pulls off his gloves to hold his brother's waxy hand in his own warm flesh. The pink solution flows into the hand, restoring some colour and pliability to it. "Bro', I'm sorry. I'm so, so, so, sorry. I shouldn'a stopped there." Clarence pinches the bridge of his nose to staunch his tears. "It should'a been me, bro'. I'm so, so, sorry." Clarence lays his ear against his brother's cold, silent chest, and weeps.

"Let's take a break," says Billy. They have been working for more than two hours.

Behind the garage in the sunshine, and protected from the cold wind, Clarence lights a cigarette with a Zippo and offers one to Billy. "Indian smokes from the rez. Martin had cartons of them stashed up at his place. Musta had somebody bringing them out to him." Billy accepts the cigarette, and cups his hands around it so Clarence can light it. After it's lit, Billy holds it, pinched between his thumb and forefinger, smouldering at his side. They lean back against the sun-warmed wall, and watch the seagulls circling and squawking down near the beach.

Keeping his eyes on the gulls riding on the updrafts of air, Clarence asks, "How long you been doing this?"

"Pretty much since high school," says Billy. "You okay?" Billy's question is equal parts sincere concern, and his desire to switch the channel from how he got started in this business to anything else.

"Not really. Probably never will be okay. I doubt it." Clarence takes a hard drag on the dart, holds it and blows the smoke out. "How do you ever get over it, deal with... with the shit, the guilt, with such a total fuckup that can't never be fixed? How do you even *want* to keep goin'?"

"I don't know, how they do it," says Billy, and holds his cigarette up and just looks at it. "It amazes me that anybody... well, they never get over it. You never get over it, not really— not if you lose someone you truly love—but some people keep going, some even become grateful for life, again." The sound of a car door closing and an engine starting drifts down the street from the Ford dealership. Clarence crushes his butt out on the ground. Billy does the same and says, "This next part, with the organs, is kind of rough. Then we'll get the makeup and hair right."

- 33 -
THE SERVICE HAPPENS IN THE MIDDLE

The kitchen at Pickerel River Community Hall is fired up, in full operational mode, like a finely tuned machine. The hall itself, a cinder block and steel-girder box, is, in a pinch, large enough to accommodate the total population of Pickerel River (POP 300, give or take), plus their friends. The kitchen, however, is not much bigger than the one back at the St. Luke's manse.

Damp warmth, and the scent of hard-boiled eggs and moose stew, wafts out through the servery window. Given the flurry of moving bodies, hands and sharp knives, Catherine can't get an accurate count of the number of women stacking sandwiches four high and slicing them into triangular thirds, stirring pots and loading trays. She estimates twenty. Forty hands and arms, sliding loaves of premade, uncut sandwiches from bread bags, levering knives and stacking them cut, onto cookie sheets and plastic trays. Twenty voices calling out: "egg salad," "ham," "meat-n-pickle," "peanut butter and jam." The scene calls to Catherine's mind the poster of Rosie the Riveter tacked up on her office wall and the black and white photographs of war-time factory women—sleeves rolled up their muscular arms, hair held back with kerchiefs from their damp faces.

The faces bobbing around the Pickerel River Hall kitchen island are shades of brown and white. Connie Stinson had heard from Ernie Caird's wife Bev, that their preacher had been asked to take the funeral at Pickerel River. So, she put the St. Luke's Ladies Fellowship chain on standby. When the phone call came from her friend, Sandra Lapier of Pickerel River, inviting St. Luke's to help out, they scrambled into action like fighter pilots.

Sandra, and Connie, circulate in the kitchen offering words of encouragement and gratitude—and when absolutely necessary, quietly coaching ladies from among their own ranks.

The countertops are piled near to tipping with rice and noodle casseroles, paper plates, serviettes, plastic cutlery, and Styrofoam cups. Cases of Pepsi and bottled water are stacked waist-high in the open fronted cupboards, underneath the counters.

Pickerel River's been on a boil water restriction—and drinking bottled water—since a cyanide spill by a fly-by-night mining operation. The reserve's water has been poisoned for more than a decade. The mine is long gone and the company no longer exists. To date, neither the mine's insurer, nor the government, have been legally compelled to do anything about it. The Pickerel River claim languishes in the courts.

Twin stainless-steel coffee urns percolate on the counter. Four industrial-sized pots of moose stew simmer on the stove. The two ovens are so packed with fry bannock, wrapped in tinfoil, that the doors won't completely close.

Connie spies Catherine, watching the action through the servery window, and joins her outside the kitchen. Connie pushes a hank of errant hair from her forehead with the back of her wrist and reports that, "Everything is under control."

"It's a beautiful thing, Connie." Catherine meant the words to come out lightly, with a bubble of laughter perhaps, but something more poignant catches in her throat. Her eyes well up with tears. She composes herself, before continuing, "Seeing all of you in there, working together like that..." Catherine waves her hand, lost for words. She and Connie watch the action through the servery window, listen to the buzzing hive of efficient conversation. "Any problems?"

Connie crosses her soft arms above her ample breasts, and indulges a quick, proud smile. "There was a little skirmish over trimming or keeping the crusts, but we play by home team rules."

Catherine can see that the home team rule is crusts on. "It's amazing, really. All of you working together like that," Catherine imagines a great coming together of nations, a healing and reconciliation of centuries of trauma and colonial injustice, brought about by women working side by side—by the power of egg salad sandwiches, bannock, and grief. "If politicians spent more time cutting sandwiches, and stirring moose stew, together it could change the country."

"Oh, we're old friends," says Connie. "Us girls all went to the same high school—some of us got to be friends. It's like a Grade 10 Home Ec. reunion in there." She chuckles, "And we haven't changed a bit, except most of us take up a bit more space in the kitchen than we did in the tenth grade." She grips Catherine's elbow and steps closer to whisper, "You doin' okay, Rev?"

Catherine's eyes threaten to spill over again. She is moved by the novelty of Connie's affection, and by her budding familiarity revealed in the casual use of the abbreviated honorific, "Rev." Caught off guard by her own emotions, Catherine stems another flow of tears with the heels of her hands.

Connie pulls her into a warm, doughy hug, Catherine's alb and stole slung over her forearm between them. "Don't start crying now, Rev. That mascara doesn't look waterproof. You'll end up looking like Alice Cooper before things even get started." A tremor of silent laughter quakes between them.

Some of the plastic folding chairs in the hall are reserved with coats and scarves for Elders. A line of men in pressed jeans and tucked-in western shirts leans against the back walls smoking. Toddlers dressed in frilly pastel dresses or miniature tuxedos with clip-on bowties—outfits, purchased one size up, for the previous summer's weddings—break free of their parents to roam among the forest of legs, every pair belonging to their kin. A country gospel band in matching black Levi's and leather vests are at the front of the hall tuning guitars and checking microphones. "Check. Check. One. Two. How'zat Ronnie?" Ronnie, listening from the back of the hall, gives two thumbs up.

A queue of mourners wends its way along the far side toward the front of the room. They pause in clusters around the open casket, to confirm what just doesn't seem possible has actually happened—that it is, undeniably, Gilbert's body, visible from his waist up, laid out in the casket. Every one of them have survived countless traumas, but that doesn't make it any easier. *Not Gilbert. It just can't be.* They offer a prayer. Their shoulders quake. They move on, still shaking their down-turned heads in disbelief. Elders press wads of Kleenexes to their mouths to staunch their sorrows, weeping silently the way they learned to cry as children in Residential Schools.

Florence, standing only a foot taller than the polished oak coffin resting on its draped cart, greets her community. She is flanked by Bernadette on one side and by Monica, tall as a pine tree, on the other. Florence holds their hands like a lost child. The three women invisibly share strength with each other. When the poverty of unbearable grief overtakes one of them, another passes some spare coins of hope into the palm of her hand. The coins are returned, when the benefactor becomes the beggar. Such is the economy of mourning.

The skin around their eyes is raw, but dry. They have wept themselves dry at the three-day fire leading up to the funeral. They are wearing long skirts with ribbon-blouses and moccasins. Even Monica is dressed in the traditional manner. Last night, she was adopted and named *Akoozi Miigwaan*—Tall Feather— by the sisters.

"Do you need somewhere to suit up?" It is Billy, dressed in the same well-preserved morning suit he wore on the day of Mr. Martin's funeral. He appears to have left the white framed sunglasses in the car.

"Oh, hi Billy." Catherine detects the softness in his eyes, a gently rumpled mourning in them that matches his suit. She resists an inclination to stoke his fulsome sideburns, to take his face in her hands. She wishes that Canadians greeted one another with a kiss, like the French do. She lifts her cream coloured alb and the purple stole slung over her arm. "I thought I would just scoot into the bathroom to put these on."

"Over here." Billy sets out through the crowd toward a set of double doors on the far side of the hall. "You can use the equipment room." People clear a path for Billy, and Catherine follows easily in his wake. She passes in front of a row of chairs where seven or eight white kids are seated. They're wearing matching navy coloured sweatshirts, Lakehead University in bright yellow emblazoned across the front. The hall is jam-packed, but to the left and right of the students, there is an empty chair. A huddle of leather-skinned men, leaning against the doors to the equipment room, step aside. Billy drops the smoldering butt of a cigarette into a Pepsi can, and opens one of the doors.

"You're smoking," says Catherine. "I haven't seen you smoke since Mr. Martin's funeral."

"I only smoke at funerals," says Billy. "You can hang out in here if you want to, uh, collect yourself or what not." *Take a moment.* Billy flips a switch and the lights flicker to life. The room houses a net bag containing a dozen, worn basketballs, two floor-hockey nets, a pile of sticks, and a pallet of ten-litre water jugs, sealed with blue plastic caps. "You can leave your stuff in here if you don't want to carry it around. No one will bother it."

Catherine drapes her stole and alb over a hockey net. "Did you bring the sander?" She asks, a friendly reference to an inside joke they share, a point of camaraderie, but her neck blossoms red, recalling the disastrous morning she dropped by to return the sander to Billy.

Billy pats his left vest pocket and nods. "All set. I'll hand it off to you on the way to the cemetery. Unless you want to practise on your Bible." Straight faced, he scans the growing crowd and purses his lips. *Did he mean that as a joke?* Catherine wonders. *Is he teasing me? Affectionately?*

She risks a tinsel of laughter and says, "Thanks. I'm good."

"Okay," says Billy, visibly distracted now, still scanning the hall. "If we get separated, I'll meet you back here at say," he consults his watch, "eleven-twenty."

"Eleven-twenty? Aren't we supposed to start at eleven?" Catherine steps closer beside him, trying to follow his gaze. *Who is he watching for?* Her shoulder presses up against his. She can feel his warmth radiating between them. She thinks that's what she is feeling. Maybe it's just her.

Billy sweeps an arm—the one not attached to the shoulder pressing against Catherine's shoulder—indicating the mingling mourners, and the line-up of those paying respects. "It's already started."

They remain standing, side-by-side inside the frame of the open double doors. Their shoulders are still touching, neither of them is pulling away. "You want a Pepsi or a water?" asks Billy. He continues to scan the room as if he is unaware of, or unaffected by, or comfortable with, or maybe enjoying, their physical contact.

"I'm fine. Not right now, thanks."

"I'll put a water up front for you," indicating a portable lectern beside the casket. It looks to be made of particle board, chipped. The top is slanted, mounted on top of a chrome plated stand. Someone has carried it over from the school. There is a microphone, secured with duct tape to a separate stand, next to the lectern. Its cable is taped across the floor, and disappears into a snake-ball of similar cables, where the band is setting up. There is a goose-necked lamp fastened to the podium, its brown power cord lies on the floor twenty feet from the nearest outlet.

The Bear Clan doodem—a black paw-print painted on a twelve-inch square of varnished plywood—is mounted on a staff, between the casket and lectern. An expanse of beige tiles lies between the front row of chairs reserved for family, and the makeshift pulpit. Catherine feels that distance to her soul. *What am I, who am I, being here? I should be seated at the back, not up front talking.*

Billy is still scanning the back of the room.

Following his gaze, Catherine asks, "Who are you looking for?"

"Clarence."

"Didn't he come with you?" Their shoulders are still touching. He isn't pulling away. Catherine tries not to think about kissing him.

Billy sighs. "No. He's scared to see Florence. Well, her and everyone else. He thinks this is his fault. Nobody here even knows he's out of jail, or that he was with Gilbert when he died. Just Florence and Bernadette. And Monica."

"Florence will be heartbroken if he doesn't come."

"I called her, for Clarence. So, she knows he's okay, and understands he's probably not ready to face this. She gets it, I think. But I left keys to the van in case he changes his mind. He might, you never know. Some people have to make it hard—the way back—have to make it difficult. Some people find their way back, some people not for a long time, some of us never do."

Catherine wants to ask what Billy means by "us," but says, "I think I'll hang out here, until we're ready. I want to go over the service one more time." She digs into her bag for her notes, wondering how she can possibly bridge the tiled canyon separating that lonely pulpit from the assembled mourners, and feels sick to her stomach.

"Okay. I'll see if the programs are ready. Someone's trying to find more toner for the photocopier." He walks two steps out into the hall and then returns, lowering his voice. "You know where the bathroom is, right? Probably a good idea to use it. Hard to tell how long things will go."

- 34 -
LIGHT A FIRE AGAINST THE NIGHT

Half an hour passed, during which time Catherine lined up for one of the stalls in the women's bathroom. What was no doubt intended to be a respectful silence fell upon the lavatory when she entered; the sad, friendly banter among the women came to an abrupt stop as she stepped into the line. Catherine was so self-conscious in the packed, yet soundless, bathroom that when her turn came, she was unable to relieve herself.

Billy closes the casket and retreats to listen to the service, from the doorway to the equipment room.

Terrified, Catherine takes up her place, behind the pulpit, robed in her alb and purple stole. The hall is pin-droppingly quiet. The boom of the big community drum has stopped, the keening honour song is silent. The silence is expanded by their absence. Sweetgrass, sage and tobacco mingle in the air. A low canopy of smoke drifts above the seated mourners. The shuffling of chair legs has stilled. Children are nestled in the nests of their grandmothers' laps. Infants, soothed with bottles, have been lulled to sleep by full bellies and the warm hall.

An expectant tension descends onto the room, as though each and every mourner is holding their breath, waiting to inhale what Catherine has to offer. Her heart beats staccato, like the tight skin on a little drum. She grips the sides of the lectern, so she won't be washed overboard by the storm churning her guts. She flattens her papers, unable to bring their typed words into focus. She blinks to clear her eyes, but blindness persists, like Saul not yet Paul, on the road to Damascus. She feels the rapid pulse of blood in her neck, hears it surging in her ears. She starts, "I…" The sound of her amplified voice echoes off the back wall, startling her and she stops.

Again, she looks to her notes, but the words continue to swim around on the page. All those words that seemed wise to her, and rich with compassion, when she typed them back in the church office. Now they feel trite and limp, insulting to the drum and the singers, to the Elders and healers, and to the mourners. Her knees tremble beneath her alb. Her full bladder threatens to let go. She is certain that she is going to faint.

Bernadette, Florence and Monica are seated in the front row, waiting. Catherine wants to kneel down in front of them and beg their forgiveness for her arrogance, for the empty bowl she has brought to the feast. She wants to lie, to tell them she is unwell, unable to continue. That would not be a lie. She will beg their forgiveness, and run.

Her eyes find Florence's eyes—imploring, desperate and, at the same time, they are sparkling brown pools of strength and trust. Their eyes form a tunnel of clear, red light that flows between them. Catherine can see only Florence's eyes; the rest of the room has gone black. The two women perceive one another through a brilliant tunnel of crimson light.

It is not the calmness that Catherine prayed for that settles on her. It is not serenity, or the peacefulness to which she aspires, that overcomes the debilitating sense of the impossibility of the task set before her. No. She is filled instead with fire. She becomes fire, a pillar of fire. A fire burns within her, but does not consume her; a fire rises from her feet, devouring her robe and stole and lighting her up, to the top of her head. It turns her dry pages, set neatly on the lectern, to ash; then it reduces the lectern to cinder, eliminating the barrier between herself and everyone, everything.

An unfamiliar voice pushes at the back of her throat, like the roar of a mother bear for her cub. So, she releases it—a sound of rage and defiance, a grunt which refuses to surrender to the darkness pressing in on the hall.

She strides into the no man's land separating mourners from the one mourned, rejecting the illusion of the chasm separating life and life beyond death. All illusions collapse within her.

She finds herself—unsure of how she got there—with her back turned to the mourners, facing Gilbert's closed casket. Her fingers slide along the lip of the casket, find the latch and levers it open. She raises the lid, bends down and rests her lips on Gilbert's forehead. A flock of sobs—like the flapping of a thousand wings—are expelled around the hall. Catherine lowers the lid. The sound of the latch, a heart-shaped locket clicking shut, can be heard at the back of the hall.

Catherine turns, straightens her spine, and casts out all impediments to the telling of truth, impatient to be told. She scans the rows of chairs, looking into each person's eyes. The mourners are no longer a single, amorphous creature, but each of them a particular hurting human, perfect and precious in their individuality. Each of them, and she herself, a miracle, created in the image of Creator. She allows herself to fall into The One, who is called Love, with them.

She unleashes her words, like wild dogs straining and howling against their captivity. "Gather up what has been broken." Her voice clarion as a loon's call across a still lake at night. The men at the back of the hall lean in, lean away from the wall, respectful of the Creator's presence in her voice. There is no need for amplification. Catherine pauses, and looks again into the hungry eyes of the multitude waiting to be fed. Words pour out of her as poetry. Not her words. Not her voice.

> "Gather up what is been broken
> Bring what is wounded
> Bring the long winter
> and the impossibility of spring.
> Bring hearts cracked open
> by sadness, by defeat, even guilt.
> Bring your whispered prayers
> your raging souls,
> your pain-filled memories
> and your dreams stolen.
> Bring your doubt and anger too.

Bring the lie, bring the lie
about the finality of death.
Bring it all, bring it all, bring it all.
Together we will carry it, like kindling.
Stack it high, brittle stick on stick
and rub those bones together,
to light a fire against the night."

Outside a clap of thunder breaks the sky. The men at the drum respond in kind.

- 35 -
MISSING VAN AND MISSING MAN

When Billy arrives home from Gilbert's funeral, he hoists the
garage door to find the garage empty (except for the ten-speed,
leaning against the wall on flat tires). The van is missing, and
Billy deduces that Clarence—ipso facto—must be missing with
it.

Billy pulls the hearse inside and hurries to close the door
behind it. He doesn't want the entire town to see what a fool
he has been, is. The absent van, and the absent young man,
embarrass him. His naiveté, his glaring lack of common—small-
town—sense has resulted in a missing van, likely piloted by
Clarence. The empty space in the garage is proof, to anyone who
notices—and Billy is pretty sure everyone will notice—that he
is just a soft-headed, gullible guy. Fooled again.

You what? You left the keys to the van with Clarence? The
*Clarence Bearchild? Crank? Crank the just-released-from-jail
criminal?* Billy's inner voice, shrill with past failures, and secret
guilt, piles on. *Did you consider for one minute that Clarence just
might steal your van and head west, like so many other miscreants,
in search of a geographical cure to their fucked-up lives?* No, this in
fact, had not occurred to Billy, not until just now. *Man up, Billy.*

Standing in the van-less bay, Billy surveys the concrete floor,
where the van should be located, and tries to think. He shoves
his hands into his coat pockets. He persists in his self-flagella-
tion. No need to beat a confession out of himself. "I'm an idiot."

But he reasons, *Okay, okay, Clarence has the van—fair
enough—it's not here, not right this minute*. He doesn't know
where the van is, or where Clarence is, but he is pretty sure that
if he finds one, he'll find the other. The van is not technically
stolen. Billy *gave* the keys to Clarence. *Brilliant. Shut up.* Maybe

he just borrowed it to go for smokes, or to his grandmother. Maybe he didn't *steal* Billy's van to flee Twenty-Six Mile House and Pickerel River—where his every sin is a matter of narrative record—for the promise of anonymity on the gritty downtown east side of Vancouver. *Maybe not. Who knows, right?*

Billy decides it best not to report the possibly stolen vehicle, or the previously missing person missing again, to the police. Not yet. Clarence will be back. Billy is sure of it, sort of.

Inside, Billy hangs up his coat, then carries the cellophane-covered paper plate of leftovers into the living room. The thin plate bows beneath the weight of the stack of sandwiches, and assorted cookies and squares. The ladies did the plate up for him. When it comes to dibs on fellowship time leftovers, the immediate family of the deceased are afforded first priority, followed by the preacher, the funeral director, and then bachelors in general. As the funeral director, a bachelor and an orphan, Billy is a reliable beneficiary of leftovers.

The bread is a bit dry from sitting out on the tables all afternoon. He opens and sniffs an egg salad sandwich, trying to recall the unrefrigerated shelf life of mayonnaise in a warm hall before spawning salmonella. It smells fine, as fine as hard-boiled eggs ever do.

He watches *Cheers* on television while he eats. In this episode, Diane is falling for Sam's handsome and successful brother, Derrick. During commercial breaks, Billy turns the volume down and listens for the sound of tires in the parking area, or garage door opening. Those sounds would lift a great weight from Billy's mind. He would shake his head and chuckle with relief. *Silly me, always worrying about nothing.*

During the next commercial break, Billy goes to the kitchen window to see if—at that very instant—Clarence is rolling into the parking lot with his van. It is dark out. He can see his face mirrored back at him in the window. The face of the Spanner house, across the road, mocks him behind his own. The light in the basement window flickers like a silver tooth in a leering skull. Billy bares his teeth, repositioning his reflection to align his image with the tooth in the skull across the road.

The *Cheers* episode ends, with Diane and Derrick flying off on a date in his private jet. The words "To Be Continued" appear on the screen. "Oh, come on," Billy protests, and throws his arms above his head. The empty paper plate slips from his lap, spilling crumbs onto the carpet. He didn't see that coming: To be Continued. Billy hates not knowing how things will end. *Who knows if I'll even be* home *to watch the next episode, or even alive a week from now! No one knows! To be continued. Geez.*

Billy brushes his teeth and goes to bed, still irritated about *Cheers* being To Be Continued. He can't sleep. Big surprise. His mind squirrels again, manufacturing one horrific scenario after another. He imagines the phone call, instructing him to collect Clarence's body, where the police have found him, parked out by The Crack. One end of a garden hose duct-taped to the exhaust pipe, the other end inside the van, secured by the closed rear window.

He forces himself to picture knocking on Florence's door, telling her, "I left the keys with him." His stomach clenches. He found Clarence just like Florence knew he would. Technically, Clarence found Billy but, this is no time for splitting hairs. Billy found Clarence, Clarence found Billy, and Billy lost Clarence.

- 36 -
Please, Don't Shoot the Ravens

The digital clock beside his bed reads 4:11 AM. Billy drags a blanket and pillow from the bed and relocates to the couch in the kitchen. He pushes his nose into the crack at the back of the couch, breathing in the reassuring aromas retained in the fabric. The couch, however, provides no consolation tonight. Nor do his threadbare fantasies deliver their previously reliable sense of calm.

He thinks about Catherine, pressing her shoulder against his shoulder, in the doorway of the equipment room at the Pickerel River Community Hall. Or was he the one doing the pressing? He rolls over, to feel the couch press the shoulder against which Catherine's had pressed. He lies that way for a while, attempting to recreate the sensation of Catherine's shoulder touching his.

He gives up and gets up, boils water for tea, and pours it over the bag, while standing at the counter. He leaves the tea to cool in the cup and wanders through the funeral home in his pyjama pants and T-shirt. It would be soothing to vacuum the chapel, but he doesn't want to turn on the lights, doesn't want anyone to know he's awake and start them wondering why. He doesn't want to spark a wildfire of gossip. Gossip, like wildfires, gets out of control fast. *Saw Billy Buffone's lights on over at the funeral home last night. What d'spose he was up to?* Speculation, fanned by lack of actual facts, becoming common knowledge by the end of the day. Some of the kind citizens of Twenty-Six Mile House are just curious about each other that way. Others, however, deal in the power of knowledge, truth be damned.

Billy walks his fingers over the Braille dots on the bathroom door sign across from the embalming room. He makes the rounds of the embalming room, hoping to find Clarence once again, stretched out on the table there. Alive. He touches each implement like a talisman, each bottle of solution and cleanser a potion, the table and the trays totems of his undertakings. He opens the door from the embalming room that leads into the garage, and flips the light switch up and down once. The van isn't there.

Billy drinks his tea. Then he boils a pot of quick oats, stirring it with his wooden spoon. The oatmeal thickens quickly as advertised. He pours milk and sprinkles brown sugar—cue Mick Jagger—into the pot, and looks out the kitchen window while he eats. Light is beginning to bleed into the dark.

It's garbage day. Billy can see Spanner's trash cans are set out to the road. Billy's can is only half full. He'll put it out next week.

Billy fills the sink to wash the dishes. He floats the upturned pot lid, spins it on the thinning suds. The spinning is calming, hypnotic. He spins it again. The lid whirls around and around. Billy whistles the sound of a falling bomb and plunges it under the water. He shakes the water off and adds it to the dish rack.

There is a bang across the road. A bear has knocked over one of Spanner's metal garbage cans. The lid is off and the contents spill out onto the driveway. The bear sorts the trash with her nose, sniffing and pushing her head inside the can to extract plastic grocery bags with her teeth. The bear looks heavy enough to be a boar, but her narrow forehead and tall ears lead Billy to believe it is a sow, maybe the one he saw with twin cubs last summer, and more recently up at the cemetery.

The bear drags knotted grocery store bags out of the can onto the driveway. She knocks the second can down with a swat of her paw. Famished, by her long hibernation, she roots frantically for gristle, bone, anything fat; tearing bags open, feverishly gobbling her way through Spanner's rubbish. Eventually the bear lumbers off into the bush behind Spanner's place, a clear plastic bag swinging from her teeth. It looks to be full of fish guts, spines, tails, and heads.

Seven ravens are perched on the crest of Spanner's roofline, waiting patiently for the bear to depart. They descend to scavenge what the bear has left. They screech and caw and bat one another with their wings. They tip chip bags and cracker boxes over their heads with their beaks, to shake out the crumbs. They peck at the salty bits tipped out onto the cement. Newspapers, magazines, cereal boxes, blood-stained meat trays, and an eviscerated vacuum cleaner bag, are scattered on the driveway and out into the street in an expanding radius of carnage.

The front door swings open and Spanner steps out onto the stoop. Dick Spanner is in his late fifties. His barrel-shaped torso balances on top of a pair of pale, stork-like legs, sticking out below a short, brown, velour housecoat. He flips a handful of mouse-coloured hair over the top of his balding head and shouts, "Hey, hey, git, go-on, git, git, hey, hey, hey!" The ravens concede only an indifferent glance in his direction and return to their buffet.

Billy leans forward above the sink. He cannot recall the last time he actually laid eyes on Dick Spanner. Were it not for the flickering basement window, Billy would wonder if Spanner had left town or if he was perhaps dead inside his house.

The cement stoop is fuzzed with a coat of hoarfrost, so Spanner descends the three steps, hopping from one bare foot to the other. At the edge of the yard, he scoops up a fistful of stones and sidearms them at the birds. Still, the ravens grant him only the briefest of glances and return to foraging in his trash.

Billy's warm breath condenses on the cold window pane, obscuring his view. He wipes the moisture from the glass with his dishtowel.

Spanner, his housecoat flapping, charges the ravens, shouting "git, git." He hurls a baseball-sized clump of dirt, and it remarkably finds its mark, stunning one of the birds. It tips over onto its side, staggers back to its feet, hops sideways on one leg across the driveway, and stumbles again, while ineffectually flapping its enormous wings.

The other ravens lift off in a pulsing black cloud of wings and rage. After achieving an altitude of about twenty feet, they commence to serially dive-bomb Spanner. One by one, screeching like banshees, they box his ears with their wings and claw at the unprotected top of his head.

Spanner spins on his heal to retreat. The frantic dash, combined with the inertia of his substantial girth and the slick condition of the concrete stoop, make cutting right in through the door impossible. He plants his feet in a bid for traction, but slides across the frost-coated porch. Arms windmilling, he manages to snatch a hold of aluminum door handle. Big mistake. The first knuckle of his middle finger pops from its socket as he flails off the far side of the stoop, landing hard on his back in frozen dirt.

Billy grimaces and considers the bounds and duties of neighbourliness. Is he obligated, for example, to pull on some trousers, cross the street, and enquire as to Dick's well-being? Before Billy reaches a conclusion to his question, however, Spanner bounces back to his feet with surprising agility. Dick is clearly winded, but walks purposefully around the stoop. His housecoat is dragging on the ground from one arm, and his jockey shorts have been wedged, by the force of his landing, into a parody of thong underwear. His back and buttocks are covered with angry red scrapes, as if a cheese grater had been involved in this mishap.

Clutching his injured right hand to his chest, Spanner opens the door with his left hand and disappears inside. The ravens resume their scavenging. Billy pulls the plug from the sink and returns to worrying about Clarence's whereabouts.

But wait, there's more! Spanner may have lost the battle, but apparently has not conceded the war. He reappears, now sporting black rubber boots. The tie on his housecoat is cinched and knotted at his waist. His face is twisted into a mask of crimson rage and he is cradling a rifle.

He marches along the walkway, stuffing rounds into the clip and levering a bullet into the chamber of his 30-30. The dislocated finger—pointing in the completely wrong direction—causes Billy to suck air between his teeth and unconsciously flex his fingers. *Yeow, that's gotta hurt.*

Sensing their imminent imperilment, the ravens hastily gobble a last bite of garbage and head for the skies. Billy's foresight and reflexes are much slower than those of the birds. He remains standing, framed in the kitchen window, stunned like a proverbial deer in the headlights. He is transfixed by the fury fuelled drama playing itself out across the street. Eyes wide, Billy watches Spanner empty the clip in quick succession, ripping three thunderous holes in the quiet morning. The first bullet passes neatly through one of the fleeing ravens. It bursts it into a chaos of feathers and drops like a rock to the ground. The second round buries itself in the tailgate of a brand new Econoline Van parked up the road beneath the red, white, and blue pennants at the Ford dealership. That bullet will be located during the police investigation.

During the millisecond in which Billy begins to consider the wisdom of taking cover, the third shell—travelling at approximately 2,500 feet per second—pops a spidery hole in his window, spraying glass into the sink and onto the kitchen floor. All of this unfolding, as these things do, stretched out like a rubber band, proving the relativity of time. Billy has a premonition of the shell coming toward him. He hears and sees the pop of the glass, catches a whiff of cordite, feels an ominous whip of air. Time elapses even more slowly, and Billy observes the hot round of ammunition sailing toward his face. He snaps his head around and twists his body in a final, but futile, spasm of instinct. It feels to Billy as if he is snapping and twisting with all the hustle of a sloth. The acrid smell of gunpowder scorches his sinuses, and his mind explodes in a burst of a thousand particles of bone and blood.

- 37 -
BILLY DOESN'T GET TO THE NETHERLANDS

Looking down from the window seat in the airplane, Billy sees
fields of tulips stretching to the horizon in every direction,
disappearing around the curve of the earth. The flowers are
the bright red of highly oxygenated blood, bumblebee yellow,
Barbie-doll-accessory pink and pearly white. There are deep
purple petals, dark as the Concord grapes that Billy's father
crushed for wine every autumn. There are buttermilk and lemon
drop coloured tulips, too. Infinite. Row on row on row on row
on row on row. Their black stamens, erect and humming, like an
orchestra of horny tuning forks. Billy recognises the melody, its
title is on the tip of his tongue, but he can't quite name it.

The flowers—their colours and their pollen-hungry stig-
mas, their lusty vibrations—sting Billy's eyes with happiness.
He blinks and presses his forehead against the cool glass of the
oval window. He tucks his nose and mouth into the crook of
his elbow to muffle his ecstatic gasps. He touches the tip of his
tongue to the skin of his arm and savours the salty gladness of
his tears. *The first thing I'll do after landing is taste some of those
tulips with my tongue.* The flowers look lollipop sweet.

This must be the Netherlands. Billy has never been to Hol-
land, but he recalls the travel poster, sticky-tacked up on the wall
in Mrs. Dirksen's Geography classroom, displaying the endless,
orderly rows of tulips. Late winter rain slid down the classroom
window. His desk, pockmarked by compass gouges, and the air
rank with chalk dust, children's feet, wet mittens and half-eaten
peanut butter sandwiches. The poster, an explosion of colour on
the bone-coloured wall, evoked in Billy a delicious longing for
the world. He thought at the time, if he was someday fortunate
enough to travel to this land of endless floral beauty, he would

lie down on his back between the rows of tulips, let them blush his cheeks with pollen, and paint the cloudless sky with colour.

A runway comes into view; the asphalt strip is carpeted with seductive petals, as if scattered to lead a bride to the altar. The runway, like the tulips, stretches out, curving around the horizon. Billy is filled with a lightness he has not known since those mornings he sat caressing yellow dandelion manes with the palms of his hands. His feet and knees—he realizes he is wearing short pants—churn up and down in anticipation of running through the flowers, their satiny petals brushing against his sun-browned shins.

Billy turns toward his seatmate, to share his excitement, and is not surprised to find that it is me, sitting next to him. "Matt, this is amazing!"

"Yes, it is amazing." I reply. "But it's wrong." My chest aches with sadness.

"Wrong? What are you talking about, Matt?" asks Billy, "Look out there!" He turns back to the window and shields his eyes against the unearthly brightness.

"Not yet. It's just not time," I tell him. There is a click—like a door closing—in my voice. I look toward Billy's chest, knowing his eyes will follow mine.

For the first time, after all these years, he can see the umbilical cord that still connects us to one another. Finally, what has tethered us together for more than a decade is visible, tangible to him. It snakes its ugly way between the buttons of our shirts, binding us heart to heart, to each other. It is a blue and purple muscle, ripe with blood, and thick as a garden hose. Both of us suffer the ache of it—have felt its bruise since I left—wedged like a root growing between our ribs, prying them apart. It is a familiar ache, so familiar that we have become accustomed to it.

Before Billy can object, I produce a pair of golden shears and cut it. The cord crackles, spews angry sparks, and then it shrivels. It falls, as cold as last week's ashes, into our laps, mixing with our falling tears.

Billy is falling. He falls for a long time. It is not an unpleasant sensation. He has always savoured the sensation of falling in his dreams. He has never subscribed, as some people do, to the notion that if one does not awaken from a dream about falling, before impacting with the ground, you will die. How would anyone know whether or not it is true? In fact, Billy usually prolongs these falling dreams as long as possible. There is, to him, a rightness of falling, a righteousness to it. Now, severed from me, he just doesn't care. He wishes the myth was true. This falling fills him with unbearable sadness, about where he is falling from and to.

Meanwhile back on Earth

Billy's fall stops on a stretcher in the emergency room at the Anderson General Hospital. He tries to return to the dream, the airplane, the Netherlands, the tulips, me. But a cavernous throbbing in his chest, and an ice pick of pain in the centre of his face, blocks the way.

He pries his swollen eyelids open. The harsh light above the stretcher drills into his eyeballs. Billy closes his eyes, but the brightness—red with the blood of his shuttered eyelids—persists. He listens. Voices. Rubber-soled shoes squeaking on waxed tiles. A phone rings. These sounds reach his ears from far away, through a thick, cottony baffle.

Close by there is the sound of pen scratching on paper and a woman's voice, "Well, there you are, Billy." He recognizes the voice, but can't pair it with a face.

"Do you know who I am? Can you tell me how many fingers I am holding up?"

Billy slits a single eye open, long enough to ID Elaine Bisterquake, a grade or two behind him in school, his sister Mary's age. He's known Elaine most of his life. It was obvious to everyone, except Billy, that Elaine had a crush on him in high school.

He tries to say, "Oh, hey, Elaine." But his words are garbled, and speaking intensifies the twisting knife of pain at the centre of his face.

"Fingers?" she asks.

"Doo."

"Do you know what day it is, Billy?"

"Debens."

"I beg your pardon? Oh, *depends*. Depends on what?"

"Howong I 'een ou." Billy winces.

Elaine pauses to decipher his words, chuckles, looks at her watch and writes something on her clip board. "You've been in and out of it for a couple of hours."

Ursay?

"We have a winner," says Elaine. "Yep, still Thursday. You're a lucky man, Billy."

"I wa shod id da faith." Billy speaks carefully from the back of his throat, trying not to trouble his lips.

"Well, on the bright side, you could be dead. By luck or by crook, you just lost the tip of your nose. You're lucky to be alive, mister. Dr. Janzen thinks you might have had a wee little bit of heart attack though. A TCM. I forget what TCM stands for but sometimes a shock can stop the old ticker for a minute or two. Like, for example, if you got shot in the face," She chuckles again and smooths Billy's hair back from his forehead. "Not to worry. Still a good-lookin' guy. We'll know for sure about your heart when the blood work comes back."

Billy takes shallow breaths through his mouth. He tries out a tiny inhalation through his nose, and it feels like a white-hot rod of steel is being rammed up into his sinuses. His toes clench reflexively. He grips the rails of the gurney and sips air between his pursed lips.

"Do you need something more for the discomfort? Dr. Janzen will freeze you up before he stitches, but I can hit you with some Demerol if you need it." Elaine checks the round-faced clock on the wall of the examining room. "You know what? Probably a good idea. Get it going before Dr. Janzen starts poking around with a needle." She fills a syringe from an upturned bottle and injects the solution into the intravenous port taped to the back of Billy's hand. He feels the medication, like a cold creek trickling up his arm, a droopy numbness flows into his body. He thinks, *I could be dead in the Netherlands.*

- 39 -
BILLY BROUGHT BILLY

Billy is conscious, and again unsure about how much time has elapsed since Elaine doped him. Someone is holding his hand, the one without the IV port in it. He offers a weak squeeze to inform whoever's hand is holding his hand that he is alive. He's not yet an organ donor candidate. He's heard stories.

"It's Catherine, Billy. We're just waiting for Dr. Janzen." She releases his hand, and pats his arm. "I came as soon as I heard."

"You brought me here," slurs Billy. His lips and tongue feel numb and inflated. His mouth is dry as a toad. "You picked me up in your arms and..." He stops, hoping Catherine couldn't understand what he started to say. It sounds absurd—even to him—when he contemplates saying it out loud. He remembers it clearly, but it couldn't have happened: Catherine bursting into the kitchen, the sound of crunching glass beneath her boots, picking him up in her arms like a baby. He is tiny and she is big; a cinnamon-haired giant. He must have been dreaming, again or still. Thick liquid flooded his mouth and nose. He couldn't swallow fast enough. He was choking, drowning, but couldn't turn his face away from her freckled breast. He didn't want to. *It must have been the blood*, thinks Billy.

Like most dreams, it seemed real in the dreaming and impossible after waking. Also, like most of Billy's dreams, the emotions of it linger long after waking. Despite knowing the contents of the dream are impossible, it *feels* real. Obviously, Catherine didn't load him into the hearse, drive to the airport and kiss him on the lips before he boarded a flight for the Netherlands. The disturbing mixture of arousal and confusion, however, persists. As does the shameful eroticism of nursing at her breast like a toddler. *This is the preacher for God's sake!* No point denying those feelings though—even if denial has been his heretofore *modus operandi*—because even if he *chose* to lie to himself, the stirring of an erection beneath the sheet testifies to the truth. Billy decides it might be best to just sleep some more. So, he does.

- 40 -

THE DOOR CLOSED ON DICK SPANNER

Billy startles awake. Catherine is still holding his hand and he holds hers back. He tries to ask, *How did I get here?* but his lips are numb and his tongue flops in his mouth like a fish in the final throws of death.

"You're back," says Catherine. "You had a little nap."

He picks up the conversation where they had left off. "How did I get here?"

Catherine pauses to decode the sounds Billy is making, and then replies, "You apparently drove yourself to the hospital. It's lucky you didn't kill Mr. Spanner."

Billy rolls this information over the folds of his brain. *Wasn't it Dick Spanner, who had nearly killed him?* "What do you mean?" Billy struggles to harness his uncooperative lips and tongue.

"I guess when you swung out onto the road you drove across Mr. Spanner's yard and clipped his car door. He was getting in the car."

"The beside house," Billy words jumble. "Car."

"From what Elaine tells me, he was on his way to the hospital too, with a dislocated finger, when you hit him," says Catherine. "The door was open, and his leg wasn't in yet. Sounds like it got crushed pretty badly."

"He shot me in the face."

"True," says Catherine. "No one's saying you did it on purpose, Billy."

"How does it look?" Billy wants to know.

"Like I said, it's pretty bad. They're getting ready to fly him out."

"Not Spanner. My nose," says Billy.

"Your nose? It's covered up with gauze, but Elaine said," Catherine's searches for the most reassuring words, "uhm, she says it's not serious."

"What? What did say she?" Billy is frustrated by the effort of lining his words up in their proper order.

"She said it wasn't serious and, well, it doesn't look like much cartilage was lost. Which is a good thing," Catherine gives Billy's hand a reassuring squeeze, "but where your nostrils are ... I guess where they were ... may need a little touching up. They can't say for sure yet how much of your septum will..." she makes that the end of the sentence.

"What about Spanner?" asks Billy.

"Both bones in his lower leg are broken. They've sedated him because he was fighting them about being flown up to the Lakehead. Elaine says they can't deal with breaks like his here. A compound break? That's when the bones are through the skin, I think. He was screaming blue murder for them to just put a cast on, and let him go home. Probably just the shock talking. Sounds bad, though. Elaine said he'll likely need some plates and pins and traction."

Tibia and fibula, thinks Billy. He can hear a helicopter landing on the pad behind the building. A burst of air from its rotating blades push the swinging doors to the emergency room open a few inches. Cold air flows in the room and Billy pulls the thin blanket up over his shoulders. His feet poke out at the end of the gurney. Catherine tucks in the blanket around his feet.

She raises her voice above the noise of the helicopter outside. "They've got him pretty knocked down with drugs now, so he can't cause trouble on the flight."

"Maybe one of those tranquilizer darts, like Mutual of Omaha's Wild Kingdom." Billy's words are still stumbling out of his mouth like drunks after last call. They are drowned out by idling engines and the chop of the rotating blades. "I don't like that guy."

Elaine is back and telling Billy, "Dr. Janzen said that he'll be in to stitch you up as soon as he gets Dick squared away on the helicopter." She injects another dose of something into the IV port and it trickles up his arm.

- 41 -
BILLY GIVES HIS STATEMENT

Billy dreams that his nose has been transplanted with the snout of a pig. He is awakened by his own painful snort. Catherine is gone, and Dr. Janzen is stabbing a syringe into Billy's nose, working the needle around, distributing Lidocaine around the shredded tissue. Billy groans, but seconds later an anaesthetized vacancy empties itself into his face. He feels the lift and tug of each suture, hears Elaine and Dr. Janzen chatting, but can't sort out what they're talking about. *Are they flirting?* That might be the Demerol thinking.

Billy is, again, confused by the passage of time. Constable Ryan is tapping his shoulder. "You awake, Mr. Buffone? Doctor says you're okay to talk." Billy feels like he is waking from a restful sleep on a Saturday morning. Whatever he is getting for pain is doing its business. He yawns without moving his jaw and rotates his shoulders.

"Okay if I ask you a few questions, Billy?" asks Ryan.

Billy nods and tells Constable Ryan about the bear and the ravens scavenging in his neighbour's trash, and about the shooting, but not about Catherine driving him to the airport or the flight to the Netherlands. Ryan records Billy's version of events in a spiral-bound notepad flipped open on his knee. "Anything else?" Billy shakes his head; no. Ryan slips the notes into the chest pocket of his uniform jacket and buttons it closed. "If you think of anything else, Billy, give me a call. I'll leave my card here for you." He produces a card bearing the Twenty-Six Mile House Police Services logo, and sets it on the bedside table, next to the plastic water jug and cup.

Billy says, "Check inside the house, inside Spanner's house."

"Why do you say that, Billy? We collected the rifle as

evidence, and Mr. Spanner understands that he'll be charged at the very least, with unlawful discharge of a firearm within town limits. Probably reckless endangerment causing harm, too. Not sure there's any legal reason to turn his house upside down, though." That's what Ryan is saying, but he leans closer to Billy. He looks like he is hoping Billy can give him a legal reason to search. "Can *you* think of a reason, Billy?"

"Something bad in there."

"Can you be a little more specific?" asks Ryan.

Billy crosses his hands on his abdomen the way he places the hands of the deceased, and says, "It's a feeling I get."

"A feeling? Huh. I hear ya, Billy, but I can't take the heebie-jeebies to the JP for a warrant to search." Ryan teeter-totters his pen between his fingers, tapping it on the table top. He takes his lower lip between his teeth and sounds disappointed when he says, "Let me know if you can think of anything specific. Anything at all. Okay?"

"You've got a feeling, too," says Billy. "Isn't shooting me in the face a good enough reason to have a poke around inside?"

"I'll need you to sign your statement. Dr. Janzen says you're going home later on. So, I'll type this up," Ryan taps his jacket pocket, "and bring it by your place tomorrow, if that's okay with you."

On his way out of the room, Constable Ryan hesitates, patting the door frame like Detective Columbo used to—like he has just thought of one last question he meant to ask that will break the case wide open—but, having nothing more to ask, he leaves.

"Probably cause, that's what it's called. That's what you've got," Billy says to his empty room. "Probable not Probably. Cause."

- 42 -
CATHERINE BRINGS EASTER LILIES

Billy dozes, while his liver and kidneys filter the Demerol out of his blood. He wakes more alert, due in no small measure to a fresh buzz of pain in the middle of his face. The Lidocaine seems to have packed its bags and checked out. His eyelids are completely swollen shut. He peeks out between their gluey lashes. There are flowers on the counter beside the sink, white lilies, planted in plastic pot. Catherine is sitting beside the bed on a vinyl covered chair, one foot tucked beneath her. She is holding his hand. Billy grasps her hand before speaking, in case she pulls it away.

He carefully shifts his head toward her and asks "Did you bring me flowers?"

She shrugs, "Hope they're okay. It was lilies or a spider plant. The stores are all closed."

Billy tries out a diminutive smile, testing for pain. "I bet they smell good. Not that I can tell." Then he asks, "Closed?"

"Good Friday," says Catherine while checking her watch. "Service is at seven. Can I assume you're not coming?" She grins.

Billy realizes he's lost a day somewhere. Garbage day is Thursday.

"I forgot." The display of bunnies, chicks, and chocolate eggs at Steadman's Department Store has been up since Valentine's Day. Since then, he has become so desensitized by their constant presence, he lost track of the actual date of the Easter weekend. Store displays, Billy concluded, are increasingly less helpful landmarks for Christmas and Holy Week. Nor has there been any real climatological evidence for the arrival of Easter. Winter still has spring in a headlock. Billy, however, does remember the full moon on the night he found Clarence in the embalming room. *Paschal,* he thinks. *The Paschal moon. First full moon after something.*

"You don't go to church, Billy? Not ever? Not even on Christmas or Easter?" asks Catherine. She tries to convey genuine curiosity, rather than judgement. "Sorry. People assume I'm taking attendance, when I ask. I'm just genuinely curious, that's all. What about as a kid?"

"My mother and father were kind of Catholic, I guess. Italian, so Catholic or recovering. When we were kids, my sister and I went to St Luke's for Sunday school for a little while." The long sentence causes Billy to wince with another hive of stinging bees in the centre of his face, so he thinks, rather than say, *Our parents came to see us in the Christmas pageant.* He sips air through his clenched teeth.

"Well, the Good Friday service is tonight, and Easter is at eleven on Sunday. You'd be very welcome." Conversation over. She knows she sounds like someone trying *too* hard to keep it light.

"Elaine says you can go home whenever you're ready. I'll drive you."

Then, rummaging in her bag beside the chair, she grins and says, "I brought you another present."

- 43 -

BILLY COULD HAVE AN OPEN CASKET

For the first time ever, Billy is seated in the passenger seat of his hearse. Prior to getting in the car, he inspected the surprisingly minor dent in the bumper where he had allegedly crashed into Spanner's driver's side door. Billy braces his hand on the dash, and presses his foot down on an imaginary brake pedal. Catherine is behind the wheel.

Elaine insisted several times, that he "could *not* drive or operate heavy machinery of any kind" until the Demerol was completely out of his system. "That means *at least* 24 hours, Billy. Are you paying attention?" *Why did she sound so far away? Weird.*

So, it is Catherine who turns the ignition key—the key only Billy has previously turned—and levering the long-armed shifter—the lever which only Billy has ever levered—on the steering column from "R" and to "D." Driving, at the proverbial pace of a snail, she manoeuvres the vehicle through the parking lot. Billy wonders how stressful this drive would be without Demerol riding shotgun.

At the exit from the parking lot onto the street, Catherine punches the brake pedal a little too enthusiastically, and the car lurches to a stop. The rear end heaves upward, the front-end dips slightly, and the tires scrabble momentarily for traction on the sanded parking lot. A winter's worth of ice sanding has not yet been swept up. "Power brakes are a bit touchy," Catherine comments. She checks to her right for traffic. Then left. Then right again, as she was instructed to do in drivers' education back in Cleveland. She rotates the oversized steering wheel to the right, her hands gripping it at precisely two and ten o'clock. She pulls out onto Main Street and accelerates—Billy notes appreciatively—to a funereal pace. Still he remains vigilant, perched on the lip of the bench seat.

"It's only a couple hundred yards, Billy. Relax." Catherine rolls her eyes. Billy keeps his own, swollen eyes, trained on the road. "I've driven across Toronto, in a blizzard at night, during rush hour," she reassures him. "Pretty sure I can pilot this yacht up the street to your place in one piece." Catherine pets the steering wheel and adds, "Besides, even crashing into Mr. Spanner's car barely made a dent in this big ol' gal."

Billy lowers his hand from the dash to his lap, feigning a relaxed and confident demeanour, but continues to radiate tension like a tightly wound clock spring. His left hand rests on his knee ready to grab the steering wheel, should it become necessary to do so. He tries to whistle a happy little tune, but his upper lip is too swollen, and his mouth too dry.

Billy's kitchen is cold. The blind above the shattered window sways inward on the late morning breeze. Catherine locates his broom and sweeps up the shards of glass. She duct tapes a square of cardboard into the window frame. She makes chicken noodle soup from a can, and instant butterscotch pudding from a box. They eat the pudding first while the soup cools.

After they finish eating, Billy sits on the closed toilet lid in the bathroom, so Catherine can remove the gauze taped over his nose. Blood has soaked through the dressing, and the tape is no longer securing it in place. He is thankful to discover that Catherine is of the "pull it off slowly," rather than the "rip it off fast" persuasion, when it comes to Band-Aid removal. She drops the clotted dressing into the wastepaper basket.

Billy insists on examining the exposed injury in the mirror before she replaces the dressing. He flattens his hands on the counter and leans in for a close inspection. The end of his nose is puckered. The fine stitches—20 or 25 according to Elaine—are mostly hidden by scabbing blood. There is a thin glistening at the edges, and the scab appears to be drying nicely. Given what he had to work with, Janzen's done a respectable job.

Billy turns his head from side to side, looking out the

corners of his eyes, to assess the damage. About 80 per cent of his nose is still there—swollen, purple, green and brown—but attached to his face. His upper lip is bloated, fat as a sated leech. *With a little putty and proper make-up,* he consoles himself, *we could have an open casket.*

Billy pretends to be continuing to inspect his nose, so he can look at Catherine in the mirror behind him. Their eyes meet, and Billy flicks his gaze back to where the tip of his nose used to be.

"You know, it doesn't look that bad," says Catherine. "Once it heals, they'll send you to a plastic surgeon, for a little touch up. It'll be good as new."

"It's gonna look like a belly button in the middle of my face," says Billy. "Like where they cut the cord." Suddenly, the forgotten dream—about sitting next to me on the flight to the Netherlands—floods back into his pharmacologically addled mind. He pokes two fingers between the buttons of his shirt, probing for a scar left by our severed bond. He feels the pulse of his heart, beating steadily beneath his undershirt, but finds no scar.

"Are you okay?" ask Catherine.

"Good. Yep, I'm good."

"You're not having a heart attack? Denial is one of the common signs that you're having a heart attack, you know."

"Heart? No. *No!* I'm fine and I'm not in denial. I guess I'm just feeling... kind of disconnected." *Disconnected! Why did he say that?*

Catherine meets his eyes in the mirror. "Disconnected?"

"Not from you!" Embarrassed, Billy quickly retreats, "I don't know what I'm talking about. I think the drugs are still dumbing my brain. Sorry."

"I think you mean *numbing* your brain," smiles Catherine.

She looks away from Billy's reflection in the mirror and actually giggles. "You're something else, Billy Buffone. I look forward to someday figuring out what that something else is."

Billy wills himself to keep his mouth shut to avoid saying something he might later regret.

He turns around and sits back down on the toilet lid. Catherine sits on the edge of the bathtub, their eyes level, and their knees interlocked. She leans in close. *To kiss me?* thinks Billy. *No, Buffone, to patch up your face.* Billy wonders what her breath smells like. She tears open one of the paper envelopes of gauze. "Does it hurt a lot?" asks Catherine, leaning close for a better look. She drapes a doubled square of gauze over the end of his nose.

"They gave me some Tylenol 3s and something else," says Billy. He winces, in spite of her gentle application of the tape, fastening the gauze to his cheeks.

Catherine cups Billy's ears in her hands, to inspect her handiwork. She kisses him on the forehead. Her lips are warm and soft, and they linger a little longer than is medically necessary.

"Well, it's a miracle, really" she says, hands still holding his ears, "that you're alive. Think about it, Billy. Just think how much worse this could be? An inch this way or that?" Her voice trembles.

"Ya, without me around, who would put the fun in funeral?" Billy's laugh comes as a single hoot from the back of his throat, followed by a flinch of pain.

Catherine laughs, too. "Oh, we'd have to find someone, *to be the last person to put you down.*"

With that, Billy pulls a large Band-Aid coloured nose and moustache suspended from pair of plastic eye-glasses, from his shirt pocket. Caterpillar sized eyebrows perch on the top of the frames. He rests them across the bridge of his nose, and hooks the arms over his ears. He mimes a wagging cigar, "I plan to live forever, or die trying." He bobs his own eyebrows up and down above the glasses.

The nose and glasses are the other present—other than the lilies—Catherine brought to the hospital for Billy. She found them with the dress-up clothes in the tickle trunk, in the Sunday school cupboard at the church.

She brought them as a joke, a little levity after Billy's brush with mortality, but Billy insists with genuine gratitude, "I love these! They feel good, thanks."

Catherine laughs. "Well, they are quite becoming on you."

"No, seriously," Billy insists. "I mean it. They are great. I like them." And he's not just being polite.

"Billy, it was joke. You can't wear those around town. People will think you are... I don't know. Nuts."

"But I like them," he says. "They're like a nose shield." The prosthetic nose is like a clam's bone-case, protecting its gooey internal organ from seagulls. "Thanks. Seriously, they're great. What if I got stabbed in the face by a seagull's beak?" He taps a finger nail gently against the plastic, testing its protective qualities. "See, I barely felt that."

Catherine laughs louder, "Pecked by a seagull? Billy, seriously, you cannot wear them. It was a joke. People will think you've lost it. Completely."

But the plastic cup, combined with the gauze padding, provides Billy with a sense of security. It will shield him from any reflexive nose scratching on his part. Even the slightest stirring of air has, up until now, sent needles of pain radiating up into his nasal cavity and sinuses. "It's like a bandage, but stiff. Like an eye patch. A nose cast." He taps it again, testing.

"Okay, okay. At least let me trim them up a little. The mustache and eyebrows have got to go." Catherine carefully removes the glasses and heads into the kitchen, calling out as she goes, "And don't tell anybody you got them from me! Where do you keep the scissors?"

Billy, somewhat bewildered, trails into the kitchen after her. "I'm not sure. In one of those drawers on the right."

Catherine rummages in the top drawer and finds a pair. "The moustache looks ridiculous." She snips it off from beneath the nose. "It makes you look like Groucho Marx or Adolf Hitler. I can't decide which." The eyebrows are glued to the frames with rubber cement and peel off easily. She rubs the residual glue until it rolls into balls.

The freshly trimmed nose-shield back in place, Billy insists he will be fine on his own, and that she should attend to her

Good Friday worship preparations. He's taken too much of her time already. His sincere brown eyes peer from behind the glasses, which strangely accentuate his earnestness. Catherine kisses him on the forehead again, and then on his cheek, her nose brushing his sideburns and his ear. She covers him with the crocheted throw from the back of the couch, and leaves him resting on the couch in the kitchen.

He keeps the novelty nose in place while he naps. Should he roll over in his sleep, and press his face into the cushions—as is his habit—the prosthetic will fend off the resulting fiery swords of pain, and prevent any tearing of his sutures. Billy knows, from professional experience, there is not a lot of excess skin on a nose to stitch.

Catherine walks along the side of the road, back toward the hospital, to collect her car. Ernie Caird, chair of her property committee, slows his Buick and offers her a ride. She thanks Ernie enthusiastically, and waves him on, beaming a suspiciously radiant smile. Even Ernie, takes note of a fresh spring in Catherine's step. In spite of the overcast and gloomy Good Friday sky, Catherine skips along the side of the road like it's already Easter.

- 44 -
BILLY ALMOST GOES TO CHURCH

Billy is awakened from his nap by a snore that launches a torpedo of pain up his nose into his forehead. He runs his dry-as-a-lizard-tongue along his likewise reptilian lips. His upper lip is fat, and tight as a drum. He takes another Tylenol 3 to douse the tongues of flames licking the back of his eyeballs.

He refills the water glass, and gulps down what doesn't dribble off his chin onto his shirt. He decides that he better take one of those other tablets Elaine gave him. *What did she say they're called?* "Take these as needed," she said. He remembers that. "Something a little stronger for the pain, Billy." He definitely needs something a little stronger for the pain. He swallows one of the chalky tablets, but the pain continues to throb in his face. So, he takes another one. *As needed.*

Shortly thereafter, Billy starts to feel pretty darn good. *Probably survivor's high, post traumatic gratitude,* he thinks. *You walk away from a car crash, or dodge a bullet to the face, and you're bound to feel hyper happy, jazzed.* Strictly speaking, in Billy's case, it was a hit to the face, not a near-miss, but his thinking is a bit jumbled at the moment. He demonstrates just how jumbled his thinking is by deciding to attend Good Friday services at St. Luke's. He taps the plastic nose shield and thinks, *Damn, I feel good.*

Billy owns one suit. The morning suit he wears when directing funerals. It is a bit formal, even for Good Friday, and perhaps a bit morbid. His fellow worshippers might find the outfit disconcerting. *Don't want to freak anyone out.* So, he dresses in a white shirt, a striped tie, and pressed chinos. He brushes his hair and, ever so gently, his aching teeth. Bending over to tie his shoes boosts the blood pressure in Billy's head, activating a fresh round of stabs in the face, with each pulse of his heart. So, he slips one shoe on at a time, and then raises each foot onto a kitchen chair to tie the laces. Then, holding onto the edge of the table for balance, he gives each shoe a quick polish on the back of the opposing pant leg.

Billy checks the garage, but the van is still AWOL. Not that Billy expected to find it parked there, next to the hearse. It just feels like a long time—what with being shot and all—since he last verified the van's absence. He wonders once more about reporting the missing van to the police, and he wonders if he should report the missing Clarence, as well. Could he report one and not the other? If he did report, what exactly would he report? Missing person? Grand theft auto?

He decides to defer any and all reporting until after church. Maybe he will receive a message from God, some spiritually inspired wisdom about what he should do. "I'll keep my ears open, God." Surprised by the foreign sound of his own voice, Billy quickly searches the garage to be sure he is alone, to be sure it was him speaking. He finds no one hiding in, or behind, the hearse. *Don't be paranoid!*

Billy will ask God for the return of the prodigal Clarence. And the van. He puts his elbows on the hood of the hearse and presses his hands together to pray. *Please watch out for Clarence and bring him back face. I mead safe. Mean.* It will be an experiment, to test for the existence of God. *God, if you answer my prayer, if Clarence shows up in one piece with the van—also preferably in one piece, but this doesn't have to include the van. If Clarence shows up, I'll start going to church. I'll keep going for at least... for a least... let's say one year. Okay, two. Final offer. That's fair, right? If Clarence shows up face, I mean safe, and sound, I'll go to church for two years. And I'll believe you exist. Amen.*

Billy thinks he might have heard God reply: "As if I care whether or not you go to church." I can assure you, had it been Catherine hearing it, while writing in her journal, she would *definitely* have bracketed that phrase with quotation marks.

The analogue clock on the dash of the hearse seems brighter than usual. It reads 6:45 PM, when Billy pulls up to the curb in front of St. Luke's. The neon orange hands appear to be pulsing, as well as being super bright. Billy is wearing the lens-less glasses, plus the plastic nose, minus the moustache and eyebrows. He does the math—sum total negative one—and considers other life predicaments to which he could apply mathematical equations. His chin falls to his chest, his eyelids close, just for a moment.

His presence, and that of the hearse docked in front of St. Luke's, does not go unnoticed by the congregants arriving for Good Friday worship. Most of them double-take, smile, and wave. Generally, they are older, and numerically sparse. They climb the front steps, clutching the handrail, and disappear into the little church. Ernie Caird stops at the bottom of the steps to nod his toque-covered head sagely in Billy's direction.

They're not entirely surprised to see him there. Near death experiences have, on other occasions, temporarily bumped up their congregational membership numbers. A brush with mortality can induce religious sentiments in even the most recalcitrant backslider.

Word is also circulating that something might be going on with Billy and Catherine.

Beverly Anders and Connie Stinson, bundled in their parkas, come around the hearse, stand by the driver's door, and wait for Billy to roll down the window. "Would you like to come inside?" asks Connie.

"You would be very welcome to join us," adds Beverly, sounding strangely formal, given she has known Billy since he was born. Neither of them remark on Billy's nose and glasses, or his swollen upper lip. No need. They are fully apprised of the shooting, the splintered bones in Mr. Spanner's shin, the restraints required to fly him to Thunder Bay, and the beyond the call of duty pastoral care Catherine has extended to Billy. News travels fast in Twenty-Six Mile House, especially news involving shootings, and budding romances. It is doubtful that Billy—a key player in the aforementioned events—has an iota of useful detail to contribute to what Connie and Beverly have already gleaned via dependable networks.

They chat with Billy, as if the presence of the nose and glasses, and his apparent intention to attend worship, is just business as usual in Twenty-Six Mile House. No big deal. Just another Good Friday.

Billy is flustered by their hospitality, by their readiness to overlook what is as plain as the nose on his face. "Thanks, I think I'll uh," he stares out the windshield, "smoke a dart first." *A dart? Smoke a dart? Jesus. Who says 'smoke a dart?' Where did that come from?*

"Okay," says Connie, reaching her mittened hand through the open window to rest it on Billy's shoulder. She presses her lips in a straight line, gives a short nod, and squeezes his shoulder, meaningfully. One of Connie's go-to figures of speech is, "Keep a stiff upper lip." For obvious reasons, she doesn't say it to Billy.

"We'll save you a seat," says Beverly, which causes her and Connie to laugh, so that they have to wipe tears from their eyes.

Why are they laughing? What's so funny? Billy feels even more conspicuous, and preposterous, sitting in the hearse outside the church. He imagines everyone inside, including Catherine, laughing at him.

Billy's only real exposure to church has been for funerals, when attendance tends to trend high. He doesn't know that Good Friday congregations are comprised of the tiniest smattering of the remnant devout. Even Christmas Eve services—which used to pack the sanctuary well past regulatory fire capacities, chairs crammed into all three aisles, hundreds of candles burning in close proximity to highly combustible fur coats—no longer fills the pews. Lacking the good cheer and inebriation of Christmas Eve, Good Friday vespers are strictly the province of the devout, and the desperate, which is all to say, ninety-five per cent of the pews will be empty.

Which explains the ladies' mirth: "We'll save you a seat" is a joke. That is why Beverly and Connie are cracking up about holding a seat for you, Billy—to attend a service which commemorates a gruesome, bloody, and violent religious spectacle. Believe me, there is no lineup to get in. It wasn't that funny, and even less so after having to explain it. But it kills Connie and Beverly.

Billy, however, doesn't know this, and is busy battling his opioid-induced paranoia and parsing possible veiled meanings to Beverly's invitation. He watches them disappear into the church and checks his pockets for smokes. Of course, he doesn't have any. They are, as always, kept in his morning suit jacket. Funerals only.

He equivocates, one hand on the door handle, and the other on the transmission lever ready to vamoose. Go inside. Go away. At 7:05ish—the dashboard clock continuing to bedevil Billy's vision—Beverly pokes her head out the door. She offers a frenetic little wave. He smiles, winces and returns the wave. The door closes. *Deal's off, God.* Billy pilots the hearse away from the curb.

- 45 -
EPIPHANY AT THE INTERSECTION

Billy cruises aimlessly around town for half an hour before parking in the lot above Pebbles Beach. A misty film of ice particles smudges the horizon. That will likely change soon. A north wind is tipping the white caps backward off the tops of the swells. Snow is on its way.

A compact car is parked at the far end of the gravel lot. The windows are draped by condensation, but given the shadows within, and the motion of the vehicle, Billy assumes that the occupants are squeezed into the backseat. He considers fooling around with Catherine in the back of the hearse. It would be much more spacious, and private, than the cramped quarters of a car. The hearse has drapes. At thirty-two years of age, Billy has not fooled around with anyone, ever, anywhere... outside of his head.

Depressed by the certainty of coming snow and his virginity, Billy resumes his tour of town. He drives past the home where he grew up; past the unkempt house where my Dad now lives alone; past the houses with their brown lawns and NHL jerseys hanging on coat hangers in front windows, declaring allegiances to *Les Canadians*, or the *Bruins,* the *Oilers* or the *Maple Leafs.* The hearse rolls past the post office, past the hardware store—where I was last seen alive.

With no other logical destination in mind, Billy points the car toward home. A hearse, idling through town, is conspicuous. It gives people the heebie-jeebies, a hearse stalking the streets, like the grim reaper. It gives people the creeps, especially on a grey Good Friday.

Lost in his pharmacological fog, however, Billy glides right past the funeral home, up the hill, past the cemetery. He only appreciates that he has overshot the mark when he finds himself stopped at the intersection with the Trans-Canada highway.

It is here, idling at the corner—wondering whether to turn left or right or make a multi-point U-turn and head home—that Camp 12 Road pops, unbidden, into Billy's mind. Camp 12 Road is a decommissioned logging road. It has been almost entirely abandoned for more than a decade. The entrance to it is about five kilometres west of the turnoff to Twenty-Six Mile House. Camp 12 Road, up from town and down the highway, is at least a ten-kilometre drive. But, because of the way it curves sharply south and east from the highway, it doubles back close to town through the bush. Billy can picture it on the old forestry maps. Given the switch-back, it must come within a kilometre or two—as the crow flies—of his funeral home. A bush trail, from Camp 12 Road into town, would cross some rugged terrain, but if you knew where you were going, it would be a snap.

- 46 -
DOWN CAMP 12 ROAD

Billy, having deduced the relative proximity of the Camp 12 Road to town, is feeling smugly dismissive of Elaine's precautions against driving with the remnants of the Demerol on board. *And the other one. What's it called? I think this stuff might actually be making my mind sharper. Loosening my mind up. Did I take two or three T3s? Right. 3Ts, I took. Or was that other ones?* He drives five kilometres west, at fifty kilometres per hour, and turns left into the overgrown entrance to Camp 12 Road.

The moose population is sparse in the area. Hunters abandoned the road years ago. It affords access to a few shallow lakes, but they are stingy, and over-populated with saw-toothed jack-fish which have eaten all the pickerel. So, fishers don't bother with Camp 12 either. It attracts a birder or two each year, that's all.

Once upon a time, trucks, dozers, haulers, and skidders thundered up and down, clear cutting and transporting limbed timber to the mill. Graders kept Camp 12 Road smooth as pavement in those days. Fresh gravel was spread in the summer, and snow was plowed down to the hard pack all winter. The mill is mothballed, and forestry operations have moved on to more easily accessible wood fibre. A scrubby forest of poplar and black spruce has reclaimed the landscape. Nature is swallowing the road, narrowing it. What was once a thoroughfare now barely qualifies as a trail.

Billy yawns—tight-jawed in deference to his nose—and guides the hearse down the narrow passageway. He tries, without success, to circumnavigate potholes and rocks heaved up by freeze and thaw cycles. Leafless raspberry canes and red willow wands scrape along the side panels of the hearse. Billy shudders, and his grip on the steering wheel clenches with every screeching, paint-peeling branch, with every hammering of the undercarriage.

He decides, too late, to turn back. There is nowhere to change direction. He creeps forward, his foot riding the brake pedal, and watching for an opening in the trees big and flat enough to turn around. Eventually, having pushed deep into the woods, it also becomes impossible to reverse out. The turns are too tight, the ruts too deep, the laneway too narrow. He would just end up stuck in the mud or turtled on a rock. It's starting to get dark.

Dusk comes early among the dense stands of black spruce. Day fades, and exhaustion wraps itself around Billy like a blanket. The sleepless nights, and the long days that followed, are gaining on him. His legs and arms are heavy. He yawns, trying again to remember what Elaine said about how long it would take for the Demerol to be out of his system. He creeps further into the bush.

Billy finds the van parked in a patch of winter-flattened grasses. He pulls up behind it, cuts the engine, closes his eyes and leans back against the headrest. The scraping and bouncing and banging, and the clattering of his teeth and the concomitant whingeing, have intensified the throbbing in his face. He can feel the pulse of blood in his nose; can hear it surging in his ears. He empties the little paper envelope into his hand. He pops the last T3 into his mouth, intending to dry swallow it, like they do in the movies. His mouth though is dry as cotton and he can't work up a trickle of spit for the tablet to ride down his esophagus. The pill lodges in his throat and eventually dissolves there. He rests, just for a moment.

- 47 -
Trick or Treat

Billy wakes, confused and chilled. It is more night than day now.

He walks around the van, peers through the rear window. He leans in close and his nose guard taps against the glass. He sucks cold air between his teeth, and his toes curl inside his polished shoes. He should have worn boots. When he set out, he was on his way to Good Friday services, not a night in the bush.

The gurney is latched to the floor inside the van, where it should be. The cardboard carton of body bags and stay straps is there too. Billy half hopes to find Clarence sleeping on the stretcher. He cups his hands beside his face for a second look, just to be sure. Clarence is not there.

Billy circles the van, trying the door handles and—his shoes sinking into the mud—wishes again for his rubber boots. The doors are all locked. The keys, Billy can see, are dangling in the ignition.

Had Billy an operational nose, he would detect the scent of smoke drifting in the air, and the faint aroma of a nearby privy. Even without these olfactory clues, he easily discovers a path that can only lead to Mr. Martin's cave. The van is like the X on a pirate's map, pointing the way to buried treasure. Without the van, the otherwise unremarkable entry to the path would be easily missed. It could be disregarded as a game trail; an insignificant parting of the foliage by a fox or a lynx in its nocturnal hunt for voles or hares; a trail travelled by a creature less substantial than a bear or moose.

The path is less than fifty yards long. It is the sly turns and the stretches where it crosses naked granite, not the distance, that keeps the secret of its destination. A skiff of low mist hovers in the shallow dips along the trail. Billy's foot disappears into one of these depressions, and he is rewarded with a wet sock and a sucking shoe. Dead wildflower stalks and rosehip buds brush their wetness onto his trousers. Thistles—fiercely dedicated to dissemination of their progeny—hitch rides on the cuffs of his pants.

The path ends abruptly at the base of a cliff. A wisp of smoke drifts up the curving hill at the top of the rock face. Billy can hear the sound of running water. He locates a pipe, driven into a fissure, a few feet from where he stands. Spring water pours out, splashing onto a flat rock.

There is just enough light remaining to make out an oddly shaped wooden door, fashioned into an opening in the face of the cliff. It looks organic, as if it grew there. The frame and lintel are fitted into the exposed rock below the hill. The door is obscured by a fallen boulder, and by the bottom-most boughs of a stand of cedars. It is stout to the ground, like the entrance to a hobbit carpenter's shop. A seam of brass screws secures the upper and lower crossbars to the wider vertical planks. The wooden handle has been rubbed smooth by many years of use. There is a latch mounted on the outside of the door, allowing it to be secured with a padlock when the occupant is away.

Billy pulls off his glove and knocks on this door. He hears faint scuffling inside. The door cracks open, and a slice of Clarence's brown face appears in it. Seeing Billy, he pulls the door open, and light spills out into the darkness. Billy squints. Clarence scrutinizes Billy's plastic nose and glasses. "Aren't you s'pposed to say trick-er-treat?"

"I got shot in the face," replies Billy.

"Shot? Seriously?" says Clarence. "Jesus."

"Long story. Can I come in?"

Clarence nods. "Watch your head."

- 48 -
Inside the Cave

The cave is much larger than the elfin-sized door suggests. Inside, it is warm and dry. It looks to be an abandoned mine from the days when anyone with a pick axe, and a dream of striking it rich, could stake their claim.

An old Coleman naphtha-gas lamp hangs on a chain, bolted into the cathedral ceiling. The lamp hisses, and casts a yellow light onto the rock walls. There is coffee perking on a pot-bellied stove. The stove's chimney is elbowed, and wedged up into a high fissure. A stack of split firewood is at the ready next to the stove. There is a wooden chair and a table. A black bear hide is draped along the back of a low sofa. Vintage soda crates and a military footlocker serve as shelves and cupboards. The stacked crates are provisioned with tins of Klick, corn, peas. Gallon-sized pickle jars are hand-labelled Ries, Zucker and Mehl. Two moose hides carpet the stone floor, one by the stove and the other in front of the couch. There is a transistor radio on top of a crate, its wire antenna snaking up alongside the chimney into the crevice.

There is a sleeping loft—more nest than bed—on a ledge at the back of the cave. A pile of grey, wool blankets are spread on a mattress of cedar boughs. A soda crate serves as a step up to the ledge, no doubt a concession to age by Edison Martin.

"Coffee?" Clarence offers. "Just made it." Without waiting for a reply, Clarence fills a tin cup from the pot. "Sit down." He motions toward the couch with the cup and sets it down on the footlocker. "Careful. It's hot. Your lip looks pretty sore."

Clarence pours a cup for himself, and sits on the chair, facing Billy across the footlocker. "You want some fry-Klik and bannock?"

Billy raises his mug, "No thanks. I'm good." He sounds like a man suffering a severe cold.

They blow across their cups and sip coffee. The firewood in the stove snaps and, like the silence, radiates companionable warmth.

Clarence asks, "So, ah, what's up with the nose?"

"Dick Spanner shot me in the face," Billy shrugs, "Pretty sure, not on purpose."

"Huh," says Clarence. "I guess you're pretty lucky then."

"Lucky? I got shot..." Billy stops and changes track, "You took my van."

"Sorry about that. I figured you wouldn't mind. I wasn't gonna keep it. You can have it back."

"Thank you. You could have left me a note or something, Clarence."

"It was kind of spur of the moment. I was heading to Granny's place, but I changed my mind at the corners—hung a left instead of a right and came back here."

"Chickened out."

"I guess," Clarence concedes.

"The keys," Billy points out, "are locked inside the van."

"Ah huh. That's how come I didn't bring it back yet. You got some more keys, eh?"

"At home."

"We're good then, eh?"

Billy can't think of anything else to say on the matter of the van. So, he says nothing.

"I'll help you bring it back dude, relax."

"Then what?"

"Then what what? What d'ya mean, then what?"

"You know what I mean." Billy looks down and discovers he can see his distorted reflection, mirrored on the surface of the coffee in his cup.

"You mean, am I going back? Back to my granny's and the rez, where everybody hates my guts, but—to my face—they'll pretend they don't? Where everyone knows I'm a jack-off who got his brother—the good brother—killed, because I parked on the wrong side of the road to climb up the fucking Crack—a total fuck-up now and forever, but they won't say it? You mean that, *then what*?"

By the time Clarence has finished his tirade, his face twists with pain, with self-hatred. His words ricochet, sharpening themselves on the stone walls. Saliva sprays from his mouth. Then he sobs, covering his face with the pulled-up front of his T-shirt.

Billy puffs his cheeks, cautiously releases the air between his swollen lips and sighs, "Not exactly, but something like that. Dumb question."

Clarence bends forward, drops his head between his knees and clutches the medicine pouch hanging from his neck. He flattens the palm of his hand on the stone floor. He murmurs, repeating the words, "Grandfather, Grandfather, Grandfather." Ghosts of past failures enter the cave, skittering, like feral creatures, in the shadows cast by the yellow light.

Billy reasons with Clarence, "This is no life." He indicates the cave with his mug, but Clarence does not raise his head, does not look up. Billy can't tell if Clarence hears him, can't tell if he has gone somewhere far away. That's what Billy would do, but he persists with Clarence anyway. "You want to live the rest of your life all alone, like Mr. Martin?" Billy raises his voice, "By yourself? Hiding out here like a lonely old hermit? That's not going to bring Gilbert back. It won't make anything better for your granny. It takes more guts to keep living than it does to give up. This," Billy's voice quivers with emotion, the last drops of his coffee splashing from the cup shaking in his hand. "This is for cowards." He surprises himself, by the anger in his voice.

"Don't talk to me about fucking guts, Billy." Clarence— growing accustomed to Billy's glasses and plastic nose—sits up and locks eyes with Billy. "Everybody knows about your friend Matt Collins, and about you, Billy. About *Churley's boys*. And what happened." Clarence throws down the gauntlet, countering Billy's advice. There is venom in his voice. "What that... that pervert did to them and how Matt—*your best friend*, Billy— killed him and then killed himself. People talk on the rez. They say that's when you checked out, when you left town, and never came back. They say you disappeared but didn't go anywhere. They say you were maybe there. The Elders say you are a ghost walker. They can see through you. Like you're here and you're not here. So, don't talk to me about being a fucking hermit. At least I would still live in my own skin. Your friend hacks a guy's head off, jumps in front of a train, and you been living some-place else ever since. Fuck you, Billy. You only relate to dead people, and their friends, dude."

"You don't know what you're..." Billy is flustered by the nearness to the truth in Clarence's accusations. He stops and starts again. His heart is hammering. His voice shudders. "*I* know this much—and you're right, I do live in a cave in my head," Billy thumps his chest, rummaging for words. "It won't, *this* won't," he flails his arms around at the interior of the cave again, throwing the tin cup onto the floor, "this, this punishing yourself is not going to get Gilbert back. I can guarantee you that. Believe me, I know what I'm talking about." His eyes sting with tears, and he doesn't try to hide them by looking away.

"You. Can't. Even. Say. His fucking name," Clarence shakes his head. "*Matt Collins!* Let's all say it Billy, Matt Collins. Matt Collins! He must a been a helluva guy."

Billy, spits back, "Coward!" and is rewarded by a fresh stab of pain to the face.

Clarence counters, "ME! ME! Fuck you! Coward!"

"CHICKEN!"

"PUSSY!"

"Loser."

"Dickweed."

"Fuck it."

"Shit."

They sit, staring down at their feet, for a long time, chastised by their own childishness. Light from the lamp glistens on their wet cheeks. The air begins to cool. Clarence lifts the round lid off the stovetop and drops in a few splits of wood. The fire pops and crackles back to life. The stove iron heats and pings, radiating warmth into to the room.

Billy unzips his parka and smooths his necktie. He sighs, "Matthew Collins. His name is Matthew. Was Matthew. I can say it. And he, Matthew, would tell me, 'Don't waste your life. Don't waste my death.' If he was here that's what he would say, but he's gone and I'm not."

Of course, I am indeed here, but I am denied, by death, the capacity to speak for myself, but Billy's not far off on what I would say to him, if I could.

"He would say the same to you, Clarence. So would Gilbert. Don't waste your life. That won't bring him back, and life is too short, too precious to waste. Take it from me. I know. I'm an expert. My life, the way I live, the way I *don't* live it, is a blasphemy to Matthew's death." Over the years Billy has offered this similar, but less personalized, advice to the bereaved, but his words never sounded as true to him as they do now.

"It's different," says Clarence, "it wasn't your fault, Billy. It's not the same. What Matt, what Matthew did, he did it to himself. That wasn't your fault. You didn't cause it. It's not the same. I did it. It's *my fault* Gilbert is dead. *I did it.* I parked where I parked." Elbows on his knees, he presses his forehead against the heels of his hands.

Billy opens and closes his mouth. Stops and starts several times to say something, teeters on the cusp of admitting the truth. Then he says simply, "Gilbert's gone and you are here. Those are the shitty facts, Clarence. That's the deal. He died. You lived. You live. You'll never be the same. Not ever. Trust me. But you've gotta choose. Like I said, it takes guts to keep living. It takes more courage to live—and I'm not saying I've got that kind of courage. But I know, the real cowards are the ones who bail."

At this point, in Clarence and Billy's conversation, I lean closer. Is Billy proffering advice for Clarence, or is he talking about himself? Or venting at me, the one who bailed? Are his accusations of cowardice mine to wear like a coat of shame? Billy seems confused as me on this count, as well.

Clarence says, "Guts like you?" His voice compassionate now, kind. All the hot air is gone out of both of them.

Billy raises his hands, defeated, "I've been a coward and ungrateful. Guilty as charged." It is a confession: *Bless me Father for I have sinned.* What else is there left to say? There is no excuse for his rejection of the gift of my death. He has refused my sacrifice. "I guess, I want you to do better than me, Clarence; want to see you open the door of sadness, instead of locking yourself inside it. Like I did."

They are quiet, both of them taken up with failure. Finally, Clarence chuckles and declares, "Well, we could *both* stay here, if you want, Billy."

- 49 -
LET'S SPEND THE NIGHT

"You wanna head back?" Clarence asks. He and Billy are peering out through the diminutive door, into the night. The lamplight behind them flings their shadows out onto the ground. The luminosity spilling from the cave splinters among the cedar boughs. Dense cloud cover obscures the light of the stars and moonbeam. The blackness of night pushes back against the feeble light, so much so the light seems to be retreating into the cave. Billy's and Clarence's meagre candle is no match for the dark, bearing down on the forest on nights like this.

Billy squints, but can't make out a single shape beyond the cedar boughs. "I don't think we could find the cars, let alone drive out." Just the thought of crashing nose-first into the trunk of a tree, or taking a twig to one of his swollen eyes, sends a stab of pain rocketing up into his forehead. Even if they found their way to the vehicles, they likely will destroy the hearse trying to get to the highway. "Could you?"

Clarence considers it. In the past, he's picked his way along this path by moon light, but not on a blacked-out night like this, not without a flashlight. The batteries in Martin's old torch are long dead. "Probably not."

"We'd end up lost in the bush all night," says Billy. Clarence nods, and latches the door closed. They agree to wait out the night, and leave in the morning.

Clarence twists the slotted key around a tin of Klick, slices the meat onto a dollop of lard already sizzling in the frying pan. He mixes flour, more lard and salt in an empty coffee can for bannock, and drops spoonfuls of the batter into the spattering grease with the Klick. "Wish we had some baloney."

He divides the bannock and fried Klick into two portions, and passes one to Billy on a metal plate. Clarence eats from the frying pan. They split a can of tinned peach slices for dessert. Clarence drinks half of the peach syrup and passes the tin over to Billy. "That's okay," Billy declines, "you have it."

The food, the drugs, the drive, being shot in the face, the insomnia, all drop down on Billy like a felled tree. His head wobbles on his neck. His body tips over on the couch. He stretches out on his back and stuffs his hands into the pockets of his parka. His muddy shoes, still on his feet, stick out over the end of the couch. He's too tired to take them off. Clarence spreads the bear hide from the back of the couch over Billy. On his tiptoes, Clarence stretches up and extinguishes the lantern. Billy is deep in sleep, and snoring through his open mouth, before Clarence has rolled himself into the blankets on the sleeping ledge.

It's difficult in a cave to know when its morning. Clarence wakens first. He opens the door, admitting a wash of thin grey light and a cold draught of air. The wind is coming hard from the north now, clattering leafless tree branches like bones, the spruce needles and cedar boughs are humming an ominous tune.

Billy pulls his arm out from beneath the bearskin to consult his watch. It is after ten already. He can't remember when he last slept so soundly, or for so long at a stretch.

His nose feels like two bees stinging around under the bandage. In other words, there has been a remarkable improvement since yesterday. Healing is underway. He adjusts the plastic nose and rolls cautiously onto his side. The thin light and cold continue to leak into the cave, while Clarence pulls together a weather report.

The door closes, and darkness is restored. Billy can hear Clarence adding wood and stoking the stove.

"Looks like winter's not done," says Clarence in the dark. Billy recognizes the sound of the brass plunger pressurizing the lantern. Clarence counts twenty pumps, then opens the valve, and scrapes a match on the striker. The single match lights up the cave. The mantle pops, and Billy has to shield his eyes against the sudden light.

"Temperature's dropped and the wind is outta the north. It's gonna snow. Probably, a lot. Believe it. We better get going," says Clarence. "Or plan on being stuck here for a few more days."

Clarence takes the time, though, to boil some coffee. They finish the leftover bannock, dipping it in the reheated pan of Klick fat and lard. When they're done eating, Billy helps Clarence set things in order. He spreads the bear hide neatly on the couch, scrubs the dishes with a spray of cedar and a pot of water heated on the stovetop. Clarence is dampering down the fire, when he asks, "Billy, don't tell anyone about this place, where it is? Okay?"

"Okay."

"I guess the preacher, and the girl, Monica, know about it."

"Catherine. Not *where* it is, but about it, yes." says Billy.

"Martin was a good guy," says Clarence. "I think maybe he used to be a bad guy, but he got good, out here. He was always kind to me and Gilbert. Anyway, I might need to come back here sometimes."

"Okay," says Billy. *Maybe I'll need to come here sometimes too.*

- 50 -

BACK AND FORTH AND BACK AND FORTH

Clarence and Billy spent the remainder of the day floor-pan-pounding, and paint scraping the hearse, up and down Camp 12 Road to retrieve the van. First, they drove into town to collect the spare key to the van. They bounced their way back down the road, only to discover that the van battery was dead. By this time, it was starting to snow.

"I mighta left the lights on," Clarence allowed. "I was pretty upset when I got here."

They drove back up the road and into town to get Billy's jumper cables. They went back and forth and back and forth—on the road, and in their resolve.

By the time Clarence pulls the van in to the garage next to the hearse, it's after four o'clock and snowing hard. Slabs of wet snow slide off the vehicles, and puddle on the cement floor. A fierce wind rattles the closed, aluminum garage door.

"We better drive this," says Billy as he inventories the hearse's paintjob, scourged by the lash of branches and brambles.

"Sorry about wrecking the battery," says Clarence.

"It's not wrecked. It'll be fine," says Billy. "I just want to get it fully charged before taking it too far."

Clarence trails Billy into the funeral home. "It's coming down pretty bad out there. You know, maybe we should wait? Go tomorrow?"

Billy ignores Clarence's procrastination, pulls on his boots and trades his gloves for the beaded mittens Etoile Pelletier made for him after her father's funeral. He stuffs a toque into his coat pocket and notices Clarence's Blackhawks cap. "You want a warmer hat?"

"I'm good, but the storm. Seriously, maybe we should wait? You think?"

"Your granny's been waiting too long already. She needs you there, needs you with her. You want me to call ahead, or surprise her?" asks Billy.

Clarence blows out his cheeks and says, "Surprise. I guess. You can be the Easter Bunny and I'll be the cracked egg."

- 51 -
BILLY'S FALL FROM SPACE

Clarence's return could not be a more prodigal event had there been a fatted calf to slaughter, robes to wrap around his shoulders, and rings to put on his fingers. It is a tearful, happy, and bittersweet affair. Florence and Bernadette's home inhales relief and joy, and exhales sorrow, like it had been holding its breath with the sisters.

Clarence's brother's name—Gilbert's name—and the heart-wrenching fact of his eternal absence, are left unspoken, for now. What needs said about Gilbert will be said, in the morning and on many mornings thereafter. There will be endless days to bear the weight of their shared grief for him. He is tangibly present in their sorrowful smiles, in the softness of their eyes. What else could be said, could speak so eloquently? On nights like this, words are insufficient in any case, to carry the burdens of remembering.

Florence heaves a roasting pan—filled with bubbling moose stew, and capped with dumplings—from the oven. Clarence sits in his place at the table, the place where he sat as a little boy. The women insist that Billy stay and eat stew and dumplings before heading home. Bernadette pulls a chair up to the table for him, next to Clarence. Gilbert's absence is acknowledged, by the empty chair across the table.

"I knew you would find our boy," Florence says to Billy, while wrapping her arms around Clarence from behind his chair, stretching to rest her chin on the top of his head, inhaling the smokiness of the cave lingering in his hair. He smells of wood smoke, forest, of fried Klick and bear hide. All comforting odours that settle her soul.

Bernadette dishes stew into a bowl for Billy. "We knew you would bring him home today. That's why we got the stew ready." She fills a bowl for Clarence. "We'll go to Easter Mass in the morning. Everyone will be so relieved to see you alive! There is too much dying here." Clarence closes a hand around his medicine pouch, silently asking the Creator for courage to face his community, courage to accept the forgiveness he knows they will offer. "Chief says she'll ask the Elders about hosting a healing ceremony for you, at the Turtle Lodge."

The kitchen is warm and steamy from cooking. Rivulets of moisture trickle down the insides of the window panes, like tears.

At the door, after supper—her arms wrapped around Clarence—Florence says, "I knew you'd find him for us, Billy. Now you've got to find yourself."

Billy had known, that first morning with Florence at the funeral home, that something cosmic had come knocking on his door, and it would lead him to Clarence. He sensed, though he did not understand, that Catherine was part of this journey of searching and finding. But time passed, and doubt seeped in, leaking second thoughts and arguments anchored to things like logic and rationality into his certainty. He kept looking anyway. What was the alternative? All other options, felt flat and two dimensional, felt too small and cowardly. Clarence was missing and found, and missing and found again. That's how life goes.

Now Florence is opening a door to a more terrifying possibility, one he had not considered—finding the self he had lost. A blizzard raged outside. On any other night, Florence would have insisted he stay put. It was dangerous, even foolhardy, to set out in a storm like this, but she knew it couldn't be helped.

Fat flakes of snow ride in on the gale-force winds from the north. Ferocious gusts of wind thump the panels of the hearse, push it sideways. Whiteouts obscure the road.

In 1969, Billy and I watched Neil Armstrong's one small step on the moon on their black and white television. The broadcast pre-empted *The Flintstones*. We watched the full three hours. We ate dinner on TV trays, and watched. Mr. Buffone used a full 36 shot roll of film, taking pictures of the television screen. I can't remember if the pictures turned out when he had them developed. I slept over at the Buffone's place. Billy and Mary and I stayed awake late, marvelling at what we had witnessed. When Armstrong planted the American flag in the monochromatic dust of the moon, everything appeared to be so still, so quiet up there in outer space.

Tonight it is more like the *SS Enterprise*: William Shatner calmly issuing orders as imminent destruction raced toward them. "Activate Navigational Deflectors, Sulu." A billion meteors fly at warp speed towards Billy's Star Ship. He pilots it through a maelstrom of snowstroids, swarming in his head-lights, exploding against the windshield.

Billy grips the steering wheel like he is hanging from it. The snow is falling in thick clumps. The hearse bucks, plows, drifts, skids, and sinks in the snow. Late spring blizzards, on the north shore of Superior, bring battering winds, and heavy, mois-ture-laden snow.

It takes nearly forty minutes for Billy to crawl the hearse up to where the Pickerel River road and the highway intersect. The wiper blades shovel side to side across the windshield, unable to keep pace with the falling snow. Billy leans forward in his seat and squints out into the pelting abyss. There aren't any tire tracks packed in the snow on the highway for him to follow. No other vehicles have passed this way. The police have likely closed the road at Twenty-Six Mile House all the way to Wawa, maybe as far down as the Sault. There is no way for Billy to know.

He decides to have a closer look before deciding to push on, or to backtrack to the reserve. He zips his parka up, pulls his toque down over his ears, puts on Etoile Pelletier's mittens. Billy lifts the door handle and the wind whips the door from his grip, as if to hurl it spinning into the woods. The snow is so deep that it pours into the car, onto the floor mats.

Outside, Billy leans into the door to close it. He spreads his feet, steadying himself against the car for balance. Snow spills over the top of his boots, packing around his thin socks and numbing his ankles. His pants flap around his legs like flags in a hurricane. He turns his back to the wind to pull his hood up and tie it around his face. Needles of ice tick at the plastic nose and sting his cheeks. He tents his mittens over his mouth so he can breathe. *Jesus, it's April!*

The hearse's headlights penetrate only a metre or two into the storm before bouncing back off the swirling wall of whiteness. The buffeting air causes Billy's eyes to run with tears. His long eyelashes clump with snow, freezing them together.

He wades to the rear of the car to see if turning back might be the lesser evil. The tail lights are cups of red, in an otherwise black and white universe. His tire tracks have already blown in, erased in the few short minutes since Billy stopped.

He leans back against the hearse, imagining being lost in space, the sole survivor of a failed intergalactic expedition. Abandoned on a hostile planet, battered by its pernicious lunar winds. The story of the brave astronaut will become legendary. His body wants to lay down in the snow and sleep.

Instead, he struggles back inside the warmth, and provisional safety, of his craft. His coat and pants are sloppy with wet snow. He brushes it from his shoulders. Tipping it out of his hood, it ends up sifting down into the back of his sweater. He shakes the snow from his toque onto the floor on the passenger side.

The rearview mirror is black as coal. To the front, the blizzard continues to riot in his headlights. Billy enumerates his choices: go back, go forward, stay put. Staying put seems the simplest option, the least demanding, like not having to make a choice. "Not choosing," his father was fond of saying "*is* to choose."

Billy leans close to the windshield, his prosthetic nose hovering above the steering wheel. He shifts into drive and lightly touches the gas pedal. The rear tires spin. The hearse remains stationary. Billy wishes he had a three-hundred-pound cadaver in a hardwood box in the back, for traction.

He shifts to "R" and then to "D" and then to "R," rocking the vehicle, inch by inch until he's packed a short runway in the snow. The car, finally, begins to slide around the corner onto the highway. The tires spin and speedometer needle swings wildly up and down, between ten and eighty miles per hour. The back end of the hearse fishtails, and Billy begins his assent up the first hill toward Twenty-Six Mile House.

He calculates the general trajectory of the road, based on the location of the rock cut to his right, estimating the width of the ditch, and adds a few metres to account for the shoulder's approximate distance from the ditch to the rock face. He steers a course along this line of reference. At normal highway speeds, it takes about five minutes to climb this first hill. Tonight, it takes Billy a white-knuckled twenty.

The rock cut disappears at the top of the hill, where it crests. Based on the absence of the rock cut, and his inner gyroscope, Billy concludes that he has begun his descent. Without the familiar landmarks, however, he can neither confirm nor deny that this descent is taking place on or off the highway. Billy has often mused in the past, "I've driven between Pickerel River and Twenty-Six Mile House so many times, I could do it with my eyes closed." Turns out he can't.

The terrain levels out. Whiteouts continue to obliterate all points of reference as to the whereabouts of the road and ditches. The bush line is cut so far back from the highway that it is no help in land marking the road. "Okay Billy-boy, it's all downhill from here." This is what he tells himself, and it's true, but he has well-founded doubts about finding the turnoff, let alone maintaining control of his two-tonne vehicle, as it careens down the hill into town.

His anticipatory worries are circumvented by a more immediate calamity. The snowflakes whirling like dervishes in the low beams hypnotize Billy, and confound his perception of depth. That, and a misremembered curve in the highway, conspire against him. Billy continues straight when he should curve left. The front left corner of his bumper clips the leading end of a guardrail hidden beneath the snow. This guardrail was installed to mark the curve in the road that Billy has missed. On the other side of the guardrail lurks a substantial ditch into which Billy is crashing. Even at fifteen miles an hour, a hearse can plow a long way down into a deep, snow packed, gully.

The crash is like a diving submarine. The hearse submerges into the water—water crystallized to snow. A wave crashes up the hood and over the windshield. Billy is no longer in space. He is falling from the sky, and splashing down into an Arctic sea. His space capsule has become a diving bell, coming to rest at the bottom of the ocean.

Billy reflexively pulls up on the handle, to open the driver's door. Even as he's doing it, he knows it is a futile enterprise. The door budges an inch, maybe two, against the snow that is cemented against it by the impact. He winds the window halfway down. In the glow of the car's dome light, Billy pats the wall of packed snow with his mitten.

He considers using the windshield brush to dig his way out. Then what? Climb up into a blizzard and start walking? In what direction? It's ten kilometres to safety, in either direction, and no one else is coming along the highway to rescue you.

People, in shock, behave irrationally. They panic, endangering themselves and others. They stumble from their crashed cars, for example, out onto the highway, only to get run over. They jump out of the boat to rescue a loved one, fallen overboard into the water, and double the drowning, even though a rope or a lifejacket was within easy reach.

Billy has undertaken their funerals. He is no match—and he knows it—for the snow pressing the door closed, trapping him inside. The snow is burying the car, burying him in it. He is no match for the snow or the panic pressing in on him.

In spite of the storm, the radio has excellent reception. Alone is playing. Billy—like Ann Wilson, Heart's lead singer—can hear the ticking of the clock and hopes the night won't end alone.

Billy sighs, "Perfect." He flips the radio off. It would be a great soundtrack for one of his fantasies, an escape hatch into his imaginary life. Not tonight. Tonight, his fantasies feel ridiculous, like they always were.

Billy has also buried people who unintentionally asphyxiated themselves trying to stay warm in their cars or trucks. No need to run a hose from the exhaust to the driver's side window or roll a blanket along the bottom of a garage door. The seal of snowpack could be just as lethal. He turns the key and the engine falls silent. To conserve the battery, he shuts off the dome and dash lights.

There is a quilted blanket, like the ones used by moving companies to protect furniture from scratches, in the back of the hearse. When Billy has the sad task of transporting two caskets together, he drapes the blanket between them so they don't ruin the finish. He crawls over the seat, feeling around in the dark for the blanket.

Back in the front, Billy rolls up in the blanket, like a worm in a cocoon, and flops across the seat. He tugs his toque down to his eyebrows, taking care not to bump the nose shield. The blanket, closed over his head, traps the warmth of his body and breath. He hugs himself, his mittens under his arms, and his knees drawn up to his chest. The storm above is almost inaudible, here at the bottom of the sea. Silent as a tomb.

THE UNDERTAKING OF BILLY BUFFONE

Alone in the hearse, beneath the snow, Billy is hectored by memories. He's got nothing with which to hold them back. He can't seem to conjure a potent enough fantasy with which to whitewash the badgering images of that last summer, that last night. There is no situational song appropriate to his circumstance to hum. No rock and roll loud enough to fill the silence that interrogates him, demanding he confess, at least to himself. Billy's magic tricks have lost their mojo.

He watches it all unravel from above, sees himself, like he is someone he used to know. He is a character in a gruesome story he heard a long time ago. A once familiar but forgotten teenaged boy, a distraught adolescent, is furiously cranking the pedals of a ten-speed bicycle. The chain whirs, propelling this boy along the highway. His forearms and calves are summer brown, their muscles cabled by exertion. His hands grip the curved, taped racing bars.

Those must be someone else's hands, that body a stranger's body. This is some other boy who Billy is watching. A boy Billy could have never possibly been. He must be a boy Billy dreamed. It can't be him.

At the boat launch, this not-Billy boy crushes the brake levers and the bicycle's rear tire skids sideways in the dirt. The boy can smell the scent of August—dust, lake, fish, 40:1 gasoline to oil mixture—floating on the warm breeze. He hears water, lapping up against the aluminum boats, hears the waves knocking them against the old tires tied to the dock.

He dismounts the still rolling bicycle, letting momentum carry it into the brush beyond the boat launch at Birch Lake. He stows his backpack—provisioned with two days of food, by his mother—in the bushes, where the bicycle tips over. He scavenges among scrubby bushes and tall grass, looking for a canoe. No one locked their houses in Twenty-Six Mile House, and they don't chain and padlock their canoes at Birch Lake.

The boy finds a fibreglass canoe and drags it down to the water. The canoe is green and patched in places. A set of paddles is secured with bungee cords up under the seats—at the ready for a quick paddle out onto the lake for an evening of fishing. He slips the bow into the low chop and starts up the lake, towards Churley's camp. It is just past noon. Paddling solo, it will take at least two hours, maybe more, depending on wind direction and waves.

✆

Billy rests the paddle across the gunnels, and coasts to shore, just south of Churley's camp. He rolls the canoe up onto his shoulder, and carries it up onto the beach at Spanner's camp, next door to Churley's. Normally, like anyone else, Billy would just drag the canoe up on shore, but today he carries it, so there is no possibility that the sound of the hull skidding across the sand will carry through the woods. He hides the canoe in some tall beach grasses.

There are two freshly caught pickerel on a stringer anchored to a rock in the shallow water. The steel clips are set in through the gills and out their mouths. The fish swim listlessly, heads weighed down, tipping on their sides, revealing their smooth white bellies. Startled by the presence of the fish, Billy spins toward Spanner's camp, looking to see if it is occupied. It appears to be empty. The windows are shuttered with nailed plywood, loose shingles curl on the roof, aspen saplings have overtaken the yard. Billy decides to take the fish, for his mother, when he leaves. That's as far as his planning goes, just that he will bring the fish home.

He wades around the rocky outcrop separating Spanner's beach from Churley's. The water is clear and late summer warm. He stands for a moment, watching a school of minnows swim around his shins. At the tip of the point, the lake bottom becomes muddy. It sucks at his running shoes and turns the water the colour of tea. A water bug skates ahead of him on the surface of the lake.

He scampers low, up onto Churley's beach, and sits down behind an upturned boat, to empty his shoes and wring the water out of his socks.

The late afternoon sun is diffuse in a sky, the faint blue pallor of skim milk. Deerflies buzz around Billy's head and unprotected legs. One lands on the back of his neck and bites. To avoid the clap of a slap, Billy raises a hand, stealthy as a cat, and rubs the fly to death against his skin.

Kneeling on the far side of the wooden boat, Billy scoops out enough sand to squeeze himself under the gunnel. He will wait under the boat. He isn't sure what he is waiting for, not yet. To confirm his suspicions? To confront me? To rescue me? He is waiting for dark—that much he knows—when he will be able to see without being seen.

The hollow boat amplifies sound. Our drunken shouting up at the camp is, paradoxically, both muffled and amplified. Billy can hear everything. He hears a door slam. Someone vomits over the porch railing. It might be Anthony. He hears us roaring, and pounding our fists on the tabletop, when Larry is the first to forfeit his underpants in a round of strip poker. One of us weaves down the rotting steps to take a piss—so close that Billy can smell the stink of urine mingling with scent of the rotting boat.

Billy—still without a plan—remains hidden under the boat, long past the time when night has drained all the light from day. He feels a spruce beetle crawl over his hand in the dark and shivers, but lets it be. Eventually, the shouting and laughing, the pissing and puking, give way to the sound of our shameful groans. The cry of a loon echoes from across the lake.

∽

Back in the hearse, Billy reasons that this boy—*that he*—could not possibly have heard all that, not from under the boat. Nonetheless, the sounds persist, tattooed in his aural memory. He has spent every day since that night trying to drown those sounds out. Now he is just too weary—too damned tired of his fantasies—to fight hearing, seeing, and knowing what comes next.

 ℒ

Keeping to the shadows, Billy crawls on elbows and knees—the way we did when we played war in the woods at the end of our street, winning imaginary battles, and the hearts of girls—up toward Churley's camp.

When he reaches the deck, he stands, still as a tree on the windless night. It is a humid, sticky night. His T-shirt is pasted to his back with perspiration. He ignores the mosquitoes drilling into his exposed legs and arms.

By the light of the moon, through the torn screen hanging in the frame of the sliding door, he senses movement inside the camp. He sees enough, more than he wants to see, to confirm his suspicions about the perversions that had wedged themselves between his life and mine.

It is hard to say how long he watched, or what exactly he saw, or imagined. Hard to say how long he remains motionless, there in the dark, outside the door, before coming through it. Like many victims of trauma, Billy's memories of time and detail are unreliable. He is certain of this, he is at once sickened by and unable to turn his face away from what he sees.

Alcohol numbed me to what he witnessed being done to me. My own drunkenness that night, like many nights prior to it, distorts the chronology of time and blinds me to what Billy must have watched happening through the clear eyes of sobriety.

The propane lights were extinguished by the time Churley was enacting his debauchery on me—the drunkest boy, again. But the moon was nearly full, and bright as a yard light. Billy sees our silhouettes moving, hears our animal grunts of pain, and relief. He wants to close his eyes, to stop up his ears, to turn his head and run, but he doesn't. Was it the paralysis of fear, or the courage of steadfast friendship, that kept him there?

I believe that he was rooted there by love. Stumped like a felled tree, by the love that had always flowed in him like the sweet sap of a maple. What he observes, however, turns his love to lava. It boils, erupts, and flows down over his mountainous spirit, seething and, as it cools, turning to flint. The scalding flow of grief in him solidifies into rage. It was the fierceness of love that possessed him.

Billy slides the door open, and steps lightly across the threshold into the camp. Churley and I are asleep; that's what we called passed out drunk. Asleep. Billy is carrying an axe he collected from the woodpile, a splitter with its broad cutting blade and a heavy maul, mounted on a thick hardwood handle.

Churley is splayed on his back, snoring. In the moonlight, his smooth fat belly rises and falls, white like the pickerels' bellies outside on the stringer. I am on the floor, jumbled in a blanket and self-disgust. My back is turned to Churley. I passed out while trying to untangle, in my mind, the *me* on the bed from *me* in town. I rolled to the floor as always with the taste of bile and self-loathing in my mouth, determined this night was the last. I wanted to rinse my teeth, but the floor canted steeply when I rose to my knees, and then I was out.

Billy paces on the other side of the bed with the axe, willing us to wake so that he can confront us, utter some redemptive threat. He is panting, fast and shallow. His heart beats, like the wings of a caged bird, in his chest.

His pacing comes to an alarming stop. The absence of his steps is instantly filled by the swishing sound of the arching axe, and by the bounce of bed springs. There is a wet thunk the sound an axe makes when driven into a punky stump. Blood fountains. A squeal of air escapes Churley's windpipe.

I startle awake. Yes. I did wake, momentarily. I saw Billy, his foot is braced on the mattress reefing up on the axe to dislodge it from Churley's throat. Churley's neck rises off the bed. His head, still on the pillow, dangles from the axe. Billy pries it free, and Churley's neck falls back in line with his head. Billy sees me watching and says "Go back to sleep." And, testimony to shock and drunkenness, I do as I am told. It is just a bad dream, a nightmare.

Billy drops the axe, headfirst, at the end of the bed. It tips over and the handle bangs on the floor like a gavel.

He collects the canoe and the fish on the stinger and paddles by the moon back down Birch Lake to the launch. Mist hovers over the lake, and the night becomes more grey than black. He returns the canoe and paddles. In an hour, the sun will rise in the east. It will be warm on Billy's back as he cycles toward Twenty-Six Mile House, but Billy won't be able to feel its warmth.

₨

In the hearse, buried in snow, Billy weeps. He has wasted my imperfect sacrifice on fantasies and isolation. He floats now in his snow-stayed cocoon. Spent by the rigours of surrendering to memory, he sleeps.

He dreams of the bear, burrowed in her den, at the back of the cemetery. The den is beneath a stone shelf, guarded by the massive dead tree that has fallen across the opening. Billy crawls inside the den, and lies down with the bear. She spoons her warm body around his, and he sleeps.

- 53 -

GREATER LOVE HATH NO MAN

The morning after Billy killed Churley, I honestly did not remember Billy being there, or what had happened during the night. It's hard to believe, even to me, but true. I awoke with only lingering fragments of what I assumed was a nightmare about Billy showing up at the camp. I genuinely believed I had killed Churley. It was the only logical explanation. I wanted to kill him, and I must have been drunk enough to do it. I was horrified and sickened by what I had done, but I also felt freed by his death, and ennobled even by my conviction that I had brought it about.

It was a day later, lying sleepless in my bed at home, that I recalled Billy telling me to go back to sleep. Until then, I thought Billy's face, floating over me in the dark, was a random sequence in a nightmare. The gory details returned to me over the following days—images as blinding as the light on Churley's Super 8 camera. I wished I had not seen what I saw. The spools of memory, however, were captured, developed, and archived in me—and in Billy—forever.

Walking down the tracks after Churley's partially eaten body was discovered, I sorted out what I needed to do to save Billy. People would accept without question that it was me who killed Churley. Anthony and Larry would testify to it, if necessary. Everyone would accept, without doubt, that I had been the perpetrator. In a way, even I felt that I was guilty of Churley's death. I may have lacked the moral conviction to wield the axe, I thought, but I was the force that brought it down on Churley's neck. I was the cause of death. There is no point in arguing this point with me. I bear the fault. I am not saying it was the right thing to do, or that *I* should have done it. It was then and is now and will always be true, however, that I am culpable for Scouter Churley's murder. Billy an accessory to the crime, at worst.

The police were out looking for the perpetrator, out looking for me. When they found me beside the tracks, they did the math, stopped looking, and closed the case. By then they had taken down Anthony's and Larry's eyewitness statements.

My shirt was damp with fog when I heard the locomotive blasting its horn as it crossed the road at Pickerel River. Greater love hath no man than this. I loved Billy enough to lay down my life for him. As the wheels thundered and the tracks shook beneath my feet, as I braced for the engine's crushing impact, I took consolation in the notion that I was exercising this greater love.

If we're being totally honest, however, I didn't kill myself solely to protect Billy. It was a less noble, and more complicated, act than that. I would like you to believe I lay down my life with purely altruistic intentions. I would like you to remember me that way—as an exceptionally good and noble human.

But, I also did it because I was ashamed that I *hadn't* killed Churley. I was ashamed of my ambivalent weakness that allowed me to succumb to evil. I was ashamed of my cowardice and of the self-deception that found me at Churley's camp in the first place. I know, you will say that it was not my fault—I was the victim—but feelings of shame are immune to reason. I was ashamed to be the victim.

It was worth it, or so I thought. I would spare Billy from prison. I had not considered, however, another kind of incarceration to which my death condemned him. The day I left the hardware store—walking down the rails to where some of Churley's other boys had boarded the freedom train—I sentenced Billy to a life on death row.

The police told Mrs. Buffone that I hadn't suffered. It was quick, yes, but just before the lights went out, I did feel an excruciating, and redemptive, crush of pain. I am both grateful to have suffered in the end, and I'm glad they lied to Mrs. Buffone.

WHERE IN THE WORLD IS BILLY BUFFONE?

The telephone on the table beside Billy's unrumpled bed is ringing. The telephone on his desk in the funeral home office is also
ringing. So, too, is the one mounted on the kitchen wall beside
the sink. The sun is high in the midday sky. It slants down in
through the kitchen window, lighting and shadowing—like a
gallery painting—the three items in the dish rack. The plaque
beneath the painting would read: One porcelain bowl with blue
band, one spoon, and one upturned coffee mug. Multimedia.
Loneliness.

The snow storm that had brawled across northwestern Ontario during the night has lost its punch, and is discharging what
is left of its fury further to the east. A more peaceable, warm
front has ridden in on the tempest's coattails. The temperature
rose precipitously during the early hours of morning.

The sound of melting snow, dribbling from the eaves at the
manse, awakened Catherine at dawn. She raised her bedroom
blind to discover a rapidly liquefying snowdrift sliding down
the side of her car—crying "uncle" to spring. Sunshine was busy
healing the bruised sky. It was a perfect Easter Sunday sunrise.

The service at St. Luke's was resurrection joy-filled. The
congregation sang on key and attendance was bumped up by
Connie's visiting daughter, son-in-law and their six children—
three each, from previous marriages. The sanctuary felt positive-
ly packed. Catherine's mind, however, was elsewhere.

"Insanity is doing the same thing over and over again and
expecting different results." It was Einstein, I think, who said
that. And falling in love comes with its own special brand of
crazy. So, you will not be surprised to hear that it is Catherine
who is setting off the ruckus of ringing telephones over at Billy's

place. She skipped fellowship time after church, and the Easter egg hunt in the basement, and has been calling Billy's place like a stalker ever since—each time expecting different results. She wonders: *If a phone rings, and there's no one to hear it, does it make a sound?*

Following the Good Friday service, Ernie and Beverly and Connie had each, quietly and separately, taken Catherine aside to inform her that Billy had been parked outside the church before the service. She feigned a strictly pastoral interest in this news, but the red blotches on her neck betrayed her. She dialed Billy's number several times that night, and pretty much all day Saturday, without success.

She is calling, she tells herself, just to check-in. *Friends do that right?* When Billy eventually answers she will lightly enquire—as if it is her first, not her fortieth, attempt to reach him— "Hey, how are things going? Happy Easter." The way friends, or family members, do when calling one another on the holidays.

She'll casually invite Billy over for dinner, if he doesn't have plans, or to go for a drive together in the hearse to the Sault and on down the I75 to Cleveland and the Rock 'n' Roll Hall of Fame. Then to Florida or Peru, someplace warm and anonymous. Catherine has always wanted to go to Peru. They could drink Mai Tais, and get brown on a beach. Catherine's plan ignores her propensity to sunburn like a lobster. They could convert the hearse to a funky camper with purple tas-seled fringes around the windows and a mattress in the back to sleep—or whatever—on at night if it rains. These musings are how Catherine passes the time, waiting for Billy to answer his damn telephone.

The phone rings six times and his answering machine clicks in, again. On the cassette tape Billy's voice sounds kind, if some-what formal. He speaks slowly; chances are the person calling is bewildered by the loss of a loved one. "Hello, you've reached Buffone's Funeral Home. I am truly sorry that I am not available to take your call right now." He sounds sincerely truly sorry, to

Catherine. "Please leave your name and phone number after the tone and I will return your call as soon as I possibly can." *Beep,* and the second cassette tape is activated to record her message.

"Hi Billy. It's me, Catherine, again. Give me a call." She hangs up. *No, "Howzit goin'?" Just "Gimme a call."* Did she come across as too abrupt? Too Demanding? Entitled? The jealous girlfriend? Did she sound nervous? Should she call back and leave another message, apologizing for the perfunctory nature of the previous message? Another call would only make matters worse. She has already left six messages over the course of the weekend—one message every third time she called. Eighteen calls. She has kept track.

Catherine locates her canvas bag, hanging from the knob of her bedroom door. She rifles through the scraps of paper lining the bottom of the bag, and finds Florence's telephone number. Florence answers, yelling, on the first ring. "Hello!"

"Sorry to interrupt," says Catherine. "It's Catherine. You're probably cooking."

"Happy Easter, Reverend!" Florence's voice chirps like a robin. "I'm cooking up a feast for my boy. Can you smell the ham?"

Catherine smiles. She can hear loud talking, and even cautious laughter, in the background. "It sounds like a crowd over there."

"Some people came by after Mass, to welcome Clarence home."

"Clarence is there?"

"Yep, Billy brought him back last night." To someone in the kitchen, Florence says, "It's up there." Then to Catherine, "You should come for dinner. I heard the highway's opened back up. Bring your boyfriend."

"Thanks, I'll ... my boyfriend? What are you talking about?" Catherine voice flutters and her hand goes to her blushing neck. *Shit.*

"My eyesight is fine. Us ol' ladies see things, Reverend. Plus, I'm Indian. You know we're very spiritual that way." She laughs,

"You wanna tell me I'm wrong?"

Rather than denying her burgeoning affection for Billy, Catherine changes the subject to the closure of the highway. "Do you know? Was the road closed, all night?"

"I'd say," says Florence. "We haven't had a spring blizzard like last night since 1956. My cousin came by this morning, on his snow machine, to check on us. He says they just reopened the highway a couple hours ago. Everything's melting so fast. Come see us. Bring Billy."

Catherine promises to drive out later on, hangs up, dials Billy's number and gets the answering machine. She changes out of her dress into jeans and a bulky green sweater, and tries one last time to get Billy on the phone.

She makes a peanut butter and jam sandwich to eat in the car on the way over to Billy's place. *Maybe he's wearing those massive headphones and can't hear the phone ringing.* If that is why he isn't answering, it would mean he's been wearing the headphones for nearly two days straight. Wishful thinking is trumping logic at this point.

There are no tire tracks in the melting snow in front of the funeral home. She trudges around to the back, peeking in the windows as she goes. *Please don't let someone see me doing this, especially Billy, especially Billy dancing with the vacuum cleaner.* The main doors are locked, but the backdoor, leading into the living room, is not. She stamps the wet snow from her boots and leaves them on the rubber mat by the door.

The house is dead quiet, obviously unoccupied. So empty that it does not even occur to her to call out Billy's name. Clearly, nobody is home. She searches for clues as to Billy's whereabouts. The kitchen is empty. The sofa there is cold. The bowl, cup and spoon in the rack are dry. The bathroom and bedroom doors are open. The sight of Billy's un-slept-in bed shifts the worry in Catherine's mind down into her chest.

She passes through the kitchen again and down into the office. She checks the chapel, taps on the door to the embalming room. No answer. She reaches her arm around the door frame, feeling for the light switch and flips it on. She crosses the room to the door leading out to the garage. The van is parked there, the hearse is not. Billy's old ten-speed bicycle is there, leaning against the wall on its deflated tires. The bike looks tired to Catherine.

Short on other ideas, Catherine drives up the hill out of town. The pavement is wet but bare. Sunlight flares off the watery blacktop. The fast melt flows like a river down the shoulders of the road. She turns right, east toward Pickerel River. *He probably spent the night at a friend's place out there, she tells herself. By the time I get to Florence's, she'll know where he is.* She checks her watch. *He's probably already there, eating ham and potatoes, with Clarence.*

- 55 -

A Conspiracy of Ravens

The highway is wet, and bracketed by plowed and melting snow. Water puddles in the runnels, compressed by heavy trucks into the pavement. A tow truck and a police cruiser are pulled off on the side of the road, their red and yellow lights flashing. Catherine parks behind the cruiser and walks up to join Constable Ryan at the side of the road. He is watching the tow truck operators working. "Morning, Constable."

"Afternoon, Reverend. Happy Easter."

"Right. Afternoon. Quite the storm last night."

"Ah uh."

Danny, one of the tow truck guys, wades into the drift and down the ditch with a shovel. He clears snow away from the rear bumper of a blue sedan. The front of the car is completely buried beneath the snow. He reaches under the bumper up to his shoulder, and hooks the cable to the chassis. Back at the truck, his partner engages the winch and the rusty cable rises taut above the snow.

Catherine raises her voice above the growl of the diesel engine. "Are there others?" she shouts to Officer Ryan. "Other cars to be towed out?"

"A pick-up, further up that way." Ryan points to a truck, only the cab is visible above the snow. "We got the highway closed off pretty early. Not many people out here last night."

A transport truck slows as it rolls past the cruiser. Catherine attempts to inject a tone of nonchalance into her voice, "You haven't seen Billy, or the hearse, by any chance?"

Ryan turns to face her for the first time since she arrived. "Nope. Why?"

"Okay. It's probably nothing." Catherine nibbles her lower

lip. "Well, what I know is this, he left Pickerel River during the storm, and it doesn't look like he made it home. I just checked his place." She hates how easily her pale skin blossoms red.

Ryan raises his eyebrows as if to say, "Well, well, well," as Catherine concentrates on scanning the highway, as if Billy might suddenly appear. "We'll be done here in a couple of minutes," says Ryan. "We better do another drive by, just in case. You can do a ride along, if you like."

Catherine joins Ryan in the cruiser. He drives slowly, scanning the left-hand side of the highway for signs of Billy, or of the hearse. Catherine focuses her search on the right side. They drive all the way down to Pickerel River and make a circuit of the reserve, past the community hall, the church and Florence and Bernadette's place but don't see any signs of Billy.

Back out on the Trans-Canada, they head back west toward town. They pass Catherine's car and the tow truck. "What the heck?" Catherine points through the windshield. "Look at that. Holy..." To the right of the highway, a cloud of ravens funnel down from the sky, like a black tornado. "There's gotta be a hundred. More. Way more." She shivers and the hairs on her arms and neck stand to attention.

The birds spiral down and land on the ground, forming up into a hippity-hopping circle. Their tail feathers sweep the snow behind them. Thirty or forty of them remain airborne, circling above the looping formation below, like sentries.

"Huh, at *least* a hundred?" Ryan disagrees. "More like at least five hundred. I'd go a thousand. Holy cow, that's a lot of ravens. Gotta be some kinda road kill buried in the snow there."

"What do you mean there's got to be...?" Catherine's voice comes out strangled, the blood drains from her face. "What are you...you mean? Are you saying? Oh God, oh God."

Ryan cuts her off. "Whoa, whoa easy there, Rev. I'm saying there's probably like a moose or a something. I didn't mean Billy."

He pulls the cruiser off onto the gravel. Slack-jawed, they watch the circling hive of ravens. The birds march with the precision of a brigade on parade, in a wide loop, typing twiggy footprints in the snow. They hop clockwise, like one, dark organism. The birds that are still aloft coast on an updraft in the same direction.

"When it's a bunch of crows, it's a murder," says Ryan, "What's a bunch of ravens called?"

"An unkindness or a conspiracy, a conspiracy of ravens," says Catherine. In spite of being mesmerized by the circling avian regiment, she manages to summon some seminary Latin. "*con* means with and *spirare* means breathe: they're breathing together. Have you ever seen that many ravens, or birds of any kind, in one place before?" She turns to Ryan, "Or marching around all orderly like that?"

"Not that many, no way, not even close. That's one hellva conspiracy, if that's what you call it," says Ryan. "And, for sure, never seen one all organized like that."

"Me, either."

They get out of the cruiser and approach the guardrail to risk a closer look. The ravens gurgle, clock, and chortle from their gullets. Marching forty across, they flatten the white canvas of snow with their two-thousand—give or take—taloned feet, like a black whirlpool drilling down into dark waters.

Then, with regimental discipline, as though the raven drill sergeant had shouted, "Company halt!" the birds freeze in place. Catherine hears other, smaller, birds chirping in the distance. She hears water running beneath the snow somewhere. The warm breeze flips random feathers up off the raven's backs. The conspiracy holds its position like statues, eyes forward.

Then, with terrifying, soundless synchronization, one-thousand, purple-black ravens pivot their heads to stare directly at Constable Ryan and the Reverend Catherine. Their unblinking, black bead eyes bear down on the cop and the clergy.

Without consultation—and spooling scenes from the Alfred Hitchcock classic in their minds—they beat a hasty retreat to the cruiser. Locking their doors—even though they are dealing with birds—does not strike either of them as an unnecessary precaution. They had peered into those ravens' eyes, and saw that these were not birds to be underestimated.

Without dithering, Ryan keys the radio transmitter. The mic shakes in his hand while he transmits, "We've got a bit of situation here." He hadn't considered how he would describe the "situation". There is no numerical radio code for a terrifyingly massive and highly organized conspiracy of ravens.

"Go ahead, vehicle two." A woman's tinny voice replies.

"Uhm, we ah might need some back up out here. We're well, in a bit of a..." Ryan stumped by what exactly to say, swallows and presses onward, "We're into a bit of a stare-down with about ten-thousand birds." He hears the words coming out of his mouth, and immediately regrets them. He sounds crazy, even to himself. Catherine, on the other hand, is nodding emphatically.

- 56 -
The Conspiracy Draws a Crowd

Fifteen minutes later, a crowd is gathering along the highway to witness this avian anomaly. Ryan's peculiar broadcast lit up every emergency scanner in Twenty-Six Mile House and Pickerel River. On an otherwise unoccupied Easter afternoon, a transmission such as Ryan's is sufficient to activate not only emergency personnel, but a substantial representation of the general citizenry. Volunteer firefighters, ambulance crews, and the merely curious, whose emergency band radios are always scanning, are arriving on scene. The quiver in Ryan's voice, seeking backup for a bunch of birds, was clearly audible above the static. Was it a joke? It didn't sound like Ryan was joking, nor does he seem to be the joking type.

His broadcast—that he was in stare-down with a thousand birds—and the urgency in his voice triggered a stampede. Ryan is not a young man, nor is he given to hyperbole—or humour as I said. There was notable alarm in his wobbly voiced broadcast. People were coming to see either a remarkable aberration of nature, or if Constable Ryan had flipped his nickel. Either way it was worth the drive.

The professionals arrive dressed in uniform, the spectators in casual attire—coats pulled hastily on over dressing gowns, pyjama cuffs tucked into rubber boots, and children, their pockets provisioned with chocolate eggs and bunnies.

Travelers stop too, to see what roadside attraction could be garnering such a large audience on an Easter Sunday afternoon. Cars and trucks and campers are abandoned on the road. Armed with cameras, they jockey for sightlines along the guardrail, keeping their voices low, so as not to break the ravens' spell. All curbside doors are—understandably—left strategically ajar, at the ready, should a rapid retreat become necessary.

Constable Capperi—most recent recruit to the local constabulary—has also scrambled out to the highway. He has parked the second cruiser diagonally across the road, its flashers lit, bringing traffic in both directions to a standstill. He steps up beside Ryan, who has emerged along with Catherine, from the safety of the cruiser. "Maybe we sh, sh, should sh, shoot a couple a, a couple, rounds, over their heads?" suggests Capperi. "Over the birds' heads. B, b, b, break thi, thi, this thing up." Capperi stutterers when excited.

"Probably not a good idea," says Ryan without wasting a glance at his fellow officer. Catherine, however, cannot help turning to stare in disbelief at the young Constable: *Did you just say maybe we should fire a couple of rounds?*

An elderly man, sporting a leather bomber jacket and a New Jersey accent declares, "Well, somebody's gotta get over there and take a look see." His camo-green ball cap says *Army* in bright yellow letters above the bill. He hops over the guardrail with surprising agility for a man of his age.

"Sir, please step back," Ryan says, because that's what you say when civilians involve themselves in police matters. The man, already over the guardrail, knee-deep in snow, considers Ryan's request. Ryan re-issues it in the form of an order, "Stand down now, sir!" Chastened, the man climbs back over to the roadside of the rail.

A college student, his hair plaited in straw-coloured dread-locks, squeezes his Subaru into the traffic jam of parked vehicles. The car is packed floor panel to ceiling liner with what appears to be all of the boy's earthly possessions. A sticker, pasted inside the rear window, advertises the University of Alberta.

He scoops up a handful of snow, packs it into a ball with his bare hands, and lobs it, under-handed and high. His aim is good and the projectile lands squarely in the centre of the ring of glaring ravens. Instead of a whispered *phiff,* one might expect to hear when a snowball lands in the snow, it lands with a hollow *whump*, like a felt mallet hitting a timpani drum. The boy blows warm air into his cupped hands and says to Ryan, "For sure there's something's under there, dude."

Some of the other bystanders follow suit, lobbing snow balls into the middle of the circle of ravens. Quite a few miss the middle, but the ravens have no trouble neatly dodging the errant projectiles. What looks like the wet ragtop roof of a station wagon—or hearse if you happen to be Catherine looking for Billy—surfaces in the melting snow.

57

BILLY HAS SEEN HIS SHADOW

The ravens spiral off, in a reversing tornado of thundering wings. Some perch on the boughs of a nearby stand of black spruce and balsam. So many, in fact, that the branches sag, and turn black as pirates' beards. Still others wing off to the north.

A rectangular patch of vinyl, like a black carpet, rolled out on top of the snow. The sheen of wetness on it turns to vapour in the sun's warmth. The snow, beside the black steaming patch, lifts, like a bubble of air rising to the surface of a lake. The crowd holds its collective breath. The bubble bursts and collapses back into itself, leaving a tunnel in the snow. A windshield brush, wielded by a mittened hand, sweeps back and forth, widening the hole. The brush and the mitten are closely followed by Billy Buffone, wearing his nose and glasses

He flops up onto the snow, and pulls his toque off to scratch his head. His hair points madly off in all directions. Blinded by the bright light, he squints behind the lens-less frames, giving him the appearance of an intellectual mole. As his eyes adjust to the sunlight, Billy takes in the crowd lining the guardrail. He waves them off and looks away.

The crowd explodes with hoots and whistling and clapping, as if they have by stroke of luck, witnessed a birth. Anticipating death, they are greeted by Billy's oddly unassuming and peculiar manifestation of life. Strangers congratulate one another with back slaps and bouncing hugs, as if they had not only witnessed, but played some small part in the miracle. Constable Ryan, hands stuffed in his coat pockets, leans over to Catherine and asks, "If he sees his shadow, do we get six more weeks of winter?"

The distance, from the hearse to the guardrail isn't far, but wading chest deep through the sloppy snow is more akin to swimming than walking. The crowd shouts words of encouragement to Billy as he thrashes his way toward them. "You got this!" "Almost there, bro,'" and "Dig deep, only twenty yards to go!"

Halfway there, someone has found a rope in their trunk and thrown it out to Billy. An impromptu tug-of-war team forms up across the highway. They pull, and Billy slides up the steep incline of the ditch. Constable Ryan reaches out to steady him as he climbs over the guardrail. The spectators fall silent, circling close to hear whatever Billy might have to say about his time beneath the snow.

Catherine flings her arms wide, intending to throw herself into Billy's embrace before considering who she is and where she is. Billy looks confused. Catherine freezes, her arms outstretched like a parka-wearing statue of Jesus. Even in this moment of exceptional relief, and personal enthusiasm, she realizes that it is best not to announce to the entire town the preacher is crushing on the funeral director. Her mind churning, Catherine subtly transforms her posture to the one she assumes when pronouncing the blessing at the conclusion of worship on Sundays. "Well, Billy, we're so happy you are all right. Bless you!" She bows her head, drops her arms to her sides and thinks: *Dear sweet Jesus, take me now.*

Billy smiles a wobbly, fat-lipped smile in which Catherine detects more sadness than joy. For a man just rescued from his buried hearse, Billy looks more downcast than uplifted. The crowd, and the ravens, begin to drift away. Travellers anxious to be on their way start their cars and wait for the traffic jam to sort itself out. Emergency personnel—unspent adrenaline draining from their systems—load the jaws of life back into their truck. The citizens of Twenty-Six Mile House remember their Easter dinners, possibly burning, in their ovens at home. A few of the men give Billy's shoulder a friendly squeeze as they pass. "Glad you're okay there, Billy." They politely withhold remarks on his plastic nose and glasses, until they are out of earshot.

Everybody is smiling though, like they've been to the circus, like they've seen Hugo Zacchini shot out of the Ringling Brothers' cannon. They make their way to their cars, recounting the marvellous thing they have witnessed. It is a story they will tell and embellish, for years to come. People who weren't there will have trouble believing it, especially the nose and glasses bit. Also, like a crowd leaving the circus, they laugh nervously, while casting wary glances toward the departing ravens, confirming that the lions are safely locked back in their cages. The ravens are chuckling too.

To Catherine, Billy looks like he has seen a ghost. "You okay?"

Billy considers his response, then he says, "Not right now. No, I'm not okay, not yet, but I think I'm going to be."

Constable Ryan offers Catherine a lift back to her car and Billy a ride into town. "Danny'll tow the hearse out later on, Billy. Said he wants to wait 'till more snow melts so he doesn't do any damage."

Billy insists that Catherine sit up front with Ryan, and climbs into the backseat. "I'm good in the back." His knees crush up against the steel security panel between the seats. He lays his head back and removes the glasses, taking in the cloudless blue sky.

Catherine wants to say things to Billy, but doesn't want to say them in front of Ryan. Billy needs to tell Constable Ryan something, but isn't ready for Catherine to hear it. Ryan is debating with himself about telling Catherine and Billy something. So, they ride in awkward silence.

Finally, to relieve the palpable tension, Ryan says, "Must a' been quite the night, Billy, the storm and all."

"I was okay," says Billy. "It's a big car. Lots of air. I rolled up in a blanket."

"Sure, you must think about life and death and what not, though," Ryan presses, "I mean at a time like that, when you don't know, you know you're wondering: 'Am I going to make it?'"

"Yep, that's true." Catherine detects a catch in Billy's voice, but he doesn't elaborate.

Another long, excruciating silence follows this brief exchange.

Catherine's stomach growls.

Billy says, "Bart Ryan. Bartholomew?"

"Right. Who told you that?" says Ryan.

Billy shrugs, "Just a guess."

"Okay. Listen, I probably shouldn't be telling you this," says Ryan, "but I figure we owe you a word of thanks, Billy."

Without missing a beat Billy replies, "Spanner."

"Spanner?" asks Catherine.

"Spanner," says Ryan. "We did a search on the house, after all. In case, you know, he had other guns around, or left the stove on, or something." Ryan forgets he is wearing sunglasses and winks at Billy in the rear-view mirror. "What we found was a shit-load—excuse my French, Reverend—of kiddie porn. Really raunchy stuff and a lot of it. Violent, some of it. Kids tied up, sick garbage like that. Made me puke. Literally." Ryan sounds old, tired of being angry. "It's going to take a few stiff drinks to get that shit—those images—outta my head."

"In that room downstairs?" Catherine is not surprised by her prescience. "Oh, my God. I knew something wasn't right. The other morning..." She stops herself, to avoid having to explain to Ryan what she was doing over at Billy's, the morning after Gilbert died. A completely innocent situation, but she doubts she could say it without blushing beet red. It was a professional encounter spread thick with unprofessional desires.

Ryan purses his lips and tips his head side to side, "You're talking about the home theatre." Spanner had it all pimped out in the basement. La-Z-Boy and stacks of homemade VHS tapes. Magazines. Where do you even get this crap? He had one of those old Super 8 projectors, too."

After a glance at Billy in the rear-view mirror he asks, "This doesn't leave the car, right Reverend? Billy?"

"Uh huh," Billy replies absently. He removes the glasses and covers his eyes with a hand.

"Of course," says Catherine, "anything you tell me in confidence stays that way."

Ryan is relieved to be sharing what he has kept to himself since Friday. "There were quite a few Super 8s. Anyway, the movies are all of naked boys." He pauses, considers how much detail he should be sharing. "Sergeant's been around the detachment a long time you know? He had a look, Billy. Says they're all from up at that Scouter's camp. All local boys. Some pretty nasty stuff."

"Churley." Billy's voice is flat, coming from far away.

"Right. Churley. That's the guy. Sergeant says one of the boys is who killed him—Matt somebody. Said, you two were friends, Billy."

"Matthew Collins," Billy's voice, still empty as a readied grave.

"So, you knew him?" asks Catherine.

"He was my best friend."

"Jesus, sorry, Billy," Ryan shakes his head, again.

"It's was a long time ago. It's been too long."

"You'll be glad to hear that the Thunder Bay kiddie porn cops are filing charges on Spanner tomorrow, before he gets out of hospital—straight to remand that way. Possession of child pornography, plus shooting you, at the very least. Maybe more. They've got his computer, too. Looks like he had it hooked up through the phone lines to the world wide inter-web. The tech guys up at the Lakehead told me you can send this garbage to computers all over the world, like a fax. Anyway, I thought you had a right to know, Billy."

Billy exercises his right to remain silent.

They pull off the highway behind Catherine's car. Ryan starts to get out, "I'll pop the back door, so you can hop up front, Billy."

"I'm fine here." There is a tremor in Billy's voice.

Catherine pokes her head back inside the car, and examines Billy through the mesh cage. "See you later on?" She searches his face, his eyes, for a clue to what is going on. His skin looks slack. He puts the nose and glasses back on, like a disguise.

"Sure. That would be good. Nice," says Billy.

"I could stop by later," offers Catherine. *The heck with what Bartholomew Ryan thinks.*

"Okay." Billy looks away, failing to hide his tears from her.

58

I'll Make Hot Cross Buns if I Can Find the Recipe

Catherine drives back toward town, following behind the cruiser. She taps her left boot on the floor mat. Ryan is driving exactly 90 kilometres per hour and she can't bring herself to accelerate past a police car.

Suddenly, the cruiser's brake lights flare ahead of her. It swerves across the highway, skidding to a stop at the cemetery gate. Catherine slows down and pulls over, across the road, twenty metres further down the hill.

She watches as Ryan jumps out of the cruiser and flings open the rear door. He is holding his palms out and angrily motioning for Billy to get out. Catherine can't hear what Ryan is saying, but he looks ticked. He is pointing at the pavement, like someone disciplining a dog that just pooped on the carpet. *Bad dog! Bad dog!* Billy is trying to interrupt, but Ryan keeps holding a palm up. *Stop! Don't say another word. Talk to the hand. I can't hear you!*

Billy steps away from the cruiser, looking not unlike a chastened puppy. Ryan slams the rear door, spins on his heel, swoops back into the driver's seat, slams his door, and peels away without looking back. He accelerates past Catherine. His eyes remain steadfastly forward. His jaw is visibly clenched.

I suspect Ryan might let dead pedophiles lie. He will no doubt worry the beads of morality from time to time. Scouter Churley was, after all, some mother's child, a human being, entitled—in spite of his poisoned soul—to some kind of justice. That said, if I get a vote, Constable Bartholomew, I vote that you find a way to let it go. Otherwise, my imperfect sacrifice, won't be worth a hill of moose scat.

Billy watches the cruiser disappear down the hill into town. He puffs his cheeks, his shoulders sag, and he scratches his disheveled head. He walks over to the cemetery gate and leans against the wrought iron rail, facing the field of grave markers. His arms crossed over his chest, he scans the bush line for the bear—she's not there—closes his eyes and tips his wounded face up toward the healing warmth of the sun. To Catherine, with the sun shining down on him, it looks as if Billy's face is glowing.

Early this morning, she had called out, "Christ is risen!" And the congregation, their voices crackling with age, and with defiance over the powers of death, had responded, "He is risen indeed!" Her chest aches with love for them, for the sun and—above all in this moment—with love for Billy.

She crosses the road and joins him in the cemetery. Coming around the gate, she leans against it beside him. She presses her shoulder against his and he leans into her. "What happened?"

Billy's face is wet with unrestrained tears. "I told Ryan I killed Churley. That it was me." Tears wash down his face behind the glasses. There is no storm in them, no deluge or wracking or bursting sobs. These tears, held in for so long, finally roll down his cheeks, warm and soft as a summer rain. Like a cloud burst—long anticipated—unburdening itself and bringing relief from the pent-up heat and barometric pressure.

Catherine is stunned. She must have misheard. "What?" She wonders if Billy is suffering from oxygen deprivation, having spent the night buried in the hearse. Is he carbon dioxide poisoned? Could there be brain damage?

Billy steps away from the gate to leave, but Catherine puts an arm around his shoulders to pull him back.

"I killed him. I killed *Scouter* Rupert Churley." Billy's voice breaks like an adolescent boy. "With an axe."

Catherine's stomach flips. "I heard about all that. Everyone says it was your friend who did it. Matthew."

"Matthew Collins. That's what they all believe," says Billy. "That's what Matthew wanted them to believe. That's what I let them keep on believing. Everybody was more than happy to sweep the whole thing under the rug. Pretend it never happened, that *nothing* happened, but it was me. I killed Churley. Then Matthew killed himself—to protect me. I did it. I killed Churley, and I let Matthew take the blame, after... after he was gone."

"Why now?" asks Catherine. "Why, after all these years?"

"I've wanted to confess all along, but it felt like spitting on what Matthew did trying to protect me. His death would be meaningless. But I'm just too tired, tired of lying, especially to myself. I can't keep it up anymore." Billy slumps back against the gate rail. "I'm exhausted and I'm lonely, from lying."

"What did Ryan say when you told him? What will he do?"

"Probably nothing. He kept saying, I did not hear that, and you did not say it, over and over. He was dropping the f-bomb between every other word. He's pretty angry, I guess. I tried to tell him I wanted to own up. To tell the truth. He said something like: Not on my watch! You're not dumping that on me, Billy. That's when he pulled off the road and kicked me out of the car.

"I'm more afraid of what you'll do, Catherine, than of what Ryan will do. I'm scared to death of what you will think of me. Feel about me."

"What I'll feel?"

"Now that you know... what I did. Now that you know who I really am."

"I guess, I..." Catherine stumbles over her words. She has no easy or quick answer to Billy's fears. She still can't quite believe what he's telling her. "I guess," she starts again, "I want to hear what happened. I'll listen, I promise. And I promise I won't walk away."

"You'll hate me. I hate me! I can't forgive myself. How could you?" The words catch in Billy's throat, again. He takes the glasses off, stuffs them in his coat pocket, and covers his eyes with his sleeve.

Catherine steps in front of him and holds him in her arms. "I promise not to hate you, Billy Buffone. I won't ever hate you. God, you were what, a fifteen-year-old boy?" And there, up against the cemetery gate, she tips her head to the side and gently touches her lips to his. Billy kisses her back. She can taste his tears, feel the firmness of his bruised upper lip. It is not a chaste kiss, there pressed up against the gates of the cemetery. It is a wet and hungry kiss. It is a kiss wet with tears of passion and pain.

Forgiveness, Billy can see, is the opening of a door. It takes courage to step through it. Mercy and redemption come, subtly wounding us with humiliation and unbearable joy. They slip away and return again, when we least expect it. He vows to himself that he will take the first step, in spite of his unworthiness.

Danny drives past the cemetery, towing the blue sedan, and pops two toots on his air horn. He rolls his window down and shouts, "Get a room!" His words, and his partner's laughter, fade. They're gone before Catherine and Billy can step away from one another, so they don't bother.

"Come on, I'll give you a lift home." Catherine is unable to supervise the smile that waltzes on her face.

Billy's smile is more complicated than hers, but equally irrepressible. "I need to walk. I need to walk back, find my way back." says Billy. "Will you still come over later?"

"Yes." She holds his hand, to look into his eyes, "Billy, it's going to be okay. We'll find a way back, together."

Over Catherine's shoulder, Billy spies the she-bear lurking in the shadows at the back of the cemetery. "Okay. I'll make hot cross buns if I can find the recipe."

GRATITUDE

To everyone who listened to me talk about this novel for years, and still believed I would someday publish it, thank you. I want to name a few of the places where I learned about writing: the Haliburton School of Fine Art; The Collegeville Institute; and The Humber School for Writing. Thanks too, to folks at Latitude 46 who have created a welcoming place for northern Ontario writers. I am especially grateful to friends and neighbours in Marathon and Biigtigong Nishnaabeg, who are the bearers of trauma, and of healing. As always, and forever, thanks to my beloved Pearl, fountain of grace, love and beauty.